NOTHING HAPPENS
UP THERE

NOTHING
HAPPENS
UP THERE

LAURIE ROGERS

Troubador Publishing Ltd
Unit E2 Airfield Business Park,
Harrison Road, Market Harborough,
Leicestershire LE16 7UL
Tel: 0116 279 2299
Email: books@troubador.co.uk
Web: www.troubador.co.uk

ISBN 978-1-83628-114-6

British Library Cataloguing in Publication Data.
A catalogue record for this book is available from the British Library.

Printed and bound in Great Britain by 4edge Limited
Typeset in 11pt Adobe Garamond Pro by Troubador Publishing Ltd, Leicester, UK

This novel was conceived during the first Covid lockdown. The parliamentary constituency of West Lincs does not exist and the main characters in this story are fictional. The political events referred to as well as the developments in research into the human genome are real. Gene editing is now in the mainstream news following the vaccine breakthroughs that occurred immediately after this story was written.

My thanks go to Caroline Batchelor for her editing skills and advice on how to develop the characters and to my wife Sue for her constant support and encouragement.

1

DECEMBER 30TH 2019, LINCOLNSHIRE

They saw the car go past and pulled out of the layby to follow. There were still nearly two miles of the straight road until it turned left abruptly towards Otherby. It had been dark for some time and the heavy rain was flecked with snow. The wipers on the big Land Rover groaned as they swung back and forth clearing the windscreen.

The driver accelerated to catch the small car and soon was right up to it. He edged the Land Rover closer, and closer. Now they were just inches behind and he smiled as the small car started to accelerate. He followed, still inches from the other car's bumper.

"We're getting close, maybe 400 metres," said his companion in Albanian

He nodded and flicked the switch to illuminate the two spotlights mounted on the bonnet. They lit up the inside of the car ahead and silhouetted the driver whose hand rose to adjust the mirror. He pushed the accelerator pedal down and the jeep nudged against the car's bumper and started to propel the car even faster. He accelerated harder, then hit the brakes. The car ahead shot away brightly lit by the Land Rover's spotlights. They saw the brake lights illuminate and the car slide as the driver desperately tried to negotiate the tight bend. Then the car was rolling over and over before disappearing down the bank of the deep water-filled ditch.

The jeep drew up close to the ditch. The car was upside down in the water, just one wheel protruding above the surface. There was no movement. The man grunted and put the jeep in gear and carried on. Job done.

2

JANUARY 2020, LINCOLNSHIRE

Andrew Eastwood was a worried man. This weekend he would make the biggest decision of his life. A decision that could make or break his career, and his marriage. He glanced at the man sitting next to him, silent for the past hour. In the back of the car the man's wife sat, stoically mute.

The Murco sign was illuminated and appeared ahead out of the mist rather as a runway landing light does at Heathrow. Andrew lifted his foot off the accelerator and the car slowed as it approached the light. It was only three in the afternoon but the January days were short here with the mist suspended in the cold air.

The garage was still open which was important. Andrew had been running on the reserve tank since turning off the A1. Thirty miles of twisting, snow-flanked road and deep dykes lay behind him. He hadn't passed a petrol station. He was used to that by now; the relative isolation of his constituency. The lack of traffic, of shopping malls, of industry.

When he had first moved here, not long after winning the by-election, he had gazed for a long time at the flat landscape, the wide skies, the vast green fields with their Charolais cattle, the other fields already turning a creamy caramel colour as the wheat and barley rocked and rolled in the breeze.

He had marvelled at the emptiness of the landscape set out before him; such a contrast to the busy streets of Wandsworth where he lived with his family. There it was often difficult to see much sky for all the high-rise buildings that crowded around you. Here, on a fine day, with the sky a clear blue with just the odd cotton wool of cumulus, there seemed space to breathe, and time to appreciate the richness of nature.

It had been Spring and Andrew had arrived with Stan, his agent, for the candidate selection meeting. The sunshine had, of course, made everything seem better, brighter and more welcoming. Since then, Andrew had come to know that such days were rare. He'd become accustomed to the cold easterly winds blowing in from Scandinavia.

Now, as he eased the car up to the pump, the landscape was a dirty grey, mist-laden and cold. The sort of winter's evening when you wanted to shut out the world and sit inside, warmed with a good fire and a glass of single malt.

But Andrew had come to love the place, its serenity, the feeling that the rest of the world was bustling by leaving Otherby to muddle along by itself.

Nothing important seemed to happen here. Well not until now. Depending on his decision all that would change on Monday.

3

MAY 2018, LONDON

"Is that really what you want to do?" Claire looked at Andrew as they sat opposite each other in the Côte Brasserie in Wandsworth. "I mean wouldn't you have to spend some time up there with your constituents?"

"Quite a lot of time, I expect. Especially at first. But most of the week I'd be in Westminster."

"Only when Parliament is sitting. They have a lot of long breaks."

"Anyway I'm not elected yet, not even selected as the candidate so it might never happen."

"But leaving Templeton. You've done so well there."

It was true. Leaving university with a degree in Industrial Economics, Andrew had found himself a job at RBS in Edinburgh. Two years later the Bank having collapsed due to the antics of its CEO, Fred the Shred, he was headhunted by a leading fund management company in London where he met and married Claire. That was one decision that wasn't the result of careful analysis. He had been infatuated with Claire. She seemed to breeze through life with a casualness that he envied. She was sociable, got on well with everyone and clearly liked the attention she received. That made it all the more surprising that she had agreed to go out with him. It wasn't that Andrew was unattractive. He was tall, well-built with the eyes that a previous girlfriend had described as 'kind'. But he wasn't the fast-talking, jocular type that typified many of his fellow traders.

Initially he had put his degree to good use as he researched various companies in which the Fund was invested. Later he became a fund manager of a new 'green' fund that Templeton had launched. He had been successful at picking a number of winners. Andrew liked facts. He liked to have all the facts. Only then did he feel confident to make a decision. So he researched the companies extensively. He looked at the management team, the market, the likely ramifications of government policy.

Recently, however, the Fund had performed badly, largely due to the uncertainty of Brexit and the anti-green agenda of President Trump. Andrew hadn't foreseen the success of the Brexiteers. In this he was not alone but the fact that he had failed to offset the risk of a leave vote still irked him. Andrew was both a firm 'Remainer' and an advocate of taking measures to prevent global warming. Andrew took life seriously. Someone who liked certainty, predictability. That didn't make him the typical fund manager who enjoyed the frequent and often unpredictable ups and downs of the market. He lacked the gambler's excitement of betting on an uncertain outcome.

Brought up in County Durham, he was not a 'townie'

like Claire. The metropolis had been an eye opener to him. Edinburgh had been fine, small enough to relate to. But London had seemed just so big. He didn't know where London ended. Was it Surbiton or Watford or did it just keep spreading out like some enormous inkblot? London and his job at Templeton had been undeniably exciting and challenging. He had risen to the challenge. He had a good brain. He was organised and analytical. He had a strong work ethic and he was young.

Life had changed since he came down to London. Now he was married, relatively rich and father to twin boys. But something was lacking. He no longer felt he was achieving. To date achievement had been measured in money, the bonuses he had earned and the assets he had been able to acquire as a result. A happy marriage and two healthy children were other achievements. But what next? He had a responsibility to Claire and the boys. But it was more than just earning enough money. What sort of future could he build for them? His analytical research had led him to the conclusion that the economy couldn't keep growing. The planet had only finite resources and these were rapidly being used up. Nine billion people on a single planet. They couldn't all live in a big house, drive a couple of cars and jet round the world looking for a sandy beach. Things would have to change. This was what was driving him now to seek a different career.

"Templeton is going through a difficult time right now. Until Brexit is decided I think the glory days are over."

"I thought that all those Tory voters in East Anglia voted to leave. They won't want their MP banging on about the benefits of staying in Europe."

The couple on the next table looked across. Claire lowered her voice. The problem with London was space. Never enough of it. The tables crammed together afforded little privacy. On the other hand that was what made London so exciting. The constant rush and hurdy-gurdy made one feel alive. It made her feel like she was in a living history book. The people around her were important. They influenced the way the country ran, the way business developed. London was a melting pot of ideas. A melange of different races and cultures. Here people jumped on aeroplanes in the morning and attended conferences in other capital cities, flying back the next day. Here was where the dinner parties were fuelled by informed conversation, where the woman's voice was just as important as the man's next to her. London was a place of equal opportunity (well for the educated it was) where women juggled home duties with stellar careers and men shopped for Pampers on Saturday.

She glanced at her watch. Half-past two. Another hour and they'd have to pick the boys up from their prep school. A short cab ride and then home. Home to a large Edwardian house facing the common. Their 4 x 4 would be gathering dust pollen from the trees as it sat in the road outside. A car was more of a liability than an asset in Wandsworth. There was nowhere to park and if one wanted to take advantage of the wine bars and brasseries then a taxi was the safer bet.

Her opposition to Andrew's desire to become an MP was fuelled by her concern about money. They were doing well, very well. Andrew's bonuses had been more than enough to put down a substantial deposit on the house and pay the nursery fees. Now she had landed the job with a

City PR firm there would be even more coming in. So they would be able to enjoy the skiing, the Caribbean summer holiday and the babysitters to enable them to go to the theatre and gallery events. An MP's pay was not a fortune by comparison. In fact it was very little, she thought. But Andrew had been looking stressed recently with work and she too was worried about how business would survive a hard Brexit. Maybe it would be good for him to become an MP. It would give him the opportunity to find out what was really happening in Mrs May's government. And, she had to admit, the social benefits of being an MP's wife were not inconsiderable. It could open doors for her.

The thought pleased her and she motioned to a passing waiter for another bottle of St Veran.

It was a long time since she and Andrew had lunched together on a weekday. A combination of a week's holiday to prepare for his selection board and the boys' presence at full time school had enabled it. Claire loved London. It was exciting, busy, a happening place. Claire loved entertaining and being entertained. She loved the dinner conversations with friends who were in the know, who were in the places where it all happened. Maybe she would get to know all the gossip from the corridors of power if and when Andrew was elected.

Andrew glanced at her as the waiter poured from the new bottle of wine. "I've got a lot of reading to do when we get back. I don't want to be falling asleep."

"Don't be such a spoilsport. How often do we lunch together like this? Anyway there's not much to mug up on in Lincolnshire. Just farming and fish!"

"Not much fish now and Grimsby's up in North Lincs."

"So, all you've got to do is watch a couple of episodes of *Countryfile* and you'll be fine. Just don't mention Brexit!"

Later that evening with the boys in bed, Andrew settled down to read up on the economics of East Anglia. Claire had gone out with friends to a reception at a new art gallery in Sloane Street. Just the sort of evening she loved.

Three pages into the forecasts of wheat yields his eyes closed as the effects of the heavy lunch took their toll.

4

JUNE 30TH 2018, LINCOLNSHIRE

Winning the safe Tory seat had never been in doubt. Tories had held the seat since the war. In the past 20 years support for the Tories had risen from 42% to over 60%. It was getting selected that was hard.

Andrew had been the youngest candidate at 32. He was up against two women one of whom had lost her Midlands seat in the disastrous 2017 election. The other was a former teacher who was now an important county councillor and well known in the area. Both had played to the local conservative association's historic support of Brexit and talked of the dangers of immigration and the necessity to protect Lincolnshire's white population.

Andrew had talked about prosperity. He talked about opportunity for more jobs for their constituents, of support for farmers and the need to get more inward investment. He impressed the panel with his grasp of statistics, his knowledge of the finances of farming and his positive thinking. There were some members who worried about his 'remainer' leanings but the difficulties the government were experiencing in getting a suitable deal had softened their resolve to leave. With the support for each of the two women cancelling each other out, Andrew, the tall blonde man from Durham, was the narrow winner.

He was appointed MP for West Lincs a month before the summer recess on July 24th.

He resigned from Templeton without regret. The firm was awash with news about a takeover and redundancies so his departure was swift and cordial. His task for the summer was to find a house to rent within his constituency.

He left Claire in London with the boys. Claire was enjoying working again and looking forward to starting the new job she'd taken in the City. It meant making arrangements for the boys to be picked up by a child-minder but as that removed the necessity for Claire to make tea for them, she was not unhappy.

On Monday morning, Andrew drove the Nissan up to Holbeach where he had arranged to meet his agent. Stan would be invaluable for advising him on suitable areas to find a property as well as introducing him to many of the more-important locals. Holbeach was in easy driving distance of Andrew's constituency.

It took Andrew more than an hour to get through the rush hour traffic in south London and onto the bottom of the A1, the road to the North. With stop-start traffic he crawled through Battersea and across the river before heading East. The congestion charge introduced years ago by Ken Livingstone had been a great success in getting traffic off London's roads but still the going was slow and painful.

He was glad when he reached a spot north of the M25 when he could open up the car. He wondered how many times he would have to do this journey and whether he would ever get used to it. He had looked at taking the train up. Then he discovered there was no railway station at Holbeach or rather there was but it had been shut down in 1959. The only way was to take a train from Clapham Junction to Waterloo, an underground to Kings Cross and a train to Peterborough. Changing trains at Peterborough he could get to Spalding from where he could take a bus to Holbeach. He began to realise why people had referred to his new constituency as 'in the wilds of nowhere'.

It was nearly two o'clock before he finally arrived in Holbeach at the Horse and Groom where he had arranged to meet Stan. The cream-painted façade of the old pub gave right onto a narrow pavement. On the right an archway led through to a small car park and the few buildings that had been converted into guest rooms.

The main bar was dominated by a long wooden table at which four men in their sixties were drinking coffee having obviously finished their meal.

There were a number of small wooden tables with wheelback wooden chairs. He saw Stan sitting at one, a pint in his hand. He rose to greet Andrew as he strode across.

"I'm so sorry …. the traffic."

"Don't say a word. You're still in time but we need to get the order in quick." Stan pointed to the blackboard screwed to the brick-faced wall listing the daily specials. "They stop serving at 2.00. I recommend the chicken and ham pie."

It was obvious to Andrew that Stan was a regular in here and by the size of his stomach indicated he enjoyed not only the family cooking but the local ale. It was a far cry from the Côte Brasserie in Wandsworth or the Portofino Wine Bar in Clapham. It was a lot quieter for a start.

Andrew nodded approval and Stan called out to the young barman for two pies and two pints of Yorkshire bitter. "Great pub. Free House. Always a good choice of beers."

Apart from a quick toilet break on the A1 where he grabbed a Costa coffee, Andrew hadn't eaten and as he tucked into the pie he realised how hungry he was. Stan explained that they would drive 'in convoy' across to Ancaster where there was a house he thought might suit Andrew. It's actually in your constituency although, as you know, your constituency spreads over a wide area."

"Yes, a wide area but not many people live there!"

"There's a hotel in Sleaford I've managed to book us both in for the night. Then tomorrow we can drive around a few more villages and see what's available."

"I've been looking at Rightmove back home but there don't seem to be many decent properties to rent." Andrew had, as usual, done his research. He had drawn circles on a map, listed the villages and searched Rightmove. He'd found surprisingly little.

"That's because the best ones go by word of mouth up here. Internet is fine but up here it's more about who you know than getting Google to search for you. People up here don't move around like they do in London. They stay put. Houses stay in the family. Passed down through the generations." Stan moved the remaining lump of mashed potato around his plate mopping up the last of the gravy. "Coffee?"

The drive from Holbeach to Ancaster reminded Andrew both that Lincolnshire is a large county and that the different parts of it have their own characteristics. Down in the south of the county it is horticulture rather than agriculture that keeps the economy working. The area is famed for its flower growing and a few months earlier the fields would have been a sea of yellow daffodils. Further north the bright yellow fields were not daffodils but rape seed, while all over the county large flat farms were growing acres and acres of wheat and barley that added a yellow gold to the spectrum.

Not all of Lincolnshire was flat though. The famous Lincolnshire Wolds near Louth were hilly while the west of the county was also more undulating.

Ancaster, as its name suggests, was originally a Roman settlement on Ermine Street the major Roman road from London to the North. It boasts a population of 1317. Andrew was pleased to see it had a working railway station. "It's on the Nottingham to Skegness line," said Stan. "Not many trains though."

"I've heard of Ancaster." said Andrew. "There's a hall of residence named after it at Nottingham University."

"Is that where you did your degree Andrew?"

Before he attended the selection committee Andrew had researched the whole area of his constituency and reckoned he knew as many historical facts about the places as Stan. What he didn't know were the people and here he would have to rely on his friend.

As they neared Ancaster, Stan was describing the nearby Cranwell RAF station. "Brings in some income, that does," he said. "Close to Sleaford too."

"Isn't there a good nature reserve near Ancaster?" Andrew delved into his mind for some facts he had read.

"Two to be precise – Ancaster Valley and Rauceby Warren, although that's closer to Sleaford – just by the golf course. You should join Sleaford Golf Club if you get a place around here – lots of good Tory voters there!"

There were advantages to Ancaster, thought Andrew. The countryside was not yet bleak like the fens and the A1 was not that far away. Sleaford was a good market town and had a golf club. Finding a suitable house to rent however was impossible. Not wanting a modern semi-detached on an estate there was nothing remotely to interest him, or more importantly, Claire.

The next day they travelled further East. "It gets pretty remote out here – especially for a townie like you," said Stan.

"But it's more like where my constituents live. Anyway I wasn't a Townie. I mean there were a couple of big towns like Sleaford but mostly it was just small villages, almost hamlets."

It was as they were leaving yet another estate agent that the agent called out to them. "I don't know if this might be something you'd consider?" He was holding the telephone with his hand muting the mouthpiece. "It's not for rent though. Could you consider a purchase? Nice house, old but in good nick. Small village."

Andrew shook his head. "No I'm not sure where I'm going to be living but I'll only be up here for weekends. A rental makes much more sense."

"Give us the details anyway," said Stan looking hard at Andrew. "What are they asking?"

Outside Stan turned to Andrew. "Look, I didn't want to

say this before but you need to have something better than what we've been looking at. OK if you are just looking for somewhere to lay your head on a Saturday night a rental might do, but that's hardly going to impress the punters is it? Another absentee MP who knows nothing about the life here and cares even less. We need to feel our MP is dedicated to the place. Remember what Gordon said at the Selection meeting. We deserve more than a poncey city-type looking for a safe seat."

Andrew looked at Stan's face. The expression was determined, almost truculent. He had never seen him so worked up. He thought of remonstrating but didn't want to fall out with him. After all he would depend on Stan to watch over the constituency while he was away in London. On the other hand the way Brexit was going Theresa might be forced out by the leave campaigners and that could spark another election. Upsetting the selection board might not be the cleverest thing to do.

So he nodded and followed Stan to his car.

Not for the first time Andrew's thoughts turned to his reasons for giving up his job at Templeton. Yes it had provided a very good income. Yes he enjoyed the fast-moving pace in the office, the feeling of being on the inside of big business. But there was also the nagging feeling that all he was doing was making informed bets on companies' futures, staking other people's pension money on a bet that the market price would rise. There was something, if not immoral, then certainly ephemeral about his job. He wasn't actually adding any value. He wasn't helping to make things, or to create things or help people.

He thought about Claire's brother. He was an actor/

singer. He had enjoyed roles in several large West End shows but now spent most of his time running comedy clubs in and around Manchester. He rented rooms in pubs and put on performances. It was hard, and certainly not financially rewarding but he seemed only too happy to be helping aspiring performers and entertaining people. He talked animatedly about his work when he came to London and stayed with Claire and Andrew. By comparison Andrew had nothing interesting to say about work at Templeton.

As an MP he could help constituents, do something for the area and maybe, just maybe, influence the government in its approach to Brexit and Climate Change. Then he'd have something worthwhile to talk about. Then he would feel he was helping to build a better world for his sons. Growing up in Northumberland with his mother, Andrew had enjoyed being in a small community. A place where you knew most of the people, and they knew you. Somehow places like that, felt more real than Wandsworth. In London you were right in the midst of things, important things happened all around you. Yet you didn't have that sense of belonging, of being part of your environment. Everything was transient, people and time rushed by. People were so busy living the life that they didn't realise that life was passing them by.

As soon as Andrew drove into Otherby he knew this was the sort of place he was looking for. Totally different from his home in Wandsworth, rural yet part of a community, albeit a small one. There was even a slight rise in elevation above the low-lying wheat fields and deep dykes. Unusually there were some trees to break up the flat wide landscape.

Entering the village they passed a road to the right. A row of identical bungalows, probably built in the seventies, bordered it on both sides, their gardens neatly tended. Stan drove on into the centre of the village passing a scattering of red-brick Victorian houses, their front doors opening onto the pavement. A church with a square Norman tower lay back from the road. They reached a crossroads where a hanging sign in front of a large white-fronted building with a grey slate roof announced The Barley Mow was a Free House. There was a small SPAR shop opposite which doubled as the sub post office.

Stan turned left and within a few yards they headed towards open fields. After a few hundred yards Andrew saw a hedge and stone wall shielding a building from the road. They had arrived at Limetree House.

The house turned out to be a Grade II listed village house incorporating the former village blacksmith forge. White painted walls with a front door of slatted dark oak. The top of the door was shaped into a pointed arch mirroring the leaded windows. It gave the house an ecclesiastical air. Either side of the door were large pots with some scarlet geraniums. The colour of the geraniums matched the red tiled roof which looked in good repair. The house stood back from the road and had a gravel driveway which led to a garage at the side. Flagstones formed a path directly to the front door.

Large bushes shaded the path and a tall tree stood to the right. Andrew didn't know much about bushes and trees, but they looked nice. Maybe the big tree was a lime tree.

As they crunched up the gravel drive the front door was opened by a very old man wearing a checked shirt and a tie under his tweed jacket. He held a cane in his left hand. He looked at the two men.

"I thought the agent said it was a couple who were

interested? You're not a couple are you?" He looked with distaste at Stan's ever-increasing stomach.

"No we're not," smiled Stan who was obviously more used to the somewhat non PC views of country folk.

"No it's me who's interested. For my wife and me." Andrew tried his best vote-winning smile. "And our two boys."

"You're not from round here then? Has your firm moved you up here? Are you with Stellagenix?"

Andrew was taken aback with the man's directness. It was not something you came across in SW18. In Wandsworth he would have been shown around by a pretty young girl from the Estate Agency reading off a script and telling him how well the property met his requirements.

"Mr Eastwood's your new MP." Stan waved his hand in Andrew's direction as if introducing a performer onstage.

The old man looked up at Andrew. He shook his head slightly. Obviously he expected MPs to be older. There was a long silence while he seemed to evaluate the information Stan had given him. Finally with a barely perceptible shrug of his shoulders he spoke. "I suppose you'll be wanting to look around then?" He tapped his cane on the tiled doorstep, turned and shuffled back inside. Andrew turned to Stan. "Friendly sort!"

"Oh he'll be fine once he's got to know you. Just doesn't like outsiders. A lot of rural folk don't."

They stepped inside. The house might be a listed building but had obviously benefitted from a great deal of modernisation. The ground floor rooms were spacious, the kitchen as well equipped as Andrew's in Wandsworth. Andrew recalled the problems he had encountered from

Wandsworth Council when he wanted to put on a conservatory. His wasn't a listed building, yet the paperwork and appeals had been a minefield to traverse. Here, the occupier seemed to have altered the inside of his house exactly as he wanted with no such restrictions.

Upstairs there were four bedrooms including a large en-suite which Andrew knew Claire would love. There was no sign of anyone else living in the house. There were no flowers in vases or pretty cushions. The house, for all its amenities seemed to lack any feeling of life.

The man showed them round with barely a word. Just an occasional grunt as he opened a door to show them another room. It was only when they went downstairs again and he opened the door to his 'library' that he became more than monosyllabic. "This is where I work. Or where I used to. I've still got all my books but my eyesight's not as good as it was. This was very much my room. Martha had her kitchen. She only came in here to dust."

The room had one wall painted a dark burgundy red with dark wood shelving housing hundreds of books. On the opposite wall was a very old long-case clock while a French ormolu clock ticked away loudly on the mantlepiece above the fireplace. A Victorian, leather-topped desk sat before the window. It looked out on a Turneresque picture of gently-rolling pastures of waving grasses. Andrew loved it immediately.

The man explained that he was having to move into a sheltered apartment in Peterborough near his daughter. "I shall miss the garden and the view." He gestured to the back garden. "Can't manage more than a few potted geraniums now. They were Martha's favourite." There were raised beds with a few plants and a lot of weeds. Beyond, the ground fell away into an unbroken vista of golden fields of barley.

"Those wheat fields certainly are a sight," said Andrew trying to draw attention away from the weed-stricken vegetable plot. "That's barley, not wheat. They sell it for beer-making mainly."

Andrew realised that his knowledge of arable farming had better improve if he were to represent the local farmers in Parliament.

"So you're the new MP? Know much about farming do you? There's not a lot else around here. Do you plan to live here then?"

"Well I'm hoping to serve the interests of all my constituents, not just the farmers." Andrew realised that he was sounding as if he were trying to convince the selection panel all over again. He decided to change the subject.

"And what business were you in Mr Hetherington?"

"Me? I used to have Hetherington's in Sleaford, sold it back in '98 and bought this place. Martha loved growing things."

Andrew had no idea what 'Hetherington's in Sleaford' was and turned to Stan for enlightenment.

"Big furniture store," whispered Stan.

Andrew looked at the rows of books on the shelves. There were many on clocks and clock-making interspersed with volumes of Miller's Antiques Handbooks and Price Guides stretching right back to 1964.

"Was it mainly antique furniture that Hetherington's sold?" asked Andrew.

"Not at all, we sold lots of contemporary pieces too. It's just that some of the new people liked antiques – the more expensive the better." For the first time he smiled. "It was good back then, lots of farms being sold to investors with more money than sense. Bought old houses and did them up with antiques. All different now. Not many newcomers" He looked at Andrew accusingly. "The locals mainly have inherited furniture and the youngsters would rather go to Ikea than have some decent furniture – although they are mostly still living with their parents in their house so they don't really buy at all. Can't afford their own house."

Andrew nodded encouragingly. "Yes it's so difficult for young people to get on the property ladder. Even here."

"Even here?" scowled the man.

"I mean with property prices so much lower here."

"You men in London have it easy. I read about your bonuses. Earn a fortune you lot. It's different here. We work for our living."

It is Stan who now changes the subject.

"Well Mr Hetherington I'm sure Mr Eastwood will be in touch with your agents if he's interested. We won't keep you any longer. You got anything else you want to ask, Andrew?"

As they walked up the drive to the car Stan asked, "Well, are you interested? He's wanting £500,000 but he may take less."

"More than interested. I can't wait to get Claire up here to look. Then it's just a matter of sorting out the money."

"Well don't forget what you can claim for on your MP's expenses – just don't build a moat and put a duck house on it!"

5

JUNE 2018, LONDON

Claire was the busy person everyone turned to when they needed something doing. She found it hard to sit still, even harder to sit out. She wanted to be involved. She wanted to be doing things.

So the five years she had taken off from work to have and start bringing up their two boys had been hard. It wasn't that she was bored. Two young boys demand a lot of attention. She had had to go through the rigours of IVF in order to have them but had coped. Then there had been the purchase of their new house in Wandsworth which had been made possible by Andrew's incredible bonuses but undertaken by her.

It had been she who had arranged the sale of their flat and the removal. It was she who had arranged for plumbers, decorators and electricians to turn their Edwardian house into a 21st century residence.

And it had been she who had been responsible for

keeping their social life so active. She was no Nigella Lawson but she had a selection of recipes she had perfected and which she could alternate to serve at their many dinner parties. So what if the deserts were often brought in and just presented as home-made? Life was for living and wasn't it Jilly Cooper who once said life's too short to spend stuffing mushrooms?

The au pair had helped for the first year or two, enabling Claire to get out during the day and catch up with her friends and former work colleagues. A year ago she had taken a part time job with Red & Green, a design agency in Putney. She was happy to be working again and found the creative environment in marked contrast to the pressurised atmosphere of Templeton. She found she was good at dealing with the agency's clients using a mixture of her feminine charm and analytic brain to convince them to develop their corporate 'persona' as her boss liked to call it.

It was nonetheless difficult working part time. She could never feel quite part of the team. She missed the after-work socialising and hated letting people down when she was forced home for some domestic crisis with the boys. But now they were in full-time education and they could afford the services of a child-minder she wanted something more.

The job at Repute Communications seemed perfect. It was like a mixture of her work at Templeton and Red & Green. The best of both. Repute Communications was all about taking a structured management approach to building a company's reputation. It was not just a PR consultancy that advertised the charitable donations or good works performed by its clients. It went deeper. It worked, often on secondment in house, to influence staff to believe in the company's mission statement and values and in a lobbying capacity to push the company's achievements or aims with the media and politicians.

Claire had endured, or even enjoyed, three interviews before being given the offer. She had worried that her parental break of five years might be seen as a disadvantage. However, it seemed that Repute had seen it as a positive. She was unlikely to be having more children, they considered, and that meant she could develop a career with the firm. The fact that they had recently won a lucrative contract for a major insurance company who were keen to develop their market with young professional women, may also have influenced their decision. Claire fitted the bill perfectly.

Nevertheless she was feeling nervous that Monday as she set off for her new office in Finsbury Square. She was pleased that Andrew had sorted out the boys for school that morning so she didn't have to, but less happy that he wouldn't be there in the evening to hear how she had got on. He would be away at least two days, maybe three, sorting out accommodation in Lincolnshire. When the House was sitting he would be around in Wandsworth to help out, particularly in the mornings, but she worried that he might have to be away in his constituency many week-ends.

Her day didn't start well. Signal failure at Vauxhall had delayed her train on its short journey to Waterloo. She endured 45 minutes standing in a hot cramped carriage with hundreds of fellow commuters trying steadfastly to ignore each other, talk on their mobile phones and balance a cup of coffee.

She decided, at Waterloo, that taxi would be the best way to make up time only to find the queue nearly fifty yards long. When she did finally get her cab it struggled through city-bound traffic at a pace barely faster than walking. She arrived nearly half an hour late for her first day.

The receptionist on the ground floor smiled at her and politely asked whom she had come to see. Frustrated, Claire explained that she worked here – or would if she could just be let through the electronic gate. Another ten minutes passed before she was greeted by a smart woman who had been one of those at her first interview. Miss Leonora Kemp was the head of the department that she would be working in. Armed with a visitor's badge she ushered her through the glass gate towards the lift.

"Sorry about all this, but we have to maintain strict security. Our clients expect us to keep their secrets." She gave Claire a conspiratorial smile. Claire surmised that she had used this 'joke' many times before.

The day passed in a blur. A tour of the offices to meet various staff was curtailed before halfway when the fire alarm sounded. Everyone looked around at each other before moving. It was as if they didn't want to be the first to panic, or because they thought their job was so important that it really couldn't stop for a fire alarm which was probably false anyway. But after a few more seconds people started to head for the emergency stairs. The lifts automatically stopped when the alarm went off. Many of the staff grabbed laptops or coats but some left empty-handed confident that they would soon be back at their desks.

Claire and Leonora trotted down the stairs together. Just before they came to the ground floor reception they were met by four men in black padded uniforms and helmets coming up the stairs, forcing the descending crowd out of their way.

"Must be the fire brigade," said Leonora. But Claire didn't think so. As they finally entered the ground floor atrium they saw the police cordon and the two silver panel vans.

"It's the anti-terror squad," said one of the Repute executives. "There must be a bomb!" He headed for the door followed closely by Leonora and Claire.

Two hours later the all-clear was given and the staff of Repute filed back into the building and queued for the lifts to take them back to their offices. The call to the police had been one of four to be made that morning advising that an explosive device had been left in the toilet of an office block. The police had found no devices in any of the four buildings and had concluded that it was a malicious hoax.

It was now nearly 12.00 and Claire still hadn't sat down at her desk.

"Look Claire, I haven't got time now to introduce to everyone and show you round. I've got a lunch in Mayfair with a financial journalist at one – just a quick one as 2.30 we've got Prospect Insurance coming in for an initial briefing. You'll be working on that and I'd like you to sit in on it. I'll give you the file with their original approach and our subsequent proposals. Read it up so you're up to speed and I'll see you at 2.30."

Before Claire could reply she stepped into her office, picked up a memory stick from her desk and handed it to Claire. "It should all be on there. I copied the files across this morning before you arrived." She gave Claire a critical look.

"There was a signal failure at Vauxhall," stammered Claire.

"Yes, well, can't be helped. Prithi over there will show you your desk. Must dash."

Claire walked across to the young Sri Lankan whom she'd been introduced to earlier. She was relieved to find that Prithi did have time to show her where her desk was and sort out the computer for her. "Don't worry about Miss Bossy Boots, she's a workaholic. She's very good at strategy though so listen and learn."

Claire hung her coat on the hook and opened her briefcase. She looked inside at its sparse contents, just her trainers and a spare pair of tights under which she noticed a large pink envelope. Surprised she picked up the envelope and took out the card. The message read *"Have a great day and show them how good you are! Love Andrew."*

She smiled as she replaced the card in its envelope. So typical. She did love her husband.

6

Claire stepped into the carriage at Waterloo and walked down the train looking for an empty seat. She didn't find one and resigned herself to standing. It was only two stops, six or seven minutes, so she couldn't complain. Many commuters had to stand for an hour or more.

It was only the end of her second day working back in central London and already she was beginning to adopt the zombie-like approach to travel. Build a little world of your own, cocoon yourself in it and avoid contact with everyone else. Look to take any advantage you could, get to that empty seat first, position yourself on the platform just where you knew the doors open, walk up the escalator rather than stand on it so as to gain a few precious yards on the crowd. Life in London was fast-moving, competitive. Survival of the smartest.

She was only just beginning to understand her role in the new job. So far she seemed to be shadowing Leonora, meeting two clients and sitting wordlessly in a creative meeting. She had had little time to talk with the other employees who always seemed too busy anyway. Prithi had helped her with basic necessities and tried to explain the company's complex cloud-based filing system and recommended a good deli where Claire had gone for lunch.

What she had seen so far encouraged her. She was enjoying the cerebral challenge of analysing clients' companies to ascertain what their 'image' was and what it should be. Companies were getting more and more worried about their public image. How were they seen by the public, by the media, by the investors? No longer was PR about organising press launches of products or writing press releases about personnel moves. Now it was trying to show how companies were good for the environment, or helped the under-privileged, or were ethically motivated. The obverse was to keep them out of the media when something happened to undermine the desired image. It was great publicity when a water company announced it was donating money to bring fresh water supplies to an African village. It was not good publicity when it was found that lack of security had meant sewerage effluent had contaminated a city's drinking water.

The train slid smoothly out of the station and gathered speed towards Vauxhall. She held onto the top of the seat back to steady herself and bent down to look through the carriage window. On the right she would once have had a view of the river and the Houses of Parliament where Andrew would be working. But in the past twenty years so many high-rise apartment blocks had been constructed that the view was totally obscured. The buildings were so close together that she wondered what sort of views the tenants had. Not all the rooms could look out onto the river, many must just look across to the next block. Still, if you were working in the world's most cosmopolitan city you would just have to put up with it. These apartments could easily cost a million pounds each. The compensation was their proximity to all that London had to offer. The restaurants of every type, the theatres, the bars, the markets, the museums and art galleries. Claire smiled. She was glad to be part of this teeming anthill of humanity and to enjoy the very best of cultural experiences. It was exciting, invigorating – it was what living in the fast lane was all about.

She was looking forward to seeing Andrew tonight and telling him all about her new job. Last night had been anti-climatic. She had arrived home, collected the boys from the child minder and, having put them to bed, made herself scrambled eggs on toast. She had been unwilling to order herself a take-away being just one person and her culinary skills didn't run to elaborate dishes. She had watched a little television, had a bath and tried to sleep.

Tonight she hoped they could get a take-away in and open a bottle or two and tell each other how they had been getting on. She hoped Andrew wouldn't be home too late.

While Claire was travelling the two stations to Clapham Junction, Andrew was speeding down the outside lane of the A1 near Peterborough. He too was looking forward to sharing his news. The idea of buying a house had not been raised before. He and Claire had just assumed that he would find a small apartment or house to overnight in when, occasionally, he had to be in the constituency. Now, following his ear-bashing from Stan he realised that his duties as an MP were more demanding than he had thought. He would not be an absentee MP, one of 'them men in London'. He would have to spend more time understanding the unique problems of his Lincolnshire voters.

Finding the house in Otherby had been a revelation. In value terms compared to London it was a bargain. It wasn't just the price that was in stark contrast to houses in the metropolis. It was the surrounding space, the vastness of the landscape, the closeness of the villagers' lives. After he and Stan had left Mr Hetherington they drove a few hundred yards to the pub, the Barley Mow.

Stan was anxious to get a pie and a pint and Andrew was keen to meet some other locals. Would they all be as frosty as Mr Hetherington?

"Not at all bad," intoned Stan as he supped a glass of real ale. It looked a little cloudy to Andrew who had ordered himself a soft drink. "It's a local brew. There's a micro-brewery in Lower Thorpe just over there." Stan waved an arm in the general direction. "Wouldn't be at all surprised if it isn't made from that barley growing at the back of your new house."

"Steady on, I haven't even made an offer yet. I've not even decided whether I should. I'll have to run it by Claire."

As the miles ticked by on the south-bound A1 Andrew found himself thinking more and more about the house. He really had fallen in love with it. Love at first sight, he chuckled. But how would the love of his life feel about it? He'd have to broach the subject carefully. Claire had liked the idea of him being an important MP, if not the MP's salary, but she hadn't liked the idea of him spending a lot of time 'up North' when he should be at home with his family. Well, thought Andrew, now the family can come up here too. The boys will love the space and the countryside. Claire might miss the plethora and variety of restaurants and bars of South London though. Still, it would only be at the weekend – nice for her to get away from all that pollution.

He was forced to go round the block a couple of times until he found a parking space and even then he had to do some nifty toing and froing to fit the large vehicle into the small space between a BMW X5 and a little VW Up!

He grabbed his overnight bag and the bunch of flowers from M&S at the services near Stevenage and walked down the street, round the corner and up to his house. It was 7.30.

The boys had just gone to bed and Claire told him he was not to wake them. She was still in her business clothes and suggested he organise a take-away while she changed and showered. "I've got so much to tell you," she said, as she turned to him one foot on the stairs. "But I need to freshen up – I feel grimy after the tube and the train."

Andrew went to the fridge and took out a bottle of Champagne. He wondered whether he should open it right away or keep it until Claire came down. He wanted to celebrate, but he also needed a drink after driving 165 miles. He compromised and dug a can of Youngs beer out of the fridge.

The beer was welcome but had a rather different taste from the beer he'd had with Stan. He went into his study which was little more than an alcove off the main lounge. He opened the post that lay on the desk. There were two invitations to drink receptions the following week. Claire was included on one of them, the Wandsworth Conservative Association one. He leafed through the other letters without much interest.

He turned as he heard Claire enter. She was carrying the Champagne bottle and two flutes. "Are we going to open this to celebrate my new job?" she smiled.

Andrew took the bottle and popped the cork. "To us and new beginnings!"

Claire began to tell him about her last two days, the train delays, the bomb scare, her new boss, the challenges of her new job. Andrew sat patiently and was pleased by the way she let none of these things dampen her enthusiasm.

"I've got us two tickets for the new Romeo and Juliet at Sadlers on Thursday," she announced proudly. "It's sponsored by one of our clients and they gave the tickets to Leonora but she has something else on that evening. Oh, and Glen and Christine have invited us round to theirs for dinner on Friday. So that's two nights running we need a babysitter. I seriously think we are going to have to have an au pair living in."

"I've got some news too." Andrew poured a refill. "I've found us a house."

"Us a house?"

Andrew explained the need to spend more time in Lincolnshire and the unsuitability of a rented flat. He told Claire about the 'fantastic' house he had seen and the fact that it was only half a million pounds. As he spoke he enthused about the benefits of the rural location compared to the grimy city.

Claire was silent. At last she said, "I didn't think we were going to have to move. I like the 'grimy city' and I've got my new job. Lincolnshire? Nothing happens up there"

"No we're not getting rid of this place. It's just that we need something good as well up there. "

"But can we afford it? I mean we've got the mortgage on this place and you're not earning what you did at Templeton."

"Stan reckons we can get the mortgage payments paid for on expenses and I'm thinking of cashing in my share portfolio. All this drama over Brexit is doing the market no good. I can only see it going down the closer we get to a no-deal."

Claire sipped her Champagne. She wasn't excited about the prospect of spending weekends in the frozen north. The idea of Andrew becoming an MP was fine and would add to their status at the round of drinks parties and dinners that formed their social life. Because most of their friends worked in the City, the weekends were precious time for socialising. If she had to head north on a Friday night it would seriously impact on her social life. And the upkeep on two homes, with the two boys. Andrew hadn't thought about that, had he?

7

JULY 2018, LINCOLNSHIRE

They left early that Saturday morning. The boys had been woken, washed and dressed. The car was packed with their toys and a large overnight bag. The Travel Lodge in Sleaford had reserved a family room. Andrew was excited to show Claire the house and talk with the venerable Mr Hetherington again. Claire, feeling tired after her first week back at work, was quiet and went about things in a zombie-like way.

It was still just a little after six as Andrew double-parked the Nissan outside the house and bundled the boys into their car seats. They, at least, were excited by the prospect of a 'holiday' and staying at a hotel.

Andrew had been keen to leave on Friday afternoon but Claire said she couldn't ask to leave early in first week and anyway the Friday evening traffic would be horrendous. Added to that had he forgotten they had a supper invitation?

The traffic in London was lighter at this time of the

weekend but it still took over an hour to manoeuvre their way round the North Circular and onto the A1.

Living in the centre of a big city you are less aware of the weather. You rarely get more than a glimpse of the sky to see if it's blue or cloudy and the noise and pollution is much more imposing on your senses. Most residents in the Eastwood's road spent their life in their house, travelling in crowded trains or underground and working in large, anonymous air-conditioned offices. The weather made little difference to their lives.

As they crossed the M25 and the A1 turned into the A1M motorway, Andrew accelerated. Suddenly they were in open country and the early morning July sun was already climbing into a bright blue sky. He glanced in the mirror and saw the hazy outline of Barnet and the north London suburbs. The haze was caused by the traffic on the orbital M25, already busy with lorries heading for the Dartford Crossing and the Kent ports. It was a reminder of the volume of trade England did with Europe. Andrew shook his head as he thought about his last few days at Westminster.

He'd been back in time for Prime Minister's Question Time on Wednesday when Theresa May had to fend off questions on Brexit. The Withdrawal Bill had come back from the Lords with amendments but the government wasn't having any of that. "Brexit means Brexit," she had said on more than a few occasions. The problem was, no one had actually worked out how Brexit could be implemented.

"Where have all the houses gone, Daddy?" Miles piped up from the back seat.

"We're in the countryside now, Miles. They have fields and farms and not so many houses as in London."

"Oh," said Miles as he continued to look out on the flat Hertfordshire landscape.

They had arranged to meet Mr Hetherington at 2pm after they had checked into the hotel in Sleaford. But they had to stop twice on the way up for the boys' bladders and the adults' coffees and then the hotel room wasn't ready. It was nearly half past two when Andrew eventually drove up to the house in Otherby.

The boys were already excited by the sight of cows and tractors and anxious to stretch their legs. As Marshall got down from the car he looked around at the big garden. "Is this garden all ours, Daddy?"

"Hang on, we haven't even bought the house yet!" said Andrew.

"And we might not," said Claire. She had still not embraced the idea of staying in Lincolnshire. The coffee and sandwich in Sleaford had failed to recharge her batteries.

Mr Hetherington was only marginally more welcoming than previously. He watched as the two boys ran around the front garden. "Been cooped up, have they? The country air will sort them out."

Later that evening, with the boys fast asleep, Claire and Andrew sat down to a pizza and a bottle of wine in their room.

"Well, I have to admit the house is lovely," said Claire. "It's bigger than I imagined and the décor is much better than I expected. Might need some work on the kitchen though."

Andrew smiled. At least she was considering the place. "Of course it will mainly be me up here but I think the boys will love the space to run around in when they come up in the holidays. Tomorrow we'll take a drive around the constituency and then meet Stan at the pub in Otherby. You'll get a chance to meet some of the neighbours."

Claire gave him a look that said 'do I really want to meet the neighbours?'

"I didn't think Hetherington was particularly sociable," she said. "We were there for over an hour and he didn't even offer us a cup of tea. Can you imagine that back in London? Don't they know how to entertain up here?"

"I don't think he thought about 'entertaining'. He's an old man, on his own, just wanting to sell the place."

"Well if I'd been him I'd have made a bit more of an effort. There's nothing like the smell of real coffee brewing and maybe some fresh bread. It makes the house seem more welcoming. I read that in House Beautiful. They had all sorts of tips on how to present your house to get the best price."

Andrew grinned. "I've noticed that they don't seem to go in for fancy arrangements or displays up here. Did you see that dress shop along the street from the hotel? The window displays looked like someone had just hung a few dresses on some old mannequins."

"I'm sure that's exactly what they'd done. No imagination at all."

Andrew thought about this. He needed to understand these differences if he were to be successful as the local MP. He'd done a report on anticipated changes to the High Street when he was at Templeton.

As high streets the length of Britain were suffering from the combination of high business rates and internet shopping, those in London went to great lengths to entice shoppers in. To make the visit 'experiential'. Outside the main cities, in rural areas like the one in which Claire and Andrew now found themselves, there was not the competition, not the cosmopolitan influence. Most of the shops were independently owned rather than part of a national chain. The buying decisions were made by the shopkeeper based on what he or she felt the clientele liked. More store was put on quality and wearability than fast fashion.

The next morning after a full English breakfast the family's mood had improved. Certainly Claire's had. Andrew drove across the Fens from Sleaford and showed off his newly-gained knowledge of the local terrain and the differences in farming. The boys looked with amazement at the wide, high vistas of the Lincolnshire countryside. The lack of shops and houses didn't faze them at all.

They met Stan in the Barley Mow. The weather was warm and sunny but the pub did not have a garden or tables outside so they took the boys into a corner and sat them down with colouring books. Claire stayed with them while Stan and Andrew walked up to the bar.

It was Sunday lunchtime and the pub served a choice of beef or lamb with all the trimmings. Chicken nuggets and chips were offered to the boys. Claire watched Andrew at the bar talking with some of the customers. He was shaking hands and smiling. Stan continued to introduce him to the men before taking him across to a couple of families sitting down with their Sunday lunch. He seemed relaxed and happy. Maybe this was the change he needed. He had a good financial brain but he also seemed to have a way of connecting people. She smiled to herself. So this is the life of an MP, thought Claire. She was glad that she had insisted on Andrew wearing his new chinos and a Boss polo shirt.

She had bought them for him only the month before in preparation for their holiday in St Lucia in July. Yes, just another few weeks and they'd be jetting off to the Caribbean. A whole lot hotter and more sophisticated than this place.

8

JULY 2018, LONDON

Andrew sat down on the green bench. It was the highest bench, up by the back wall. Appropriate, because as a new boy to Parliament he was supposed to sit on the back bench. The chamber of the Palace of Westminster was already filling up with MPs. This was the time when the chamber was at its fullest. That meant there weren't enough seats for everyone. In fact nearly a third of MPs would be forced to stand if the whole complement of elected members were present. It was one of the quirks of the Mother of Parliaments. It had long outgrown the building and the building itself was crumbling.

Already the government had announced it was going to have to move to new premises. The new premises, however, would be only temporary while the Palace was restored. Then all the MPs would return to the inadequate chamber and no doubt continue to spurn anything modern like electronic voting. Instead they would shuffle off down the corridor and into one of the two lobbies. Two MPs would stand at each lobby entrance and count the number of MPs entering. Then everyone would shuffle back to the chamber, seats would be retaken or disputed and the Speaker would be given a piece of paper with the results of the count. It made for good pageantry but slow governance.

Andrew was new to all of this. In the few days since he had been elected he had spent time in small offices around the building, meeting the Whips, chatting with other MPs and occasionally even getting to speak with a junior minister. But his sole responsibility had been to vote on various motions and, in particular, on Brexit-related issues.

Theresa May was having a torrid time. Having picked up the baton dropped by David Cameron after the unexpected referendum result she was trying, and failing, to find a way of satisfying half of the population without upsetting the other half. It wasn't helped by the fact that she had no control over the extreme right wing of her party, the European Research Group, who were hell-bent on leaving without a deal.

Every vote in Parliament had therefore become crucial and required the attendance of everyone.

Not everyone would be here today, although the chamber would be uncomfortably full. Wednesday at noon was time for Prime Minister's Questions which was like a prize fight between the Prime Minister and the Leader of the Opposition with baying supporters on each side drowning out both people's arguments. It gave MPs an opportunity to shout and jeer and gave the public, who watched the televised proceedings, an opportunity to see how childishly their elected representatives behaved.

Andrew looked up to see one of the Conservative

Whips approaching him. "After PMQ there's going to be a statement from the new health minister. I think you should stay around for that. The Minister knows your background on Green energy and would like a word after."

Andrew had been wondering to himself exactly why he had agreed to give up his well-paid job to represent a constituency in the back of beyond. Just what difference could he make to policy? Everything seemed to revolve around Brexit to the exclusion of everything else and his Remain leanings did not match those of the majority of his constituents. He wanted to get working and if a meeting with the Health Minister could lead to some work for one of the many committees he would jump at the chance.

His decision to stand for Parliament had been almost an impulse. Andrew had always thought of himself as cautious, methodical even. His economics degree had taught him to look at situations objectively, to weigh up the pro's and con's and decide which way would have the best outcome. But his life had been marked by sudden lurches in direction which made him look impulsive. He had decided to apply for Nottingham University rather than one of the fine Scottish universities or even Durham. He had seen the prospectus (among dozens from other universities) and decided it was more relevant to the current world than some of the others. That had led him to a job with a Scottish bank where he toiled diligently and was marked for rapid promotion. Then the offer from Templeton had arrived and he had fled the Scottish city for the great Metropolis of London. He liked to argue that he only left because of the havoc being reaped by 'Fred the Shred', but truth be told he wanted a bigger challenge that offered far higher financial rewards.

The Templeton job had led to him meeting Claire and their romance had been a whirlwind affair that quite shocked the cautious Andrew. Claire was very popular at Templeton. She seemed to enjoy the repartee and coarse comments that the young traders indulged in. Andrew was quieter than most of his colleagues. He worked diligently on researching companies, building financial models and planning his strategy. He liked to think he took his job more seriously than some of the others. So Andrew had been surprised one day when she had come over to his desk with a file and asked him out for a drink. Just like that. So typical, he now knew, of Claire. Claire was a thoroughly modern woman and wasn't hampered by tradition or convention. Their drink had led onto a pizza dinner and afterwards Andrew felt like he had been interviewed for a job. The questions she asked! But the attraction quickly grew and it was only a few weeks before he had driven north to present his fiancée to his mother.

The Brexit Referendum result had come as a shock to most people in the City and the resultant uncertainty led to massive falls in the value of Sterling and the share prices of many of the major companies making up the FTSE100. It made Andrew reconsider his career. Once again he had felt that this was the right time to move, to change direction. Now a parent, his views on the future development of the country, in which his children would grow, were more nuanced than before. Whilst still a believer in capitalism, and retaining a puritanical work ethic, he wanted the country to maintain its connections with Europe, its biggest trading partner by far, and an area with similar cultural values as

Britain's. He feared the consequences of a headlong rush to embrace America and China. Indeed he wondered whether Britain could simultaneously suck up to China and the US. He had a nagging fear that, having burnt its bridges with Europe, the country would fall between two stools and end up without the support of either China or the US. Maybe I can help the Tories get a good Brexit deal or even force a Referendum to overturn the decision to leave, he thought.

Then there was Climate Change. There had been a vicious campaign by certain American companies, and the major oil companies, to disprove the scientists who were warning against carbon fuels. Then there was the little girl from Sweden who wanted the politicians to act, and act fast, to switch to renewable energy. It was one day when Andrew was walking with the boys along Wandsworth High Street and Marshall had started to cough. The diesel fumes were noticeable. It convinced Andrew that something had to be done to preserve the planet. The best way might be to join the government. The best way for little Britain to influence world climate change would be in concert with its current EU partners.

It was while he had been contemplating a move that he had, one lunchtime, met George Osborne in a wine bar near Templeton. A just-resigned chancellor and now editor of the Evening Standard, he had been a staunch supporter of Europe. It was unusual for George to be on his own at lunchtime and Andrew apologised for interrupting his sandwich lunch. How he had had the nerve to 'doorstep' the former Chancellor and then to pour out his ideas of standing for the Tory seat in West Lincs, Andrew still didn't know. But he came away from the meeting firmly believing that there was a chance, if only a slim one, of getting another referendum. He decided then and there, to elbow his way onto the West Lincs candidate's list.

Now here he was, a few months later, MP for West Lincs and sitting on the famous back benches. A meeting with the Health Minister was promised and who knew where that could lead?

The noise got louder and he looked up to see Theresa May enter the chamber escorted by several members of her cabinet. Smartly-dressed in Tory blue she got into the ring with Jeremy Corbyn. The resultant contest did not cheer Andrew. The 'Chequers' agreement announced 11 days earlier had been withdrawn, the Foreign Secretary had resigned and there was yet another Brexit secretary appointed. Mrs May seemed to be bowing to the power of Rees Mogg and the ERG. "We'll have no freedom of movement, no border in the Irish Sea, no customs union, no single market and no further referendum."

Andrew wondered just what we would have, but there was no answer forthcoming. Not for the first time he began to wonder about the merits of standing as a Conservative MP.

In the few days remaining until Parliament recessed for the summer, Andrew felt that he was chained to his desk. Or he would have been more than metaphorically, had he got a desk. But he didn't. He didn't have an office. He had been promised one and in due course he would be told which of the tiny rooms in the Palace of Westminster and neighbouring buildings would be vacant for the member for West Lincs. But the Whips were too preoccupied with orchestrating the voting on the various Brexit amendments to bother about sorting out offices. Only the meeting with the Minister of Health had made Andrew feel wanted, or at least noticed.

The meeting had been brief, no more than a few minutes and conducted, not in the Minister's office but in a corner of the lobby. The Minister had pointed out that there was a growing disquiet about the air quality in the city and in particular its effect on children who went to school in London. Perhaps Andrew might like to 'get a handle on this' and let him know how real the danger was to children and what measures could be taken to reduce the risk. 'Without affecting the sales of petrol and diesel cars, of course. We're not ready to splurge on electric-car infrastructure at the moment and the tax we get from petrol and oil sales isn't insignificant."

It was Andrew's first rung on the ladder. It was also the first time he realised that politicians cared more about perception than reality and more about keeping their jobs than caring for their constituents.

Andrew diligently set about discovering the facts behind the headlines of asthma-suffering children being slowly poisoned. He had a vested interest. His twin boys went to school in London too.

9

The holiday in St Lucia had been a complete and happy break from work and responsibility. The boys had loved the beaches and the exoticness of the place. Claire and he had enjoyed the great food and a chance to get away from Westminster and the City. Escapism summed it up and surely that was what holidays were for.

Back from the airport and unpacking in their Wandsworth home, reality checked in. There was a package waiting for Claire from her new office. The documents and brochures inside related to a new client that she would be meeting on Monday, tomorrow!

There were no work papers for Andrew. Parliament was in recess. There were no committee meetings – Andrew wasn't yet on any Parliamentary committees anyway. Stan hadn't sent any urgent requests from constituents. But there were letters from his solicitor, a building society and the estate agent in Sleaford. Everything was proceeding on the purchase of the house in Otherby, but forms needed to be signed and funds obtained. He realised that Monday would be busy for him too. He would be a house-husband looking after the children since the new au pair wasn't arriving until the end of the month. He also had to sell part of his share portfolio to raise cash for the house and transfer the rest of his shares into Claire's name to prevent any risk of conflict of interest as an MP.

He had a lot to do before Friday when he was due to drive up to the constituency and hold his first weekly 'surgery' in Ludthorpe, the largest of the small towns in his constituency and the site of his constituency office. He had been told by Stan that he would be expected to host two surgeries a month to deal with constituents who wanted to talk over their problems with their MP. This weekend would give him a chance to look around Otherby in more detail and hopefully get to know some of his future neighbours. Claire would stay in London with the boys.

The boys thankfully slept in, exhausted from their long-haul flight from St Lucia so Andrew had an hour or two to sort out his week before they woke. Claire had left very early for her PR firm hoping to read up on her new client when she got to the office.

With little or no food in the house, Andrew elected to take the boys out to McDonalds for 'brunch'. The boys were delighted and skipped along happily as they walked the half mile to the High Street. The weather was cloudy and the pavements wet from overnight rain. They had to pick their way past several vans parked with their wheels on the pavement, some still with their engines running. Their drivers were delivering nearby or simply waiting until there was a space to park legally. The boys seemed oblivious of the fumes. Andrew was not. His mind returned to his research before the holiday.

He was concerned about the pollution. But those concerns would be pushed aside by far greater health concerns in the coming months. And the source of those concerns would be 150 miles further north where the air was clean and fresh.

10

Andrew peered through the windscreen as the wipers briefly cleared the heavy rain. The headlights illuminated the flat straight road ahead. Andrew was uncertain whether there were hedges on either side or deep ditches. He was watching out for the sudden bend in the road that would signify he was approaching Otherby. On a clear day he would be able to see the village from here as it was on slightly higher ground, but tonight with the rain he couldn't make out any lights.

The roads would go straight for a couple of miles and then suddenly swerve around for no apparent reason. Many a driver on these uncrowded roads had failed to navigate these sudden turns. Accidents were surprisingly high in this rural community according to research that Andrew had dutifully done.

Finally the lights picked out the directional arrows and Andrew slowed the car to take the bend. As the car straightened up he saw faint yellow flashing lights ahead and brought the car to a stop behind a small stationary car. The car door opened and a figure climbed out pulling up the hood of their parka. The figure approached Andrew who was anxiously looking in his rear-view mirror to see if another vehicle was approaching. He put on his hazard lights.

The figure crouched down to look at Andrew through the side window. Andrew rolled it down. The girl spoke in a soft voice with a distinct Spanish accent. "I was on my way back home to Otherby when the car just came to a stop. I thought it was petrol but there's plenty."

The rain was dripping off the peak of her parka and onto her nose. The wind drove the rain into the car as Andrew listened.

"It's only a mile down the road," said the girl hopefully.

It was half an hour before they arrived at the Barley Mow and it was still raining. Andrew turned into the car park carefully with the little car following at the end of the tow rope. Both drivers got out. Andrew lifted his overnight bag from the back seat and followed the girl into the bar.

Tired from the long journey, soaked from fixing the towrope, Andrew was looking forward to his room in the pub. It wasn't palatial but had a good shower and served him fine until the house purchase went through.

Once inside the bar they both removed their wet coats and shook them before hanging them on the stand near the door. The pub was quite full with Friday night drinkers and many of them turned to see who had arrived so late in this bad weather. Andrew looked at the girl as she shook her long damp hair. He could see she was in her late twenties, a little older than he had thought, with large heavy-lashed eyes, and the aquiline nose he had noticed as she had leant into his car. Her lips were full but bore no trace of lipstick. She smiled now at him and her smile was in her eyes as well as her mouth. Andrew grinned back. "I think we should introduce ourselves," he laughed, "I'm Andrew, Andrew Eastwood."

"I know," she replied. "You're our new MP. Well you get my vote, just for the lift! I'm Sara. Sara Mendoza." She held out her hand and Andrew shook it rather embarrassedly watched by a group of men at the bar.

The few tables were all occupied but there were two vacant bar stools and they headed across to them. Sara's long legs were clad in tight jeans poked into the tops of brown mud-splattered leather boots. Her damp black hair fell over the shoulders of her thick checked shirt. She certainly didn't look dressed up for a Friday night.

"What kept you out so late in this weather?" Andrew asked as the barman handed them their drinks.

"I had to deliver twins out at Skegby."

"Oh, so you're a midwife?"

"No, not exactly," she grinned at Andrew and he found himself staring into her large dark eyes. "I'm a vet! The twins were calves and their mum was having a hard time delivering them."

Andrew was a good listener and learned that Sara had lived in the village for the past two years after finishing her veterinary training. Her mother was a schoolteacher, her father a lecturer and they lived in the walled city of Salamanca. Sara had got the job with the local veterinary practice and appeared to like the rural English life.

The landlord came up and spoke to Andrew. "Good to

see you Andrew. Your room's ready but the kitchen's closed now. I could rustle you up a couple of ham sandwiches." He turned to Sara. "You look like you could do with something to eat too, Sara. Sandwich?"

Andrew's surgery went well the next morning. Only four constituents called in and two of them were more out of curiosity than a desire for action from their MP. Only one visitor stood out and he wasn't technically a constituent.

George Krasnik was an American from Nebraska.

After shaking hands the American introduced himself as the Vice President for Stellagenix in Britain. Stellagenix was a large international conglomerate that specialised in agricultural bioscience. He explained that the company ran a large laboratory and testing centre in the constituency and hoped that Andrew would find time in the coming weeks to visit. He would be pleased to show him around and explain their work including genetically modifying wheat and barley.

At 12.00 Stan and Andrew closed the office and headed for the local pub. "It's a chance to meet more constituents and then I thought we could pop into one or two local shops to introduce you."

By three o'clock Andrew managed to get away from Stan and head back to Otherby. Whilst the day had been very fruitful in terms of meeting so many total strangers whom he represented, Andrew was keen to pop in and see Mr Hetherington at the house. Everything was proceeding at a fast pace, the mortgage, the legal stuff. It seemed that being an MP had an effect of speeding up certain services and Andrew wasn't going to complain. Neither was Mr

Hetherington who had already made plans to move into his new supported-living accommodation.

The storm from the night before had passed through and the sun was doing its best to dry up the puddles in the driveway leading to the house. This time he found Mr Hetherington in the front garden waiting for him. The welcome was considerably warmer than previous ones and he had even put a plate of biscuits out to have with their tea.

They sat in the study – Mr Hetherington's room where his wife had only been allowed in to dust. Looking out at the garden and the fields beyond Andrew could see that part of the barley field had already been harvested.

"They had hoped to get it all in on Thursday before the rain came but although they worked until it was quite dark on Thursday they couldn't finish," said Mr Hetherington. "They'll have to wait a few days now for it all to dry out well before finishing."

Andrew already loved this room. He loved the view. He loved the peacefulness of the pastoral scene, so different from the traffic-clogged view from his Wandsworth study or the blank wall of his pokey office in Westminster. Here he felt he could get away from the constant demands of urban living. He might even start learning about gardening. Or farming, he thought. That might be very necessary if he were to develop a rapport with some of his constituents.

Mr Hetherington seemed to be in no hurry to see the back of him. Neither did he feel the necessity to make idle conversation. They sat together looking out at the view and sipping their tea. After his hectic day Andrew was glad to unwind. He knew that he would have to get back to the Barley Mow and get ready to go to the Conservative

Association dinner that evening but for now he was content to sit back and enjoy the peace.

Lincolnshire certainly seemed to have a lot to offer, he thought. So different from the frenetic pace of life back home. Some people find the constant competition to get through traffic, to find the last parking place or a seat on train, stimulating. Here life rolled on at a calmer pace. There was time to reflect, time to look at your surroundings. Although the people seemed a little brusque at first He appreciated their straight-talking and was already finding that there was warmth behind an initial off-handedness.

Later Andrew would adjust his judgement. He learnt at the Conservative Association dinner that there was a surprisingly high crime rate in the area, albeit not the gang warfare to be found in London. There was also a major problem with the youth and drugs. Unemployment wasn't high among the young compared with some London boroughs but there was a lack of variety of jobs, particularly well-paid ones. The same 'old-fashionedness' that had pleased him also made people less adaptable and less competitive when it came to looking for jobs.

11

Claire looked at her watch surreptitiously. Her client was still explaining the meaning of an organisational chart on his Powerpoint presentation. Leonora was smiling at him as if he were revealing some universal truth. She was like that. Very good at making clients feel that they were really interesting. Claire just wished he'd get on with it so she could get off home.

It was Friday afternoon. Who fixed meetings for Friday afternoons? It was POETS day – 'push off early tomorrow's Saturday'. She needed to get home in time to make the boys their tea. Andrew had to get away up to Lincolnshire and had hoped she'd be back in time to relieve him of child-minding.

Her head hurt. It had been a tough couple of weeks back and she was still getting used to full-time work. She had spent the days either researching the markets of her three clients, reviewing the media coverage the Agency had achieved for them, or actually presenting new ideas to those clients.

She had been so busy that the terrorist attack that had injured three people at the Houses of Parliament on Wednesday had passed almost unnoticed. It was just something you got used to in a big city like London.

She had eaten lunch only once that week – and that was with one of her clients. Other days she had made do with a sandwich grabbed on the way into work. Nevertheless it had been a good week. She had got on well with the client she had presented to and who had taken her to lunch afterwards. Wasn't it the role of the Agency to take the client for lunch? Gregory had been most chivalrous in first proposing lunch and then insisting that he paid for it. He was a few years older than Claire and divorced from his wife. No children. (Claire's research had not been restricted to the company's performance).

The lunch, including sharing a bottle of wine had been extremely pleasant and the conversation flowed easily. If Claire had expected him to have ulterior motives she was disappointed. When the lunch was over he complemented her again on the presentation, said how much he'd enjoyed their lunch and then rather formally shook hands. She felt good to be back in a world where she was treated as an equal, as an intelligent person whose opinions were worth listening to. Motherhood had its benefits but she had missed the intellectual challenges that business in the City threw up.

She wondered how Andrew was enjoying his time being a house husband. With Parliament recessed he was free to work at home or wherever. In fact he didn't have a lot of work, other than keeping his constituents happy and that he would be attempting to do this weekend. She wondered if he was missing the intellectual challenges of Templeton as she had.

She was brought out of reverie by the sound of Leonora thanking their presenter.

"I'm sure that has given us a most useful insight into the ethos of Prospect Insurance and I'm sure Claire and I will be able to get together some ideas to promote that to the public." She looked pointedly at Claire who realised that she had been less than attentive.

"Indeed. There's a lot of useful information. I wonder if you could email me a copy of the Powerpoint in case there are points I need to check back on?"

She saw Leonora smile and then stand up to shake hands with the client. She too must be wanting to head off home, thought Claire. Let's hope so anyway, she's such a workaholic.

The City wasn't so busy in August with many of the workers on holiday. Nevertheless the tube was full and she had to stand for the few stops to Waterloo, and again on the train to Clapham Junction. Despite her early departure she was caught up in the mass exodus of office workers anxious to head off for the weekend.

There would be no weekend away for her though. She'd be catching up at home with the boys while Andrew swanned off to his lovely Lincolnshire. Not for the first time she wondered if she really wanted a life as an MP's wife.

If he hadn't had to go to Lincolnshire she would have fixed up a dinner party for Saturday and they'd have been able to go to Simone's drinks bash tonight. That was the joy of living in a place like Wandsworth, there was so much going on all the time. She'd take the boys out on the Common on Sunday morning but she knew they preferred a kick around with their Dad.

12

Andrew was waiting for Claire as she arrived home on the Thursday evening. He was beaming and the two boys were jumping up and down behind him. There was a rich appetising smell coming from the kitchen and the dining table was laid out with four settings. There was an ice bucket with a bottle of Champagne poking out of it.

She put down her briefcase and slipped off her jacket, looking all the time at Andrew who was still grinning but saying nothing. As she walked over he held something aloft in his right hand.

"It's the keys! We're now the legal owners of Limetree House, Otherby. We can move in tomorrow!"

Marshall broke in "We're going up to the farm tomorrow and spending Bank holiday sticking up our posters in our bedroom! Daddy says we can ride a horse!"

She'd managed to get the Friday off in case the house purchase did get completed on schedule and leaving early

Friday morning would at least avoid the Bank holiday traffic. Andrew was clearly pleased with himself, announcing that he had arranged for beds to be delivered on Friday so they would have something to sleep on. The old Mr Hetherington had negotiated an amount for a lot of the furniture he couldn't take with him and while Claire was anxious to put her own stamp on the place it meant that they could at least live in the house in moderate comfort.

Now it was confirmed she wondered whether she could take Tuesday off too. She'd have to ring Leonora in the morning on their way up to Lincolnshire.

Andrew poured lemonade into glasses for the boys and uncorked the Champagne. "To our new life in Lincolnshire!"

"To our new 'holiday home," replied Claire rather pointedly. She still had no intention of leaving her busy Wandsworth life.

13

Andrew gazed out of his study window in Limetree House. It was his favourite part of the house. Most of the view consisted of sky. Sky was something that was only glimpsed in London. Glimpsed between high buildings. Even at Westminster where there were rooms that overlooked the Thames and the sky was not obscured, Andrew did not have a view. His pokey office offered him no view of the sky.

The harvesting of the barley had been completed. The fields were just stubbled brown now. Soon the tractors would be out ploughing the rich earth ready for the next planting. Barley is a two season crop with harvesting in Spring and Autumn. The recent harvest was earlier than usual and Mr Hetherington had maintained that it hadn't been fully ripe when they cut it.

"I'm sure the farmers know what they're doing," Andrew had responded.

"Not that one," Mr Hetherington had grumbled.

"Always looking for something new. Very pally with those guys at Stellagenix. I've no truck with them myself."

The view from the window was uninterrupted for miles. Otherby was on a rise rather than a hill but this gave it a panoramic view of the fields and villages for miles around. Past the barley field were fields full of sugar beet, potatoes and other vegetables.

Lincolnshire was where a good proportion of the UK's vegetables and cereals were grown. Here children knew that peas came from pods and beans climbed up poles. Back in Wandsworth most kids thought peas came from Iceland (the store not the country.)

Andrew's boys were back in Wandsworth. Claire had taken them back on Tuesday morning and had arranged for her mother to look after them for a few days. Andrew wanted to sort out the house and get around more of his constituency. He promised to be back for Friday evening when they were due out for dinner with friends.

The sun finally dropped over the horizon as he gazed out. Sighing, he got up, picked up his coat and headed out. Pub grub at the Barley Mow was beckoning.

It was half an hour later when she came in. Andrew had been half-hoping she would. This time she was wearing a dress rather than the jeans and sweater. Once again he noted her shapely figure as she walked across to the bar where he was sitting. She tossed back her long dark hair and welcomed him with a broad smile.

"I hoped I'd find you here," she said.

Andrew hid his surprise. Truth be told he had hoped that she might be in the Barley Mow too. He had enjoyed their short time together a couple of weeks before. He still

66

felt as if he were working when talking to the men in the pub, his constituents. He felt he was still on trial. With Sara it was different. She was an outsider too.

"It's great to see you too. I'm staying up for the week because we've just bought Limetree House."

"I know. News travels fast around here. Is your wife back in the house with the boys?"

"My! You are well-informed. No she's had to go back to London, the boys too."

"I want to ask you something," she said.

"Fine. Look, have you eaten.? I was just about to ask Sam what's on the menu tonight. Care to join me?"

They sat at a small table in the corner. One of the farmers winked at Andrew and gave him a thumbs up. Really, thought Andrew, no one in London would turn a hair if he was having a meal with a woman. Here in the country it was obviously something to be remarked upon. He was sure it would be too.

"What's the problem?" he asked Sara trying to act professionally but still finding her dark eyes disconcertingly attractive.

"It's not a problem exactly. It's just something I'm curious about. I wondered if, as an MP, you might be able to get me some information."

"What exactly are you after?" Andrew was intrigued.

"I want to know what the incidence of multiple births is with cows in England nationally."

If Andrew had been expecting an inquiry about how Brexit would affect Spaniards who wanted to live here, or how she could handle her tax return, he tried not to show it. What a bizarre question.

"Can I ask why?"

"Well, as I said, I'm curious. You remember that night we met?" She paused and looked at him with those smiling eyes.

"How can I forget?" he joked.

"Well, if you remember I had been helping a farmer with his cow which gave birth to twin calves. It was the first time I'd done it. Last week he called me again and another of his herd had twins. One of my colleagues was over at another farm towards Sleaford where a cow was in difficulty. In fact it died and the two calves were stillborn. It just seems like, well, quite a lot of cows having multiple births."

"Well I'm afraid I haven't a clue about cows. Maybe there are records kept, I don't know. But I can ask someone who works for Defra and get back to you."

"Thanks. I don't want to put you to any trouble."

It's no trouble thought Andrew and it is a reason to see her again. Professionally of course!

When they left the pub around 10 pm it was quite dark. Andrew turned down the offer of a lift with Sara pointing out that it was only a few hundred yards and the walk would do him good. He watched her as she drove off in her car. She waved out of the window as the car made its way, rather uncertainly, down the road away from the lights of the pub. It's a good thing there's not much traffic, thought Andrew. They had finished a bottle of red wine between them after an initial glass of white wine for her and two pints of local ale for Andrew.

He switched on his torch as he walked down the road towards Limetree House. He was still coming to terms with how dark it was in Otherby. Away from the pub there were no houses lit up and unlike Wandsworth there were no street lamps. The moon was obscured by clouds and the torch was a necessity.

He opened the front door and took off his coat. The house was quiet and still. Without Claire and the boys it felt empty and for the first time Andrew felt lonely. He was glad he had met Sara at the pub. The evening had passed quickly and he found her easy to talk to. She told him stories of visits to farms and the attitudes of some of the farmers to a foreign, female vet.

He remembered his promise to find out about cow births – very bizarre. He opened his laptop and scrolled through the lists of committees. He found the names of two MPs he knew slightly who were on the Agriculture Select Committee. Hopefully they were not on holiday. He made a note to ring them in the morning.

Andrew was woken by the sound of heavy rain resonating on the window. The bedroom windows were not double-glazed so there was nothing to deaden the sound. He glanced at his watch and saw it was just 6.30. Groaning, he turned over and put a pillow over his head and tried to sleep.

After an hour he gave up and rolled out of bed. He dressed quickly and went down to make breakfast. His head felt heavy and cleaning his teeth hadn't been enough to get rid of the stale taste in his mouth. He thought back to the evening. Two pints of Fentastic Ale and most of a bottle of Valpolicella had left their mark. He needed coffee.

The meagre furnishings they had brought up, together with some crockery, did not include a coffee maker. Andrew looked at the jar of Nescafe with disgust. This morning he needed real coffee and there wasn't a Costa or Starbucks for miles. He'd have to make do with tea. He made a mental note to add a Nespresso machine to his shopping that morning. He was due to attend a Rotary business lunch in Sleaford. Stan had told him that he should make a short speech about the local economy and the effect Brexit would have on it.

He took the teapot and mug into his study and looked out at the garden and fields beyond. The view was obscured by the heavy rain cascading from the sky. The green fields, the golden ones too, all seemed to have dulled to an almost monochromatic tone. Not for the first time Andrew remembered that this was the North of England.

For a couple of hours he worked on his speech. The problem was he really had no idea what the effect of Brexit would be on the farmers and businessmen of Lincolnshire. No one yet knew what sort of Brexit Theresa would achieve, or if indeed any deal could be reached. Most of the people in Lincolnshire had voted in favour of Brexit despite the subsidies they received from the EU. He knew immigration was a touchy subject in the area but the majority were migrant workers from Eastern Europe who stayed for a few months to help harvest the crops. You had to go as far as Leicester or Bradford before you had the high incidence of Asian permanent immigrants.

The Rotary Lunch was at a modern hotel in Sleaford. There were around 30 guests, all but one were male. The lady was a director of the local radio station and was seated on Andrew's left. On his other side was a farmer from near Boston who was also the Chairman of the local Conservative Association.

"So how do you find little Otherby after the delights of Wandsworth?" asked the lady who introduced herself as Sonya Arkle.

Andrew smiled, impressed at her homework. "It **is** quite a contrast, I must admit. But it's actually nice to get away from all those 'delights' you mention. They come at a price."

"You mean the houses cost a fortune in London."

"I was actually referring to health. There's just so much pollution. That's a real problem especially for kids, and it's getting worse." He knew he had facts at his fingertips if need be. His report for the Health Minister would not be wasted.

"I understand that you're not in favour of Brexit," she grinned.

"Well I must admit that I have concerns about our future relationships with Europe. But in London we are surrounded by Europeans and so many of our friends are involved with business there. They hop on a plane to Paris, Amsterdam or Frankfurt at the drop of a hat and get back in time for dinner the same day. It's a rather different matter up here. I do understand that people up here may feel that Brussels is making all the regulations and is so far away that they have no influence on it."

"I don't think it's just Brussels. Round here people feel pretty disenfranchised from Westminster."

Their conversation was interrupted by Nigel Underhill, the farmer on Andrew's right. "There's no doubt that European farmers get a lot more than the British ones. Especially the French. Keeps the prices artificially high. They're bloody inefficient too. Over here we've got big farms, well-run, latest technology. They're all scrabbling around on small-holdings and wanting Britain to pay for them."

"I'm not sure that's quite accurate," said Andrew wondering if he might ever be able to start on his soup. "If we leave Europe and scrap the food hygiene and animal welfare regulations etc., won't we be swamped with low-cost imports? That wouldn't help your farm?"

"No, no. We will insist that any of the countries we deal with adopt the same standards as us."

"But that's what we do with the EU at the moment – that's what you said you want to change."

Andrew turned his attention to his fast-cooling soup. He was aware that Nigel was glaring at him. Brexit was causing deep divisions in the whole country. Families were divided. It wasn't a matter of Labour supporters and Tory supporters. The Brexit argument railed across party lines.

"All these regulations against fertilisers, and GM crops. It's a nonsense. If Brussels wants us to feed our expanding populations it needs to let us farmers use every tool in the box to produce enough at the right price. The Americans know that. That's why they can export so much food."

Andrew looked up from his soup at the large farmer. He certainly looked well-fed. And he had a point. The world's population was rising fast and there were only limited resources. Britain was already overcrowded and more immigrants were arriving every day – legally or illegally. They all had to be fed. Making agriculture more efficient by using fertilisers and developing better crop strains was surely a good move.

On the other hand he thought about what Claire said. She was always trying to buy organic. She hated all 'E-numbers' and tried to cook family meals rather than order takeaways. Their neighbours in Wandsworth would wax lyrical at dinner parties about the purity of food and how it was worth paying extra for organic produce. But they could afford to be choosy. Here in Lincolnshire household incomes weren't at the stratospheric levels of City bankers. Those Wandsworth families would still take their kids to McDonalds or Pizzahut, would still eat out at expensive ethnic restaurants or the new trendy street food outlets. You didn't know what went on in those kitchens.

When he sat down after his short speech, Andrew didn't know how it had gone down. There was a round of applause and a nod of approval from a few but he knew many of the diners remained unsatisfied. He had tried to be even-handed agreeing that some EU laws were restrictive and expensive. But he also pointed out the importance of having a very soft Brexit that would enable people in Lincolnshire to continue to enjoy many of the current benefits. There was no doubt that many in the room wanted their cake and to eat it. The advantages of membership without the responsibilities and Andrew saw no way of squaring the circle.

His one consolation was that Sonya had given him a pat on the back and suggested that he agree to be interviewed on her radio station. "The Tory landowners around here and their cronies all hark back to the days of empire," she said. "The rest of the population doesn't feel it matters what they think, the politicians in London will do what suits them. That's why they voted to leave. It was a protest. It would be good for them to hear a Tory point out some of the benefits they might lose."

He had allowed himself just a small glass of white wine, aware of the journey back to Otherby and his responsibilities as an MP. It was still raining and the flat landscape looked uninviting. He was glad to get back to Otherby and Limetree House. He unpacked his new Nespresso machine and made himself a cup. He took it into the study and switched on his laptop. Among the emails was one from George Krasnik. It was an invitation for him to visit the Stellagenix offices the following week.

"I don't know how I'll fit it in," he mumbled to himself. "Next week I'm back in Westminster, and the following week. Then there's the Tory conference. That just leaves the weekends.

He wrote a brief reply thanking George and explaining the difficulties.

After a long phone call with Stan who was anxious to know how his speech had gone down, Andrew dialled Claire's number. He wanted to speak with her and tell her about the lunch. But the phone went to answerphone immediately. It must be switched off or maybe she was on the Tube, underground and out of signal range. He tried the home landline. The call was answered by Analiese, the au pair. She assured Andrew that the boys were fine, were having their bath before bed and everything was 'cool'. She said Claire had rung her and explained that she had an evening event to go to so wouldn't be home until late. Andrew thanked her and hung up.

He noticed that the rain had stopped although it was already getting dark under the cloud-filled sky. Despite the lunch, at which he had only picked, he felt hungry. And he felt like company. He grabbed his anorak and headed for the Barley Mow.

14

SEPTEMBER 2018, LONDON

Andrew and Claire left together on the first Tuesday of September to go to their respective jobs. The boys had been still asleep and in the hopefully capable hands of their new au pair.

It was the first day of the new Parliamentary session and Andrew was anxious to be involved. During August the government had come under increasing media pressure to get results on both Brexit and the other hot potato – the Windrush scandal.

He listened from the crowded back bench to Dominic Raab reporting on progress, or lack of progress on negotiations with Michel Barnier. October was the deadline for the Chequers Agreement to be finalised with the Europeans and it appeared to Andrew that Raab's insistence that they could have no border in the Irish Sea and none on the land border was untenable.

Theresa May was fighting battles everywhere. She was not only trying to get her Conservative MPs to back her deal but also trying to extricate herself from the Windrush scandal where Jamaicans who had lived here for 50 years or more had been deported because the government had destroyed their landing cards.

The next month or so in Parliament looked like involving a lot of late-night sessions and arm-twisting by Tory Whips. But Andrew began to realise that there was a lot more to Parliament than what happened in the chamber of the Commons. There were hundreds of committees and sub-committees covering all sorts of things and MPs of all the parties were represented on them. This is where a lot of the detailed work was carried out. He realised that he would soon be spending a lot of his time on one or more of those. He wondered how Claire would react to all the inevitable late-night sessions followed by weekend trips to the Lincolnshire constituency.

The same thoughts crossed Claire's mind as she sat at her desk in the City. The idea of being married to an MP had seemed good at the time. Now she had found herself a really satisfying but demanding job she wasn't so sure. She worried that their social life would go to pot. She had already had to turn down dinner invitations and an offer of theatre tickets.

Her short time at Otherby had convinced her that, nice though the house was, it was really in the middle of nowhere and that any neighbours were unlikely to be hosting celebrity dinner parties. She had agreed with Andrew that the countryside was much healthier than Wandsworth and offered something different for the boys, but they weren't about to move up there. His weekday job took place in Westminster, hers in the City and the boys had just managed to get into a really good school.

15

George Krasnik stepped out of the cab. He turned up the collar of his raincoat and hurried across the crowded pavement and into the Finsbury Circus office. He had done his homework well and hoped that the Agency would impress him as much as its website had. There were big plans for the UK after Brexit. George would be in charge of the expansion and the liaison with the laboratories back in the US. What he needed now was some favourable press comment on Stellagenix and its work to improve the yields of cereal crops in Britain.

Leonora's secretary led him to the boardroom where Leonora and Claire were waiting. There were fresh croissants, a fruit bowl and the smell of strong coffee.

"You guys are sure going to miss Europe when you leave," he said holding out his hand to Leonora. "French croissants, Spanish fruit and, I guess the coffee's Italian?"

He had planned such a remark. He needed to test them

on their allegiance to Brexit. Europe's 'big pharma' including GSK, Sanofi, Bayer and Novartis were the companies that Stellagenix hoped to rival soon. It had been hard for the American company to break into Europe but the UK was easier and a trade deal between America and Britain after Brexit would make things a lot easier.

Claire bit her lip. As a 'remoaner' she was against the decision to leave the EU and still hoped her husband might bring her news of a second referendum one day.

"We like to believe we are open for business with the whole world. If the French make the best croissants we'll buy them, if you Americans prefer bagels I guess we'll have to start serving them too," smiled Leonora before introducing Claire.

The introduction was unnecessary for George although he didn't let on. He knew who Claire was from the agency's website and the fact that she was married to Andrew was another reason to choose this agency.

Later, as they waited in reception for his cab, he turned to Claire. "I believe your husband's our local MP. I've been trying to get him to visit our laboratories there but he's been too busy. Maybe now you're going to work on our account he'll be able to find the time."

At that moment, Andrew *was* busy. He was squeezed onto a back bench watching Theresa May face questions from the leader of the Opposition. Mr Corbyn had to repeat the question as his first attempt had been drowned out by the baying of Tory MPs and the cheers of their Labour opponents.

Andrew shook his head. Prime Minister's Questions

was more like a pantomime than a debating chamber. Every question was prefaced with archaic references to Mr Speaker and right honourable members. Every answer to an opposition question seemed to avoid any admittance of responsibility and instead attack the performance of the Opposition questioner. Sycophantic questions from the government MPs were welcomed and these MPs would add them to their speaking records.

Today, as nearly every Wednesday, the questions were mainly about Brexit which seemed to be dominating Parliament. Negotiations were foundering with the EU. Hardly surprising in Andrew's view since there appeared to be no agreement in Parliament about what the British really wanted. It all seemed so removed from the real world – his world now of cereal farmers, teenagers in dead-end jobs, poor transport links and slow broadband. Yet again he thought about the efforts of people like Greta Thunberg to make the world a healthier, more sustainable place. There was very little appetite for that here in Westminster.

Andrew still hung to the belief that his presence was important and in any tight division his vote might lead to a softer Brexit. But the Irish border problem was proving intractable and Theresa May was trying to walk a tightrope held between the trembling hands of the DUP and the ERG.

After PMQs Andrew left the Palace of Westminster and walked to a riverside wine bar near the Tate Gallery. Two of his friends who still worked for Templeton had agreed to meet him. The on/off progress of the Brexit deal was making the stock-market very volatile which is something the guys at Templeton loved. Stocks were rising and falling, shares were being shorted and currency dealers were switching their bets with increasing frequency. Overall there was a lot of money being made by the brokers and the hedge funds.

His two friends pushed him for inside knowledge of what various MPs were thinking and whether Theresa would be able to hold the party together. In truth, Andrew knew no more than they did. Most MPs kept their own counsel and he was, anyway, a new boy in Westminster and had yet to form alliances.

It was a parting comment from Yasseem that held Andrew's attention. "Have you managed to get any directorships yet, or consultancy fees? You can't exist on an MP's salary."

Maybe, thought Andrew, I should look at some additional ways of making money. I don't have great hopes of influencing the Brexit deal, I'm not on any of the committees, so maybe I should concentrate on what's going to help my constituents.

As he walked back to Westminster his mobile rang.

Claire was anxious to tell him her good news. The Stellagenix account would have the second-highest monthly fee in the agency. She was to be the account manager on it and if it worked out well she would be promoted quickly to account director and a substantial rise in salary. Couldn't he skip Parliament for one evening and take her out for dinner to celebrate?

There was to be a debate on the Salisbury poisoning incident but Andrew saw no reason to stay late with that so readily agreed.

Over dinner Claire mentioned what George Krasnik had said about him not visiting the laboratories.

"Well I haven't exactly had time," he protested. "It's been full on in Westminster. "

"But there's the recess next week and then the party conferences. Surely that'll give you time to visit them? I think it would really help me. They are going to be an important client for the agency and any support you can give would help. Anyway they're planning to expand their operation in your constituency so you should be pleased too."

"Maybe we could go together?" said Andrew. "Why not come up with me on Friday night and stay over Monday?"

16

Claire did not accompany Andrew to Stellagenix. On Friday morning the au pair had discovered a rash on Marshall's chest and it was quickly confirmed that he had chicken pox. So once again Andrew set off late Friday afternoon up the A1 alone.

As ever, he was relieved when he finally reached the first bit of A1 motorway having crawled his way through the heavy London traffic. It had been an eventful week. Claire's new client and expected promotion was great news and Andrew was pleased for her. He was also pleased that the family would soon be getting an increased income. He had also been surprised when, just before Recess, he was called to a meeting in Smith Square with Michael Gove. In a short meeting he learned that he had an additional job. It was to work with APHA, the executive agency for Animal and Plant Protection and Health.

"This could be a major issue when we leave the EU. You

represent a big agricultural constituency so it should be right up your street. I need to know what the problems might be, what the opportunities are. You get the picture."

And that had been that. Not exactly a ministerial post but a definite step on the ladder.

Andrew was someone who enjoyed gathering information. He was cautious in his decisions normally. His decision to leave the City for Parliament had been an exception. Now he was determined to become an expert on animal and plant matters and work out strategies to help British agriculture. It might also help him in his quest to 'save the planet'.

He would start with the visit to Stellagenix on Monday, but tomorrow he had his surgery in Ludthorpe.

He saw the lights of Otherby winking in the distance as he turned the sharp bend and he smiled. He checked his watch. 8.42 pm. Not bad. Once he'd got through the central London traffic he'd been able to cruise a comfortable 10 mph above the legal limit all the way up the A1 to Colsterworth.

He was hungry and thirsty and headed for the Barley Mow as soon as he had parked the car at Limetree House.

Sara was sitting at the bar, a glass of white wine in her hand. She was wearing a dress, the same dress as before. Her long legs were bare and ended in smart low-heeled black shoes. Her hair was down, the dark strands falling in gentle waves down her back. She saw Andrew's reflection in the mirrored optics and turned to greet him.

Without thinking, Andrew bent and kissed her on both cheeks. A normal greeting in Wandsworth.

She smiled and her smile lit up her whole face. Her eyes sparkled.

Andrew nodded to the group of farmers by the bar, one of whom gave him a big grin and tapped the side of his nose. The vet being kissed by the local MP! That would be something to tell his wife later.

He ordered a pint of Fentastic and another glass of wine for Sara. "How's your week been?"

"Oh, busy as ever. I had to do some TB tests out on a big farm towards Boston. But it all turned out clear. We had a very old Labrador brought in but he was too bad to save. We had to put him down. Oh, and we had another case of twins."

"Calves?"

"No, this time it was foals. The mare was okay afterwards but we couldn't save the foals."

"They were stillborn?"

"Yes and they weren't due for another couple of months. Probably as well. They didn't seem to be growing right. The farmer was pretty upset. That's him over there."

She nodded towards the group of men along the bar.

Andrew got up and went over to them. "I hear you had a problem with one of your horses, stillborn twins."

The man who had grinned at him earlier nodded. "Yeah it was real touch and go whether she would survive. Pretty good job your young friend did there. But I don't know what caused it. The stallion is healthy enough and she had a foal two years ago, no problem. Sara said she was going to look into it. Anyway, thanks for your concern. Now get back to your girlfriend!"

"She's not my girlfriend," stuttered Andrew but the men merely laughed.

Sara was laughing too as he turned back. "The men up

here aren't used to all this continental kissing. You'd better not do it again!"

Andrew told her about his new role in animal and plant protection. "I haven't managed to find out about the incidence of multiple births in cows yet but now I've got this new job I should be able to find out something. Do you think there's a link between the horses and the cows?"

"I don't know. It's probably just a coincidence. I'm going to ask around at other farms, see if I can get any statistics. There's the Young Farmers dance over in Horncastle tomorrow night and I'll get a chance to meet a lot of farmers there. Do you fancy coming with me?"

17

SEPTEMBER 2018 ,LINCOLNSHIRE

On his way to Stellagenix Andrew was still deep in thought. All day yesterday he had been going over the implications of Saturday night. It had been a mistake to go to the Young Farmers dance. Perhaps if he hadn't allowed himself to be driven by Sara then he wouldn't have drunk so much. As it was, he had consumed rather too many beers and although he had ostensibly gone so he could question farmers about multiple births, he had enjoyed holding Sara close as they danced.

When she had dropped him at his house, near midnight, the village was in darkness. He shouldn't have invited her in but the attraction was too much. She had seemed happy and one thing led to another. She had left mid-morning on Sunday with Andrew hoping that no one from the village had noticed her car parked there all night.

Guilty? Did he feel guilty? Yes of course he did. After all, if Marshall hadn't gone down with chicken pox he would have spent Saturday night sleeping with his wife. He could blame the alcohol but really he knew that he had always found Sara attractive and, given the opportunity he would never had said no. After all, she had suggested the Young Farmers' Dance, not him.

Nevertheless he regretted it. There could be big repercussions. What if the villagers found out? They were desperate for any tittle tattle and this was right up there. What if it was more than a one-night stand? He enjoyed Sara's company, enjoyed being with her. Would the fact that they had gone to bed change all that?

Still pondering these issues he drove up to the barrier outside Stellagenix's offices. A security guard checked his name on a clipboard and then waved the car through. He parked in the visitors' space outside the main building.

The facilities were impressive. The buildings were two storey constructions built in a 'U'-shaped layout. The main offices fronted the complex with two long wings projecting behind to form an open-ended piazza.

As he waited in the sparkling-clean reception he could look through to the piazza. There were fountains and manicured flowerbeds. Stone benches had been placed near the fountains and Andrew saw some workers sitting on them. The whole place had the air of a smart corporate high tech company. He half-expected to see Mark Zuckerberg walk by in his T-shirt.

Instead it was the overly large figure of George Krasnik who strode across, hand outstretched. "So glad you could find time to visit us, Andrew."

Andrew picked up his briefcase and followed him to a small conference room off the main reception.

George pointed to a chair and asked if he wanted coffee or tea. "I'm afraid we don't have any fresh croissants here like your wife's agency but there's some Snickers bars if you want one. I'm sorry Claire couldn't make it today. I gather your son's ill."

"Yes I'm afraid he went down with chicken pox on Friday. It's not too serious but she has to stay with him."

"No problem. I already spoke to her and she's going to come up next week to see the place."

Andrew wondered when they had spoken. She hadn't mentioned it when he spoke to her on Sunday afternoon. They had talked about Marshall and whether she should keep Miles off school too. Andrew had not mentioned the Young Farmers Dance or Sara. He just spoke about his Saturday morning surgery and his hope to get stuck into some research.

A young girl in tight jeans and T-shirt entered with a tray of coffee. She was followed by a similarly-dressed young man with crew-cut hair. "I've asked Dylan to run through the corporate video, it will give you some background to the work we're doing here."

Andrew was used to corporate presentations. He had sat through countless videos and Powerpoints while working at Templeton. This one was very slick. There were shots of the American headquarters, of lab technicians, of vast fields of cereals, and close ups of seedlings. Then the video turned to pictures of starving African children, followed by graphs showing population growth and then predictions of global warming. Finally there was a shot of the Lincolnshire facility and a smiling George Krasnik shaking hands with Theresa May.

The video finished and the lights came up. The T-shirted employee departed.

"Well what do you think Andrew? Pretty impressive eh? And the UK arm is right here in your constituency. Stellagenix is the future for mankind. We've got a really crowded planet and if we're to feed all those guys then we're going to have to have far more productive farms – particularly the arable ones."

Andrew took a sip of his coffee. He couldn't deny that George had a good point. Andrew had been born just as Bob Geldorf and Midge Ure launched Live Aid. It was to provide help for victims of the Ethiopian famine. Since then there had been countless other famines. Some caused by natural phenomena – drought or locusts. Others by man himself in war-torn countries such as Syria, Chad and Yemen.

The world was growing weary of providing food aid for such countries. There was a feeling of hopelessness, that starvation for some of the world's population was inevitable especially as the birth rates in such countries continued to rise. Scientists believed that such problems could be overcome by developing drought-resistant plants, and plants that resisted insect attacks.

Andrew's job at Templeton had been to analyse company reports, question the bold statements corporations made and his training kicked in.

"George, that really is a very impressive presentation and there is no denying that the world needs to be producing more food. But people are still wary of GM foods, particularly here in the UK. There are protest groups who oppose the American-led crusade to doctor foods."

"Hey, hang on Andrew. We're not doctoring foods. We're

simply carrying on the work of people like your Charles Darwin – natural selection. For years British growers have been propagating hybrid plants. Look at your beautiful rose gardens!" He gave Andrew a wide grin and pushed the dish of Snickers closer. "What we're doing is just taking that one-step further. We're going into the building blocks of the plants, their DNA if you will. We're finding out why certain varieties resist infections, or grow more quickly and then synthesising that gene and incorporating it into other plants. Well that's a bit simplistic but you get the idea."

"So what, in particular, is the role of this facility here in Lincs?"

"Well that's what's so exciting. You have some really good scientists over here. A few that think outside the box. Plus you grow a heck of a lot of cereals and vegetables here. The future lies in large-scale farming, not the small family-run set-ups you find in many parts of Europe. The EU is spending a fortune through the Common Agricultural Policy propping up the small farmers. Here in Britain you see things differently. Look at the ownership of the land here in Lincs. There's millions of acres owned by corporations, Universities and the like. They're interested in yields. You may not have the Great Plains of Mid-west America but neither are you bothered about supporting Welsh hill farmers."

"I'm not sure that's true. Welsh farmers are voters too."

"Yes, but not Tory voters I guess. Britain owes its place at the top table simply because of its finance industry. And the money in farming is in big acreage here in Lincs. The EU grants are based on acreage – the bigger your farm, the more money you get. The more efficiently you produce food the more money you make. So big fields, full utilisation of space and more robust plants is what is called for."

Andrew didn't need to be told how much wealth was produced in the City. He had been part of that Big Bang success. He could see the attraction of George's argument. Lincolnshire and neighbouring Cambridgeshire were the heartlands of what remained of British agriculture.

As if reading his thoughts, George continued. "We looked at Cambridgeshire of course. Great links with the University there and quite an incubator for hi-tech companies. But we got a good deal on the land here and your predecessor helped get the planning permission through in record time. I hope we can count on you to support our expansion."

"Expansion?"

"Oh yes. This is just the start. We've been concentrating on your wheat and barley principally but we're looking at the root vegetables now – the beet, parsnips, turnips. Then there's peas and beans – great sources of goodness if only you Brits would eat more than five a day!"

"What does that mean in terms of employment?" The MP for West Lincs asked.

"Well it should be a great help. Obviously the top scientific jobs, the specialists, will still come from the US but the lab guys will come from universities in the UK. In fact there'll be a need for more UK graduates since many of our current technicians are European and they'll all be going home after Brexit. "

"But what about the local population? What jobs will there be for them? "

"There'll be opportunities for some in the planting and harvesting although that will mainly be the current farmers. But you don't suffer from much unemployment here anyway."

Andrew thought about the people he had met over the past few months. Sure, there was not mass unemployment. But neither were there many opportunities to earn good money in the area. Young people who stayed in the area had precious few openings. He thought too of Sara. She was typical of the well-trained, educated European working over here. Would she look to return to Spain when Brexit went through or would she still feel welcome?

"Let me show you our research labs. Very secret really but I guess as you're our MP it's Okay. Leave your phone here though. No photos please"

Later, as he walked Andrew back to his car George put his arm around Andrew's shoulder. "I look forward to seeing you with Claire again, end of next week when you're back from your Tory Conference. I'd like to take you to lunch over in Stamford. There's a great place there serves really traditional English food – Yorkshire pudding and all. We're all in this together now, you me and Claire. We can make a real difference."

18

SEPTEMBER 2018, LONDON

Claire wrote and then rewrote a paragraph in her proposal document. She was sitting at her kitchen table with her laptop. Marshall was lying on the couch in the living room watching cartoons and feeling sorry for himself.

Analiese had taken Miles to school and was doing some shopping. Claire was taking the opportunity to finish her proposal for her Insurance client. She was still new to her job. She was in a way still on trial and she didn't want her bosses to think that parenting made her unreliable. She would go back to the office tomorrow, with the finished proposal and leave Analiese to watch over Marshall.

She was excited to get to grips with her latest client too. Stellagenix was set to be the Agency's biggest client and she was the main person working on it. She knew that a lot depended on it. If Marshall hadn't contracted chicken pox then she'd be up in Lincolnshire now, with her husband and her new client. Still, Andrew had gone that morning to the plant and that would please George. She'd get up there next week and have a good look around at all the facilities. She had already developed some ideas about how to increase the press coverage of Stellagenix. It helped that they seemed to be so well connected with so many senior Conservatives. Photo opportunities were always useful.

Andrew had been pleased when he announced his appointment to APHA, the executive agency for animal and plant protection and health, but she had been even more pleased. At last Andrew's new job was proving beneficial. She had little doubt that being the wife of the MP had had a bearing on her Agency's appointment to the Stellagenix account.

She wondered how Andrew was spending his time up at Otherby. Such a remote place with no decent restaurants or any entertainment. She felt sure he was regretting leaving Templeton and the vibrant social life of Wandsworth. Still, he'd be back tonight and getting ready for the Tory Conference in Birmingham at the end of the month. She wouldn't be able to go with him because of her job, and the children. But he had promised to come to her office do this Friday evening and spend the weekend at home rather than in his constituency.

That was not what happened however.

On Friday, Miles succumbed to the inevitable chicken pox and more worryingly, so did Analiese. The result was that Andrew stayed at home that Friday evening while Claire attended the office party.

The party was held at a small, but trendy nightclub in Westminster and was to mark the fifth anniversary of the founding of the Agency. All the staff and their respective partners were there as well as some of their most important clients. There were several representatives of the media too of course.

Claire had taken great care to dress appropriately. She had booked an appointment with the hairdresser for Friday afternoon and her blonde hair was now cut in a very modern fashion that she felt suited her. She wore a newly-purchased cocktail dress in electric blue. Her high heels emphasised her shapely legs and the neckline of the cocktail dress was low enough to reveal an adequate amount of cleavage while remaining professional.

For the first hour she congregated with her colleagues, enjoying the canapes and the Champagne. Paul Devorian, the Agency's charismatic CEO gave a short but very amusing speech about how he came to found the Agency and some of the trials and tribulations he had endured since. Then the DJ upped the tempo and volume of the music and people began to take to the dance floor.

Stellagenix had been invited but George was not there. In his place was a young American woman whom Claire had never met. She introduced herself as Vice President Corporate Relations UK. A grand sounding title that failed to impress Claire. She was well aware that US companies were littered with VPs. But her role in corporate affairs was interesting as that would mean she would be working with the Agency. They exchanged pleasantries and Amber, as Claire learned was her name, said she would be seeing her when Claire visited the plant next week.

Their conversation was interrupted when Claire felt a tap on her arm and turned to see Clifton from Prospect Insurance.

"You're not going to refuse your favourite client a dance are you?"

Clifton was the son of the chairman of Prospect. Marlborough-educated, he was six foot two but looked taller because of his slim frame. He had dark hair and dark eyes and a reputation for being a flirt. Claire had only met him once. He didn't appear to have a major role at Prospect but was listed as 'Development Director' on the company's website.

Claire smiled and took his hand as he led her to the crowded dance floor. After the first dance when the crowd gyrated manically to a thumping South American beat the DJ switched to a slower number and Clifton took advantage of it to hold Claire close around the waist. They moved rhythmically to the melody and Clifton's grip grew stronger. Her head was resting on his chest and the scent of his cologne was intoxicating. "No husband tonight?" He bent his head to bring his mouth closer to her ear.

"No. And no girlfriend for you?" Claire knew of his reputation as a party animal and being one of the most eligible bachelors.

"I'm very happy with the one I'm dancing with right now!"

Smooth bastard, thought Claire but made no move to unentangle herself. In fact, after the week she'd had it was rather nice to be flattered.

They finished dancing as the DJ spun a new disc with a loud fast beat. He led her across to the bar and ordered two glasses of Champagne. They perched on two leather-topped bar stools.

Away from the dance floor the music was not so loud

and it was possible to talk. After some banter he suddenly turned serious. "I hear you are interested in art." Claire was surprised. It was true that she had studied art at A level and enjoyed visiting galleries but how did he know? Who had told him?

She had assumed that Clifton was just a playboy who would spend the evening dancing with as many of the attractive ladies as possible. There were a lot at this party and many were not married like Claire. She was curious to find he had been genning up on her.

"Well I like looking at it. Some modern stuff interests me but a lot of it is just sensationalist. It tries to shock rather than inspire." Claire took another sip of Champagne. That sounded quite intelligent, she thought, pleased with herself. The Champagne went down a little too fast and caused her to cough. Clifton immediately patted her on the back and passed her a napkin.

Recovered, she looked at him. He was smiling in an amused way. "I love it when you wrinkle your nose like that," he said. She ignored the flippancy and tried to bring the conversation back to art. "Do you have a favourite artist?"

"No, I like many sorts of art. Some of the classicals but more of the modern scene. Do you know Pavel Torchevski?"

"I'm afraid I don't. He sounds Polish."

"He's actually Hungarian. His paintings are politically-inspired. Lots of imagery. Has a bit of a fixation with boots. They're a bit like Chagall's cows that seem to pop up unexpectedly in his paintings."

"Boots?"

"Yes, he uses the boot as a symbol of control. Controlling a downtrodden population for instance."

"Sounds interesting but maybe a bit threatening."

"You should see them. In fact why don't you? There's an exhibition of his work in a gallery just off Bond Street. Why don't we go together and see next week?"

Claire looked at him as the disco lights played across his face turning it alternately red and purple. She realised that her head was spinning a little like the disco lights. The champagne was having an effect. She shook her head. Had he just asked her out on a date? Clifton? The rich playboy with a colourful reputation?

Clifton was waiting for an answer. He is a client, one of my main clients, she thought. It's not a date. It's a visit to an art gallery. Probably at lunchtime. No harm. In fact almost obligatory.

"I'd love to."

"Great, how about Tuesday?"

"Yes that's fine Andrew will be up at Birmingham for the Tory Conference and I'm not going up to Lincolnshire until Thursday."

A smile passed across Clifton's face at the mention of the Tory Conference. "Right then, Tuesday. I'll pick you up at the Agency after work, the gallery stays open late and we can get a meal afterwards."

19

SEPTEMBER 2018 – BIRMINGHAM AND LONDON

Andrew was in the bar at the Metropole when the Minister approached him. "Andrew, thanks for your work on the air pollution in London. Good job. I need you to look at something else for me. As you know we're getting a lot of stick on this contaminated blood fiasco. You know, the HIV-infected blood transfusions. It may have happened forty years ago but the inquiry is reminding everyone about how cavalier politicians can be with the public's health. Of course we're not now but I think if you could dig up some facts about blood transfusions, whether we still import supplies of plasma etc it would be really helpful."

Andrew looked at him. "Of course I'd be happy to but isn't that something more for your intern?"

"Well Andrew I see a role for you in the ministry. After Theresa's performance today I think there's going to be some reallocation of roles and I'd not be surprised to see you joining my team. It could be good if you'd gen up on some of these technical issues."

So this is how it happened, thought Andrew. The first step on the ladder had been his appointment to the committee on plant protection , now there was a possibility of a junior minister's job in the health department. Andrew's interests lay more in agriculture than health but nevertheless nutrition was closely linked to health.

The minister ordered a tonic water and offered Andrew another beer. "Thank you. Not quite up the standard of my constituency's beer – Lincolnshire Fentastic! Still it's very welcome after all those speeches."

"I hear you were over at Stellagenix last week. Big donors of ours you know. See what you can do for our Mr Krasnik will you?"

Before he could comment another MP arrived and shook hands with the minister. "Forgive me, Andrew. Need to sort something out with Alistair here."

Andrew took his beer and moved out of earshot. How did the minister know he'd been to Stellagenix? Was someone checking up on him? Had he spoken to George Krasnik? Andrew made a mental note to be careful how he behaved in future. His thoughts turned to Sara. He hoped that liaison wasn't on the Westminster grapevine.

He joined a couple of colleagues and a little later they took a cab together into the city where they enjoyed an Italian meal. It was nearly eleven by the time he was back in his hotel room. He decided it wasn't too late to phone Claire and tell her about the meeting with the minister. Her mobile rang for several seconds before going to answerphone. Maybe it was a bit late, he'd ring first thing in the morning.

Tomorrow, Wednesday, was the final day of the conference and he would be taking the train back to London.

In London Claire heard her mobile ring. It was in her handbag which was under the table. By the time she had moved her chair back and rummaged in her bag the phone had stopped ringing. She looked at the missed call – Andrew. At least it wasn't Analiese phoning about a problem with the children.

She glanced at her watch. It was nearly eleven. Clifton was watching her carefully. Now he reached across the restaurant table and took her hand. "Everything all right? No problems I hope?"

"No everything is fine – it was just Andrew. He probably thinks I'm tucked up in bed."

"Talking of which," said Clifton, "perhaps we could stop over at my flat. I've got a couple of paintings I'm sure you'd enjoy."

"Clifton. Stop it. You'll be asking me to see your etchings next. But it's late and I need to get back home. It's been a lovely evening and a delicious meal. Thank you so much."

"So there's no prospect of me seducing you tonight?"

"Not tonight, no."

"Another night then? I'll hold you to that." He laughed and called for the bill.

As she sat in the taxi back to Wandsworth Claire thought through the evening. She had enjoyed it. Clifton had been very attentive, very complimentary. They had flirted a little but he hadn't been insistent and she had not had to fight him off. In fact it had been a thoroughly good evening. She was humming to herself as she inserted her key in the lock.

The alarm woke her at 6.30 and she groaned. Her head was muzzy and her body was covered in sweat. She desperately wanted a glass of water. She put it down to the cognacs that Clifton had ordered to follow the meal. The wine she could deal with, no problem. But two large cognacs was another matter. She thought back to Clifton's suggestion that she come back to his flat. Was he really serious? Had she offended him by refusing? After all, he was her largest client. Well Prospect and Stellagenix were her only two clients. She couldn't have been that drunk or she just might have agreed. He was rather dishy.

She heard Marshall yelling at his brother. She was back to earth with a bang. She slipped off her wet nightdress and tossed it in the laundry basket and wrapped a gown round her. She went down the stairs ignoring the noise from the boys' room. In the kitchen she poured herself a glass of cold water. Her head was still buzzing. No. it wasn't her head, it was her mobile. It was in her handbag on the table. Still in silent mode from the restaurant it was vibrating quite loudly.

For the second time in the past seven hours the Andrew heard the answerphone. He started to leave a message when Claire picked it up.

"Did I wake you? Sorry"

"No, I'm up. Just. A heavy night last night." She drank the rest of the water.

"You sound awfully croaky. You're not going down with chicken pox are you?"

"No, just too much cognac last night."

"Oh? Who was that with then? I called you around 11 but you didn't answer."

"Oh it was just a client do I had to go to – an exhibition

and then a meal. Anyway, how's the Conference going – Theresa's big speech this morning isn't it?"

Claire wondered why she was feeling guilty. She hadn't lied. There had been an exhibition and a meal. And Clifton was a client. Still, best not to go into detail.

Andrew told her about his meeting with the minister. Claire was pleased. "That's great Andrew. It could be the first step on the ladder to a stellar career!"

"Talking of stellar – we're due to meet your friends at Stellagenix next week, don't forget."

20

When Andrew got out of the cab, he looked at his house. It was indistinguishable from the others flanking it, yet it was worth a seven-figure sum. He contrasted it with the house in Otherby. It lacked the grounds, the detachedness, and it certainly lacked the country views. The roadside was lined with parked vehicles and the house lights reflected in the vehicles darkened windows. He looked up as another plane passed overhead destined for Heathrow.

After his few days in Birmingham and now his return to suburban London, he realised that he was missing the rural peace of Lincolnshire.

Claire was happy to see him and threw her arms around his neck as he entered. There was a delicious smell coming from the kitchen and the table was laid for four with candles flickering. There was no sign of the twins.

"Analiese is putting them to bed. I've invited Justin and Lucy over for supper. They're due at eight."

Andrew looked at his watch. It was already 7.30. He needed to shower and change. He rather wished they weren't entertaining this evening. It would have been nice to sit with Claire and tell her all about the conference and his hopes for the role in the Health Ministry. But Claire was a social animal and he knew only too well how she loved entertaining and being entertained. Her days were always full. She had obviously recovered from last night's heavy drinking, had done a day at the agency and was still busy preparing what would undoubtedly be a delicious meal. That's what he liked about his wife – her boundless energy.

Lucy and Justin had arrived and were drinking champagne by the time Andrew returned downstairs, freshly showered and changed.

"How's our budding politician doing?" joked Justin who had spent the day in Canary Wharf studying currency movements.

"Shall we put on an ABBA record and all sing *Dancing Queen,*" laughed Lucy.

The image of Theresa May prancing onto the stage at Birmingham to the ABBA tune flashed through Andrew's head. It had all seemed a little gauche.

"So tell me, Andrew. What's it actually like in Westminster? Is it frantically busy with all this Brexit stuff or do you all just sit around in the bar back-stabbing each other?"

Andrew thought for a moment. What *was* Westminster like? So far he hadn't got that involved. He still felt on the periphery. Stuck on a back bench listening to the cheers from his own side and the jeers from Labour. Brexit was all anyone talked about yet there seemed to be little or no progress. Perhaps there couldn't be. Half the country wanted it, the other half didn't. Whatever Theresa managed to negotiate wasn't going to please at least half of the country. It probably wouldn't please anyone. It seemed we had gone from taking back control in order to enjoy the sunny uplands of new trade deals to making the best of a deal which would inevitably cause us great disruption.

"The pound's taken a beating ever since the referendum," said Justin. "Every time she loses a vote in Parliament it drops further. I'm hoping she can sort out this Northern Irish problem and move on. Then we'll see the pound improve. I've got clients depending on that."

"Surely we'll see the benefits when we sign a new trade deal with America?" Lucy had read English at University together with American history.

"The problem," said Andrew, "is that the American health and food standards are different from the European's. If we do a deal with them it could make it more difficult to sell our agricultural products to Europe."

"Oh I'd forgotten that you're a farming expert now you represent Lincolnshire." Justin's knowledge of farming was at the Ladybird books level.

"The Americans are leaders in GM foods though," said Claire. "I've got a client who's looking to expand his operation in Lincolnshire which will bring a whole lot of jobs. That's got to be good news."

"We still have to import a lot of our food and with the pound so bad it's costing us more." Justin held out his glass for a refill.

As the evening wore on Andrew found himself thinking

about the differences in attitudes between London and Lincolnshire. Here the four of them were talking of these international issues with personal knowledge of the people and problems involved. They were engaged by politics, economics and travel. They, and their colleagues, were newsmakers, not just news watchers. For Andrew's constituents, currency swaps, Parliamentary debates, PR campaigns were things that happened 'in London' not in their world. They felt they were powerless to influence such things so took little interest in them. They were more concerned about local jobs, schools, climate change and probably who might win *Britain's got talent*.

Andrew spent the next few days in Wandsworth. He decided that he would wait until the following week before heading back to Otherby. He and Claire would drive up together and visit George Krasnik again. In the meantime he could spend some time with the twins and getting to know Analiese whom he'd hardly seen since she had started as their au pair.

It was Friday afternoon when his mobile rang. "Can you get up here as soon as you can?" It was the Minister's PA

"He's just come from the PM. The appointments are being announced tonight so we need you up here for the photo op."

Andrew was still learning how Westminster worked. He'd imagined that any appointments would have happened only after discussion, interviews and things. Instead, here he was apparently being promoted and told to rush up for his photo to be taken.

He apologised to Analiese, who thought she had a free day, and asked her to pick the boys up from school. He chose his best suit and a suitable tie and took a cab up to Whitehall . There were only a couple of journalists outside the Ministry. It wasn't a major reshuffle as it had been in January. Just a couple of minor changes.

The Minister welcomed him and shook his hand vigorously. "Very glad to have you on board. First step of the ladder eh?"

Andrew, as a Parliamentary under-secretary would now have a new office in the Victoria Street building. "There's quite a lot going on at present so best to get stuck in on Monday," said the Minister. "I've just been told that there's been an outbreak of Mad Cow Disease up in Aberdeen so you probably need to talk with Malcolm over at Defra."

Andrew smiled. Now he felt that he was finally climbing that ladder.

21

OCTOBER 2018, LONDON

Claire felt she was climbing the ladder of success too. In the few months she had been at the Agency she had worked hard and achieved a lot. She was working on two of the Agency's biggest clients, Prospect Insurance and Stellagenix.

Both companies had their problems when it came to public perception. Prospect was regarded by many as just another big financial company with overpaid executives and a disregard for the welfare of its clients. Stellagenix had little awareness with the general public but was American, rather than British. The antics of President Trump were making Americans unpopular.

Claire's job with Prospect was to generate favourable press articles showing the company as fair and decent and having sufficient assets to meet any foreseeable claims. It was largely about making sure Prospect wasn't tarred with the same brush as many other large insurance companies were. Apart from defending the company's image with the public, the company's standing with the City and the investment managers was crucial. Prospect did a lot of business in Europe and the way Brexit talks were going increased the risk that it might lose most of this business.

Claire's boss, Leonora, had warmed to Claire. The two of them spent a lot of time discussing various strategies for the two clients. Of course Leonora had other accounts to monitor as well and increasingly left Claire to manage the accounts on her own. Claire took that as a sign that she was trusted.

If Claire found her new job fulfilling and exciting, the same could not be said for Andrew's job. She had been used to talking about his job in the evenings. Evenings when they weren't entertaining or being entertained. But, since he had become an MP, things had changed. The debates in Parliament went on long into the evening and she was often asleep by the time he returned from the House. Weekends were also bad. Andrew seemed to be always leaving for Otherby on a Friday or returning late on a Sunday night.

In fact Andrew was never around. Their social diary had all but dried up and even the boys were complaining that they never saw their father.

She was thinking about this when her office door opened and Leonora came in. She was carrying two Costa coffees and passed one to Claire.

"Thank you," said Claire looking surprised. Leonora obviously wanted to discuss something at length with her.

After a few pleasantries Leonora got to the point. "Look Claire, I know when you interviewed for the job you said you had family commitments that prevented you from working overtime or taking on too many responsibilities. But we've been very impressed at how quickly you've got to grips with Prospect and Stellagenix. I'm getting great reports from both of them. Amber, from Stellagenix, is very complimentary and you've obviously made a hit with Clifton at Prospect." A smile crossed her face as she said this. She had obviously picked up on Clifton's invitation to Claire.

Claire tried not to show her embarrassment. "Yes, the work's going well with both companies. I think there's some real opportunity with Stellagenix going forward."

"The thing is," said Leonora, "the Agency is really motoring at the moment. All this uncertainty over Brexit has meant firms have started to beef up their public persona. I've never been so busy. "

Claire wondered where this was leading but took another sip of her coffee and let Leonora continue.

"I've talked to Paul and he's in agreement. We'd like to promote you to account director, handling both accounts. You'd have Prithi as your account executive. What do you say?"

"I'd say, thank you. I'd love too. I really appreciate your faith in me."

Leonora looked relieved. She had been worrying that Claire would refuse the extra responsibility because of her family commitments.

Claire was elated. She had been feeling low, missing the attention of Andrew. Now she felt valued again and looked forward to telling him about her promotion. She realised it might mean extra work, some of it perhaps outside of office hours but as usual was optimistic that she could manage it. Claire always liked to get things done. The more things she had to do, the faster she did them.

She was still excited as she came out of Clapham Junction station that evening. The commuter crowds were as dense as ever and she was half-carried by the tide of humanity scurrying out of the station. It was raining heavily but she managed to hail a cab. To hell with the expense, she'd just had a raise.

The reflected lights from the front room of their house shivered in the puddles on the pavement as the rain continued to pour down. She fumbled for her door key. Before she could dig it out of her bag the door opened and Andrew greeted her with a big smile. She hadn't expected him to be back from the House yet so was delighted that she could now share her news.

Analiese was upstairs bathing the boys so they went through to the kitchen where Andrew poured them a glass of wine. She couldn't wait to tell him her good news. Only as she was explaining her extra responsibilities did she start to fear he might put in objections. But he didn't. "That's so good darling. Really good. I'm sure you'll do an excellent job and the extra money will be good."

"You're home early for once," she said looking at the kitchen clock. "We can go out and celebrate."

"Yes, I decided to head home early. There's a rumpus going on in Westminster. Boris and his mates are stirring it all up and Theresa is reportedly going spare. I think I'll have some very late sessions in the next few days, so I'm making the most of today."

"But I thought that they'd all agreed on her new deal down at Chequers back in July."

"No. Boris and David Davis resigned if you remember. Now Theresa's got this withdrawal agreement with the EU

112

she wants to get it approved by Parliament. But there's a sizable chunk of the backbenchers who want a hard Brexit and Boris is leading them. It's all getting very nasty. Corbyn says the agreement is a load of waffle so we're in for some tense debates in the next few days."

22

News of Claire's promotion spread swiftly. On Thursday she got a phone call from Clifton at Prospect Insurance. He congratulated her and said how pleased he was that they would now be working more closely 'on strategy'. He suggested lunch the next day.

Clifton had not previously sat in on her meetings with Prospect but she could hardly refuse. In fact she was pleased to have the invitation. A good lunch would be nice. She had hardly seen Andrew in the past week. Interminable debates on Brexit had kept him late into the evening. She sometimes watched on TV to see him crammed in on the second row of the green benches. His new position with the Ministry of Health meant he was no longer relegated to the back row.

The restaurant was in Charlotte Street and Clifton was already seated at a far corner table when she arrived. He stood up, his face beaming and helped her out of her coat.

Kissing her on both cheeks he pulled out the chair for her. It felt nice to be so appreciated.

If she had expected light-hearted banter with some flirting, she was disappointed. For once, Clifton was all seriousness. "Where does your husband stand when it comes to Brexit?"

She looked at him to try and understand the reason for his enquiry. Brexit was a thorny subject. Half the people in the country were in favour of leaving Europe and Britain becoming a global powerhouse, the other half saw it as an economic and political disaster. It was best to refrain from discussing Brexit with friends and clients until you were sure which side they were on.

"Why are you interested?" she smiled.

"Well you must realise what a disaster it's going to be for Prospect if we leave the Single Market? After all, you're our account director now and you must be aware that we have a large amount of business written in France and Spain."

Claire hadn't really thought about that aspect of Prospect's business. She had been busy working on campaigns to improve their image with British consumers and London-based fund managers. Now it dawned on her. If, or when, Britain left the EU and the Single Market it was likely that UK financial firms would be prevented from doing business in Europe.

"Well, Andrew has always been a Remainer, like me. In fact one of the reasons he stood for Parliament was the hope that he could influence the government in some small way to go for as soft a Brexit as possible. He wanted financial service companies to be able to continue to trade in Europe. Passporting I think the phrase is."

"Yes Claire, passporting. But Boris and his mates in the ERG look like forcing Theresa into a hard Brexit which is why we're looking to set up a new business in Spain. And Claire, I want you involved from the start. I'm going over to Barcelona next week and I want you to come with me."

They talked over the details of the proposed trip. Meetings with some large brokers, with real estate companies to find offices and with the new legal advisors that Clifton had appointed. "You'll need to understand the Spanish and French markets, the financial media, the influencers. We'll have to work hard to retain our existing business and move it into the new vehicle."

It was after 3 by the time the lunch finished. The food had been delicious and they had enjoyed a bottle of Pouilly Fumé and brandy afterwards. Looking at her watch she gasped at the time. "Look I really need to get back to the office. I need to sort things out if I'm going to be in Spain next week."

He helped her into her coat and signalled for the bill. She left the restaurant and hailed a cab. She didn't like to be late home on a Friday, especially as she was hosting dinner that evening, but she needed to run the Spain trip by Leonora.

As the taxi threaded its way down Charing Cross Road and into Trafalgar Square she saw all the barriers being erected. "They're expecting big trouble tomorrow," said the taxi driver. "It's those Extinction Rebellion lot. They're trying to ban all us diesel cabbies. Save the planet, they say. The sooner we get out of Europe, the sooner we can forget about global warming!"

Claire smiled and nodded assent. The ignorance of people, she thought. Best not to get into an argument about Brexit.

23

George Krasnik accepted another glass of champagne and picked up the folder again. Glancing out of the window he could see the never-ending layer of cumulus beneath as the Boeing headed west.

He was looking forward to being back in time for Thanksgiving. It had been a very busy time for him in England but now he could sit back and reap the rewards. The results of the barley trials over the past two years were laid out in the report in front of him. He already knew the salient figures but it was nevertheless reassuring to see them in print. The graphs all climbed up in the right way. The steepness of the curves was amazing.

The new seeds first trialled two years ago in Lincolnshire had been treated to a subtle change to their DNA. But there was nothing subtle about the results. Yields which they had hoped might increase by a few percent had, in fact risen more than 20%. In the past year, using a mixture of newly-modified seeds and seeds from the previous-year's trial crops had been even more amazing. There was a further increase of nearly 10%. The results meant that when manufactured on a large scale and planted on the world's large farms almost 30% more barley could be produced in the same acreage. The sale of Stellagenix seeds would earn the company a fortune. And that was just the start. George's team were already working on a new modified seed for winter wheat. If that was anywhere near as successful as the barley trials it would be a complete game-changer.

George would return in a few days having received the congratulations from his bosses. He would immediately set in train the proposals for the expansion of the lab facilities in Lincolnshire. The laboratory work would continue to be undertaken in the UK where his small team, led by Dimitri had been able to work in almost complete secrecy. He still didn't quite follow all the mad Greek's explanations of what he had done to modify the seeds and produce such dramatic results. The subsequent mass production and distribution of the 'super' seeds would take place in the US of course and be exported to countries around the world including an EU-free Britain.

Once the amazing yield results were achieved in these countries even Brussels would have to succumb to pressure from their farmers to allow these GM seeds.

Claire Eastwood would be briefed to start the campaign to get support for the new strain among the media. The headlines would be about feeding the hungry and reducing the need for harmful chemicals. It was bound to play well with the environmentalists. There would be no opposition from the local council either to a massive increase in the size of the facility in Lincolnshire – her husband Andrew would see to that.

Britain's 2016 referendum had been the catalyst for Stellagenix to set up the experimental laboratories in the UK. It was disappointing that the exit deal had still not been finalised but George was assured by the Minister that there were sufficient Eurosceptic MPs who would ensure there was a hard Brexit whether Mrs May wanted it or not. Stellagenix's contributions to the Tory party (carefully disguised of course) had proved a good investment and George was sure that Britain would end up cutting ties with the EU and therefore being desperate to sign up a new trade deal with the US. That would be the green light for Stellagenix.

The choice of location for the laboratory had been influenced by the work being carried out in nearby Cambridge. There, an enormous project to map the genomes of 100,000 people was being undertaken by Illumina, a Californian biotech company. George had been instrumental in obtaining a constant stream of information from one of the chief scientists at the Cambridge facility. When the results of their research were publicised, George felt sure it could only benefit Stellagenix and their use of DNA manipulation in cereal crops.

Meanwhile another company based in North London was hard at work trying to predict with accuracy the physical form of proteins from their chemical make-up. For nearly 50 years biologists had been trying to do this one protein at a time. Last year at a biannual competition, this company, now taken over by Google, had won by using an artificial intelligence programme on a super computer. Stellagenix's scientists were also busy but using their own intelligence, 'informed guesswork', to modify plants and their seeds to improve their resistance to disease and rate of growth. Their leading scientist, Dimitri, had got very excited about something called CRISPR although George hadn't a clue what that actually was. It was an exciting world and Britain was at the heart of it.

The United Airways stewardess leant over to speak. "Have you decided on your lunch sir? We've cornfed chicken or poached salmon. "

George ordered a small bottle of Zinfandel to accompany the chicken and put the report aside. 2019 and 2020 were going to be great years for him. After which a seat on the board back in the States was a shoe in.

George wondered what his father would have said about his success. George's father, Frank, had been proud of how, in just three generations, the Krasnic family had progressed from his Albanian, refugee grandfather to a high-flying college-educated executive.

When his grandfather, Ferid Krasniqi had joined the immigration queue at Ellis Island he had spoken only a few words of English and the American officer had struggled to understand his name. In desperation Ferid had accepted a more anglicised version, Fred Krasnik.

Ferid had been relieved to become American and escape the clutches of the Albanian authorities. Life in Tirana had been hard, often brutal. He had pursued a less-than-honest career. If the needs must, Ferid had been willing to justify the theft and corruption that enabled him to afford the passage to America.

George's father had inherited Ferid's work ethic and

had built up a profitable business that paid for George to attend college. He had been proud of his Albanian heritage celebrating and boasting to his friends when Ferid Murad won the Nobel Prize for his research that had led to products such as Viagra.

Shortly before he died he had told George that one day he hoped George would become as famous and successful as Ferid Murad.

Now, sitting with his glass of Zinfandel, George looked down at the ocean 35,000 feet below and smiled. His father would certainly have been proud.

24

Clifton chose a white Spanish Rioja with his British Airways chicken salad. Claire, alongside him, did the same. The flight to Madrid was less than three hours. They would meet with a banking friend of Clifton's that evening and see two more contacts the following day before catching the train down to Barcelona.

Claire was excited to be going to Spain on business. Although she had been many times to the Costa del Sol this was different. It was the real Spain and she was working. It wouldn't be true that she hadn't thought of the implications of accompanying playboy Clifton but she tried to convince herself that she was savvy enough to resist his advances. If indeed he made any. Despite his reputation and his occasional flirting comments he had never acted improperly.

Now, as they sat side by side in business class he was all seriousness. Brexit had really affected Prospect and its share price had dropped considerably since the referendum.

Prospect now needed to set up a separate company, a subsidiary, in the EU in order to underwrite insurance for its European clients. Several of the senior employees would have to relocate to the new Spanish office once it was set up.

Clifton angled his laptop towards Claire. "This is the guy we're meeting this evening. He's handled quite a few mergers and acquisitions in our market. I'm sure we'll be able to get a lot of useful information from him on the market."

"What will he want from us?"

"Good question. No such thing as a free lunch eh? I guess he'll pitch for our business – handle us as a leading financial adviser."

"Have you got any background information on his company? Anything I should gen up on before tonight?"

"Yep. It's all on here."

He handed Claire a memory stick. "Shall I get your laptop down for you?"

The hotel in Madrid was modern and comfortable. Clifton had booked two rooms. Everything was business-like. After their dinner with Carlos they returned to the hotel. It was midnight. The Spanish eat incredibly late. Claire was exhausted. As they collected their keys from reception Clifton turned to her with a smile. "We need to go to bed! But if you're as tired as I am I suggest we go separately."

Claire laughed, more with relief than anything. She stretched up and kissed him on the cheek. "You're right, busy day tomorrow too."

25

Andrew spent the day in Cambridge where he met with the scientists who had completed the amazing 100,000 genome mapping project. With all the media attention focused on Brexit this project had not received the publicity it deserved. Having found a quick and easy way of mapping an individual's genetic code, or genome, scientists were now able to identify differences in your DNA that caused different diseases and in future the NHS would be able to design specific treatments for individuals. Britain led the world in this research.

He didn't arrive back at the Barley Mow in Otherby until eight that evening. The press conference at the Wellcome laboratory in Cambridge had gone well. The press seemed happy to have something positive to talk about after all the comings and goings on Brexit. The achievement was very worthy and, as Junior Health Minister, Andrew had expounded the benefits it would bring, not just to patients but to the NHS. "We will be able to use a patient's genome data to anticipate illnesses like cancer and apply appropriate treatment earlier. That will save the NHS a lot of money and resources." Andrew was genuinely excited by the prospect. For once he felt he was involved in something worthwhile.

He was keen to tell Claire about it but realised that she would be travelling and busy in Spain with that insurance company she handled. So when he arrived at the Barley Mow he looked around hopefully for Sara. She wasn't there.

Standing at the bar were three or four men that he recognised as locals and he joined them. One of them was a sales rep for an agricultural machinery firm. He was expounding at length the advantages of 'big farming'.

"It's all very well for this Extinction mob to go on about global warming, saving the planet and making farms better places for nature but they would moan if they didn't have enough food. In this area we've done so much to increase productivity. Taking down those hedges, consolidating small farms into bigger ones has meant we produce so much more per acre. And we're still not up to the American mid-West scale."

"And we still have to import a lot of our food," said his friend.

"Oh we've a way to go, I agree. But getting rid of the EU and its Common Agricultural wotsit will help."

"And all those silly rules about fertiliser!"

The machinery salesman turned to Andrew. "Where do you stand then Andrew? I hear you don't want us to leave Europe."

Andrew smiled and told him that it wasn't as simple as

that. He didn't want to get into an argument about Brexit, not after the week he'd had. He tried to change the subject.

"Look there's some amazing things happening in agriculture right now and Britain is leading the world in many of them. That's why firms like Stellagenix have set up their labs here. They're going to be able to increase the yields on your farms and, hopefully, cut down on all the pesticides you have to use."

"Yes, you're right. They planted a few fields of barley on my farm with their new improved seeds and they seemed to grow really well – much better than the rest of crop. Mind you, their seeds are going to be pretty expensive." Eric owned a medium-sized arable farm at the back of Andrew's house.

They continued to chat about farming until Andrew's meal arrived and he took it to a table seat. There was still no sign of Sara. I don't suppose she comes in every night, thought Andrew. It was, after all, mid-week. It had always been Friday night when he had seen her here.

As he was finishing his meal a man in his fifties wearing a Barbour jacket and cords tucked into his wellingtons came into the pub. Seeing Andrew he nodded and having got himself a pint at the bar came over. "You're Andrew Eastwood aren't you? I'm Dave Nicholson."

He held out his hand and Andrew half-rose to shake it.

"May I join you? I wanted to ask you about Sara."

Dave explained that he was the head vet at the practice where Sara worked. "I know you've talked a lot with Sara about her concerns about all these twins we're seeing being born. She's got a bit of a bee in her bonnet about that – probably just an aberration. Things happen. Bit like your London buses. None for ages then three come along at once!

Anyway it's not that I'm worried about. She's Spanish, as you know, and we don't want to lose her. She's a bloody good vet. But she's worried about whether she'll be allowed to stay in Britain after Brexit. There's talk of people like her being sent back unless they're earning a big salary. And even if she was earning enough she'd have to get a work visa and that would mean going back to Spain and applying for one there. Who knows how long that would take? What would we do in the meantime?"

Andrew tried to reassure him that it wouldn't come to that. We'd have an agreement that would preserve freedom to work and live in each other's countries, he felt sure. Or did he? The antics of Rees Mogg and the ERG were beginning to worry him. Theresa May just didn't seem able to get a soft Brexit deal through.

"I'll find out everything I can and I'll talk to Sara. I'll do anything I can to help her. Where is she tonight by the way?"

"She's back home researching I suspect. She's on call tonight in case of emergencies and we divert the calls to our homes when we're on call."

"Well I'll do some research on my own and maybe, if she's not working tomorrow evening she'd like to pop in here and I'll talk to her."

"I really appreciate you taking the trouble Andrew, let me get you a drink."

"It's no trouble at all." It was a very good reason to meet her again. He had hardly seen her since the Young Farmers' Dance. He missed her although he tried not to admit it.

It was still dark as Andrew came down into the kitchen. He

hated the short days of December. He seemed able to get so much more done in the longer days of summer. Pulling up the kitchen blind he looked through the rain-streaked window and could just make out the line between the leaden sky and the distant horizon. It wasn't black as night, more deep charcoal. And cold. The bedroom windows had been thick with condensation. Double glazing was sorely needed.

He inserted a fresh capsule into the Nespresso machine and looked to see if the bread in the fridge was still toastable.

Opening his laptop he settled down at the kitchen table as the daylight hesitantly emerged from the darkness. He wondered what Claire was doing in Madrid. It was probably even colder there right now. He had read books on the Spanish Civil War that had described the winters there on the high plateau. Still she'd no doubt have a better breakfast than he was managing. She had been excited about the trip, he could tell. She seemed to be embracing her new working life after the years house-bound looking after young children.

But what about his new life? Was he enjoying it? Was it what he had hoped? The answer, he admitted was no. Although he liked to think he was right in the centre of great things, in Parliament, mixing with the lawmakers, the strategists, he didn't feel he was in any position to influence the things he cared about.

Brexit was a disaster, a long-running tragedy that seemed to limp along from one crisis to another without any real progress. Worse, there seemed no agreement among his colleagues on the progress they wanted. Some were still gung-ho that Britain was leaving 'Brussels' and taking back control without ever being able to say what that would enable them to do which would be of benefit to the country.

Others were moodily clinging to the belief that they could achieve a Brexit in name only – stay in the single market and just get the EU to agree to some minor changes to things like the Common Agricultural Policy or state aid. Meanwhile very little was actually getting done on the pressing issues that affected Andrew's electorate.

How would farming change in the light of global warming? What about pesticides? What about all the air pollution caused by diesel cars (nothing seemed to have happened with his investigation into the problem in London) or other climate change issues that Extinction Rebellion were protesting about?

And then there were the economic issues like rolling out Universal Credit and providing more job opportunities for poorly-educated young people. He thought about the young people in Lincolnshire he'd talked to. They seemed resigned to living in a very small world with few opportunities to change things. There weren't the glittering career paths that people like he and Claire had followed in London. The youngsters here didn't think of Europe as an opportunity to work in different cultures, meet interesting people, develop new ideas. They thought of Europe (if indeed they did) as somewhere to go for a stag weekend or two weeks holiday and where they could enjoy beer and English-style food at prices lower than at home. They were very much citizens of Lincolnshire, maybe of England but certainly not citizens of the world.

Of course some of the young people were more ambitious but they escaped down to London or elsewhere leaving their former towns and villages even more introspective.

He thought about Sara. She was adventurous,

international. She had got up and left Salamanca to find a career in veterinary medicine in a foreign country that she believed would give her more opportunities. And what had she found? A nation that voted to cut its ties with Spain and the rest of Europe, that wanted to 'take back control' and rid itself of immigrants like her. No wonder she was worried about her visa. In fact Andrew wondered why she hadn't just decided to give up and go home. He remembered his promise to help her with the paperwork.

He turned to his laptop and started typing. What exactly were the rules going to be about working in Britain? Would she still be able to use the NHS? She would continue paying income tax and NHI to the British HMRC but what benefits would she be able to claim?

His searches revealed only that many of these questions had no answers yet. It all depended on the final leaving agreement and we were keeping our cards close to our chest to strengthen our negotiating position.

Frustrated, he closed his laptop and looked at his watch. Two hours before he was due to meet Stan over at Sleaford.

26

DECEMBER 2018, LINCOLNSHIRE

The Christmas decorations and lights did their best to brighten up the town in the relentless rain. But the high street was devoid of Christmas shoppers. Andrew was aware that online shopping was growing by the year and that many high streets were suffering but somehow it wasn't so noticeable in London. The West End always seemed to be busy, there were all the tourists of course and so many workers and theatre-goers. Here in a typical market town the changes to Britain's high streets were all too obvious. The weather, of course, made it worse.

He was glad of his umbrella as he ran from the car park into the bar where Stan was waiting.

Stan wanted to quiz him on what was happening in Westminster. "A lot of the local party are worried that you might be going soft. They know you weren't in favour of Brexit but think some of you MPs are stringing it out as long as possible. They want a clean break with Europe and they want it now."

Andrew was exasperated and tried to point out the difficulties that lay ahead if no deal were struck with the EU and how hard it was to replace the trading relationship we had with Europe with new trade deals with countries like America.

"Talking of America, Andrew, how are you getting on with George Krasnik at Stellagenix? Between you and me they have given a lot to the party. We need to keep onside with them. Could help with a US trade deal too."

"I didn't think the Party could take donations from foreign companies?" said Andrew.

"Not officially, no. But there are lots of ways around that, don't worry. They've been very generous."

"I believe they're looking to expand their operation over here and that's good news. I've promised George that I'll have a word with the local Planning Committee to help overcome any objections."

"That's good, Andrew. We could do with generating more jobs around here. We need the young people to vote Tory instead of listening to Corbyn. Decent jobs provided by Stellagenix thanks to the Tories could help in the next election."

"I don't think we need to worry about a new election for some time yet." Andrew smiled reassuringly.

"I wouldn't be so sure, Andrew. If Theresa doesn't manage to get a deal approved soon she could find herself on the way out."

As they lunched in the Queen's Head, talk turned to what he should say during his radio interview with Sonya Arkle. Andrew had promised her an interview on Brexit when they met at the Rotary lunch and since he had become a Minister she had been hounding him to make good on his promise.

"You don't want to put the backs up of some of the big landowners round here. And they are pretty much all Brexiteers. Maybe you should talk about the NHS?"

"It would certainly be good to talk about health and maybe global warming. Anything rather than Brexit – it's such a mess."

"Well good luck. I'll tune in and see how you do."

Andrew's spirits remained low as he drove to the radio station's studios in Lincoln. The wipers slushed back and forth across the windscreen and tried their best to deal with the spray thrown up by the lorry ahead. The arable land stretched out on either side, a flat, featureless landscape of uniform grey-brown. Here and there he could make out the furrows of ploughed fields.

As he waited in reception for Sonya he was surprised to see a large figure in a dark raincoat and broad-brimmed cowboy hat push open the street door. George Krasnik looked around and took off his hat and shook the rain from it.

Seeing Andrew he walked slowly across. The rain dripped from the brim of his hat which he held in his left hand. It left a trail of dark stains on the polished floor of the radio station building.

"Well this is a coincidence. Fancy seeing you here. Are you taking part in the programme?" George held out his right hand and shook Andrew's vigorously. "I just got back from the States this morning and your wife has lined me up with this interview already. No peace for the wicked eh?"

Before Andrew could reply the clatter of high heels announced the arrival of Sonya. "I see you two have already met. That's good. Should make for a lively programme."

"I thought you were just going to interview me about Brexit?" Andrew liked to prepare for meetings. He always had. He liked to have any facts at his fingertips. Now, apparently he was going to be discussing it with an American. No progress had been made by the government on a US trade deal since Trump had become president.

They made their way together along a corridor and into a small studio. Sonya's assistant clipped on their microphones and tested them for levels.

"We'll be starting the programme in about 20 minutes so I'll have some coffee sent in while you wait. I'll introduce the programme, read the headlines, Maisie will do the weather report and then I'll announce the two of you and we can go into the discussion. All right?" She turned her smile on Andrew who nodded stoically back.

With that she closed the door and they heard her heels tapping out their rhythm down the corridor.

Andrew looked across to George. "I thought I was doing a solo interview with Sonya talking about the effects of Brexit on the local economy. I didn't know she'd invited you." He realised this sounded a little blunt and added "great to see you though."

"Well I didn't know until I got into the office at lunchtime. Truth be told after an overnight flight and three hours up your A1 I am ready for some shut-eye rather than this. But when I spoke to Claire about the Board's decision to go ahead she said we should get the news out on local media as soon as possible. She's a fast worker, your wife.

By the time I got to the office she had already fixed up this interview and prepared a press release for the papers."

I don't understand. What Board decision?"

"The decision to upgrade our facility here in UK to become our world centre for development and production of GM cereal products. You remember I said the results on the barley crop were good? Well you don't know just how good. This could lead to massive increases in yields and little old Lincs is going to be right at the centre of its development."

They heard Sonya's footsteps and the door opened. She was followed by her assistant, Maisie, bearing a tray of coffee. They watched as the two girls examined the running order for the programme. Sonya made some notes in the margin. She poured herself a glass of water, put on her headphones and gestured to the two men to put theirs on. A blind rose behind Sonya to reveal the sound engineer. He held up his hand and three fingers to signify 3 minutes.

"Right gentlemen, we're just about ready to go. Your mikes are muted right now but your voices could be picked up on mine if you're not careful. So please keep silent until I introduce you after the weather."

They sat in silence. Andrew's head was spinning. How had Claire had time to speak with George but not him? He didn't even know she was back from Barcelona yet. In fact he was sure she wasn't back until tomorrow. He felt jealous. But it wasn't George he should be jealous of. Still in Barcelona, Claire was trying to come to terms with what was happening with her other client – Clifton.

27

Claire had woken early in the Madrid hotel. Although the first day had been exhausting she had awoken ahead of her alarm. She had joined Clifton at breakfast and together they ran through their itinerary. As she was packing her suitcase before checking out, her mobile rang. It was Prithi back at the Agency. She had just had a call from George Krasnik at Stellagenix. He was excited about plans to expand their Lincolnshire facility following the Board's reaction to the tests on a new barley seed. He wanted Claire to set up an interview with the local radio station and a press briefing for local media. He had been disappointed to hear that she was away in Madrid. Claire gave Prithi instructions about the radio station and set about writing a press release. She had little time because the first Madrid meeting was in an hour but she emailed the release across to Prithi who promised to contact George.

After three meetings she and Clifton boarded the 17.00

train at Madrid's Atocha station. The 500 kilometre journey to Barcelona took just two and a half hours and they arrived at the Sants station at 7.30 that evening.

Claire had long wanted to visit this exciting city. But it was dark although noticeably warmer than Madrid. The temperature was around 10 degrees due to the proximity to the sea. The station was brightly lit, its smooth white floor tiles sparkling under the twin domes of the roof. Everything looked clean and modern. It was a lot different from Waterloo or Victoria that she was used to.

The lights of the shop windows, dressed for Christmas, flashed by as their taxi sped them to the boutique hotel that Clifton had booked. The receptionist smiled broadly at Clifton when they arrived. "Nice to see you again Señor Travis." He was obviously a regular visitor realised Claire. "Your suite is all ready for you. Do you need me to book a restaurant?"

The hotel was a four-storey building in a quiet road towards the south of the city. It was ultra modern in décor with minimalist furniture and large artworks adorning the walls. "I know you share my interest in modern art, Claire. This hotel is a work of art in itself."

He turned his attention to the receptionist. "Thank you Daniela, see if you can get us a table at Casa Olivia. I'm sure you can use your charm to get us one." Smooth bastard, thought Claire, as Daniela fluttered her eyes back at him. Clifton had obviously made an impression on his earlier visits.

A young man in a charcoal grey tailored suit and a name badge announcing him as Miguel arrived to take their two small suitcases. "I will take your cases to your suite Senor, Senora," he said in perfect English.

"I hope you have a nice time Senorita," grinned Daniela.

Claire felt that she was enjoying a joke with Clifton. Claire's Spanish was rudimentary but she understood the difference between Senora and Senorita. She wanted to ask Clifton about their rooms but waited until they were out of earshot.

"Clifton. I hope you've got us two rooms. "

"Better than that. I've got us a suite. Much more er um well much more anyway. You'll like it."

Miguel opened the door to the fourth floor apartment. The lounge had a large picture window that looked towards the lights of the city centre. "In the morning you will be able to see the sea in the distance, Senora. You can see the Sagrada Familia from the bedroom window." He pointed towards one of the two doors on the other side of the room.

She walked over and opened the door. Inside was a large double bed, wardobe doors to the one side and an open door to the en suite bathroom. The walls were deep purple while the bedspread was a pale mauve. She kicked off her shoes and walked in feeling the soft thick-pile carpet beneath her feet. She went to the window and peered out. She could just make out the crenelated towers of the Sagrada Familia Cathedral, still unfinished after more than a hundred years. Clifton had been the perfect gentleman so far. There had been no attempt to seduce her in Madrid. But now, here in Barcelona it was like she had wandered into his world. A world where he was well-known. A place he had been many times before – no doubt with other women if the smirk on Daniela's face had been anything to go by. Now she was in his web. A fly in the clutches of a randy spider. What was she going to do?

She turned back as she heard him enter the room. But it wasn't Clifton but Miguel bringing in her case and placing it on the bag stand. She heard the door of the adjacent room open and Clifton's footsteps as he carried his own case. She followed the sound.

She padded out of the bedroom into the lounge and peered through the second door. The room inside was the mirror image of the first but decorated in deep burgundy red with pink bedspread. Clifton turned to her, a grin on his face. "I normally choose the purple rather than the pink room but if pink is too feminine for you I'll take this."

Claire blushed. She didn't know what to say. Clifton could obviously read her thoughts and his lips widened into a smile. "I think you'd prefer the purple, Clifton. Pink is fine for me. I'll move my case."

Miguel stood grinning too. He said nothing but fetched her suitcase and placed it in the pink room. Clifton passed his case to Miguel who dutifully took it into the purple room followed by Clifton. She heard muffled laughter as he spoke in Spanish to Miguel.

She opened her case and took out her sponge bag. She felt dirty after the day in Madrid and the train ride. "OK if I take a shower now?"

"No problem, let me know if you want your back scrubbed." She heard him chuckle.

Closing the door she started to undress. The shower was hot and powerful and she luxuriated in its warmth. She picked up the hotel shower gel and began lathering it on. Her skin was still slightly tanned from their holiday in St Lucia but the white patches around her breasts no longer stood out; they were just a shade lighter. Not bad for a

Mum of twins, she thought rubbing the gel over her brown nipples. She moved her hands down her body over her flat stomach. No noticeable stretch marks. Her pubic hair was bushy. She hadn't trimmed it since St Lucia when the bikini pants had required her to do some artistic shaping.

She thought about Clifton and her confusion over the sleeping arrangements. Was she relieved that she had her own bedroom or was she a little disappointed? Did she really think he had invited to Spain merely to seduce her rather than as a business colleague?

She reached for her shampoo and massaged it into her short dark brown hair. She had got her hairdresser to cut it shorter when she started at the Agency. It framed her face well yet looked more business-like than previously when she had allowed it to grow to shoulder length. It was also easier to maintain – just the thing for business trips like this.

Reluctantly she turned off the water and stepped out wrapping a fluffy white towel around her. The bedroom door was now open and on the bedside table was a misted Champagne glass. "I poured you a drink Claire. I thought we'd deserved one."

She padded to the door and stuck her head round into the lounge. Clifton was sitting on the sofa with his laptop open on the coffee table in front of him.

"Thank you. Champagne, how nice!"

"It's actually Cava but a really good one. I've had it here before. Hope you like it." He smiled at her and raised his glass in a toast. She was aware that her hair was flattened against her face and water was dripping down from it to her chin.

She stepped back into the privacy of her room and

partially closed the door. She wanted to close it but wouldn't that seem a little rude? He'd obviously entered while she had been showering, and the Champagne was very welcome.

She took a sip and pulled the stool up to the dressing-table. The hairdryer was in the top drawer and she began to dry and style her hair.

She had packed only a small case and her choice of clothes was limited. She chose a pale cream blouse and her smart navy trouser suit. It still looked a bit too 'officey' but it would have to do. She undid one of the buttons and the edge of her lacy bra showed. Fine.

She strolled back into the lounge to join Clifton. But he wasn't there The door to his bedroom was open and she glanced in. He was standing with his back to her wrapped, as she had been, in a white bath towel. He was speaking on the phone. Guiltily she turned back and went across to the Cava in its ice bucket. She refilled her glass and took a large sip. She heard Clifton saying goodbye to his caller.

"Do you want a refill, Clifton?" She grinned, feeling naughty.

"Yeah, great!"

His glass was beside the ice bucket and she refilled it. She walked across "I hope you're decent!"

He was still wearing just the towel and held a denim shirt in his hand. "Great room service. I'm not used to this."

Smiling, she handed him the glass. "Cheers!"

"You look very smart if I may so, Claire. Very professional."

Back in the lounge she looked at herself in the small mirror. Yes, very smart, efficient. But she wasn't about to go for a business meeting. It was a late dinner with Clifton in a local restaurant in Barcelona. She didn't have anything glamorous. The trouser suit was beautifully tailored with a waisted jacket. The cream blouse was nicely detailed. But Clifton was obviously going to be wearing chinos and a denim shirt. Was she just a bit too formal?

She went back into her bedroom and opened her small suitcase. She selected a white T-shirt. Maybe this would be more appropriate, more casual. The T-shirt was cut in a way that left one shoulder uncovered and had a slanting neckline. She took off her blouse, hesitated, and then took off her bra too. She slipped her head through the T-shirt and pulled it straight. Her breasts looked good, the outlines of her nipples were distinct under the tight jersey cotton material. She reached for her jacket, that would make it more chaste.

"Allow me." Clifton entered her room, picked up the navy jacket and draped it across her shoulders.

Claire blushed. How long had he been standing there? Had he seen her remove her bra? She slipped the jacket off her shoulders and turned towards him putting her arms in the jacket sleeves as she did so. She pulled the jacket across her chest.

"I've got the reservation. The restaurant is only a few hundred yards from here and the weather's dry. If you don't feel too cold I suggest we walk rather than get a taxi."

He waited for her reply.

"Of course. Yes. A walk, good."

"Maybe take your coat though? I wouldn't like you to get cold wearing such an outfit." He looked pointedly at her T-shirt.

She could feel her nipples hardening under his gaze.

The cold night air would make them even more prominent. She was glad the jacket was covering them. What was she thinking? She was flirting for heaven's sake. And she had worried about *him*!

The restaurant was warm and intimate. It certainly wasn't formal. There was an undertone of diners' voices together with a low volume guitar track playing over concealed speakers. Maybe half the tables were occupied, almost all couples. It was still early by Spanish standards although by 9pm Claire was very hungry. The two glasses of Cava had relaxed her and she was looking forward to the evening. It was a long time since she had been dined by anyone other than Andrew.

Clifton had obviously been to the restaurant several times. A man of around fifty wearing jeans and a black silk shirt came over and shook hands vigorously. "Senor Clifton, so nice to see you again. And your beautiful friend." He took Claire's hand and brushed it against his lips. "Welcome senorita to Casa Olivia."

It was almost midnight when they left. The meal had been superb and they had washed it down with two bottles of a very fine Rioja. The conversation had flowed as Clifton regaled her with stories of his travels and the people he had met. His arm supported her as they made their way back the few hundred yards to the hotel. She was aware that she was tipsy, unaware that she was more than tipsy. She felt liberated. Here she was, walking at midnight along the narrow streets of this Mediterranean city, the air still warm for December, and a handsome man had his hand around her waist. She was enjoying herself.

28

A few hours earlier, back in his office, Stan turned on the radio and poured himself a cup of tea.

"My guests today are two very important members of our local community. Neither of them, however, is a born-and-bred local. Today I shall be asking Andrew Eastwood, conservative MP for West Lincs how our local economy will benefit or suffer from Brexit and asking George Krasnik, the CEO of Stellagenix in Upthorpe about the incredible breakthrough they have made in cereal production which means they are expanding their operation here in Lincs. Good afternoon gentlemen."

Stan adjusted the volume.

"Mr Eastwood let me turn to you first. The people of Lincolnshire voted overwhelmingly for Brexit. They have had enough of rules and regulations from unelected bureaucrats in Brussels. But it seems that your boss, the Prime Minister isn't able to make Brexit happen. We haven't got a withdrawal agreement yet let alone the subsequent trade deal. What's going wrong?"

Andrew took a deep breath and launched into his prepared speech. This was pretty much what he had expected. "The problem with Brexit is that it's difficult to know what the UK was hoping to achieve when it voted to leave. Sovereignty, taking back control, writing our own laws are great sounding ideas but what does it mean in practice? We gave our sovereignty up after the war when we set up and joined NATO. If any member is attacked, the other members must go to war to protect them. I can't think of a bigger loss of sovereignty."

"So you're against NATO?"

"Not at all. I support it. I believe there is strength in numbers, in acting together with allies. But it does mean we don't have the ability to choose whether to act. It's the same with the EU. The single market of 500 million people is the biggest market in the world and has been beneficial to all its members. As a trading bloc I'm all in favour of it. "

"But it has become more than a trading block now."

"Indeed. It has become a political institution too. That can be very beneficial to us as well when acting jointly say against Russia or Iran. It helps our security services and improves cooperation on everything from fighting terrorists to catching criminals."

"Yes, but it also has meant that we've been stuck with things like the Common Agricultural Policy and giving up most of our fishing rights. Here in Lincolnshire those things are more important to voters." To Stan, listening, she sounded aggressive and he wondered how Andrew would seek to answer that criticism. In the studio Sonya gave

Andrew a smile of encouragement. She shared his Remainer views.

"Yes of course fishing and agriculture are important to us. I'm all in favour of ensuring our farmers and fishing industries benefit from any deal we do. It's vitally important that we don't ruin our economy for a vague feeling of being independent.

Sonya turned to George. "Now Mr Krasnik, you're an American, running an American company here in Lincolnshire. Leaving Europe would enable us to have a new trade deal with your country. What do you feel about that?"

"Thank you, Sonya and can I say what a pleasure it is to be invited onto your programme. We in America are always keen to strengthen the special relationship we have with you Brits. As you know we have probably the biggest and most productive farming industry in the world and we're only too happy to bring in some of our methods to you here Britain."

"And I believe your research unit in Upthorpe has just created something of a wonder product?" Sonya glanced at her notes. "Apparently your tests here in Lincolnshire have produced a strain of barley that grows quicker and stronger than traditional barley."

"Indeed we have. In fact the amazing increases in yields I was able to report to my Board back in the States was what persuaded them to back my vision to build a super large facility here in Lincolnshire that could be the envy of the world."

Sonya turned to Andrew.

"That could be really good news for the local economy here couldn't it Mr Eastwood?"

"Well yes, it's very encouraging. In fact I recently visited Mr Krasnik's research facility and was very impressed with what I saw. I am always looking at opportunities to create more worthwhile jobs in the County and the expansion of the Stellagenix works would be welcome."

Sonya turned back to George. "Now these yields you talk about are a result of you genetically engineering normal barley, are they not. Not everyone is in favour of GM foods."

"We aren't doing anything that nature doesn't do itself – over time. Natural selection Darwin called it. All we are doing is accelerating that development a little. Our new super barley is more resistant to insects and blight so won't need to be treated with all those nasty pesticides and fungicides that your farmers currently use. Much healthier."

After the interview the two men gave a brief handshake to Sonya and left together.

The rain was still siling down. It was completely dark now and the shops were long closed. George turned to Andrew. "Look I'm driving back your way and I have to tell you I'm famished. Didn't eat on the plane and just a quick sandwich for lunch. I hear you've got a decent pub in Otherby. Why don't we have dinner together there?"

They drove in convoy down the twisting unlit roads until finally Andrew turned off towards the lights of Otherby. The pub was crowded with locals, many standing around the bar drinking and chatting. There were a couple of groups sitting at tables near the far wall.

Kevin, the barman, looked up and gave Andrew a smile. "Hi Andrew, pint of Fentastic?"

"Yes I need one after that drive and the day I've had."

He nodded to George. "Have we converted you to British beer yet, George?"

"No, it's too warm for me. I'll just take a Coke."

"Can we get a couple of menus Kevin? What's special tonight?"

As they made their way towards a table Andrew felt a tap on his shoulder and a voice said "I thought you might not be coming tonight."

Oh God. He'd forgotten his promise to sort out Sara's residency papers.

"I'm sorry, I'm just a bit later than I thought because I was doing a radio interview over in Lincoln." He looked down at Sara who was, for a change, not wearing jumper and jeans but a rather smart woollen dress that showed off her slim figure to advantage. He put down his pint on the table and bent to kiss her on the cheek. She pulled away before he could kiss her. "Careful Andrew, remember the locals and their ignorance of European customs!" She stuck out her hand and rather comically shook Andrew's.

Andrew realised that George was staring. He introduced Sara to him. "George, I hope it's alright if I ask Sara to join us for a meal. I promised to help her with her paperwork for Brexit. She's Spanish. Er, she's a vet."

He found himself stammering. Why did he feel so embarrassed? Why should George not accept his explanation? That night after the Young Farmers Dance was their little secret. There had been no repeat. In fact, he had hardly seen Sara since then.

He introduced George to her. She looked at him quizzically. "I'm very interested in the work your company is doing. I've been studying the effects of GM foods on animals."

George paused before answering. "That's great and we have some really good news as Andrew will no doubt tell you. We plan to vastly increase our facilities here in Lincolnshire. Because of the work in our lab we have managed to increase farmers' yields considerably. Cuts down on the use of pesticides too. Got to be a good thing yes?"

"What products have you been successful with?"

"Well barley for a start. Very important crop around here. Now we're working on wheat. No secret that."

"Barley? What exactly have you modified?"

"Well I ain't at liberty to tell you that. Very secret. I'd have to kill you first!"

George laughed and took a swig of his Coke. Kevin arrived to take their food orders.

Andrew was still perplexed. Sara seemed unhappy. Was it the fact that she had wanted him on his own or was it something she didn't like about George? He decided to change the subject to Sara's Brexit problems.

George ate his meal quickly and stood up. "I guess I'd better be heading home. Still some drive. I'll call you Andrew. I want to talk to you about Brexit and the new US trade deal you're after but I guess this isn't the time or place." He looked at Sara. "But Claire's fixed for some of the press to come over tomorrow at 11. It would be good if you could come too. Good publicity. Get you a few more votes. That's if you're not too busy." He looked at Sara again.

As he left Andrew turned to Sara. "Sara, I get the feeling you're worried about something. Is it just the Brexit papers?"

"No. Thanks for helping me out with those. I'm sure I'll be allowed to stay with that letter from you as well as my boss's."

"So what is it?"

"Well we had another two cases of cows having twins last week. We lost the two cows but the calves survived. They were very healthy, very big in fact."

"Oh I'm sorry, that must have upset you."

"It's worried me. Why are we getting all these twins? It's not normal."

"The figures I gave you from DEFRA said that it was unusual but that small sample sizes could account for it."

"Yes, but I've talked to some of the other local vets across the county and so has David. Their twin birth figures are quite normal. It is just around here that they've shot up."

"So what do you think is causing it?"

"I don't know. I've looked at the bulls that were used to inseminate them. There were two bulls that had all the twins. The other three bulls I've looked at didn't produce any twins from the cows they inseminated."

"So you think it's something hereditary in the two bulls? Are they related?

"That's what I'm trying to find out. It's all so difficult."

"Well I wish you luck with your research."

He asked her if she wanted to come back to the house for a 'nightcap' but she smiled and said "Not tonight, Andrew." She left him perplexed. Was she tired? Was she just worried about Brexit and calving or was she giving him the cold shoulder? He said goodbye to her in the car park, kissed her on the cheek and turned to walk home. He would pick up his car in the morning.

29

Dimitri had worked for Stellagenix for four years or more. As senior scientific officer he held an important position in the company. It was Dimitri who organised the selection of DNA to be inserted into the plants. It was Dimitri who organised the field tests and Dimitri who had the first look at the results.

Dimitri had two other scientists working for him. Both were women, biologists of one type or another. The women were well-qualified and well-trained. They worked methodically and carefully. Dimitri admired this but was naturally more impulsive. He saw his job as working on the front line, not in the back office. He was driven by a desire to achieve great breakthroughs, to be recognised for his revolutionary thinking. The Nobel prize beckoned.

But today he was in a pensive mood. There was no doubting the success of his recent project to increase barley yields. It had exceeded even his inflated expectations. And it could open up many more opportunities. More cereal products. More success, more recognition for Dimitri. But he had to be careful.

Today, his boss, George Krasnik, was going to be meeting the press to announce the expansion of the facility as a result of these wonderful figures. The press were sure to ask questions. How had this been achieved? What was Stellagenix doing that competitors weren't?

Dimitri had finished writing up the project and George had taken this with him when he went over to the States. What he had done with barley wasn't unprecedented. Bits of animal DNA had been inserted into plants before. But never with such striking results. And it had been Dimitri's decision to use a section of DNA from rabbits hoping that it might increase the rate of cell division and promote rapid growth. Dimitri wanted results and wanted results quickly. Normal methods could take up to 12 years of tests before they were considered safe to be approved for human food consumption.

But Dimitri had combined different technologies of genetic modification including X-ray mutagenesis. This produced random mutations which could then be propagated and tested. Mostly the resultant changes in DNA structure of the modified plant did not produce useful traits but occasionally they did. In this case Dimitri's experiments had taken the most-promising of the mutations and tried a new technique which had hit the jackpot. The rate of cell development was greatly increased. Of course the alterations caused by the earlier mutagenesis may have caused other traits to alter and these could theoretically be harmful to humans. But there was no specific requirement to undergo years of tests and Dimitri had started field tests immediately. They had now had two harvests of the new barley seed and the results were amazing. He did tests for toxicity on lab animals but found no ill effects.

The bio firms involved in GM foods are secretive by nature but normally follow the regulations as regards testing. Induced mutagenesis of crops in most countries (including the United States) is not regulated for food or environmental safety. Breeders rarely conduct what is known as molecular genetic analysis on their modified plants so are often unaware what other traits have been modified or what their effects might be. Worldwide, more than 2300 different crop varieties have been developed using induced mutagenesis. There are no records of molecular characterisations of these mutant crops, and in most cases, no records to retrace their subsequent use.

But what Dimitri had done was to go much further. By combining protein elements from the rabbit with the mutated barley he had achieved enormous increases in plant yields.

The reason he was now nervous was he didn't want his methods to be scrutinised in case the authorities decided, in the light of the combination of methods used, it should go through many years of tests before being passed for sale. Stellagenix was in a hurry to make profits and Dimitri was not going to let tiresome regulation get in the way. He would not mention the rabbits. He hoped George wouldn't either.

Andrew had decided to attend the press conference before returning to London. It would be good for his political standing to be seen to be supporting job creation in the county. He remembered too the words of his boss, the Secretary of State who had reminded him, like Stan had, of the financial donations that the company had discreetly made to the Tory party. There was also the fact, as George had mentioned, that Claire had helped to set up the conference even though she was away in Barcelona still.

He was disappointed to find that only a handful of journalists had turned up. Yes it was in the run-up to Christmas but he would have expected more interest. The local Lincolnshire media were there including Sonya but only one of the farming journals. As a result much of the elaborate slide presentation went over their heads as first Dimitri and then one of his section heads explained different techniques that could be used to modify plants. Neither of them mentioned inserting rabbit DNA into the barley seed. They had used a very new development which had been discovered only in the past couple of years by an American microbiologist. Then it was George's turn to explain the benefits of this work and how the expertise of Stellagenix's team here in Lincoln had resulted in a world-beating new strain that would not only be good for farmers but enable Stellagenix to greatly increase its operation in the county. There was also the likelihood of large export sales which would be helpful in the new post-Brexit world.

More job opportunities, spin-off benefits for local companies involved in constructing the new buildings and more productive local farmers was the news that these journalists were interested in. George fielded a number of questions about the time frame for the new facility, the job opportunities for young people, apprentice schemes and so forth. He nodded at Andrew whom he had seated alongside him on the platform. "I'm sure Andrew here is delighted with the results of our efforts which will increase employment in his constituency. Andrew has been a big supporter or our genetic engineering programme." Andrew nodded and smiled. There were no questions for Dimitri on the methods he had used to produce this amazing result. All the talk of mutagenesis, somaclonal variation and transposons had gone over their heads and wouldn't have been interesting to their readers or listeners. Andrew had found it hard to follow too and made a mental note to talk with Claire. No doubt she was well mugged up on all of this.

After the presentation Sonya turned to Andrew. "Well it certainly sounds as if Stellagenix are going places. I didn't get all the technical stuff but there's no doubt that Dimitri guy knows his stuff. It would be really good for people round here if a high-tech company like this were to expand."

"Absolutely Sonya. Although don't get too carried away. The big new facility will boost the local economy, the building of it for a start, plus services to the increased workforce. But it is still a highly-skilled laboratory operation and that needs clever scientists. We don't have too many of those sitting around here looking for a job."

"Yes but they will also be processing all the seeds and packaging them, and marketing them. That's a lot of different, non-scientific jobs."

"You're right. Lots of opportunities over the next year or two."

"Which will be good for your re-election! George gave you a good plug there."

"It's a long time before the next election – 4 years. They'll all have forgotten by then," laughed Andrew.

George had asked Andrew to stay for lunch after the presentation and came across now, a broad smile on his face. "Well here we three are again. Small world!"

"Looks like you might be taking over the world though Mr Krasnik. Your barley results sound like a real 'game-changer'. Good for us yokels around here. We need American investment."

"And I'm sure you'll get plenty more of it once Andrew and his colleagues have got you free of Brussels. Now if you'll excuse us, Andrew and I have much to discuss."

Over a light lunch the two men discussed the plans for the expansion of the Stellagenix facility. George asked if he could count on Andrew to ensure that the local council would fast-track the planning process. Andrew saw no reason to delay something that would enrich his constituency and agreed to talk with councillors immediately.

"It's a shame Claire couldn't be with us today – she'd be excited about the news. But I gather she's abroad with another client?"

30

DECEMBER 2018, SPAIN

The cool Barcelona air and Clifton's arm around her waist kept Claire walking purposefully back to their hotel. But once in the warmth, riding the lift to the top floor she started to feel light-headed. She turned towards Clifton whose arm was still supporting her and reached up and kissed him. "Thank you for a wonderful dinner," she whispered.

She rested her head on his shoulder breathing in the scent of his cologne. It had been a wonderful dinner. She couldn't remember a nicer one. She felt really alive – the food, the wine, the Spanish atmosphere and the lively conversation. After the past four or five years of playing nursemaid to two children she felt rejuvenated. She had worked hard, this was her reward.

The lift doors opened and still clinging to each other they crossed to their suite. "I really enjoyed this evening too," said Clifton taking her shoulders in his two hands and looking into her face. "It's not often I get to spend an evening with such a beautiful, intelligent woman."

If Claire hadn't drunk so much she might have laughed at the cheesiness of his remark. It was classic Clifton, the playboy she had heard about. But she had drunk a lot, and with the romance of the restaurant and the hecticness of the last three days she just blushed. She was intelligent, she knew that. She had always been attractive, men had told her many times. But it was so good to know she was *still* attractive.

She gazed at him and then lifted her head bringing her mouth up to his and kissing him again. This time the kiss was longer and more passionate. She felt his tongue exploring hers. She felt his hands sliding across her shoulders and slipping off her coat. He bent his head and kissed her bare shoulder. She laughed, a deep liquid laugh. She pulled away and turned towards the bedrooms. His arms wrapped around her waist and his lips started to caress the back of her neck. She tensed. Everything was tingling. She knew at that moment there was no turning back. She didn't want to. She rolled her head from side to side with pleasure. She felt his hands rise from her waist up to her breasts. She vaguely realised that her nipples were hardening and then she felt his fingers plucking at them and a small moan escaped from her lips.

They stumbled across to the pink bedroom. Without the lights it was illuminated only by the light from the lounge and the curtains weren't drawn. The lights of the sleeping city sparkled in the clear December air and just for a moment she saw the silhouette of Gaudi's masterpiece. Then Clifton was spinning her round, kissing her mouth, running his fingers through her hair. She pulled at the buttons of his shirt and exposed his smooth chest. She peeled his shirt over his shoulders and it fluttered onto the deep maroon carpet. She kicked off her shoes and turning away slipped off her trousers. She hesitated for a second before pulling the T-shirt over her head. Clad only in her small white knickers, her breasts, in shadow, bare and standing proud. The light from the doorway into the living room framed her as she tipped her head back to look at Clifton..

He was standing by the bed, watching her. He moved his hand to the bedside lamp and a soft golden light threw his shadow across to the window. His body was tanned and his muscles toned. Her gaze lowered from his torso. His desire was only too obvious. He held his arms out to her. She slipped off her knickers and crossed to the bed.

31

DECEMBER 2018, LINCOLNSHIRE

By the time they had finished discussing the plans for the new laboratories and production unit it was after three. Andrew had considered driving back to London after the press do but now, as he looked out at the grey, rain-laden clouds hanging over the flat wide fields he decided to leave it until morning. In truth, he wanted to have some time to think about all he had seen and maybe call up the head of the local council to see what the planning position was.

So, taking his leave of George he got back into the Nissan and set out for Otherby.

As he drove he started to think about Claire. He hadn't spoken to her since she left for Spain. He had been busy of course and no doubt she had too. Still he would have liked to know how it was going. She had obviously found time to talk with George about the press do. He had thought about ringing her last night when he had got back in from the Barley Mow but he realised it was late, and even later in Barcelona. She would be flying home this afternoon so there wasn't any point in trying now. He would phone her tonight from the house. Her mother had come down to help Analiese with the boys and if there had been any problems he would have heard.

When he arrived at the village it was already dark and he made himself a cup of coffee with his new Nespresso machine. Stan had given him some letters from constituents to look at and there were a number of emails on his laptop including a couple from the Ministry that needed dealing with.

The problem with being an MP, thought Andrew, was that you have two very different lives. On the one hand you were supposed to represent all your constituents and sort out problems in the area as diverse as new bypasses or welfare payments. On the other, as a minister, you were supposed to be working on grand strategies to improve the health of the nation. The first required you to spend time in Lincolnshire, the other to be available in London to have interminable meetings with civil servants.

All that as well as sitting through late night debates on Brexit in the Houses of Parliament. It left little time for family life. For the first few months, before his promotion, and when Brexit wasn't becoming all-consuming he had been able to get home at a reasonable time, hear all about Claire and her new job, see the boys and even enjoy some dinner parties with friends.

Now, he realised, Claire and he were seeing less of each other. His evenings had been spent too often sitting on the sticky green leather benches while she put the children to bed. Weekends were often taken up with trips to

Lincolnshire where he held surgeries on Saturday morning. His idea of her accompanying him on these weekends had soon become obviously impractical. She was working all week and needed the time to sort out domestic things at the weekend.

He was looking forward to Christmas. Parliament would be in recess, constituents would not be wanting to see their MP over the festivities and civil servants were certainly not expected to be at their desks over the two weeks leading up to the resumption of Parliament in January. He could spend quality time with Claire and the boys.

As he worked through his emails he found one from his friend in the Home Office. There was a link to an update on the requirements for EU nationals currently working in Britain. He clicked through and started to read it. After the first two pages he gave up trying to read it on the screen and printed off a copy. He would study it to see if and how it affected Sara.

Among the letters that Stan had given him was one from the chairman of a local conservative association complaining about the lack of sports facilities in the area and asking him for a meeting to discuss how they might get central government to provide more funds. Andrew doubted any more money would be forthcoming. He made a note to raise the issue with Stellagenix. Maybe they would chip in some money for new facilities when their planning permission came through.

His mobile rang. As he reached for it he glanced at his watch. It was nearly seven. Probably Claire ringing him to say she was back.

It wasn't Claire, but Sara. The evening before she had

seemed on edge and reserved. Now she sounded more like her usual self. "Andrew. Are you still in Otherby or have you gone back to London?"

When he confirmed that he wasn't leaving for London until the morning she asked if he was free to meet at the Barley Mow. He readily agreed.

First he must phone Claire. He rang the home phone and it was answered by Claire's mother. "Hello Andrew, are you on your way back?"

"No my meetings went on longer than I thought. I'll be driving back tomorrow morning. I'll be there for lunch. Is Claire back from Spain yet?"

"She got back about an hour ago. She's gone up for a shower and a change. Shall I call her down?"

He waited while he listened to his mother-in-law calling out to Claire. Eventually he heard Claire's voice. "Hi darling. How are you? I just got back, did Mum say?"

"Yes. I'm afraid I won't be back until tomorrow – things overran here and I didn't fancy a long drive tonight in this weather. Are the boys okay?"

"They were very excited when I got back but seemed to have enjoyed Mum's company while we've both been away. I bought them each a Spanish donkey from the airport and they're playing with those."

"Not real donkeys, I hope?"

"No straw ones. Probably made in China anyway. Typical tourist rubbish but they seem to like them."

"How did you get on in Spain? Get things sorted?"

Claire paused. The guilt feelings flooded back. Water dripped from her wet hair onto the phone. She straightened up. "Yes it was good. Very successful, I think. Very hectic though, lots of meetings and a long train ride from Madrid to Barcelona."

"You've always wanted to go to Barcelona. Did you get to see much?"

"Not really. We didn't have time for sight-seeing."

"Oh that's a pity. Maybe next time."

Next time? Would there be a next time? Clifton would be going back but would he want her to go with him? If he did would she accept? She still hadn't managed to come to terms with that last night in Barcelona. She'd had little or no time to think about it since.

She had woken that morning in the big pink bed. The winter sun was streaming through the window. She was alone in bed. She tried to sit up but her head was heavy. She rested back on the pillow. Her throat was dry and felt like rough sandpaper. She shook her head to try and clear it but that made things worse. She realised slowly that she had the mother of all hangovers. She tried sitting up again, more gingerly this time. Successful, she pulled off the covers and swung her legs over the edge of the bed. She stood up and saw her reflection in the mirrored door of the wardrobe. She was totally naked. Memories of the night came flooding back. She crossed to the bathroom and turned on the shower. The water, warm at first, and then progressively hotter as she turned the dial, began to revive her. She let it cascade onto her hair and massaged her scalp with the shampoo gel. She worked the gel down her body over her breasts and down between her legs. The strong citrus perfume revived her and her head cleared. Her throat was still unbearably dry.

She turned off the shower and stepped onto the marble-tiled floor. She picked the fluffy white towel off the heated towel rail and rubbed her hair dry. Still naked she picked up her toothbrush. The toothpaste did its job and her mouth felt a little fresher. Picking up the towel she walked back into the bedroom.

She stopped dead as she saw him. She instinctively clasped the towel and pulled it up in front of her. She saw him smile. That same smile she now knew so well. He was holding a cup in his hand. "I thought you might need some coffee?"

He held the cup out for her. She reached with one hand, the other still trying to hold the towel in place. He was dressed in dark trousers and an immaculate white shirt. He had shaved, his hair was combed and he looked all set for the morning's business meetings. Claire, by contrast, had not a stitch of clothing, towel-dried hair that stuck up in all directions and a real dilemma. Her left hand still held the edge of the towel but it no longer covered her. She was certain that her right breast was uncovered. Her right hand held the saucer but she could not lift the cup to drink without letting go of the towel.

For several seconds they stood facing each other. Then Clifton laughed and turned to go. "I think I'd better let you get dressed, we're due at the Bank in half an hour."

Now, just a few hours later, back in Wandsworth, here she was again clasping a towel around her but talking to her husband.

"Love you," she said.

The Barley Mow was crowded with the usual suspects. Andrew was beginning to feel at home. He stopped to talk briefly with two or three before reaching the bar where

Kevin passed him a pint of Fentastic without being asked. "This one's on young Sara. She said you'd be coming over. She's at the table there, in the corner." He gave Andrew a knowing look. "You're a lucky man Andrew!"

Andrew lifted the glass carefully and bent to sip off the top inch before turning back to the room. He nodded to a man seated at the bar whom he hadn't seen before then turned his gaze to Sara in the corner, a glass of red wine in her hand. She smiled.

Before he could go to her he heard his name being called. He recognised the voice of Colin, a stalwart of the pub's darts team and the mechanic who had fixed Sara's car the first time he'd met her. He was in his thirties, no older than Andrew with dark hair that had been clippered to within a quarter of an inch of his scalp. He was wearing his usual dark fleece with the hood hanging down and a broad grin on his face.

There were three other men at the table with him and Andrew recognised them without being able to recall their names. "Will you join us? We're on a bit of a celebration."

"Yes, Colin's just found out he's going to be a father. About bloody time too." One of the group cried.

"Yeah and he's married to the mother!"

There was a roar of laughter from the three men.

Andrew lifted his glass to his lips in response. "Congratulations Colin. When's it due? Your wife well?"

"She's four months gone now. We waited until we were sure but the hospital say it could be twins!"

"Making up for lost time – he's been five years getting around to it." His friend shouted over and the other two collapsed in laughter again. It was obvious that they had been celebrating for some time already.

"Come on, sit down let me get you a drink," said Colin.

"I'd love too but I've got to sort out something for Sara over there first."

"Good for you. I'd like to give her a good sorting too!" The loud friend was unstoppable, egged on by his well-oiled mates.

Extricating himself from the raucous group Andrew made his way over to Sara.

She stood up as he got to her table and held out her hand. Andrew, bemused, shook it formally but was pleased when he felt her squeeze his hand before releasing it.

"Thank you for coming, Mr Eastwood." Her eyes twinkled and she barely contained her smile. The reticence of the previous night was gone. The handshake was merely a vain attempt to persuade the locals that this was a business meeting not a date.

"De nada senorita!"

She reached in her bag and extracted some papers. "I've filled in the form you downloaded for me. Perhaps you can check it's alright before I send it in. They want £65 from me just to register!"

"OK, I'll take a look at it but we don't have to send it in yet. There's a lot of opposition to the £65 charge. I got some news from my friend at the Home Office just now. They may be changing that. Let's hold on until we know more." He folded the papers and slipped them into his jacket pocket.

He picked up one of the menus on the table and started to study it. "Thank you for the drink. I'm starving. What are we going to have?"

"I'm sorry about last night Andrew." She looked up at him, her dark brown eyes searching his face for a response. Once again he found himself captivated by this vivacious

Spaniard with her olive skin and black tumbling hair. He couldn't ignore the effect she had on him. He found himself wanting to confide in her, to seek her approval to his ideas.

"You seemed not to take to my friend from Stellagenix. I could sense there was some tension there. Am I right?"

"It wasn't him. He was OK. It's just that I'm really fascinated by the work firms like his are doing. I've been studying the developments in animal genetics. It's part of my course I'm doing. Over at Sutton Bonnington."

Andrew knew Sutton Bonnington from his days at University in Nottingham. It was the agricultural college attached to it. "I didn't know you were still studying?"

"Yes, there's so much changing in the veterinary world. You have to keep up. I'm taking a degree course. It's mainly distance learning but next month I'll be attending college there for three days every week. Exams in June. I've got to submit my thesis on methods for improving cattle strains through introducing novel genes into animal embryos."

"Sounds frighteningly complicated. You lost me after 'novel genes'. But what's that got to do with Stellagenix. They aren't involved with animals. Their work is about improving yields and pest resistance in cereal products." Andrew dredged up phrases from the morning's press briefing. He hadn't really followed all the stuff that Greek guy had been explaining, but understood enough to know that Stellagenix's attention was purely on crops.

"Yes, Andrew, but some of the methods used by Stellagenix for introducing improved genes into plants are the same techniques as animal researchers use."

"Well I've heard of Dolly the sheep. But that was cloning wasn't it?"

"Yes, it is now possible to clone animals, to produce replicas of existing animals but the techniques I'm interested in are ones that improve the bloodline of cattle, not just reproduce it." She paused as Kevin arrived to take their order. Andrew ordered a bottle of Malbec. He marvelled at the way people like Sara could understand all these scientific things and her ability to discuss them fluently in a foreign language. Now Britain was extricating itself from the EU, he doubted that the British would improve their language skills and worried that the multi-national laboratories that were to be found in Cambridge and places like the Crick Institute would relocate. Sara was continuing with her explanation.

"Let me try and put it more simply. The modern breeds of cattle differ markedly from their ancestors. Why is this? Well going right back to Darwin we've understood the natural selection of the fittest. So you had a strong healthy bull that had a good milk-producing mother and you tried to get him to sire your cows rather than other bulls. But this was a bit haphazard. Now, thanks to being able to freeze sperm and artificially inseminate cows we can spread one bull's genes into hundreds of cows, so the bloodline improves."

"OK, I get that but that's not really genetic engineering is it? It's just a more efficient way of selecting the fittest?"

"No, but now we can take things much further. We can take immature eggs from cows and mature them in the laboratory and fertilise them and reinsert them in the cows. This means we can alter the DNA of the cells themselves. There are laboratories where they microinject DNA into the nucleus of cells. Most of the times the results are disappointing but just now and again it causes a change that is really effective."

Sara was growing more and more animated. Andrew was struggling to keep up.

"You know that we can now map people's DNA, they mapped 100,000 people in Cambridge. Well we can map individual animals and manipulate their DNA – introduce variations. We can see what the DNA of good milking cows is and how it differs from the poorer milkers. Then we can modify their DNA to introduce the better milking trait. It's so exciting."

She stopped as Kevin arrived with their meals. Andrew was relieved. He marvelled at her knowledge and her enthusiasm. He loved the way her forehead creased when she searched for the exact word. In fact he found himself loving her presence. But he had had more than enough on genetic engineering for one day. He tried to change the subject.

"Are you going home for Christmas?"

"Yes I've got a flight to Madrid next Friday. It'll be good to see my parents again."

"And nice to get some warm weather after England."

"Well not really. Salamanca is on the high plain in Spain. We have snow there most winters and the temperature is often around freezing at this time of year."

"I'd like to go to Salamanca sometime," said Andrew.

"I'd love you to." She looked at Andrew with her dark brown eyes. He returned her gaze. For several seconds they sat in silence. Andrew broke the spell, looking down and cutting into his pie. That wasn't going to happen. Claire might be gallivanting off to Spain but he wasn't. He was a married man, with children and a career in politics. His relationship with Sara must return to platonic.

His resolution lasted all of two hours. And two bottles of Malbec. The man at the bar watched them go.

Once again Andrew unlocked the door to Limetree House and ushered Sara in. This time there wasn't the passionate, headlong dash to make love. Instead they sat on the rug in front of the coal fire. Andrew had lit it as soon as he had arrived back from Stellagenix. The old house needed heating in winter. Now he raked the glowing embers and added a couple of logs to it. Soon the fire had been revived and crackled and hissed as the flames licked around the applewood logs.

They sat close together nursing two tumblers of brandy. Andrew had yet to equip the cottage with a range of glassware. She talked about life in Salamanca. He talked about his upbringing in Cumbria. He noted the similarities. The sense of community. The simpler pleasures of life – good food, good company. He noted the absence of traffic problems, of hustle and bustle.

He was intrigued by her descriptions of the academic life of Salamanca, home to one of the oldest universities in Europe. Salamanca was a place renowned for learning. The site of true Spanish where students from around the world came to learn in its ancient buildings.

What had brought her from such a place to this remote little village? How could she not miss the charms of this city she described? It was, he concluded, her sense of adventure, her quest for knowledge. She had been given the opportunity to work in a large veterinary practice with a huge variety of clients. She was working, and now studying, in a country which was leading the world in biological research, in genetics. The appeal was magnetic to someone as inquisitive as Sara.

Sara was not just an academic though. Not for her the cloistered buildings of Cambridge. She had the social skills that so many academics lack. She had a way with people. A way that got the most xenophobic farmer to accept her and act on her advice. It was her personality that gave her the confidence to walk into the bar at the Barley Mow, to shrug off the lewd comments of the inebriated labourers and find pleasure in others' company.

They sat there, shoulders touching, talking of the world. But each knew that the talking would stop. The attraction was not just intellectual. It was animal.

They made love on the carpet in front of the fire. They didn't notice the rain beating down on the windows. They hardly noticed as the fire spluttered to a low ember. They only knew each other and each other's bodies. His pale Northern body entwined with her olive skinned one. The heat of their bodies as he thrust into her and she pushed up her hips to help him probe further. The climax that came to them both simultaneously and dissolved into sobs of pleasure. Finally the softness of his touch as he led her up the stairs to the bedroom.

32

DECEMBER 31ST 2018, LONDON

Christmas had been a time of bringing the whole family together. With two five-year-olds the festivities naturally had revolved around their presents and Father Christmas. But it had also been a time for both Claire and Andrew to change their roles to being just 'Mum and Dad'. The high-pressure, fast-moving promotional world that Claire had been inhabiting came to a complete stop after the Agency held its Christmas lunch. For Andrew it was a relief to get a respite from the Brexit shenanigans at Westminster, the increasing workload from the ministry and his duties as a Lincolnshire MP.

With Parliament in recess he had been able to prepare the house for Christmas, to purchase many of the boys' Christmas presents and even organise a drinks and canapes event. It was a complete role reversal from the previous few Christmases.

He appreciated that Claire had been trying to juggle an

increasingly-demanding job with looking after the boys and that he had been away from home far too much. It was also the guilt that he felt following the night with Sara that made him determined to make it up to Claire.

He had been relieved to find that she didn't seem to be critical of his absences. In fact she just seemed really pleased to have him home for a bit. Indeed, she had actually apologised to him for not having done more to prepare for Christmas and said how she felt bad about having to work full time at the Agency right up to the 23rd.

He had asked her about her trip to Spain but it appeared that, like most business trips, she had been too busy running from one meeting to another to sit back and enjoy the pleasures of international travel. She didn't seem willing to discuss it in detail and he didn't push her.

Tonight they were planning to entertain some of their closest friends, three couples who lived close by. Analiese had gone back to Austria for Christmas and wasn't returning for another few days so Claire and Andrew were going to have to prepare the meal and look after the boys. Hopefully the boys would be asleep by the time the guests arrived at 8.

Amir and Indra were the first to arrive. Both had been born in England to Indian parents whose own parents had brought them from East Africa after Idi Amin had turned them out. Amir had worked for a short time at Templeton but was now making a name for himself in a Hedge Fund company with smart offices in Chelsea. He was shorter than Andrew and his hair was unfashionably long. Stylishness had never been something people associated with him. His analysis of figures and shrewd interpretations of market opportunities had been responsible for his success. As he shrugged off his parka Andrew noticed that he was a good few pounds heavier than last time they had met. He had donned an embroidered waistcoat that threatened to burst its buttons at any moment and combined it with Armani jeans and a bright pink open-necked shirt. Seeing Andrew's appraisal he laughed and handed across two bottles of Champagne in a Waitrose bag. "Thought I'd make an effort this evening as it's a special night."

Indra was everything that Amir wasn't. She was taller than him by a good three inches, slim and angular while he was a heavier, and flatter featured. Andrew had known Indra from university days. She had studied pharmacy at Nottingham and still worked part-time for a hospital pharmacy. Claire helped her out of her black ankle-length cashmere coat and kissed her on both cheeks. Beneath the coat one shoulder was bare while the other had a thin strap covered by the gossamer silk of her sari. The halter top was a deep burgundy silk with embroidered birds in gold and silver, the long skirt the same. Her bare midriff could be glimpsed through the gossamer white material that floated down from her shoulder. Her hair was long, black and lustrous pulled to one side and reaching down past her shoulders.

She approached Andrew who was still holding a bottle of Champagne in each hand. She smiled and lent forward to kiss him. The kiss was a light one on his lips. "Lovely to see you, Andrew. We've all missed you."

They had hardly entered the lounge before the doorbell rang again. It was Bob and Jane, and Connor and Caroline.

Bob was the oldest. He left school at sixteen and joined his father in the family firm. That firm had been a small brewery business with four or five pubs. Now, thirty years on, Bob's father had retired and the brewery had been sold for a large sum leaving Bob to concentrate on running over 300 pubs, many with restaurants. Despite the alcoholic nature of his business, Bob drank little and worked hard to keep himself in trim. He was in training for the London Marathon as he had proudly told Andrew when they spoke the previous week.

Jane was dark and petite and 10 years younger. Well-educated, she read biology at Manchester before training to be a teacher. Before she married Bob she worked in one of the more deprived areas of the capital. "She's my social conscience," Bob was used to saying. "She's got enough social conscience for the two of us." Married for only three years they had no children yet.

"Will you move out of the way and let a thirsty man get to the bar?" The Waterford lilt to Connor's voice broke through. Claire and Connor had been at university together and had even dated for a short time. Now he worked in London as a producer for one of the leading independent film production companies. He was a good few inches over six foot with the physique that hinted at a former rugby player. He had, in fact, gone for a trial with London Irish soon after university but they turned him down. "Just as well as I may have lost me good looks!"

Caroline had the type of red hair that you imagine every Irish heroine to possess. It was thick and wavy and seemed to change in tone under different lights. With her grey green eyes and a generous bosom she looked every bit the actress that Connor would have met on set. In fact she was from Devon and made jewellery which she sold in Portobello Market.

She wore one of her own necklaces now, a silver collar set with large semi-precious stones. Her earrings were also silver, each set with two round polished garnets that perfectly matched the deep dark red of her dress. Low-cut it showed off her pale ample breasts and stopped a full three inches above her knees thus giving Andrew the opportunity to appreciate her shapely legs.

As they sat down for dinner a little later Andrew couldn't help contrasting the group with those he'd been drinking with a week or so earlier in the Barley Mow. What a group this was tonight. Fashionably dressed in expensive clothes (Amir excepted), highly-educated and nearly all with interesting and influential well-paid jobs. Between them was a host of knowledge of what was going on in the country in business, in politics, in medicine and the arts. These were people at the centre of things. These were the people who felt connected with the characters and issues on the News every evening rather than bystanders. In Otherby, Westminster or Canary Wharf seemed as foreign and alien as Berlin or Brussels. No wonder so many had voted to leave the EU. They felt totally unrepresented by their politicians whether they were in Strasbourg or Westminster.

Andrew realised that he had missed dinner parties like this. Although he was at the centre of things as an MP in Westminster and surrounded by similar colleagues, he couldn't help feeling that his world had narrowed. The only issue at Westminster, for the time he'd been there, had revolved around the passage of the Withdrawal Act. There had been little else. Certainly the everyday things that affected his constituents were getting little attention and it was the same with more major issues like climate change and artificial intelligence. Not for the first time he realised that he was inhabiting three very different worlds.

There was Otherby and the rest of his constituency where people were involved in producing food, running small businesses or working for their local authority in a variety of jobs from health and welfare to education. Their concerns were earning sufficient money to support their family, to enable them to enjoy some sport and enjoy an annual holiday. The outside world was viewed via television. They often knew less about Boris Johnson or Phillip Hammond than they did about Lionel Messi or Taylor Swift.

The Wandsworth world was populated by younger people striving for success in the service industries. The cost of living was ridiculously high, especially house prices, but so were the rewards for their work. These were people who earned six figure salaries and topped them up with large bonuses or dividends. These were people of many different nationalities but a singular view of the world. A world that was forever getting smaller, more interconnected. A world where it was always possible to become a star performer as long as you worked hard enough and made the right connections.

Then there was the world of politics. It was as if you had just stepped back in time. The very traditions that typified politics at Westminster were from a bygone age. Debates, with their formalities of 'giving way' and addressing the Speaker, were reminiscent of school or university debating societies where the object was to show how good an orator you were rather than how strong a believer you were. It was a world that operated in a way that was oblivious to the world around it. To show one's support or opposition to something one had to get up, leave the chamber wander through a particular lobby and then return, a process taking 15 minutes or more. Andrew mused that it took longer for MPs to register their vote than for six million votes to be cast for *Britain's Got Talent*.

As if reading his thoughts, Connor leant across the table and addressed him. "Tell me Mr Right Honourable Eastwood, how do you manage to be in three places at once, or more accurately how do you manage to sort out some pigeon-fancier's allotment one minute, decide whether Britain should leave the customs union the next and still get back in time to put the kids to bed?"

"He doesn't," said Claire. "That's why we have to have an au pair."

"I don't know what you get out of it," said Amir, "it's not like the money's any good."

"I guess I'm just like one of your actors, Connor. I have different parts to play, different productions. You just have to be adaptable."

"But most actors are poor," said Caroline.

"Not if they're famous actors. They earn millions. When you get a seat in the Cabinet and write some salacious memoirs you'll make a fortune." Amir was only half joking. "But given your connections in Westminster you must get a few lucrative offers for, er, consultancy?"

Andrew was silent. So far he hadn't exactly been inundated with offers of cash for contacts. His work in the Health Ministry hadn't led to offers from major drug companies. And Stellagenix seemed to want his support in return for jobs for his constituents. Still he'd only been an MP for a few months, give it time.

Indra's voice broke his reverie. "Claire, I hear your new job is turning out very well. I heard you'd been taking private jets to exotic places in Europe with the heir to a family fortune." Everyone laughed except Claire.

"Well you're wrong. It was just Spain and we flew B.A."

"And the client? Did he treat you well?"

"Very well thank you." This brought hoots of lewd laughter from the group. Claire tried hard not to blush. She got up and started to collect the starter plates. Bob took the opportunity to talk with Amir about his plans to float his 300 pub empire on AIM, the second tier stock market.

Andrew rose and went to the kitchen to get more wine. "You can help me plate up the main course," said Claire. From the dining room they could hear the happy bubble of conversation.

"Seems to be going well; they loved that crab starter."

"Just don't let on that I got it ready prepared from Waitrose and just added some tabasco," replied Claire passing Andrew the fillet of beef to carve.

As the meal progressed and more wine was drunk, the conversation surprisingly turned more serious. Indra and Caroline had started to discuss climate change and Bob was trying to defend his choice of long-haul destinations for their holidays.

"We're all being so selfish. It's as if we don't care what happens to the planet as we'll all have died before then. But it's the kids I worry about." Indra tugged at her sari which had slipped off her shoulder. "The pollution in cities like Mumbai is terrible."

"And Paris," said Connor, "I was over there last month

and driving in from Charles de Gaulle you could see the layer of smog over the city."

"Did I read that you were doing a report on air pollution and its effect on children's health in London Andrew?" Jane was the serious one in the group. "When I was teaching in Hackney the pollution from the traffic was awful. We had to keep the kids inside some days."

Andrew thought back to his first project for the Minister. There was no disputing the high levels of NO2 and diesel-induced particulates that were present in the atmosphere around certain locations in Britain. Indeed the levels were illegally high in many cases. But the Ministry had pointedly failed to admit any linkage with children's health. The last thing the government needed was more criticism following the enquiry into the contaminated blood scandal.

"Well we've banned the most polluting vehicles from the whole of London and of course the congestion charge has done a lot to reduce traffic." Andrew knew this was a politician's answer. The truth was the traffic in London was steadily growing worse.

"I think you're all being a bit hypocritical," said Connor. "We all know there's a problem but we're doing fuck all about it. You're still driving that diesel-guzzling Nissan Andrew and don't the rest of us all have big SUVs?"

There was silence for a moment before Jane spoke.

"Look, I know we're all guilty of extravagance, too many airmiles, and wanting Peruvian asparagus or whatever, but don't let's underestimate the advances that are being made – particularly in biology. And Britain is a leader in this. Did you know, for instance that up at Cambridge they've just finished mapping 100,000 different patients' genomes?

They've worked out what causes certain cancers and diseases. It's a real breakthrough and Britain's leading the world in this type of research."

"Indeed," said Andrew, happy to be on firmer ground. "It was the Conservatives who initiated this under David Cameron back in 2012. I've been up to Cambridge and seen the work they're doing there. Very promising."

"I'd almost forgotten you were the Minister for Health," said Caroline.

"Only a junior minister. Here, have some more of this Beaune that Bob brought. It's rather good." Much better than the Malbec he'd been drinking in the Barley Mow.

Claire had been following the discussion closely. Now she chipped in. "The British aren't the best at everything. I've got this client who's American. Their company has just come up with a new strain of barley that's going to increase the yields dramatically. That's going to help feed an awful lot of people."

"And the work is being done in my constituency," said Andrew proudly.

"I'm not sure I approve of all this genetic engineering," said Indra whose pharmaceutical experience had made her wary of large foreign drug and chemical companies.

"Do we eat barley?" Connor queried. "I thought it was wheat we ate."

"Well they're working on wheat too. No doubt they'll be able to get good results there too. And the Americans seem to be able to develop these products fast. The British are great at research but then leave it to someone else to actually market it."

"That's because they put the finance behind it. It's far

easier to get finance for these type of projects in the States. We've got a lot of clients invested in bioscience." Amir had himself put money into one of just such funds. He made a mental note to talk to Andrew later about what he knew of the Stellagenix plans. A bit of inside knowledge was always useful.

33

JANUARY-MARCH 2019, LONDON

Andrew shuffled along the green bench to allow another Conservative MP to squeeze in. The Chamber was packed. Overcrowded would have been a better word as nearly 650 MPs tried to cram into a chamber more suitable for 200. It had been like this every night this week. And they had been late nights too. Andrew had gone into politics with the aim of trying to reverse the Brexit referendum, or at least get a really soft Brexit. But the past two months had proved just how divided the Conservative party was on the issue and just how ineffectual the Labour opposition was under Jeremy Corbyn.

Theresa May had suffered an enormous defeat in January when she tried to get her version of the Withdrawal Bill through. She had tried again, this month in a desperate attempt to get the Withdrawal Agreement signed before the Brexit date of March 29th. Again she had suffered a humiliating defeat. Now, this week it was a free for all as

MPs tried to take back control from the government and try to find a solution that would command a majority. There was even an outside hope that they would vote to rescind Article 50 and not leave the Union at all. At the very least the March 29th deadline would be extended.

All this had meant that Andrew had spent nearly all his time at Westminster, not in Lincolnshire. It also meant that he had barely seen Claire during the week because of the late-night sessions.

Andrew was becoming increasingly disillusioned with politics. The debates in Parliament were theatrical posturings that he was ashamed to be identified with. Most of the ministers seemed to have been public-school and Oxbridge-educated and thus treated debating as a game. Yet governing the country should not be a game. It affected the lives of 60 million people. No wonder so many of his constituents had voted to leave Brussels. They might just as easily have voted to get rid of Westminster. They had no more faith that British ministers understood anything about life outside the M25.

When Andrew had worked for Templeton in the City, he was aware that many of his colleagues had no qualms about doing what was necessary to make money. They revelled in their ability to invest other people's money in stocks, shares and derivatives and beat their rival fund managers. They understood what moved the market and they exploited that knowledge for their clients' and their own personal benefit. Sometimes they got it wrong, spectacularly wrong, and found themselves out on the street clutching their personal possessions in an Iron Mountain cardboard box. That was reality.

Politicians on the other hand, were not paid astronomical salaries and were supposedly people with a moral compass that they used to further the best interests of their constituents. Sadly, Andrew had come to realise, many MPs were out to feather their own nests. Many had wealth that insulated them from the effects of their actions. They could protect their wealth from taxation, yet change the benefits paid to those less well off. They could invoke their prejudices to support acts that dealt unfairly with those with little or no influence. The Windrush scandal had shown this only too clearly.

The thing that had surprised Andrew the most, however, was not the insensitivity, greed or even corruption of some MPs in his party, but their ignorance. They may have had a classical education, but their general knowledge of real life was often sadly sparse. Rarely were they prepared to study the detailed facts. That made things very different from Templeton where people like Andrew had researched in depth to make the right investment decisions. There was a laziness to get involved in detail. The Brexit argument was one such issue. No one seemed to have considered the effect it would have on Ireland for example. No one had bothered to look at the effect it would have on attracting low-paid immigrant labour that was so desperately needed to look after an ageing population. No one had actually identified the countries with whom Britain would sign new trade deals to replace its lost trade with Europe. No one had identified the 'Sunny Uplands'. There was an attitude of 'Forget details, it's the principle that matters'.

Britain had, of course, a well-paid civil service to do all the work that politicians avoided. The heads of these departments or ministries, however, seemed often to be from the same background as their political masters. Both politicians and civil servants seemed more interested in furthering their own careers than serving the population.

Much of the work Andrew had been doing as a junior minister had been trying to increase the efficiency of the NHS. It was an enormous 'business', the biggest employer in Europe. The front-line staff were very dedicated but the administration of this enormous operation was floundering. If it were a commercial business it would have defined its purpose and its strategy to achieve it. As a political institution it was more difficult. More and more money had been invested in the service yet still everyone was crying out for more. The pressures would only get worse, in Andrew's opinion. The ageing population in Britain would mean more and more patients requiring treatment. The advances in medical science made it possible to heal more people of more afflictions but that only increased people's expectations and the NHS costs. With only a finite budget it was necessary to choose which treatments were acceptable for the NHS to carry out and which weren't. The government had set up NICE, a body that decided which drugs were affordable and worthwhile for the NHS to use and which weren't. But no one said you couldn't have a new hip, or a new knee.

Andrew had been looking at the results of 'war-gaming' that had been carried out by the government in 2016 to test whether the UK was ready for emergencies. Many shortcomings had been identified, like ventilators for a pandemic, but the government hadn't allocated more money for them. There were far more pressing calls on the limited budget.

The cost of drugs was a major element in the government's plans. Brexiteers were very keen to do deals with the USA pharmaceutical companies. The prices of these companies' shares were rising and many MPs had investments in them.

Andrew groaned as another MP stood up to make a point of order. He felt powerless to affect Brexit and he felt that he was ignoring his constituents and his family.

He hardly saw Claire at all these days. Certainly not during the week. Claire left early to get into work leaving Andrew and Analiese to prepare breakfast for the boys and take them to school. She got back in time to put the boys to bed but Andrew would be in the Commons until very late in the evening by which time she would have gone to bed.

That left the weekend. Andrew was torn between his need to go up to Lincolnshire and sort out issues for his constituents and spending time at home with Claire.

The bad weather that had swept the country for the past two months had dissuaded him from making many trips up to Otherby.

Andrew had promised that it would all be sorted by Easter and they could then enjoy a family break. Claire hoped that meant a flight to somewhere warm. Andrew had thoughts of somewhere 180 miles up the A1.

The Gatwick Express from London was crowded as usual. Claire had dragged her small-wheeled case alongside her seat where she could keep an eye on it. Her cabin bag was on the rack above her. She gazed out the window, watching as the panorama of houses, flats and offices finally petered out as the train headed south of Croydon. Rain streaked across the windows and she could see the trees bending with the wind.

She couldn't remember what they had named this storm. Was it Greta, or Gertrude? Something like that. There seemed to be a different storm every other week, all blamed on global warming.

She was looking forward to arriving in Barcelona where the weather should be a lot more pleasant. This was her third trip in three months. This time she was travelling alone and would join Clifton who had been down there for the past couple of weeks.

Life had changed so much in the past few months, she thought, as she traced her finger down the steamed-up window.

She hadn't expected her new job to be so all-absorbing. Accepting promotion meant that she had really had to commit herself to the Agency. She had confidently told Leonora that she could manage it along with her maternal duties. Employing Analiese had been a godsend and Andrew rarely had to be at work before 10 so getting off in the morning wasn't a problem. But Andrew's absences up North and late-night-sittings meant that they had little or no time together.

We used to go up to a show once or twice a month, she reflected. And there were the circuits of dinner parties. We've had to give up fixing anything during the week.

Andrew seemed to like going up to Otherby at the weekend but she didn't. After a hectic week in London, Claire wanted time with the boys, time to sort out the house and time to socialise with their friends. She felt guilty that she had been up to Otherby only three times.

She wondered what Andrew found to do up there. 'Constituency work' he explained. "I have my surgery. It made him sound like a doctor.

The last time she went, it was for business anyway. Up to see George Krasnik at Stellagenix.

Not accompanying Andrew to Otherby wasn't the only thing causing her to feel guilty. Here she was off to Barcelona again. Off to meet Clifton.

During the week, in the office, she managed to dismiss thoughts of how good Clifton was in bed. When he phoned her, he was always business-like. It would sound like a typical conversation with one of her other clients or with other members of the Prospect team. He was just another client like George or Isabella the new telecoms client Claire had gained.

She thought that their secret was safe from her colleagues in the Agency. Prithi had quizzed her after that first trip. "How was lover-boy? Did he try anything on?"

"He was a perfect gentleman," she had responded honestly. "He's actually quite good company when he's not banging on about work. But I don't think I'm his type."

In fact, she mused, she wasn't his type. Typically he liked to have some pouting bimbo on his arm, someone who would be so dazzled by his flattery that she would willingly hop into bed with him. Life for Clifton, she felt, was a series of one-night-stands.

But wasn't that what she was? Hadn't she fallen for his flirting praise, his wealth, his easy charm? Hadn't she allowed herself to get drunk and fall into bed with him?

She thought back to that morning in Barcelona when she had woken with a king-sized hangover, naked and dishevelled in his bed. She remembered how matter-of-fact he was. In total control. His business hat on. Somehow she had got through the morning meeting with the real estate man. As the afternoon had progressed she has managed to fall back into her role as account director rather than paramour.

On the flight home he had been attentive and thanked her for all her support. He then had taken her hand and squeezed it. "I hope you enjoyed our trip?" She had looked down in her lap. Eventually she had looked at him and smiled.

"Yes. It was nice. Thank you." It seemed inadequate. Nice? Was that the best she could say for a night of sex that had been one of the most intense lovemaking experiences of her life?

"Can we still work together okay? I mean, I want to make love to you again but I also value your input for Prospect so much. I really need your support."

She had nodded. She didn't know if she'd be able to compartmentalise her life so easily. And there he was suggesting more sex. They did work together well, she knew. They bounced ideas off each other, shared the same sense of humour and the same interest in culture.

She had enjoyed the sex too, heightened as it had been by the knowledge that she was cheating on her husband.

She had tried to rationalise it to herself. It wasn't as if she was having an affair. It was just a one-off in a foreign country. And he was a client. And Andrew was too busy these days to notice. What was a girl supposed to do?

Indeed it had seemed ok. There was the second trip to Barcelona. Again it was a tightly-scheduled couple of days rushing between meetings. Then back to their little hotel.

This time she hadn't got drunk over dinner. It was the same restaurant, the same proprietor and the same romantic ambience. But she had been careful to limit her alcohol intake. She still drank enough to overcome any reservations about going to bed with him. The sex had been just as exciting as the first time. This time she woke hangover-free and enjoyed a further, quieter but satisfying screw with Clifton before breakfast.

Now, here she was again, off to Barcelona.

34

Dimitri was happy. You could tell when he was because he went around with a grin so wide on his face that it looked as if it would spread right up his ears. George could hear him humming as he walked down the corridor seconds before he pushed open the door to George's office. Dimitri was not one for protocol. It didn't occur to him to knock on the door. George was used to his mad scientist.

"It looks like over 23%!" Dimitri threw down a sheaf of stapled sheets on George's desk. "And it could be more."

"23%?" George's morning had been spent preparing budgets for the upcoming board meeting in Cincinnati. What was over 23%?

"The increased yield we're getting on Sitari 3?" Dimitri liked to show off his Greek and regularly gave Greek names to his projects. Sitari was the Greek word for wheat and the results of the second year field trials of winter wheat had just had their final analysis.

George looked up at his friend. "How sure are you? If that's true then we've done it, we've hit the jackpot."

Dimitri sat down on the leather chair and picked up the sheaf of papers. He started explaining the details of their research methods, how the same techniques used to produce the barley strain had been used on the wheat seeds. Initially, the results had been disappointing. They had modified the technique not once, but twice. It was Sitari 3 that had suddenly proved to be successful in increasing the yield. The grains in the wheat were larger than normal, much larger. They grew faster, could be harvested earlier. The results hadn't been verified until now after all the toxicology tests had been done, but Dimitri had been pretty certain since the harvesting back in September. If there had been any problems with the product it would have shown up in the tests they had carried out with their laboratory mice. The mice had shown no adverse reaction to the wheat. In fact they had gained weight. The effect on worldwide production of wheat if the Stellagenix seeds were adopted would be nothing short of revolutionary. The effect on the Stellagenix share price would be equally dramatic. The yield per hectare of the new strain had been calculated using data gathered from dozens of neighbouring farms and analysed against historical records. All this had taken time. Now, today, Dimitri was certain of the results.

"Who else knows about these results?"

"Well, Martha and Katriona helped me analyse the results so they know, and I have to tell you they are as excited as I am."

"And the farmer, what's his name? Does he know?"

"Well obviously he knows that the yield was up. In fact he phoned me to say he thought the harvesting should be brought forward. But he doesn't know exactly how good the results are."

"Let's keep it that way, Dimitri. We need to keep a lid on this for a little while. We need to be sure this isn't an aberration." George was not worried that this result was an aberration. He was thinking of the effect on the share price when the news got out. He was thinking of the effect it would have on his career. He was thinking of the house he would build back in the States, somewhere warm and a bit more civilised than this frozen outpost.

After Dimitri left, George made two phone calls. The first was to his broker in New York. The second was to London. The recipient of that call was not in his office according to his secretary. He was 'in the House' at a debate. Two hours later he returned the call. That evening he rang his own stockbroker.

After George had lunched in the staff canteen, he called Andrew. Andrew was at his desk in the Ministry. He had spent the morning looking at figures showing the performance of different hospital trusts and was shocked to see that his own Trust in Lincolnshire was very much at the bottom of the list for performance.

United Lincolnshire Hospitals NHS Trust had been placed in special measures in 2016 following inspection by the Care Quality Commission and the report that was on Andrew's desk now showed that very little progress had been made. There were criticisms of the lack of suitably qualified, competent, skilled and experienced medical and nursing staff, and of the leadership team which lacked the 'capacity and capability' to tackle the challenges.

Andrew knew how much his Ministry was spending

throughout the service and made a mental note to meet with the leaders of the Trust to discuss the situation.

The phone call from George was a welcome break. George was enthusing about the progress being made on the enlargement of their operation in Lincolnshire and thanked Andrew for his help with the local planning officers.

Out of politeness Andrew asked how the trials of the new barley were going. "Well, Andrew, this is privileged information you know but I guess Claire will be telling you soon anyway. But not a word to anyone yet OK? The barley seed operation is going full steam ahead but we have something even more exciting coming up."

"Oh yes?" Andrew's training as analyst had prepared him to discount many potential game-changers that companies reported. They were often floated to take attention off the company's recent poor performance. But Stellagenix shares had been trading quite nicely and there was no reason to suspect that George was flying a kite.

"Can't tell you a lot. Certainly over the phone. But this is going to be really big. You might like to get a piece of the action."

"Not allowed to I'm afraid. Conflict of interest and all that."

"Yeah, well I'm sure there are ways round that. A few of your colleagues seem to know how."

Andrew was shocked by George's comments. MPs were supposed to publish any holdings they had and weren't supposed to hold shares in companies whose interests could be served by political decisions. Nevertheless he had come to realise that many of his colleagues on the government benches had family trusts or other mechanisms that kept their involvement secret. More than one Member was reported to have shorted the pound in advance of Brexit and had a large investment portfolio in the Cayman Islands. If Britain ended up with a hard Brexit, let alone a no-deal, then he stood to make millions.

However, lobbyists weren't normally as direct as George. He made another note to himself. He would speak to Claire as soon as she returned from her latest trip to Barcelona.

He brought his thoughts back to George who was talking about a sports centre.

"Look Andrew, you and I know that the local authority ain't exactly flush with cash right now. You've got a lot of young people up here who don't see the government in Westminster doing much for them. That's why they voted for Brexit, for change. Anything is better if you've got nothing. Well you need to show them that you've got their interests at heart if you want to remain in government. Labour might not be electable right now with Corbyn and his looney left cronies, but if they got someone who connected with the people more you guys could be in trouble."

"So what are you telling me we've got to do?" Andrew disliked being lectured to on British politics by an American, a Republican at that.

"I'm not telling you to do anything. I'm telling you what I can do to improve your chances in the next election. I told you that the barley seed we're going to be marketing is going to bring a lot more employment to the area. We're well ahead on the building work and that's given jobs to local builders etc."

"Yes but there aren't going to be many jobs for young people in your new labs – especially the lower skilled youth." Andrew was only too aware that few of his younger constituents were qualified to be biochemists or lab technicians.

"Exactly, Andrew. We will have a few jobs in the packing and distribution end of the business which will suit them but we'd like to do something for those young unemployed voters you've got."

"Like what?"

"Like building them a sports stadium. More than a stadium, a state-of-the-art sports facility. I've had my guys look at what sporting facilities are available in the county and to be brutally honest Andrew, it sucks. Any of your budding athletes or tennis players or footballers have to travel miles away to get proper training. Now we thought that if the county council were to build a large indoor facility for tennis, athletics etc. it would help your youngsters to make something of themselves instead of dealing drugs."

"I don't think our drug problem is any worse than other parts of the country," said Andrew. "As for the county council having the money to splurge on some fancy facility – well that's just not going to happen. There are too many other priorities. Like improving the local hospital facilities for a start." He glanced down at the damning report on his desk.

"Sure, sure. But that's where Stellagenix can help. We'd be prepared to put up a sizeable chunk of cash to create the Stellagenix Sports Centre, and it would be in your constituency. That's going to make you a local hero!"

Andrew considered. Certainly such a sports facility was sorely needed and would be very popular. But what was in it for Stellagenix? Why the generosity?

"I'm not sure I understand your motives George. I mean, I agree we are in dire need of something like that in Lincolnshire, but what are you set to gain from it?"

"Well maybe you should have a word with your wife. She'll tell you that corporate image is everything these days. Not everyone is a fan of biochem and agrichem companies. Lot of resistance by those long-haired animal rights people for a start. Not that we're doing anything unethical. Just using a few mice and rats really. Anyway our improved seed strains are designed to reduce agriculture's use of those nasty chemicals they call insecticides, or pesticides. Nevertheless, as your wife points out, being seen to be doing something for the health and well-being of your British youngsters would do us no harm at all. It's better than being a shirt sponsor for Grimsby Town or Lincoln City." George laughed. He'd done his homework well even though he'd never watched a soccer match in his life.

"I see. Yes I get that."

"Of course it would be nice to know that we could count on you to push the proposal through with the County Council and the sports bodies. You know they can sometimes be a bit protective of their interests, arguments over where it is to be built, opposition by those with a vested interest in sending everyone to Loughborough etc."

"Well, of course. But where are you thinking of building it. Have you found a suitable site?"

"Well that's what I'd like to talk to you about. It's bang in the middle of your constituency, it'd do you the world of good with the locals. Could increase the value of property nearby too. I believe you own a nice place in Otherby don't you? Might be worth looking to see if there are any other properties near there for sale. Could be a good investment."

Once again Andrew felt compromised. In a single conversation he had been offered insider information that could result in a share killing and insider news on a possible project that would increase the value of houses in an area. It was unethical.

Andrew thought back to when he arrived in Westminster. He had a clear idea of what he wanted to achieve. He wanted to help people, improve their lives. Above all he wanted to stop Brexit which he saw as an economic disaster which would disproportionately impact on the poorer in our country. Then he had started to understand that the motives of many of his colleagues were very different. There was a cynical disregard for 'the man in the street'. Everything was about power. You had to be in government. You had to retain your seat in any election. In between elections it was open season for any deals that came up. After all, you weren't paid very much as an MP. You had to make it up through your contacts, your influence and your willingness to 'facilitate' things for companies in your constituencies.

Looking again at the report on the hospital trust on his desk he thought about the millions of pounds that was being wasted by mismanagement of quangos and government departments. The purchase of aircraft carriers without the planes to land on them, the commissioning of tanks that worked in the snowy wastes of Scandinavia but got clogged in the Arabian sands. The countless IT projects undertaken by government departments employing extremely expensive management consultants that then failed to work because the staff hadn't been trained to use them.

So what if Stellagenix's reputation might improve if they

financed a sports facility. Wasn't the benefit to people in Lincolnshire more important?

He realised George was waiting for a response from him. "Sorry?"

"I said I was hoping you'd manage to tear yourself away from all those Brexit debates and get back up here to see what we're planning. We really haven't seen you around recently."

"Yes, I'm sorry. It's been really difficult with Brexit. Never seems to end. And the weather hasn't really been helpful. How is all that snow up there?"

"It's melting slowly and leaving a dark grey mush everywhere. Disgusting! Anyway maybe you can get Claire up here too. I hear she's spending all her time in Spain these days"

Not for the first time did Andrew wonder how George was so well informed. He seemed to be better briefed on his wife's travels than he was.

35

Andrew's week had not gone well. He had been working long hours at the Ministry and in Westminster and he had clashed with several of his colleagues about their wish to do a deal with the USA over the health service.

A bill to promote reciprocal healthcare arrangements not only with the EU but any other country had been thrown out by the Lords who wanted it to apply merely to the current European countries. Andrew was worried about trying to retain the benefits Britons currently enjoyed, like the European health card that his constituents relied on if they were sick on holiday in Benidorm, or studying under the Erasmus scheme or just travelling there for work.

He worried about negotiating further deals with America for instance where the health system was still largely controlled by big pharmaceutical companies. Whatever the problems he was trying to sort out with the NHS, he didn't relish a half-baked Medicare programme. Britain was leading the world in genetic research for instance. We didn't need Republican Americans banning stem cell research or getting the population hooked on pain killers.

His mind turned to what George had been telling him. It wasn't a health issue, it was an agricultural one but the effect on a company's share price of coming up with a new seed strain was not that different from a drug company finding a new cancer drug.

After many hours in committee the government had accepted the Lords amendments and was proposing to concentrate just on the European aspect for the next reading. The name of the bill was changed. But the problem was, it all depended on Brexit!

Today was supposed to be Brexit Day. It was supposed to be the day that Britain left the EU for good. But it wasn't. MPs couldn't manage to find a withdrawal agreement that even half of them could support. Theresa May had now tried three times to get approval for the Withdrawal Agreement she had negotiated with the EU and three times it had been rejected. MPs had tried to come up with an alternative all week but without success. Now Mrs May would have to go back to the EU and beg for a further extension. She had already said she would stand down as leader in the next few months once a deal had been agreed.

Andrew was growing more and more disillusioned with politics. All this week he had been stuck in Westminster like every other MP. Everything was about Brexit. And Brexit was proving intractable. Andrew had given up his city job to become an MP. He wanted to try and prevent the government from forcing through a disastrous Brexit deal. He had done it because he wanted to make a difference. Not only to national politics but to the lives of his constituents. He had had enough of the amoral world of stock-market investment. He wanted to believe he was doing something worthwhile.

So this week had been the most frustrating time for him. A week of frantic debates and motions, proposals and counter-proposals which all came to nothing. His colleagues on the right wing of his party maintained that the referendum result three years previously had shown that it was the will of the people to leave the EU. Nearly half of the voters disagreed and had voted to remain. The majority of MPs wanted to remain even though they represented constituencies, like West Lincs, that had voted to leave. The problem was it wasn't possible to leave and still retain all the current benefits. Northern Ireland and its border with the Republic was a major sticking point and one that had hardly been mentioned back in 2016. There were many others. The whole thing was a mess.

He just wanted to get back to Otherby, see his constituents and start making a difference. He also wanted to see Sara again.

He hadn't seen her since Christmas. She was away in Nottingham studying and he was stuck down in Westminster. Snow had covered Lincolnshire for most of February and now the weather was becoming better he had to stick in Westminster.

Meanwhile Claire seemed to be having the time of her life, he thought ruefully. She had escaped south to Barcelona three times in as many months.

She was loving the chance to spread her wings after years of domestic chores, but that just left Andrew feeling more frustrated. With his late nights, and her foreign trips they seemed to be seeing less and less of each other.

This weekend, however, they would be together and have time with the boys. They would also have a dinner date with their friends Amir and Indra.

The taxi dropped Andrew outside his house. There were few lights on in the house. It was past midnight. The debate had gone on longer than he expected and everyone wanted to talk about it afterwards so he couldn't get away from the House. Parliament Square had been occupied by rival mobs of Brexit campaigners, some who had been hoping the day would mark Britain's withdrawal, others celebrating a reprieve.

He opened the door quietly and removed his shoes before climbing the stairs. A dimmed light shone from a bedside lamp. Claire was sleeping, her breathing deep and regular. Her pyjama-clad arm was draped across the duvet. Andrew slipped out of his clothes and quickly brushed his teeth without switching on his electric toothbrush. He gently pulled back the cover and lay down beside his wife. He turned to switch off the light and noticed her carry-on suitcase in the corner, its 'Priority Boarding' tag still around the handle. He wondered what time she had got back. He wondered what she had been doing in Barcelona. He closed his eyes and almost instantly fell asleep.

He was woken early the next morning by the boys running into the bedroom. "Mummy, Mummy have you brought us a present back?"

Claire sat up and smiled. "Well have you been good enough to deserve a present?"

"Yes, yes Mummy." The twins spoke in chorus nodding

their heads vigorously and looking expectantly at their mother's suitcase in the corner.

Marshall ran over to the suitcase and pulled it across to the bed. Claire lifted it onto the bed and turned to Andrew. "What time did you get in last night? My flight was delayed and I was so knackered I went straight to bed."

She unzipped the case and the lid flopped back revealing the contents. There were two small wrapped presents on the top, lying in the folds of the silk nightdress. The boys tore the wrapping paper off and shrieked with delight at their matching Spanish bulls. Outside, on the landing, they heard Analiese's voice calling to them to leave their parents alone and they dutifully followed her downstairs.

"How was your trip darling?"

"It was good. Yes very good. We got everything sorted."

"I had thought you were coming back on Thursday?"

"Yes we were but we sort of ran out of time." Claire coughed and lifted down the suitcase, spilling some of the contents onto the floor. "So we took an extra day. It meant I finally managed to go and look round the Cathedrale. But what about poor old you? I've been following the news on my tablet. The whole Brexit business seems to have ground to a halt?"

"It's a bloody mess, that's what," said Andrew. "I just can't see how she's going to get out of the mess she's got us into. No one likes her withdrawal agreement enough to vote for it, but no one can see anything better. Rees Mogg and Cash and the rest of that lot are getting ever more hopeful of a no-deal. But let's just forget it for today shall we? I'm totally pissed off with whole thing."

He leant across and gave her a kiss. She ran her fingers

through his hair, ruffling it. Then she broke away and climbed out of bed. "I need to shower, and so do you. I was too tired last night after all the travelling."

"I'll scrub your back."

She turned and looked at him over her shoulder and grinned. She unbuttoned her pyjama top and pushed it off her shoulder turning towards him and letting it fall to the floor. Then she span round and headed for the bathroom. She stopped once more, framed in the arch that led from the bedroom into the en suite. She didn't look round but wriggled out of her pyjama bottoms. She tiptoed across to the shower and Andrew heard the water flowing. He realised that he was aroused.

He'd been so tired and busy recently that lovemaking had become a rare event. Now, he slipped off his PJs and followed Claire into the shower. Their soapy bodies slapped out an ever-faster rhythm as he pounded into her until with one final lunge he came and they stood there, clinging together, the water streaming over his head, down onto Claire's shoulders and finding its way in a trickle down to the cleft in her buttocks.

After some moments they uncoupled and he bent to kiss her, first on the mouth and then bending further to kiss her still-stiff nipples. She moaned and raked her fingers through his wet hair. He reached and turned the water off.

"Oh, I've missed that!" he murmured.

"I've missed you," she replied. It was the third morning in a row that she had orgasmed.

They took the boys to McDonalds for lunch, their favourite restaurant. Analiese walked into the town with them before heading off to the station. She was meeting up with some German friends for shopping. She would be back in the evening to babysit.

Over the Big Macs and fries Andrew told her about the phone call from George. "He said you knew all about it. Something really big."

"I don't know if I should tell you. I'm not sure I know much about it anyway. I haven't spoken to him this week. I didn't get a chance to return his call on Friday when I was tied up with Clifton."

Andrew didn't notice that she dropped her chin and reached for a napkin, avoiding his gaze.

"But what's he going on about then? I mean he's pretty excited about the barley seed thing but that's not new. This was obviously something else, and he said it would be something really big."

"I think it must be the wheat they were working on. That's the only thing they were working on. Last week I had a talk with that mad Greek scientist of theirs. I was trying to get clearance for a press release we were doing for the farming press on the research behind the barley seed. I can get a bit confused between zygotes and transposons and mutagenesis and all that so I needed him to check what we were saying. He's a funny guy. It's like he's really proud of what they are achieving yet wants to keep the details of how they did it a secret. Can't blame him, I suppose. After all the benefits of what they've produced with that barley are amazing. It's going to make them a hell of a lot of money." She took another bite of her burger and wiped her mouth again with the napkin. "He told me that the barley was nothing to what he was working on now."

"Which was?"

"Wheat. He said he was hoping they could achieve similar results with winter wheat and that would be in a whole different league from the barley. He wouldn't tell me more but seemed very excited. I guess George knows the results of their tests. That must be what he was hinting at."

"How much, Claire, do they tell you about their research?"

"Not very much actually. It's not really our thing. We're there to improve their image with the public and their investors. With all these tree-huggers and Greta Thunberg fans, we have to be careful to portray Stellagenix as an ethical, caring company. Did George mention that he's thinking of funding a big sports complex for Lincoln?"

That evening, with the boys safely in bed, they left Analiese and strolled the few blocks to Amir and Indra's house.

Amir opened the door to them and accepted the bottle of wine proffered by Andrew. He was dressed in his more usual attire, blue jeans and a black T-shirt. Inside, their house was Kath Kidston goes to Bollywood. The wallpaper was small floral patterned while the furniture was dark brown, ornate and often highlighted with gold. In contrast to Amir, Indra was again wearing a beautiful sari, this one in pale powder blue with gold thread. She kissed Claire on each cheek before turning to Andrew and kissing him on the lips. "Well it's so good to see you both. Especially you Andrew. The last time was New Year's Eve. Have you been trying to avoid me?"

"Leave him," said Claire, "I hardly get to see him these days and I'm his wife! It's like he's imprisoned in that Palace of Westminster."

Andrew grinned sheepishly. "Well we are very tied up trying to sort out Brexit, it makes for late nights."

"Oh Brexit, Brexit, Brexit. That's all you hear these days. Switch on the telly and there's someone trying to explain how we can take back control, leave the Common Market, keep all the benefits, sort out the Irish border and do a Singapore-style deal with Trump's America. I'm fed up to the back teeth with it all." Indra sniffed at the lilies Claire had brought her. "I'll just put these in water. You go with Amir and get drinking and no talking about Brexit. It's forbidden tonight. OK?"

Amir turned to Claire. "I gather while he's been wearing out his trousers sitting on those green benches, you've been living it up on the continent?"

"I've had to go on three brief trips to Spain. Mainly Barcelona. Got a client whose relocating part of his business over there because of Brexit."

"Sssh. Don't let Indra hear you mention that word." Amir picked up a cut glass tumbler and dropped two pieces of ice in it. "Vodka and tonic if I'm not mistaken. Or have you developed a taste for Sangria?"

"Have you been travelling, Amir?" asked Andrew.

"No, not really. I'm still waiting for my invite to Davos. I just had to content myself with three days in Berlin and two days in Bucharest."

"What were you doing in Bucharest? Romania is hardly flush with investors for a hedge fund boss like you."

"Actually it was more up your street really. Now you're a country squire up in Lincolnshire. No, I was there to look at some cows. Quite a lot of cows actually. Nearly 2000 Friesians."

"The mind boggles. You in wellies milking cows in Romania. I've heard it all now. What on earth were doing there?"

"Well it was a tip off from a friend of mine at the European Development Bank. Do you know Romania produces milk at a lower price than anywhere else in the EU? Well it does. And the market for dairy products is growing all the time. But there's this one farm in Romania that is really going places. They've got all these Friesian cattle and they get them inseminated artificially using stuff from the best bulls in the world. But then they feed them some special food which makes them really great milkers. They have a contract with one of the agrochemical giants in America."

"Very interesting, I'm sure," said Claire, "But what's in it for you?"

"Well we've got this new fund. It's investing in a lot of the new biological companies as well as firms big in GM foods etc. There are some amazing breakthroughs happening right now. And there needs to be. The world needs to produce a lot more food, fast. It's alright for these Extinction Mob yesterday marching on Downing Street. Yes we've got to save the planet but we need to feed the people on it first. Going to Romania just opened my eyes to the possibilities for our British farmers. They are going to lose their EU farm subsidies when we pull out. We need to be using everything we can to make them more productive after Brexit."

"I told you not to mention that word tonight, Amir. Now pour me a drink." Indra put down the vase of lilies on the sideboard. "Two days in a muddy field and he thinks he's an expert on animal husbandry!"

"Well it is an interesting field, no pun intended," laughed

Claire. "Remember I told you about Stellagenix last time we met? They're getting great results from editing barley genes.

"Their shares are doing well at the moment, I've been watching them. They announced the results of the barley strain a few months ago and that put a shine on them. Anything else I should know?"

"Well you might like to do more than look at them. They could be coming out with some even better news shortly." Claire was revelling in the conversation. It was good to be back involved in the international world of finance again. She'd missed it until recently.

"Really? Tell me more."

Andrew looked hard at Claire. She took the hint. "No, I can't tell you any more. Sworn to secrecy and all that. But you'll read about it soon I'm sure."

Amir nodded and picked up the bottle of Grey Goose to refill Claire's glass. A nod was certainly as good as a wink. Knowing about a development before the market knew was what made Amir a success. On Monday he would take a punt on Stellagenix.

36

EASTER 2019, LINCOLNSHIRE

Andrew was glad to leave London at last. With Parliament closed for Easter it was a chance to get back to Otherby. The two boys were laughing at something in the seat behind him, but Claire was silent, gazing out of the car window as they headed up the A1.

Claire was thinking about how nice it would be in Spain right now. She could imagine that the beaches round Barcelona were filling up in the Spring sunshine. Bikini-clad girls strutting to and fro watched by dark Spanish eyes. Couples sipping wine, under colourful shades outside the bars along the promenade. She thought of Clifton and their last time together in Barcelona. It was the first time they had driven out to the beach. Although the day had been cloudy it was easy to imagine how it looked now, with the April sun shining.

She had enjoyed this year, all three months of it. After her years of being housebound with the boys, she had suddenly re-entered the fast-moving, exciting world of business. The trips to Barcelona, a new lover, the thrill of listening to Amir and his international business dealings. It was all so satisfying. At the Agency she was flying high. Paul Devorian, the Agency's chief had taken her to lunch last week to thank her for helping to win the new electric car account.

Now though she was facing a week up in Lincolnshire without a decent restaurant for miles, a load of country bumpkins who had probably never even heard of Romania or Grey Goose vodka or Kandinsky. What would she find to talk about?

She was annoyed with Andrew. She couldn't help it. She understood how frustrated he was with what was happening (or actually not happening) in Parliament. She shared his Remainer views on Europe. But being an MP's wife, even a junior Minister's wife, had not led to the glamorous social life she had hoped for. On the contrary, their social life had all but dried up. Now she was heading up North again with the prospect of a local Conservative Party dinner being the only social event planned. An evening smiling sweetly at the wives of the local burghers who probably still had straw in their hair and mud on their shoes. Ugh!

She couldn't understand Andrew's enthusiasm for the trip.

As they drove further north, however, the weather got better and by the time they arrived at Otherby there was a clear blue sky and a bright sun. She had to admit that the house looked prettier than their one in Wandsworth. As they drove up the daffodil-fringed driveway the boys were already excited to get out and explore. Three and a half hours is a long time in a car when you're only 5 years old.

Andrew pushed open the front door whose progress was hindered by the pile of mail on the mat. He gathered it all up and dropped it onto his desk in the study. Claire followed him in, bringing the box of food. They could hear the boys shouting as they ran round the back garden anxious to get their young limbs working again.

It was the first time Claire had been there in decent weather and it certainly made a difference. The shrubs in the garden and the trees didn't seem as advanced as those she had noticed at the bottom of the A1 but they all seemed to promise the hope of Spring.

At the bottom of the garden she could see the large fields, already planted with cereal crops. The field nearest the house had rows and rows of plants already a foot high. She didn't know what the crops were. Her horticultural knowledge stretched to roses, lilies and alstroemeria from Waitrose.

Her reverie was interrupted by Marshall asking what was for lunch. She hadn't had time the previous day to do a shop and had purchased some ready meals from the motorway services. In London she could have phoned for a pizza, or a burger or something. She doubted you could order a takeaway in Otherby. Andrew joined her and suggested they went down to the Barley Mow. "They'll do them chicken and chips."

The pub was very quiet and Kevin greeted them with a big smile. "Long time no see, Andrew."

"Yes it's been too long. Lots of business at Westminster."

"Yeah, I saw you on the telly last week. You looked pretty squashed in there. Some big debate about Brexit. Don't know what you lot find to talk about so much. Just sign the thing and get out of Europe."

Andrew smiled. He could understand how it must appear to people far from London. All that 'my honourable friend' and 'the member for' stuff. More like a pantomime than a board meeting.

A couple of locals that Andrew recognised gave him a nod as he settled the boys in the corner.

"He seems friendly enough, Andrew," Claire said nodding in the direction of Kevin.

"Oh yes, the locals have got to know me. I normally eat here when I'm up." He wondered if Sara might be in but maybe she was still in Nottingham. "So, Kevin, what have I missed? Anything new to tell me?"

"Only poor old Colin's wife. She is having a problem. It all kicked off last night and they carted her off in an ambulance."

"I didn't think she was due yet." Andrew tried to remember what Colin had said before Christmas.

"That's the problem. She isn't but I think she was having constrictions or something."

Claire smiled at the word constrictions. "Well I hope she gets on OK. The hospitals are pretty good at these things," she said.

Andrew asked about the hospital and made a note to find out how she was. He realised that he didn't even know Colin's surname, just that he owned the farm adjoining his house. Then he thought about the report on his desk down in Westminster. It had been pretty damning about the hospital's natal ward.

"Do you know Colin's number? I might try and give him a call and see if I can help at all."

It wasn't till Sunday evening, Easter Sunday, that Andrew returned to the Barley Mow. He left Claire at home with the boys. He promised not to stay long as she was attempting to cook a nice meal for them.

This time the pub was really full. As he made his way to the bar he saw three of Colin's friends standing together, deep in conversation. Remembering that he hadn't had time to ring Colin he joined them.

"I wanted to know how Colin's wife was. Have you heard anything?"

"The three men looked at him. Their faces were serious. None of them wanted to be the first to impart the news. Eventually Alan, the machinery salesman spoke. "It's bad. Very bad. Sandy is dead. She died giving birth to twins. It was all a rush and I don't know much more. It's just terrible."

"Oh I'm so sorry. What about the baby, er babies. Did they survive?"

"They're in intensive care apparently but I don't know how they're doing. I heard they were short of ventilators or something up at the hospital."

"It's a bloody disgrace that hospital. A disgrace." It was the older man who spoke. He looked accusingly at Andrew. "Someone ought to fix that hospital. The people who run it are bloody useless."

"I'll ring Colin. Offer my sympathy." Even to Andrew his words sounded hollow. His mind again returned to the report back on his desk in London. He had seen other documents too. The war-gaming in 2016 had pointed out the national shortage of ventilators in the event of a pandemic. He hadn't seen any report of that shortage being addressed. The government was too keen to practice austerity, to balance the books. Money was tight. All the more reason, thought Andrew, to stop wasting it on all the preparations for a no-deal Brexit.

He ordered a pint of Fentastic and stood at the bar drinking it. He needed to get back to Claire and phone Colin. It was beginning to get dark as he left the pub. He recognised the slim figure walking from the car park. Sara was wearing a thick sweater and her usual jeans and boots. April nights in Lincolnshire were still cold. She looked happy to see him and he instinctively kissed her on the cheek. He explained briefly what he had just heard about Colin's wife. "Oh no. Poor Sandy. She was always so full of life and really looking forward to having a baby. You say it was twins? I didn't know she was due to have twins."

They talked for a few moments and Andrew explained he was up for a week with the family.

"That's nice," said Sara, "I might pop round and see you all."

Andrew looked at her with surprise.

"Don't worry, it's our secret," she grinned. "But I would like to catch up with you. I've learned a lot up at Nottingham and I need to talk about something that's bothering me. Anyway, maybe you need a babysitter one evening?"

By Monday, Claire was getting very tired of Otherby. They had spent the last two days working on the garden. They realised they didn't have any garden tools. They didn't need them in Wandsworth. But here with quite large grounds they were essential.

Monday morning. It was now their third day at the house. The house that was in the middle of a field. The house that was miles from any decent shops or restaurants. Claire had only left it once, on Saturday, and driven 12 miles to Upthorpe where they had invested in a range of basic gardening tools. Then it was back to the house and cutting and sweeping and digging. She wasn't a gardener. It wasn't that she didn't like gardens. She liked looking at them. She liked walking around them for a few minutes. But she had no desire to plant things, or prune things and certainly not to weed flowerbeds.

Andrew, she noticed, was clearly enjoying it. The weather was fine so that helped she thought. But he seemed to relish the hard physical work. She supposed that after weeks of sitting behind a desk or being squashed on those green benches it was a release. And the boys definitely liked it. It was all new and fun for them. The garden was a big adventure playground for two five-year-olds used to being shepherded along polluted pavements and across busy roads.

It was, of course, a break for Claire too but she didn't find it so satisfying as they did. Claire liked the hectic pace of city life. She found it invigorating. Challenging certainly but that was the point. You always felt you were getting somewhere, achieving something. Here in the countryside there was nothing to measure yourself against. Life had a slower pace. It lacked the competitiveness. She liked 'chilling out' as much as the next person but it involved being waited on, a nice climate and cocktails. Preferably a beach or a good pool too. Otherby offered her none of those things.

It had always been the difference between her and Andrew. Andrew liked to weigh up things and to do that he loved to get as much information as possible. At Templeton his research was meticulous. Armed with that information he was very good at analysing a problem or a market and coming up with the right solution or prediction. It was this stability, this carefulness that had endeared him to her. She knew she was headstrong, allowed her heart to rule her head at times. Andrew was a safe, calming influence. Opposites attract.

She was already looking forward to Tuesday. She would take the car and drive across to see George at Stellagenix. Andrew would stay and dig his garden and play with the boys.

37

THE DAY AFTER EASTER MONDAY 2019, LINCOLNSHIRE

Andrew was busy trying to make a swing in the garden when she arrived. The boys saw her first. "Daddy, there's a lady at the front door."

He followed them round the side of the house and saw Sara waiting on the doorstep. He introduced her to the boys. "This is a friend of mine, Sara. She's very clever. She's a vet."

"What's a vet, Daddy?"

Sara laughed and tried to explain. Both boys looked at her in awe. Working with animals and going to farms was something alien to them. There weren't many vets in Wandsworth and even fewer farms.

Sara didn't seem surprised to find Claire out. It was like she knew she wouldn't be there. Had Andrew mentioned it when he'd seen her on Sunday? He couldn't remember.

He made two cups of coffee with his new Nespresso machine and carried them out to the garden where Sara was playing with the boys.

"I'm going up to Mason's Farm later. You could come too with the boys. They've got lots of animals if they'd be interested?"

As they sat drinking their coffee she started to tell him about her course in Nottingham.

"It was really interesting. I thought it would be about treating animal diseases. But they went into all the details of viruses and artificial insemination and how they can predict certain traits from the animal's DNA. We even had a session on cloning animals. You know of Dolly the sheep? Well she was one of the first that everyone talks about. They worked out what the sheep's DNA was and then they developed methods to recreate a sheep just the same as her. It's fascinating."

"And a little bit controversial, I imagine. People are worried about scientists offering to make designer babies." Andrew was well aware of the political ramifications of that.

"Yes it is a bit like playing God," said Sara watching the twins playing at the end of the garden.

"But now we're able to map an animal's DNA, their genome, it's possible to see where there are differences from the norm. So if an animal is born with a defect say. You know, even animals can be deaf for instance. Well if we can pinpoint where the genetic code differs, has something the wrong way round or missing, we could, in theory, alter it back or replace it and cure the animal."

"That sounds incredibly complicated and very expensive. There wouldn't be a case for doing it, commercially."

"No, that's true. Scientists are looking to cure humans of diseases first. The animals are a long way down the list."

"So what causes these changes in the 'genome'?" Andrew

liked to understand how things impacted on other things. He had always been inquisitive.

"Oh mostly they just happen by accident. Natural mutation. Some mutations are good and improve a species. Others are bad and they tend to be deselected – either naturally in the wild or deliberately with domestic animals. But sometimes the cell's make up is affected by viruses that can change the genome structure. A virus can cause dramatic effects – like polio did, or measles for example. "

"I really don't understand all that," said Andrew. "Biology was never my subject."

"But you are the Minister for Health now aren't you?"

"Yes, but that's all about making hospitals more efficient, or deciding which drugs we can afford. It's all about economics, not biology."

"So if I told you that an animal's, or a human's, whole genetic code could be altered by ingesting a virus you wouldn't understand? If I said, depending on the virus, a variety of genetic changes can occur in the host cell. In the case of a lytic cycle virus, the cell will only survive long enough for the replication machinery to be used to create additional viral units. In other cases, the viral DNA will persist within the host cell and replicate as the cell replicates. This viral DNA can either be incorporated into the host cell's genetic material or persist as a separate genetic vector. Either case can lead to damage of the host cell's chromosomes. It is possible that the damage can be repaired; however, the most common result is an instability in the original genetic material or suppression or alteration of the gene expression."

"I wouldn't understand a word. I am just concentrating on making the NHS work better. I mean I talked to Colin yesterday. He's in a terrible state. He's lost his wife and now he's got twin boys to bring up on his own. And I know how hard that can be!" He watched as Miles started throwing sticks at his brother.

"I'm still wondering about that. Apparently the twins are quite advanced considering they're less than 30 weeks. It's a bit like Mr Mason's cows. They had twins and they were all bigger than normal too."

"I don't think Colin would appreciate you comparing his late wife to a cow!" Andrew tried to lighten the mood. It was a warm day, the birds were singing. He couldn't take all this genetic biology stuff. He was happy though to take her up on her offer to join her on her visit to Mason's Farm.

Sara was still convinced that there was something odd about the situation around Otherby. Something wasn't right.

Claire sat in reception waiting for George. The offices seemed busier than last time she had visited. She had passed the site of the extended production facility as she had driven in. The building was already nearly complete. Stellagenix was a company in a hurry.

George strode into the reception and greeted her warmly. "So good to see you Claire. I've got so much to tell you and you're going to love it!"

He led her to his office, large room with the normal executive desk and computer as well as a small round table with four chairs. His PA followed them in and placed a tray of coffee and Snickers bars on the table.

George opened a large file and passed a sheet of figures across to Claire. She looked at them briefly and then back at George.

"Let me explain. These figures show the anticipated increase in yield for our new modified winter wheat grain. They show that we can expect an increased yield of maybe 15%. That's absolutely unheard of! If all winter wheat used our seeds worldwide we could feed millions more people, maybe bring an end to poverty in many countries."

"Wow. That's great. But just take me through it, slowly will you?"

"OK. You know we had great success with the barley trials – so good in fact that the Board signed off on the new production facility here." He waved his arm towards the window through which you could see the builders working on the new site. "Well Dimitri and his team had also been working on wheat. They've been adjusting the DNA of the wheat through some revolutionary new techniques and the result is what you see on that sheet. So far we've only done trials with two farms but there's no reason to believe this year's results across six farms won't be just as good."

Claire listened as George got more and more excited. She could see that this was a real breakthrough. Increasing wheat yields by 15%? She knew nothing about farming but that sounded a hell of a lot to her. If Stellagenix seeds were 15% better than any others then they would make millions.

"How come you've managed to get such great results? I mean, there are other firms, your competitors, genetically modifying seeds. Surely they increase the yields as well?"

"You don't understand. I'm not talking about a 15% increase over bulk standard winter wheat. The farmers were using GM seeds already. That's why we're so excited. In fact we believe 15% is an underestimate."

"So what's Dimitri's secret? He must be doing something different."

"Look, even I don't understand all the technical, biological stuff, but I know he's done something that hasn't been tried before. It's revolutionary."

"So how long will it be before you can start marketing it?"

"Oh it will be three or four years. We'll carry out more trials this year and, assuming they go as well, we'll start harvesting the seeds to build up supplies and plant even more farms in the following year. Then, once we've got approval from the FDA we can get motoring."

"What do you need to get the FDA approval?"

"Oh they just do a few toxicology tests, see if there are allergic reactions, that sort of thing. It's wheat. Not too much."

Claire paused before asking the next question. "You got FDA approval for the barley pretty quickly didn't you?"

"Piece of cake. Now let's talk about projecting the company. I reckon if we can spin this right we can get a real boost to our share price. This sports centre we're building for the locals will be just the start. I just need you to create a good presentation for me to take to the Board in the States. In fact, why don't you come with me?"

38

The boys were excited as they climbed into the back of Sara's little car. The opportunity for seeing farm animals was not something to be missed. Andrew tried to dampen their enthusiasm assuring them that there wouldn't be lions and tigers, just cows, horses and maybe some sheep.

Sara drove safely and competently down the winding lanes and it wasn't long before they arrived at Mason's Farm. The farmhouse was a substantial two-storey brick building with a red tiled roof. A Virginia creeper covered the whole of the west wall. The sash windows had obviously been replaced with double-glazed units quite recently and the driveway gravel led up to a large stone-slabbed area that seemed to surround the whole house. To the right of the house a tiled barn could be seen. Everything looked very clean and well cared for. There were neatly pruned bushes either side of the large, white-painted timber door.

"It looks very organised," said Andrew. He liked organisation but many of the farms he had visited since becoming the local MP had been what Claire would have termed a 'hotchpotch'.

"Yes," said Sara, "Mr Mason's very efficient. His farm is one of the best around here. You wait until I show you the milking shed. It's quite state-of-the-art. "

"So you know him pretty well then?"

"Well I was up here quite a bit when he had the problem with cows having twin calves. He's the one who brought in that bull. He thought it would help the pedigree of his cattle."

The door opened and they were greeted by a lady of around sixty. She bent down to speak to the two boys who had all of a sudden become shy and were peeping round from behind Sara and Andrew's legs.

"Hello Sara. Nice to see you again. Just back from Nottingham?"

Sara nodded.

"Pete's round the back, probably near the milking shed. Why don't you pop round? I'll see if I can find some biscuits for the boys."

Sara took Miles's hand and set off round the side of the house towards the brick barn. "I'm glad you got them wellington boots Andrew. Shame you didn't get any for yourself!"

Andrew looked at his loafers. He hadn't thought about walking around a farm. The yard looked dry and pretty mud-free however so he set off after Sara, acutely aware that he was more fascinated by the way her hips swayed in the tight jeans than by her green wellie boots.

Peter Mason was a large man. He must have been six foot three and weigh a good sixteen stone. The frown on his ruddy face morphed into a broad smile when he saw Sara and it was obvious to Andrew that he was fond of her.

"Damn fine vet, this one," he announced to Andrew by way of explanation. "Knows what she's at, she does. Very grateful to her when we had the calving problem last year. Rum do that was."

"How are the herd now, Peter?" Sara put a restraining hand on Marshall's shoulder as a large yellow tractor chugged into the yard

"Not so bad. We got the all-clear for TB as you probably know. Young Jim from the practice came and did the tests. We've got half a dozen in calf at the moment and as far as we can tell there's no twins and everything's normal."

Andrew decided he should look as if he at least knew something about the problems Mason had encountered. "So you don't really know why you got so many twin calves last year? I heard you thought it might have been the new bull?"

Mason looked at Sara as if seeking permission to comment. "We don't rightly know what caused it. Could have just been chance I suppose. We got the bull from a farm over the other side of Laceby. Good pedigree he had. A few others round here have used him too. He's not shy if you get my meaning, gets on with the job!" He looked at the boys to see if they were listening but they seemed far more interested in the big yellow tractor.

"But some of the other farmers had twinning problems too with that bull. I still think he could be the common link." Sara looked at Andrew. "I need to have a talk with you, Andrew. I've got some thoughts I'd like you to hear."

There was no car at the house when they returned mid-afternoon. Andrew invited Sara in for tea but she declined. "I've got some work to do and some catching up with some calls so I'd best be heading off. But maybe if you have time we could meet for a drink at the Barley Mow one evening?"

"Well we're here all week. We've got a dinner thing at the Conservative Club in Sleaford on Wednesday but apart from that..." An idea struck him. "We've been wondering about what to do with the boys on Wednesday evening. I don't suppose you know any good babysitters in the village?"

"Only one," smiled Sara, "and I'd be happy to do it!"

A few minutes after she left, Andrew heard Claire returning. The boys rushed out to meet her, excited to tell her about their visit to the farm. Andrew was glad the family were all together.

"So who's Sara?" she asked Marshall who was busy telling her all about the big yellow tractor.

"She's an animal doctor. She makes animals better when they're ill," said Marshall.

Claire looked quizzically at Andrew.

"She's the local vet. She's Spanish and I've been helping her with her residency papers. Nice girl and the best news is she's agreed to babysit for us tomorrow night when we go to the Tory dinner."

"Right," said Claire. Her mind seemed elsewhere. "I'd forgotten about the dinner. I was thinking I might have to go back to London tomorrow. But I suppose I could leave it until Thursday morning."

"But I thought this was a holiday? We were supposed to be staying until Sunday. That's what we'd organised"

"Yes I know but George wants me to fly to America

with him next week and I need to prepare things back at the Agency before then. I was supposed to be having a meeting with the Xygo people next week. I need to see if I can bring that forward to Friday." She pulled her briefcase out of the car and he watched her stride purposefully towards the house.

"Oh I guess we'll have to head back then tomorrow," he called after her. He looked at the boys.

"Can we go to the farm again Daddy?" Miles was tugging at his sleeve.

Claire turned as she reached the door. "You can stay up here with the boys if you want. If you could just run me to the station I'll take the train. Anyway, let's go in now. I want to update you on what's happening at Stellagenix, it's amazing."

Andrew was only half listening as Claire related the success of Stellagenix's new wheat tests. He walked around the kitchen, making tea, buttering bread for the boys. This wasn't what he had planned. After the hectic few months in Westminster he wanted time as a family, peaceful, in the country, not the city.

"Isn't that good Andrew? I mean it will be good for you – something to please your voters." She paused. Andrew continued to feed the boys their tea.

He turned to Claire. "I guess we mustn't mention this yet. I mean not to the Party members tomorrow. I don't want to break any confidences."

"True. But you can talk about their generosity in funding the new sports complex. After all they need something around here to liven up their lives.

Andrew nursed his gin and tonic as he surveyed the room. The noise of a dozen conversations seemed to bounce off the low panelled ceiling. He felt young, out-of-place as he watched. The diners were all elderly, well over 50 anyway. They were all white. The women were mainly draped in long dresses, one or two showing rather more sagging cleavage than he would have liked. The men looked uncomfortable in dark suits, their ruddy faces suggesting more contact with the elements than their brethren in London.

He knew that most were local businessmen, a few farmers. He tried to guess which were which. Their complexions and the fit of their suits might be indicative he thought. All were loyal Tory supporters; most had voted to leave Europe, and most distrusted politicians from London. For once, Andrew was happy for his Durham accent.

He became aware that he wasn't listening to the local chairman who had been talking to him about problems with a local factory. The man had stopped speaking and was looking at Andrew for a response.

Andrew slipped into his newly-acquired politico speak to cover up for his inattention. "So what do you think needs to happen now?"

The chairman, drew his thumb out of his waistcoat pocket and raised his hand, open-fingered in a show of exasperation. "Well surely you need to see what can be done to get the Board to change their decision. Without that we're going to have a lot of people out of a job."

Realising that his politico comment hadn't satisfied the man, Andrew brought his mind to focus on the conversation. A large local factory made drinking straws. Millions of them and exported them throughout Europe. But they were made from plastic and there was a growing move by people like Extinction Rebellion to ban plastic straws that polluted rivers and seas. Faced with an uncertain future for its plastic products it had decided to sell the business to a Finnish company who had started making paper straws, one of many paper products made from the abundance of sustainable timber available in Finland. The Lincolnshire company's connections with the catering industry throughout Europe would be invaluable to it. The British factory employed more than fifty people. Apart from a couple of sales people, none would be offered jobs in Finland. The deal was due to go through in twelve month's time, after Britain had left the EU and might no longer be bound by the rules that protected its workers' rights.

Mumbling that he would have a word with the CEO, Andrew tried to steer the conversation towards Stellagenix and the new sports facility. They were interrupted by a small woman wearing a two-piece business suit rather than an evening dress. She was clearly not the wife of a local Tory farmer.

"Now that you're working for the Ministry of Health as well as being an MP I'd like to know what you're going to do to improve our local hospitals. They're a disgrace."

Andrew gave her his vote-winning smile and held out his hand looking towards the chairman for an introduction. He felt confident that he could answer many of her questions as he had just finished studying the damning report from the Care Quality Commission. He noticed that Claire had made her away across the room and was talking to two smart-suited men. They were laughing at something Claire had said.

At last a waiter sounded a gong and the assembled members started to filter through to the dining room. With the chairman on one side and the chairman's wife on the other Andrew knew that the conversation wouldn't be scintillating. He thought back wistfully to an earlier lunch when he had met Sonya from the radio station. What would he give for some thought-provoking discourse now. He looked across the table at Claire who was making a good attempt at being interested in the shortage of starter homes in the area. The Association's treasurer was going into the detail of how the banks couldn't be expected to grant mortgages to people who had little prospect of earning enough to repay them. Andrew knew only too well that Claire enjoyed the vivacity of argument and discussion that accompanied their dinner parties in Wandsworth. The Irish wit of Connor or Amir's ability to look on every problem as an opportunity. He could hear her dinner companion explaining condescendingly how the amount of mortgages was dependent on income and not just the value of the house. Andrew knew he was lucky to have a wife who could flatteringly appear to be hanging on his every word. No doubt they would laugh about it when they returned to Otherby.

After dinner Andrew stood up and made the obligatory speech. He gave his audience a brief account of the ongoing debates on Brexit, trying not to let his frustration show. He then turned to local issues pointing out that Lincolnshire needed to react to the upcoming pressures not just of Brexit but of climate change. He finished by telling them of the exciting progress being made in both biosciences and agriculture and how he was proud that they had one of the most exciting firms, Stellagenix, here in the constituency. He gave hints that they were hoping to make big advances in GM crops and had donated funds to the new sporting facility.

The speech seemed well received although he was aware that many of the guests were disappointed that Brexit hadn't already been achieved and were critical of Theresa May's negotiations. He was glad when he and Claire were at last back in the car, on the road to Otherby.

Everything was calm when they arrived back at the house. They found Sara curled up on the sofa, shoes off watching the TV. There was an empty wine glass on the coffee table in front of her. Andrew smiled at the sight.

"Were the boys OK? Did they go down alright?" Claire was used to Analiese putting the boys to bed and Andrew noticed that she adopted a certain tone when dealing with the au pair. She was using that tone to Sara.

"They were very good. I read them a story and they both went off to sleep very well. No problem." She turned and smiled at Andrew. "How was the dinner. Full of boring people as usual?"

Andrew noticed Claire looking at her. She hadn't seemed at all interested in the fact that he knew Sara and had helped her with her visa. It had been he who was nervous about the two women meeting. It was an awkward situation, one he couldn't predict. And Andrew liked things to be predictable. But neither woman seemed to share his concerns. Sara seemed relaxed, just as she might be down at the Barley Mow. Andrew knew she must be sizing up Claire. After all she had slept with her husband. As for Claire she seemed so wrapped up with her forthcoming trip to the States that she had readily accepted the fact that Sara was just someone from the village who would babysit.

But the comment from Sara about the dinner guests had

struck a discordant note with Claire. It suggested a greater knowledge of Andrew's work than she would have expected. It certainly wasn't something Analiese would say. Andrew hurried to move things on.

"Oh it was the usual stuffy old men you'd expect. A few big farmers that you might know. The lamb was rather good though. I could have done with a good drink but I had to drive. I think I'll pour myself a scotch." He left the two women in the lounge and headed for the kitchen.

He heard the women talking as he returned. Claire turned to him as he sat down. "I was asking Sara how much we owed her for babysitting but she says she won't take anything."

Before Andrew could reply Sara said, "No, no I am just giving him back a favour. He rescued me when my car broke down. I am happy to babysit in return." She got up and slipped her feet back into her shoes. "I must go now. Nice to meet you Claire."

Claire accompanied her to the door and watched as she drove her little car away. Andrew took a large gulp of his whisky. He steeled himself for the inquisition that was coming.

"What a nice girl. I'm surprised she's working over here. She doesn't have much in common with the locals I've seen."

"Oh I think the farmers like her. Her boss, the senior partner at the vets speaks very highly of her. She's very studious too."

"And you were her knight in shining armour when her car broke down!" Andrew wasn't sure whether Claire was teasing him or not. He explained briefly how he had towed her car that night.

"All part of the job as the local MP!"

"Yes Andrew but I don't believe the Spanish can vote in our general election!" She laughed and Andrew relaxed. His secret was safe. For now!

39

THE NEXT DAY APRIL 23RD 2019, LINCOLNSHIRE

They left early the next morning to drive to Newark. The watery April sun rose behind them throwing long shadows The roads were empty and patterned with the long shadows of the telegraph poles. The sun bathed the fields with a crystal clear light. Not for the first time did Andrew think back to his research on the effects of air pollution on children. The air was visually cleaner here. You saw objects in sharper detail.

In a little over half an hour they had reached the station; in good time for Claire to catch the express to London. The boys who had been sleepy at first were now wide awake and pointing to a nearby McDonalds. They liked McDonalds. Breakfast at McDonalds would be a treat.

As they sat munching their breakfast, Miles asked what they were going to do now 'Mummy's gone home'.

Andrew thought for a few moments. Claire's sudden

decision to return to the office early had meant his careful plans had been disrupted and Andrew didn't like disruption. He had planned to take them on a drive to the sea, to Skegness where there was a seal sanctuary. Now it was too late to drive all that way. He determined to go there tomorrow. He had planned to visit the large hospital at Lincoln the next day for a meeting with the head of the Trust. The questions raised by the CQC report and by that irate businesswoman at the dinner prompted him to make an unscheduled visit. Perhaps he could do that this afternoon if he could get someone to look after the boys. That left the morning to spend with them back in Otherby.

As they drove out of Newark they passed the buildings of the famous Warwick and Richardsons Brewery in Northgate. Newark had been a centre for beer-making due to the particular quality of the water in the Trent and the abundance of barley grown locally. Today the big breweries had all but disappeared leaving just a couple of microbreweries. It was the sight of the original brewery that gave Andrew the idea.

"How would you like to see how they make beer, boys?"

He glanced in the mirror to see the reaction from the twins, strapped into their car seats. They didn't look that interested. "There will be lots of big machines and things," he added hopefully.

"Any yellow tractors?"

"Maybe."

It was not the brewery in Newark that Andrew intended to visit but the micro-brewery near Otherby that made his favourite 'Fentastic Ale'. He had an open invitation to visit it, having met one of the two owners at a local Conservative

Association do before Christmas. It would be good to keep his promise to visit as Stan, his agent, was always reminding him.

There were no yellow tractors at Bartlewick's brewery. There were a couple of green ones working on the farm alongside the brewery and a bright yellow fork-lift truck which at least gave the boys something to ogle. They were rather more interested in the chickens that hopped and clucked around the farmyard and Andrew left them with the brewer's wife while he went into the brewery.

Andrew's experience of brewing beer extended no further than the home brew kits he'd tried, largely unsuccessfully, in his student days. Jason was not much older than Andrew and had a shock of blonde hair like Andrew's that he kept trying to push back out of his eyes. The son of the farmer on whose land he had built the small brewery, he knew everyone around, including all the local pub landlords.

Brewing was obviously a passion of his rather than a job. He explained how he had always been interested in science at school and had studied chemistry at university. He worked for a couple of years at a large brewery in Tadcaster developing different ales. But farming was definitely in his genes, he explained, and he wanted to be outside rather than in a laboratory. He had gone back home to work with his farming father, looking after a herd of Friesians. He had married a local girl two years ago and they were building a house in the village. His brewing experience in Tadcaster had driven him to set up this microbrewery.

"To get a really distinctive ale you need to carefully control each stage of the process," he said. It's no use just buying in some malted barley. It's the malting that determines the colour and taste of the beer. We malt our own barley and then we add some special hops that I get from a friend in Sussex."

Andrew smiled as he listened to Jason explaining how the malting process worked. There was no doubt that he loved his work. Andrew wondered if he really made much money from his brewery but refrained from asking. He certainly wasn't going to earn the money Andrew had at Templeton. For that matter, an MP's salary would no doubt be many times more than Jason was making. Yet Jason seemed perfectly content with his life. His world was centred on the local community, the crops and animals, and that gave him all the pleasures he needed.

"You need to get the steeping of the barley absolutely right. If you don't get it long enough then you get a poor malt, but if you overdo it you can start getting mould and that's hopeless. After that it's about germination. The barley starts to sprout, if you will, but you need to stop that at just the right time and then kiln dry it to stop it germinating further." He pointed proudly to the kiln in one corner of the barn.

"And those vats over there?" Andrew pointed to three large stainless steel vessels.

"We heat up the barley with water to release the sugars and then boil it, adding hops for bitterness. Then when we judge it's right, we leave it to cool right down before we add the yeast. Simple really!"

Andrew laughed. "You get your hops from someone in Sussex. Where do you get the barley from?"

"Well there's no shortage of farms growing barley around

here. That's why the Newark breweries did so well. That and the phosphate in the Trent water. But you need a good six-ear variety for a good brew. We normally would buy it from a merchant in Grantham or Newark but we've got a good source right here on the doorstep."

"Your Dad's farm?"

"No, he's not an arable farmer. We get a lot of it from a farmer near you in Otherby. He's got some really fine barley using some special American variety seeds. He gets them from a firm called Stellagenix over towards Lincoln."

"I know them well. They've developed a very high-yielding variety I gather."

"That's right and George, the farmer, has been doing their trials. That's why he was happy to let me have it at a really good price. I guess he's being paid well by Stellagenix anyway. If we don't use it all for brewing we can use it for cattle food."

Andrew began to appreciate the skill that went into making good beer as he followed Jason around the barn. He could also see that farmers, or brewers, had to be good businessmen too if they were going to succeed. There was a pile of steel barrels at one end containing the finished product. The famous Fentastic that he enjoyed at the Barley Mow.

"Come into the house and you can try a drop," said Jason pushing open the barn door and heading across the yard. They found the boys inside, sitting at the kitchen table tucking into fruitcake. Jason's wife offered him a slice but Andrew shook his head. "I'm not sure it goes well with beer and Jason's promised me a glass."

Back home in Otherby he made sandwiches for lunch although the boys professed to being full of fruitcake. The phone rang. It was Stan, Andrew's agent. "The press are getting into a lather about the state of the local hospitals," he explained. "Apparently you mentioned it at the Association dinner on Wednesday? Now the local press have got hold of a report from the CQC apparently. You didn't give them it did you?"

"Of course not. But it's a pretty damning report. If someone has leaked that I can see why it would excite the press. I was planning to visit the Trust in Lincoln tomorrow but I can't now because I've got the boys here and Claire's back in London."

"You need to get over there pronto. You're not only the local MP, you're a bloody Minister of Health for God's sake." Stan was never one to mince words and his anger was clear to hear. "Look, bring the boys with you, I'll meet you there and look after them for an hour while you see the Trust."

It was after five when Andrew finished his meeting with the chief executive of the Trust. The meeting had been frustrating. The Trust had complained about lack of funding from central Government, of shortage of trained nurses, of delays in supply of much-needed equipment. It was a common complaint that Andrew had heard from several Trusts, yet the results here in Lincolnshire were far worse. Many of the recommendations that the CQC had made in earlier years had still not been properly implemented and the discussion had turned quite rancorous.

So he was in a bad mood as he strode through the main hospital reception. It was then that he saw Colin. He was accompanied by a nurse, each of them carrying a precious bundle, the twin boys. Colin smiled when he saw Andrew.

"They're coming home," he said. His face beamed proudly but there was a sadness in his eyes too. Andrew knew that the loss of his wife was something he would struggle to live with.

He walked with them to the main doors. Outside the visitors' car park was nearly empty. He saw Stan waiting with the boys. He walked with Colin and the nurse to his car.

"I'm so sorry about Sandy. If there's anything I can do. Do you have help at home to look after them?" He nodded at the two bundles.

"Her sister's coming over for a few days to help." He turned to thank the nurse, a young Filipina, who smiled and scampered back to the hospital. "The nurses were wonderful. But they couldn't save her. They're all short-staffed and the doctor was busy elsewhere when she went into labour. It was all so quick. We hadn't expected it for another month." He looked sadly down. "Maybe if she'd had a Caesarean it might have been different. But they're so stretched here."

Andrew reflected on the meeting he had just had. There was a shortage of front-line staff he knew, yet there was also a damning report about the organisation of the hospital. He wondered if the higher mortality rate was due to money or management.

He had just put the boys to bed when the doorbell rang. It was Sara.

"I knew you wouldn't be able to come to the pub tonight so I thought I'd call round. We need to talk."

They sat in the kitchen with a bottle of red. Andrew made them scrambled eggs. He had rarely seen Sara like this before. What's worrying her? Was it Claire? It was awkward, he knew. But she had seemed much more relaxed about it than he had.

He watched as she toyed with her drink.

"Andrew I'm worried. I think there's something strange going on. I've been trying to work out why there have been these twin births with the cows all of a sudden. And why it's just in a few farms round here. I feel sure that it is down to the bulls. At first I thought it was just one bull. But now I've studied things and checked with the farmers there are at least two bulls who've sired twins."

"Well it's not unheard of for cows to have twin calves is it?

"No but pretty unusual and this is way above average. Also the calves seem to be maturing more quickly than normal. The births have been earlier than forecast."

"So what's your explanation?"

"Well that's the point I don't have one. Except...."

"Except what?" He looked at the Spanish girl sitting opposite him. She was no longer the happy, friendly girl he had found so irresistible. But this new intensity nevertheless held him spellbound.

"Well I've been learning so much on my course at Nottingham. Not just about animals, but humans too. Genetics mainly. You know it's fascinating what scientists are doing now. It's not long since we learned about DNA. Now we know that everyone's DNA is slightly different and that has been really helpful in solving crimes. But the work that Cambridge did recently, mapping a hundred thousand different people's genomes can teach us so much more. It can help us find out which sequences of the amino acids that make up the chain are responsible for certain traits, or handicaps."

Andrew poured more wine into his glass. Sara, he noticed, had hardly touched hers. The conversation was getting a little too technical for him but he tried to concentrate.

She went on describing some of the new research that was taking place. "Take this woman in California. She's a biochemist and she has pioneered a technology that allows you to edit the life code of any organism, even humans."

Andrew shook his head in confusion. "I'm not sure I follow you."

"Well it's complicated but let me try to explain. In a person's genome you've got this long strand of four elements that make up your genetic code. It's the same for everyone except that in this long chain the order of these elements changes a bit here and there. If we know that the difference between someone who suffers, say, from high cholesterol and one who doesn't is one little piece of this sequence then if we could replace it with the healthy combination that would cure it!"

"OK, but how could you replace it, even if you did identify it? I mean we're talking about tiny, tiny things here aren't we? You can't just get a pair of scissors and cut a bit off."

"Well that's just what this woman's done. Her technique uses enzymes like molecular scissors to make changes in the genetic code."

"I can't get my head around that. I'm not even sure what an enzyme is. Anyway what's this got to do with bulls causing twin calves?

She looked at him for a long moment. Suddenly her face relaxed and she smiled. He saw the laughing, teasing Sara that he loved.

"OK, I know it all sounds like science fiction but the point is, it's happening here and now. My lecturer reckons this woman could be in line for a Nobel Prize for this. She really will be able to let scientists target specific DNA sequences and cut out the bad ones and insert the good ones. It hasn't been tried on humans yet, but she's shown it can work on animals."

"And the bulls? What about the local bulls?" Andrew had only the slightest understanding of the processes she was explaining but he liked to know why and how things happened. That's why he had been so good at research at Templeton. He didn't just look at movements in share prices but tried to understand what was causing them. That way led to better investment decisions.

"Well I think that there is something in these bulls' DNA sequencing that is changing their sperm cells which makes them more likely to induce twins."

"Hang on a minute. I've got two twin boys sleeping upstairs and I was told that it was because Claire released two eggs at once and they got fertilised. That's up to the mother, the female. Not the bull."

"I know, that's the problem. Twins are normally conceived like that, but not identical twins. Identical twins are caused by the one egg splitting into two right at the start of conception. Then both offspring have identical genetic make up."

"So are you saying that all these calves are identical twins?"

"That's what I don't know. I'd need to do a DNA test on each one and check. It's not easy to see if one black and white Friesian calf is identical to another."

"Yeah they all look the same to me," joked Andrew anxious to turn the conversation onto more layman's ground.

"It would tell us if it was the bulls or the cows that are causing the twin result, yes. But we still wouldn't know why three bulls would all have the same genetic mutation that was causing them to make the fertilised egg to split in half."

"But surely no one has gone in and snipped off bits of DNA in these bulls. I mean that would be insanely difficult and expensive surely?"

"Of course Andrew, but we know that bacteria can and do snip off fragments of flu viruses for instance and store them to help fight them off. Maybe something caused bacteria in the bulls to do this with another part of the DNA sequencing. I don't know but it's fascinating and I want to find out more. It could be part of my dissertation."

Andrew got up and went to the fridge. He came back with some cheese and the remains of a loaf of bread.

"I'm sorry I don't have anything better. I'm not really set up to entertain here, and I always eat at the Barley Mow.

"It's fine Andrew. It's just nice to be with you." She started on her red wine.

They talked more about her course and Andrew regaled her with stories of the comings and goings in Parliament.

"You've got to sort this Brexit thing out Andrew. We're all worried about what's going to happen."

"But I've told you that you'll be OK."

"Maybe, but people are beginning to say things. They don't like immigrants. They want their old England back."

"I'm sure it will all work out," Andrew lied. He felt, like her, that the mood was turning against Europe, that people just wanted Brexit to be over and hang the consequences.

They gave little thought to the effects it would have on things like education and indeed research.

As if reading his thoughts Sara said "There were lots of different nationalities on my course in Nottingham. That's what made it so good. All different but all wanting to become better vets. There was this one guy from Romania who knew everything about increasing milk yields in cows. Worked for some big dairy over there."

Andrew wondered if it was the one Amir had visited.

Sara left soon after nine saying she had to be up early the next morning to travel to a farm near Sleaford. Andrew realised he was bushed as well. He'd driven Claire to Newark, been round a brewery, had a stormy meeting at a hospital in Lincoln and looked after two five-year-olds.

As he lay in bed that night he began to go over what Sara had said. As a junior minister of health he had access to lots of information on genetics research. He had even been to Cambridge when they announced the results of their 100,000 genome project. Perhaps he should improve his knowledge. If nothing else it would please Sara and pleasing Sara was something he very much wanted to do.

40

Claire returned from her visit to the States in buoyant mood. She told Andrew all about the meetings she had had with George's Board and how the directors were keen to push ahead with both the barley and wheat seeds. The announcement of the successful trial of the wheat variety was being delayed until more statistical analysis had been completed but already some information had leaked out. The share price was now at an all -time high.

"We really should have bought shares in Stellagenix ourselves," she told Andrew. What she didn't tell Andrew, as she was sworn to secrecy and bound by a non-disclosure agreement, was that Stellagenix was in line to take over a pharmaceutical company.

Andrew thought back to his conversation with George back in March. He had been urged to invest then. The ministerial code of course forbade this but he was coming to realise that many of his colleagues on the green benches were making good money from their investments, even though they took steps to conceal them. Many had bet on the pound falling in the case of a hard Brexit and were actively working to try and achieve that.

He had to admit that his salary, even with his ministerial promotion, was far short of what he had earned at Templeton. Claire, by contrast, was not only loving her job but had been offered share options in the Agency.

She was busier than ever which meant that they were spending less and less time together. His ideas of the family spending the weekends up at Otherby had clearly not materialised. Instead he would go up on a Thursday evening and return after his Saturday morning surgery. It meant he could be home for Saturday evening events and have a family Sunday. It was a compromise, he knew. He realised that Claire had got used to Friday evening dinners as well as Saturdays. But he consoled himself with the thought that now she was so busy at the Agency all week she would probably have been too tired to entertain on a Friday evening.

It was a Sunday evening and the boys were in bed, when she broached the subject of money. "Andrew, I know we agreed that your MP's salary wasn't going to be enough and I know that I'm now earning a lot more than I expected but.."

"But what?"

"But shouldn't you be looking at using your position to make some more money for ourselves? I mean you've got the minister's job now."

"And that's giving me a healthy increase on what ordinary MPs get."

"Yes, but it's still not what you were getting at Templeton.

I mean with your background and now that you're involved with all this NHS stuff, surely there must be opportunities."

"Like what?" Andrew didn't like the direction the conversation was leading.

"Well now you've got such a good understanding of the health market surely we should be making sure we've got some investment in the suppliers who are set to do well? And what about getting a few Board appointments?"

"Not allowed."

"Well OK, not Board appointments but perhaps a consultant. Big fees in consultancy. I mean everyone else seems to be doing it."

Andrew thought about what he had learned about some of his fellow MPs. He had to admit that he still felt a little like an outsider. A new boy. He knew that many of his colleagues had outside business interests and although they were supposed to register any interests he knew full well that many didn't. He thought about George's offer. Had he invested a few weeks ago, knowing that these barley trials were successful, he could have turned a very large, very quick profit. What had he done? Nothing. Although, come to think of it, he had mentioned it to Amir. No doubt Amir's fund had benefitted from some shrewd purchasing.

He put his arm round Claire's shoulder. "You're right, I know. That's the way of politics these days. Oh it's not like in Third World Countries, all massively corrupt. But I must admit that increasingly I'm coming round to the view that half the men in the Commons are out for themselves, playing a game. And playing it to win."

"Not just the men." Claire nestled her hear head into his arm.

"It's just not what I went into politics for Claire. I really thought I could make a difference for constituents and help Theresa get a soft Brexit through. I still think she might be able to but not with the Irish problem and those buggers in the ERG."

She looked at him. Wasn't this one of the reasons she had married him? He was so grounded, so steady in his opinions. She had appreciated the way he researched everything before coming to a decision. But she wasn't like that herself. She was an ideas person. She liked to think on her feet. She liked the way Clifton seemed to be able to manipulate people, bringing them around to his point of view. She liked the way he seemed to be able to take a few notes from her and then present them at a meeting with complete authority. And she liked the way he didn't take life too seriously. Life was a game to Clifton, and, win or lose, he enjoyed playing it.

"Promise me you'll look around and see how we can make the most of your position. Maybe there's still time to invest in Stellagenix?"

41

Sitting elbow-to-elbow with his Tory colleagues on the government benches, Andrew listened as Theresa May announced she was standing down as Prime Minister and signalling a Conservative leadership election. For the past couple of months, ever since the Withdrawal Date had been extended for six months, Parliament had been unable to agree on a way forward. Andrew still clung to his belief that the Irish question was insoluble. You couldn't stay out of the EU Customs Union and yet not have border checks between Northern Ireland and the Republic.

He had become more and more critical of his right-wing colleagues who seemed to be hell bent in destroying Britain's economy for the sake of sovereignty or, in some cases, their investments held in blind trusts.

He was beginning to realise that his idea of influencing the Brexit debate, the thing that had finally persuaded him to give up his lucrative job at Templeton, was never going to happen. There were 'conviction' MPs but they were few and far between. For most, it was a job like any other. You did whatever you had to in order to progress up the ladder. Firstly you needed to be in the party of government. You had to beware of saying anything to the media that could be cut up, re-ordered and taken out of context to form a damning soundbite. It was like belonging to a football team. Every match you went out to beat the opposition. The politicians were one team, the media the other always anxious to trip you up. In between the 'beautiful game' was forgotten – it was all about money and promotion.

Not willing to treat politics as a game, Andrew had spent his time on his ministerial duties, researching ways of making the NHS more efficient. He had also taken time to educate himself on the various breakthroughs being achieved by biologists in the field of genetics. He liked research and Sara had sparked his interest.

Meanwhile he had been spending an increasing amount of time up at Otherby. Frustrated at not being able to influence the Brexit debate he had turned his attentions to improving the lot of his constituents. He found most of them much more concerned about what was happening locally than the comings and goings in Parliament. The question of global warming, climate change, seemed to be of greater interest to them than Brexit. Much of the Eastern side of Lincolnshire is very low lying and the reports of rising sea levels were something many farmers were worried about.

The other talking point with his constituents was immigration. On the one hand they were critical of immigrants who they felt were using the British Welfare State for their own benefit. On the other hand they were complaining that they wouldn't be able to get crops harvested if they couldn't employ seasonal workers from Europe. The farmers who had voted happily to get rid of the EU Common Agricultural Policy were now worrying about how the EU grants were going to be replaced by the British government.

For Andrew, the difference between the affluent London he lived in and the relative poorness of his constituency was striking. All their friends and neighbours in Wandsworth were striving to make more and more money to pay for ever-more-expensive houses and cars. Large amounts of money passed through their hands although little of it remained at the end of the month. Clothes, fares, restaurants, holidays, they all demanded more and more to be spent. In Lincolnshire the average wages were paltry by comparison. The young especially found it difficult to find high wage employment. At the same time the demands on those salaries were far less. People tended to work locally. Their houses cost far less (although still too much for many young buyers). Fewer people felt the need to have the latest model of German car. There was a greater interest in the community rather than the individual.

"That's that then. Now we're under starter's orders!"

Andrew looked at the man squashed next to him in surprise. He hadn't been really listening closely to the Prime Minister's statement.

"What do you mean?" he stammered.

"Now the fun and games start. The jockeying for position. The bookies will have a field day."

The stream of hackneyed phrases tumbled out his colleague's mouth. His face was ruddy in complexion, a consequence of alcohol rather than sunshine. Behind him everyone seemed to be whispering to each other. The leadership battle was on. Who was he going to support?

Because of Theresa May's anticipated resignation speech, Andrew hadn't gone up to Otherby. He had agreed to be back early from the Commons as Amir had invited them around for Friday night supper.

Andrew had expected other guests to be there but was surprised to find it was just the four of them. The girls took themselves off to the kitchen and Andrew could hear Claire sounding off about the disruptions in London being caused by the Extinction Rebellion movement.

Andrew walked across to the small bar area which Amir had designed in one corner of the large lounge. He took the beer offered and perched himself on a high bar stool. "How's business?"

"Pretty good at the moment. The market's still spooked by all the Brexit problems, but they'd already discounted May's resignation so there weren't too many surprises today." Amir shared Andrew's views on the economic impact of a hard Brexit and had taken precautions to protect his funds from the inevitable fall in the pound. In this he wasn't alone. The die-hard Brexiteers had made similar arrangements as they looked forward to forcing a hard Brexit. They stood to gain financially if there was a no-deal.

"So what sectors do you think will be winners?" Andrew hadn't lost his interest in share movements since leaving Templeton.

"I think pharmaceuticals, agrichemicals and infrastructure are pretty safe bets. The world's population is still growing, they need feeding. They're getting older so they need more medicines and in the UK we are seriously in need of better infrastructure. Thanks for the heads up on your Stellagenix though. It's put on a real spurt since I took an investment there."

"Well I think it was more Claire than me." Andrew didn't like to feel as an MP and a minister that he was involved in any insider dealing. He hadn't gained from his knowledge of the barley breakthrough although Amir obviously had.

The girls rejoined them. "Claire was telling me how they had closed all those roads again in the City with the Extinction lot." Andrew watched Indira as she pulled herself up onto the stool, her Armani jeans replacing her usual sari. "I must say I am as worried as they are about the planet but I'm not sure causing all this traffic chaos is the answer. It's just making more CO_2 pollution if you ask me."

Amir smiled at his wife. "Much better if we stopped going on about flying around the world and concentrated instead on what's really going to help. Like solar panels, wind farms, green energy. That's where the government should be putting its money."

"What about nuclear power stations, they would help wouldn't they?" Claire sipped her vodka and tonic through a long plastic straw. Andrew wondered where the straw had been made. It wouldn't come from Lincolnshire anymore.

"The Tories have blown the nuclear solution. They are years late. Most of our nuclear plants will be shut down in a few years and the deal we've done with the Chinese over that new one isn't going to be nearly enough – and it's too expensive." Amir was warming to the subject. He had little respect for politicians.

The conversation continued in this vein until they were interrupted by a young Filipina who came in and whispered to Indira that the dinner was now ready. They followed her into the dining room.

Later, back in their house and having checked on the sleeping boys, Claire put her arm round Andrew's waist as they headed for the bedroom. "You know it feels so good somehow , talking with people like Amir. You really feel how exciting London life is. I mean you feel that you're part of what's filling the ten o'clock news. Here we are, you've sat a few feet away from our prime minister as she announces she's standing down, I've been caught up in an enormous demonstration against Global Warming, Amir's busy betting millions on whether the pound is about to collapse and Indira's trying to tell us that the NHS is going to collapse if we don't get more Filipina nurses to replace the Europeans who are heading home."

"It is exciting, I know. Better than talking about the Eurovision Song Contest. I see we came bottom last week! Europeans getting revenge I suppose." Life was certainly moving at a pace here in London, thought Andrew.

"I'm so glad you're not up in Otherby this weekend. I miss it when we can't go to dinners like tonight's."

42

After spending the bank holiday weekend in Wandsworth, Andrew returned to his Victoria Street office on the Tuesday. There was an air of excitement. Who was going to challenge Boris Johnson for the leadership? He walked over to the Commons at lunchtime and met colleagues in the Riverside Terrace bar. It was like being at Ascot and discussing the favourite for the 3.30.

The whole place was buzzing with rumours and one of those rumours was that Andrew's former boss, Jeremy Hunt, would be standing. Andrew would happily lend his support to him as a candidate. He was sure to take a softer approach to Brexit and was an altogether safer pair of hands than Boris.

As more candidates threw their hat in the ring that week, Andrew was surprised when one of his colleagues asked him if he would support Rory Stuart. A rank outsider, a Remainer like Andrew, and recently appointed Minister for International Development he had quite extreme ideas. However, his commitment to fighting for funds to battle climate change had struck a chord with Andrew. Torn between his loyalty for Jeremy Hunt and his liking for the underdog, Andrew remained non-committal.

But the decision weighed heavily on his mind that Thursday evening as he headed north once more to Otherby.

After the hustle and bustle of Westminster and life in London, Otherby seemed a peaceful haven. He was standing by his kitchen door that opened onto the garden. The sun was shining and he watched the cotton-wool clouds sliding across the blue sky. It was one of those good days. Sheltered from the wind, he gazed at the barley field at the bottom of the garden, the green stalks bending and then straightening in the gusts, and past them to the flat green fields merging into the horizon.

He breathed in deeply. The air had such a different quality from Wandsworth or Westminster. The view too. Here you could see for miles. Miles of uncluttered fields, broken only by the occasional hedgerow. In Wandsworth your view was always restricted to a few dozen yards yet crammed with people, vehicles, buildings. Here he could let his mind range free, uninterrupted by people, noise or vehicles. Claire would have called it bleak, or monotonous or some such term. She fed off the rhythm of the city scene, the hustle and bustle exciting her, challenging her to perform better. In the city you could measure yourself against everyone around you. Were you quick enough to get that last seat on the train? Could you manoeuvre your car into that last parking spot? Could you cross the street before the lights changed?

Andrew wondered which world was better. Back down in London he was right in the seat of power. He met with the movers and shakers who shaped our world. In Westminster he was taking part in the debates on how Britain would leave the EU, how government money could be better spent on the NHS and how Britain could meet its Climate Change commitments. Surely this was living life to the full? And their friends. They were important people, running big businesses, hedge funds, or in the media. All that made for stimulating dinner conversations. Here? In rural Lincolnshire? What role was he playing as MP? Was he improving his constituents' lives? Were his constituents really interested in the details of the Withdrawal Agreement, or the Northern Irish border problem? Were they spending their waking hours wondering if NICE needed to review its opinion of cancer drugs, or whether the Chinese should be allowed to build a nuclear power station for us?

From his experience of running his Saturday morning surgeries, and his correspondence with constituents, their concerns were far more mundane. Mundane but nevertheless very important to them. While newspapers reported on the politicians' arguments over HS2, his constituents wanted to know when they could expect a decent bus service to take them into Sleaford or Lincoln. While Westminster pontificated on whether to let Huawei run the 5G network, his constituents wanted to know when they could get a broadband connection decent enough to enable them to stream songs and movies.

Westminster politics were no more, and no less, real than East Enders or Coronation Street. Who became Tory leader was no more important than who won this year's *Britain's got Talent*.

In a way, thought Andrew, they were right. Politics at Westminster was just a big game for most MPs. Full of their own self-importance they performed their role in the elaborate stage show of the Commons. They enjoyed the pageantry, the costumes of Black Rod and her associates, the ermine robes that they aspired to wear one day. They liked the formality of referring to each other as the Right Honourable this or that. It elevated them from the man in the street. They were important, they were interested in the bigger picture, they were the right people to decide the nation's future.

Andrew wondered what he had expected. Had he really believed that all MPs were conviction politicians? Politicians who understood the needs of their constituents and worked tirelessly to meet them? Oh sure, there were some MPs like that, but precious few and even rarer on the Tory benches.

Now that he was one of them, what had he done to improve life for his constituents? Hadn't he been more interested in gaining promotion, becoming a minister, influencing the Brexit negotiations? What had he done about the awful bus service, the slow broadband, the lack of well-paid jobs?

Returning inside, Andrew sat down at his desk and booted up his computer. It was time to start concentrating on local issues. He started making a list. He liked making lists. He liked to be organised. He needed to gather data on local bus routes and timetables. He needed to arrange another visit to the hospital where the report was highlighting so many shortcomings. He needed to check on Colin. These were just some of the local issues. But there were other things too.

Sara had ignited his academic interest in microbiology. He had to admit to being clueless on the subject. Yet what she had explained to him had been intriguing. The Californian woman who was able to edit minute pieces of DNA by using bacteria as scissors or glue. The work being carried out in Oxford to fill in the missing pieces of the human genome called the Oxford Nanopore system. The advances in crop development such as the barley project at Stellagenix that held the hope of feeding so many more of the world's population.

Working away, Andrew forgot about time. Around 1 o'clock however, his stomach told him it was time to eat. He hadn't stocked up with food so headed to the Barley Mow once again.

It was quiet inside. Kevin looked up as he entered and smiled. "Hello stranger. Come up for a short visit?"

Andrew felt there was a barb to Kevin's joke. It was true, he hadn't been up to Otherby much in the past month or two but you could blame Brexit for that. "I'll try and stay a bit longer this time. Lot of stuff to sort out here."

"I thought you'd be staying down in London choosing a new leader." He nodded towards the small TV above the bar where the BBC were showing a list of candidates. Andrew shook his head and ordered a pint of Fentastic.

"Have you heard anything about Colin, Kevin? How's he doing on his own with his new twins?"

"Doesn't come in here much now. Stuck at home looking after the twins I suppose. I heard they are doing fine though. In fact Julie says they've been putting on weight really well, growing up fast."

"Julie?"

"The midwife. Lives over at Tykeham."

The next morning Andrew spent planning his visit to Lincoln, to the hospital. Or at least he tried to. His mobile phone kept ringing. Each time it was one of his Tory colleagues anxious to know who he was supporting for the leadership. It seemed that every other Tory MP was completely absorbed by the campaign and buzzing around Westminster like so many bees around a hive, anxious to know who was going to replace the queen.

It seemed that the real contest was between Boris Johnson and Jeremy Hunt and these two were expected to go head-to-head in a second ballot. Andrew was still inclined to believe that Rory Stewart might be a surprise contender.

Boris was campaigning strongly on 'Get Brexit Done' and Andrew, aware of Boris's record, had no doubt he would push a deal through. Whether that deal would be good for Britain, for his constituents here in Lincolnshire, he doubted. He began to feel like his constituents – unrepresented by 'them men in London'.

He continued to make notes on the CQC report on the hospital trust, cursing every time the phone rang. He looked at his watch and realised that it was time to leave for the drive to Lincoln. He hadn't even had time to pop into the Barley Mow for a bite of lunch.

Gathering his papers together he headed for the door. His phone buzzed. He glanced at the screen. It was Sara.

"Andrew, I heard you were up. Can we meet? I've got a problem with my visa – the settled status thing. I don't know what to do."

He agreed to meet her at the Barley Mow that evening. The drive to Lincoln took less than an hour, but was interrupted by three more calls. One of them was from George at Stellagenix.

"Andrew. I hear you're up here for a few days. I really want to have a word with you about the new sports centre. There's some pen-pusher from your Lawn Tennis Association who's holding things up. Any chance you could pop over to us tomorrow?"

Once again Andrew wondered how George knew he was up in Lincolnshire. Maybe he'd spoken to Claire, yes that must be it.

The meeting at the hospital again went on longer than he expected. The mood was again hostile with the administrators insisting that any shortcomings were caused by lack of money. There had ensued a rather heated argument about whether the hospital should engage a firm of management consultants to investigate the best way of dealing with the shortcomings. Andrew hadn't felt it was worth spending money they clearly didn't have to pay people to tell their managers how to manage. What the hell were managers for if it wasn't to manage? And if they couldn't manage they should be fired.

As he drove back to Otherby he had a strong feeling that he had made a number of enemies at the Trust. He would do a report for his boss, Matt Hancock. He was also a contender for the leadership so probably hadn't the time to worry about a failing hospital right now.

His mood lifted once he got back to Otherby. The sun was setting in the pale, pale sky, a sky that stretched across the broad expanse of the flat fields of corn. There were no contrails from the aircraft. As he got out of the car he could hear the birds singing and little else. Peace!

Inside the Barley Mow a little later, there was rather more noise. Small groups of locals stood around with their pints in hand swapping tales. Seeing Andrew a man in one of the groups called him over. "Are you going to buy us all a drink and put it on expenses?"

Andrew looked mystified as the rest of the group break out in laughter. The man pointed to the television where the BBC News is on.

"One of your lot has just resigned because they found him fiddling his expenses! There's going to be a by-election in Wales. Better make sure you're not claiming for taking Sara out!"

Andrew turned to see Sara striding across the bar.

Safely seated in the corner with a glass of red for Sara, he asked her what the problem was with her immigration paperwork. Together they worked through the paperwork from the Home Office and Andrew found himself apologising for the confusion it was all causing. "It's like everything to do with Brexit, no one has thought things through properly. It's a right old mess."

Relieved, Sara put the papers away and took a sip of her wine. "I met my friend Julie this afternoon. She's the midwife I mentioned. She has been to see how Colin was getting on with the twins. She still feels terrible about what happened to Sandy. "

"Yes, poor old Colin. So tough, trying to manage the farm and the twins. How are they doing? I heard they were doing well."

"Oh yes. I don't know what he's feeding them but they are really growing fast. Nearly double their birth weight. Julie was amazed. But…."

She paused and Andrew waited for her to continue. Once again he saw the serious, concerned frown cross her face. "What? But what?"

"Well it's like they're growing too fast. And Julie says there is another set of twins she delivered recently in Cuthorpe. They're also growing very fast."

"Was their mother OK?"

"Yes, fortunately she was in Nottingham visiting her sister when the contractions started a month early. They gave her a Caesarean at the Queens Medical Centre. She's fine."

"So what's the problem?"

Sara looked down at her glass, rubbing her finger round the rim. She seemed reluctant to speak. Eventually she looked at Andrew and her dark eyes seemed to be searching for something, reassurance maybe. "It's probably a mad idea. It's just that this whole thing doesn't make any sort of sense. We've got cows having more twins, calves growing too fast and now mothers having twins and they're, they're," she looked down at her glass again continuing her finger's rubbing of the rim. "As if there's a connection. That something is causing cows and humans to have unusual births. You probably think I'm silly."

Andrew looked at the young Spaniard. The taunting, cheeky expression that he found so beguiling was now replaced by a sad, worried look, her eyes seemingly darker than ever. He didn't think she was silly. She was never silly. The idea of some connection between her experiences as a vet and those of her friend the midwife weren't fanciful. Maybe she was right. Maybe something was causing this phenomenon.

"But what are you suggesting, Sara? Is it something in the air? Is it just around here or is it happening nationally?"

"Well it certainly does seem to be very local. Julie says the birthing patterns are quite normal in Nottingham, apart from this one case. And in animal terms I was sure that it was something those two bulls had that was causing it. There haven't been any twin calves from the other bulls I've looked at and certainly their calves are growing quite normally."

"So what do you think is causing it?"

Sara picked up her glass and took a large sip. "Your wife works for Stellagenix doesn't she?"

"Well they are one of her clients. She does PR for them"

"I think this problem is being caused by them."

"What? How?"

"Well I know it's mad but there is one connection between the cows and Colin. The barley. It's used in cattle feed and it's used to make beer. That beer you're drinking right now."

Andrew glanced at his nearly-empty pint glass. He suddenly remembered his visit to the microbrewery. What had Jason said? He'd bought the barley from a farm that was doing trials for Stellagenix.

"You're not suggesting that the GM barley from Stellagenix is causing these birth anomalies and the subsequent fast growth of the calves?"

"And the babies." She nodded he head.

"It's the only connection I've been able to make. I know it sounds mad. I need to find out more about this new strain of barley. Is there something different in its make-up?"

"How will you do that?"

"I thought maybe Claire could help. If not I'll try and get someone to look at the DNA of those bulls.

43

Claire was having lunch with Amir. She had phoned him from her office the day before. He had been surprised to hear from her and even more surprised when she invited him to lunch. "Purely business," she joked. "I need your advice on something and I can't ask Andrew."

Amir was already seated at the corner table when Claire arrived. He greeted her warmly, kissing her on both cheeks. They passed pleasantries until the waitress came and took their order. The bottle of Sancerre was placed in an ice bucket and left at the side of the table.

Amir was curious about the reasons for Claire's request to meet him. But Amir bided his time waiting for Claire to speak. She sipped the Sancerre and then leant across the table, dropped her voice and started to explain.

Finally Amir looked at her and smiled. "No I don't think you're being stupid at all. And of course I'll set it up for you. After all, that's what friends are for isn't it?

Claire relaxed, sat back and picked up her knife and fork. She looked appreciatively at the delicious fish dish in front of her. It was good to be back in the real world, with the movers and shakers. Amir was such a clever operator. Stellagenix would never know what she had done. Neither would Andrew. Anyway he was far too busy with the leadership election.

Back in Victoria Street, Andrew was trying to concentrate on the latest report from the Quality Care Commission. His phone kept ringing and preventing him. The first ballot was tomorrow and the Conservative MPs were buzzing around trying to check on the likely outcome. Many had their strong favourites and were lobbying their peers accordingly. There was still a strong split between those who had voted to remain and the Brexiteers. Andrew had still to decide between Rory and Jeremy. He feared that it would come down to a two-horse race between Boris Johnson and Jeremy Hunt. Like most people in the country, he was heartily sick of Brexit. It dominated everything. The government was not tackling the routine issues, the problems with the health service, the threat or promise of Artificial Intelligence, the growing gap between the rich South and the poor Northern regions.

Andrew kept thinking of what Sara had said. He realised that despite his position as Junior Health Minister he had no medical knowledge. How realistic was it that eating (or drinking) barley could affect your sperm and cause multiple births? Wasn't this just a conspiracy theory that people who joined Extinction Rebellion propagated? As for Stellagenix, they weren't a pharmaceutical company. They just researched different varieties of seeds, picking the winners, discarding the losers. Natural selection, human selection had been occurring for aeons. It was the bedrock of the horticultural industry for a start. He remembered a visit to a large bulb grower near Boston. There he had been fascinated by how the company developed new colours and shades in different flowers by making hybrids.

He hadn't asked Claire about Stellagenix's methods. He wondered if she knew much more than him. After all George had tried to explain the methods used by his 'mad Greek scientist' without success. It was all too technical. And anyway there were checks and balances operated by the Food Safety people.

It was while he was contemplating this that Stan, his agent, called him. He was excited to tell Andrew that the local Conservative Association had received a large donation from Stellagenix. "I thought we couldn't accept donations from foreign companies?" said Andrew.

"OK, so technically you could say it was Stellagenix but actually the money came from a British company in Lincs and we haven't bothered to check on the shareholders."

"So how do you know it's Stellagenix?"

"Your friend George gave me a call. Apparently he's very keen that our members vote for Boris."

44

DECEMBER 2019, LINCOLNSHIRE

The past three months had passed quickly for Andrew. The new prime minister was determined to push ahead with Brexit and there was a plethora of bills, and counter bills, that kept MPs in London. The High Court was attacked by the right-wing press for daring to suggest that proroguing Parliament was illegal. MPs of both major parties sponsored bills to control the executive with varying success.

It came as little surprise that Boris Johnson decided to increase his ability to push things through by calling a general election. An election in December? That was something very unusual, but then these were unusual times.

Andrew had spent less and less time in his constituency. He had feared that his well-known support for a soft Brexit, and therefore his support for Jeremy Hunt, would harm his chances of remaining a minister. But despite Boris's rooting out of most Remainer ministers he was still in the same job. His boss, the Secretary of State for Health also remained in position. There was hope that after Brexit was finalised the NHS would receive much more money as Boris had promised on his campaign bus. Andrew doubted this. He had run the numbers. Numbers were Andrew's forte. The NHS was a vast organisation, probably the biggest in Europe and with an ageing population would struggle to cope. It was also heavily dependent on immigrant labour. With the Conservative's promise to cut immigration and in particular, immigration from lower-paid workers the situation was only likely to get worse.

The late summer recess and a holiday in St Lucia had been a much-needed break and Andrew realised how much he had missed family life. The boys were growing fast and he knew it was important to spend as much time as possible with them. Claire seemed to enjoy the break too. For months he had felt that Claire's mind was on her job, not the family. He had attempted to talk to her about Stellagenix and Sara's concerns. The reaction he had received shocked him. She was fiercely defendant of her client. When he suggested that she should ask George about it, and Sara's research, she reluctantly agreed. "Stellagenix is a great company. They're doing so much to develop products that will help feed the whole world and they're very good to you too."

"To me?"

"Yes, that new sports complex, the support for your local conservative association." Claire looked at him defiantly. She had many reasons to support Stellagenix apart from her job at the Agency.

Now here he was, out on the campaign trail again.

There's a good reason why general elections aren't normally called in December. It makes canvassing for votes much more difficult. The weather is cold and wet, the days are short. People don't like candidates knocking on their doors in the dark, but many aren't home during the day. Not that that would have been a concern in normal times. West Lincs voted solidly Conservative. As long as Andrew was reselected as a candidate, which he had been without a problem largely on the basis on the good job he had done with the new Sports Complex, he was bound to win. But this time it was rather different. Brexit had polarised people's views and the Remainers were likely to defect to the Liberals who were the only party still wanting another referendum. Even among Brexiteers there were those who worried that Boris was becoming something of an autocrat after his efforts to prorogue Parliament. Andrew's constituents felt their views were often ignored by 'them men in London' and worried that Boris was going to disenfranchise them even more.

So after being absent from his constituency for so long, Andrew had agreed with Stan to spend a solid three weeks canvassing. His work at the Department of Health was undemanding. Indeed many ministers found that all their time was taken up with Brexit and there were no new proposals in the Tory manifesto that affected health apart from a desire to employ more nurses to replace those who would inevitably be lost when the new immigration restrictions came into force.

Fortunately for Andrew and Claire, Analiese had agreed to stay on for another year which was just as well. With Andrew up North, Claire found herself increasingly busy with her clients. She had flown again to Barcelona with Clifton to help set up the new office. The four-day trip had been hectic as usual but once again she had enjoyed Clifton's bed. Their unspoken agreement was that what happened in Barcelona stayed in Barcelona. With every trip Claire's feeling of guilt diminished. Indeed she started to look on her illicit love-making as a business 'perk'. She still loved Andrew but they were both modern adults, busy, important people. As long as Andrew didn't find out, what did it matter?

Andrew had been so busy in Parliament and the Ministry that he had not had time to think much about Sara. In quiet moments he would occasionally think of their two nights together but more often he would think back to their last meeting and her concerns about Stellagenix. It was clear that Claire wasn't going to be much help in discovering the methods used by the mad Greek scientist. As time went by Andrew began to think that the whole idea was preposterous. Stellagenix wouldn't have launched the new strain if there had been any question of it being harmful to humans and animals. There were safety tests that had to be undertaken anyway, although Andrew had discovered that these amounted to little more than toxicity tests.

However, Andrew was nothing if not thorough. He liked facts. He was good at research. So he intensified his reading on the recent developments in biology and GM foods.

He read about Jennifer Doudna and her work on something called CRISPR. It seemed like the micro-biologists had harnessed an amazing tool that could identify specific bits of code in DNA (or more often RNA) that caused specific traits in living things. They were discovering the parts of the human genome code that affected hearing or sight, or caused malfunctions that led to crippling diseases like muscular dystrophy or cystic fibrosis. But the breakthrough had come when they were able to not only identify the specific parts of the billions-long code that controlled these functions but could use a bacteria to identify them and cut out the specific bits which could then be replaced with healthy cells. Medicine would never be the same again. Bacteria in humans had developed ways of spotting viruses and neutralising them through its immune system. Now it could be used to change the way the body's cells operated.

But it was not just medicine and human genomes that were benefitting from CRISPR. Companies were racing to improve plants or dairy products and all manner of other 'products'.

There was, of course, a worrying downside to all this. CRISPR laid open the ability, so far only theoretical, to create 'super' versions of animals and even humans. Designer babies were now a real possibility and that raised many moral issues.

So two days after he arrived back in Otherby he decided to give Sara a call and hopefully meet up at the Barley Mow as usual. He felt his newly-acquired knowledge would make it easier to understand her concerns about the 'twins issue'.

Before that he had an election to win.

He stepped out of the car and opened the boot. He took out another handful of Conservative leaflets and began to walk down the street of terraced houses. He knocked on three doors before he found someone at home. The occupant was young, maybe 17 or 18. He was dressed in jeans and a thick hoodie. He looked suspiciously at Andrew. Andrew introduced himself and said he hoped that the young man would be voting for him. He still wasn't sure that he was old enough.

"I certainly won't be!" The lad scowled. "You lot from London just piss me off. I've seen you on the telly – yelling and shouting at each other in that old building. You haven't a clue of what it's like for us up here. There's no jobs, no houses, nothing."

Andrew gave him the familiar response about the money the Tories were spending on helping people to buy homes, and how Brexit would create more jobs for English people once the Europeans had left. But even as he said it he realised that he didn't believe it. The lad was right. Andrew's colleagues in London knew little about life outside the metropolis of London. They'd had a good education, well-off parents and rarely had to worry about meeting bills.

Back in Otherby that evening Andrew poured himself a scotch and sat down in his study. He pulled the blind down. It had been dark for some hours and there was nothing to see. He thought about his canvassing that day. The most common response he had received was one of indifference. Voters were more interested in getting ready for Christmas than electing a political party. Most were completely fed up with the time it was taking to sort out Brexit and just wanted it done. Few of them had any idea of how it would impact them and most felt that whichever political party was in power it wouldn't change things for them.

"Why am I doing this job?" thought Andrew. He did want to improve the lot for his local constituents. He wanted there to be more jobs and more affordable housing. But that required a vibrant national economy and he was very worried that Brexit would not facilitate that. As ever, he'd studied the figures. In this case he had looked at the earnings levels by job type and by geographical area. The disparity between the top earners and the rest of the population was growing larger every year. And London wages were far in excess of those in the provinces. With Parliament pontificating in a 200-year-old building set in the heart of this metropolis and, with its members increasingly being career politicians rather than conviction politicians, it was no wonder constituents like the lad he had met this afternoon could see no reason to vote for them.

Everything in politics was about money. Not that MPs were paid that much. Andrew had taken a big cut in salary to be an MP. But few MPs in his party needed to rely on their Parliamentary salary. Most had come from wealthy backgrounds, inherited wealth and large investments. Although there were restrictions on what Cabinet Members were permitted to do, normal MPs could have as many other jobs as they liked as long as they declared them. Tory MPs were far more likely to have other income than Labour and not just from things like property rents. Jacob Rees Mogg was a partner in a wealth management firm for instance and was reportedly paid nearly £200,000 a year for his services. MPs and their families often had large portfolios of shares. Compared to a nurse working at the Lincoln hospital, or the delivery driver or farmer's son trying to run a micro-brewery, MPs incomes and lifestyles were so far removed that it was easy to see why few understood the needs of their constituents.

Andrew's mobile pinged to remind him of his 'date' in the Barley Mow with Sara. He glanced at his watch, swallowed the remaining whisky and headed upstairs to change.

It was good to see Sara again. The shenanigans at

Westminster since Boris Johnson's appointment had kept him away from Otherby for too long. He greeted her with a kiss on each cheek, once again raising eyebrows and a few grins from the locals. But he didn't care.

He watched her as she tossed her hair back and shrugged off her thick parka. He'd forgotten the effect those dark Spanish eyes had on him. Months of late-night sessions at Westminster, the drama of Brexit and the proroguing of Parliament had driven out thoughts of Sara, of Otherby, of his intentions to become more involved with the Lincolnshire life. He'd had the idea that Claire and the boys would be spending time regularly up with him and they would appreciate the benefits of clean air and countryside. But it hadn't happened. Claire had been totally engrossed in her new job and showed no desire to spend weekends up North. Her world was increasingly centred around business, London and the high-achieving set in Wandsworth.

Andrew wondered whether he had been selfish in wanting to give up that world in order to make a difference to the rest of the people in the country. Didn't that make him sound more like a socialist politician?

He looked across the bar at the small group of Colin's friends drinking there. Colin wasn't with them. No doubt, as a single parent now, he had to be at home, looking after his fast-growing twin daughters. For all Boris's promises to recruit more nurses and spend millions of pounds recovered from the EU, there was no sign of either happening. His meetings with the Lincolnshire Hospital Trust had shown him that hospitals were failing to meet the public need.

Now, here he was with Sara. A Spaniard. A qualified vet.

A constituent still worried about her ability to remain in the country yet more worried about what was causing cows to keep having twins. These were real world problems – not the world of Westminster where life was play-acting, posturing and selfish.

He poured Sara a glass from the bottle of red wine and watched her as she studied the pub menu. There wasn't a lot of choice and the pub certainly didn't run to a wine list. It was a far cry from Wandsworth. He watched as her furrowed brow suddenly relaxed and she smiled. Selection made, she looked up at him. "Have you chosen already?"

He gave the order to Kevin and leaned forward to speak. But, unusual for a politician, the words didn't come. He managed "How have you been? I've missed you."

"I've been OK but you look terrible! What's the matter? Is vote-winning that difficult?"

He smiled and started to recount his experiences on the campaign trail that afternoon. Soon he was describing his doubts about his role as an MP and Junior Minister. She was a good listener and he felt some of the burden lifted as he detailed his frustrations with the job and his distaste at the way his fellow politicians used their positions to make money. He described the way that some MPs managed their share portfolios, who acted on information that verged on inside information. He recounted how he could have taken advantage of his knowledge of Stellagenix's breakthrough to buy shares, but had declined.

Mention of Stellagenix prompted Sara to ask if Claire had given him any information on Stellagenix's research methods.

He explained that Claire hadn't managed to get any

details about the way the new barley strain had been engineered. He even wondered whether she had tried to get an answer. She had been very defensive of her client.

Sara explained that she certainly had not been idle while he'd been down in London.

She had been reading extensively on the subject of natural selection and the different ways of causing artificial mutations in plants. But she had also found out a lot of information on CRISPR and the work being done by food companies with that. She looked pleased and impressed with Andrew when she learned that he too had been reading up on CRISPR.

"That saves me a lot of explaining," she joked. "It's pretty hard to get your head round how we can manipulate the make-up of something so small you can hardly see it with the most powerful microscope."

"So you think that Stellagenix have been using the technique to edit the genome of a particular barley?"

"I wouldn't be at all surprised. And of course there's nothing to stop them. A plant's DNA can change through natural causes over time and those changes can affect how resistant it is to certain diseases, or how tall it grows, or how quickly. All they would be doing is changing a bit of the genetic code and see what effects it had. They must have found the bit of the genome that controls growth, the rate at which cells split and form others."

"But that doesn't explain why the bulls have started producing twins does it? Even if they did eat the modified barley it's hardly going to change their DNA is it?"

"I can't see why it would. Maybe we are what we eat but eating a tomato doesn't turn you into one!"

"There's a hell of a difference between a plant's genome and a human's."

"Not as much as you might think. It's the same four amino acids making us all up. But while we could possibly breed with another mammal it's a big leap from barley grains to bulls, let alone humans. The truth is we've only just started to understand the process and what the opportunities are to improve food crops, make humans healthier and so on. We've got a lot to learn."

"So where do we go from here?" Andrew liked answers, plans, strategies.

"I've got one of the guys who was on my course to see if he can get the genomes of three bulls mapped so we can see the differences. Two of the bulls are our suspects who were fed the Stellagenix barley, the other is the same breed of bull but from another farm who was fed differently. I don't know how long it will take though. He's in Manchester."

Kevin came across to clear their plates. "Do you want another bottle, Andrew?" He nodded to the empty bottle of red wine. "You not drinking Fentastic tonight then?"

Andrew and Sara looked at each other knowingly. "OK, why not another bottle," said Andrew.

At the end of the second bottle Andrew's mood had lifted. He'd listened as Sara spoke about the farmers she'd helped recently and laughed as she described a misfortune that had befallen one of her colleagues visiting a pig farm.

No words were spoken. It wasn't discussed. It just seemed natural that they should walk back from the Barley Mow in the direction of his house. And later, after they had made love, Andrew slept a sleep deeper than he had managed for months.

45

George Krasnik put down his phone and smiled. The deal was on. The Board had confirmed it although nothing was to be announced yet. An all-share offer for the American pharmaceutical company would be made straight after Christmas. But before that, Stellagenix would announce the latest results of its barley trials and its preliminary work on winter wheat. Some news had already leaked out and increased the share price but the Board's confirmation would send the value of Stellagenix shares sky rocketing. The increased value would make their takeover bid for Western Calapharm a cinch. The extensive manufacturing facilities of Western Calapharm, particularly sterile packaging, would enable Stellagenix to increase its production of the new strains. The company's major strength in vaccination production for everything from flu to malaria would add another string to Stellagenix's bow and immediately catapult them into the higher-rated pharmaceutical market. George's own share options would make him millions.

He walked out of his office and headed to Dimitri's laboratory. Disappointed to find Dimitri was away at a conference, he turned to the two researchers who worked with him.

Martha had been with company for just two years. A microbiologist with a master's degree from Nottingham University she had worked at the Crick Institute in London for a dozen years before leaving to have a family. She and her husband had moved to Lincoln soon after their first child had been born. Both felt that the new house and grounds were a better place to bring up their children than their terraced house in Greenwich. The job at Stellagenix was something she was eminently qualified for.

She worked alongside Katriona, a graduate from Edinburgh. Unmarried and bookish, she was a reliable and competent researcher.

George turned to Martha. "How's it all going? You got any more results from Wheat Epta yet?" Dimitri had named their latest experimental strain of wheat 'Epta' as it was the seventh variety to be developed.

"No it's too early to tell yet but Dimitri thinks it will be even better than Exi. But I'm working on the barley trials rather than the wheat. There's no doubt that the yields are up dramatically – the field tests showed that. But I'm concerned that it could have some unexpected results when it ferments."

George stared at her. "Like what?"

"Well we did all the usual toxicity tests and there appears to be no adverse reaction from any of the animals or humans we've tested but.."

"But what! If it's passed the FDA tests and the Europeans are happy too what's the frigging problem? It's not going to poison anyone."

"No it's just that we edited the genome using a formula from the rabbit genome. It helps the growth and division of cells. We get greater and faster growth that way. It's just that when we fed some fermented barley to the mice they started producing larger litters, much larger litters. And the offspring are growing bigger too."

"Why hasn't Dimitri told me that?"

"I don't know. I thought he had."

"Who else knows about this?"

"Just me, Katriona and Dimitri I guess. Unless he's told anyone else. "

"Let's keep it that way," barked George. "After all it's passed the legal tests and that's all that matters. With these increased yields the world will be able to feed millions more people. And the same for the wheat developments. So what if a few laboratory mice have more babies? No, this is not to be mentioned. It's totally irrelevant."

Martha nodded. The two researchers watched as George hurried out of the lab. "Wow, you certainly rattled his cage," said Katriona.

"I thought Dimitri had already told him."

"You know Dimitri! He likes to keep things tight. Makes him feel more important. He doesn't believe George understands anything about CRISPR or genome editing and he's not about to explain it."

46

DECEMBER 2019, LINCOLNSHIRE

General elections were good news for local radio stations. Normally in December the advertising sales team was celebrating the rush of orders from stores and hotels promoting their Christmas offerings. The news team were talking about busy high streets or predicted shortages of turkeys, or Christmas trees or some other essential item. But there was little hard news as everyone was winding down for Christmas. Normally businesses didn't announce new projects in December, Parliament was packing up for extended Christmas holidays, so short of a natural disaster happening locally news was normally thin.

But not this year. The Brexit debate had been keeping the national newspapers and television channels full with the goings on in Parliament and with the EU negotiators. Boris had promised a deal would be done by Christmas. Now he had gone to the country in order to get a greater mandate. Politics, Brexit, was the big news every day, nationally.

But that didn't help local media. If you were in a Scottish fishing port there might be a local angle to be exploited as any new agreement might lead to local fishing crews suffering but in Lincolnshire it was hard to find a local angle. Grimsby had long since lost its fishing fleet. The farmers had voted for Brexit so seemed to be complacent about leaving the Common Agricultural Programme. The only worry was if Boris allowed chlorinated chickens in from America.

It was this that prompted Sonya Arkle to phone Stellagenix. She hoped George would give her some good news on the new improved barley strain. She had covered the story a few months before at the press launch although most of the technical details had been unsuitable for the local press. The prospect of increased employment which George had dangled was more relevant to her listeners and she could probably get an update on the way the new sports centre was progressing.

George took her call. He was very upbeat about the research and said plans for increased production of the new barley seed were already being implemented. It was all good news. They were expecting similar results for a new wheat strain and that would increase production further. And yes, that would mean more jobs in the area. Much of this news had already been covered and as a reporter Sonya was looking for an angle to pursue. She decided to bring up Brexit.

"A lot of people in Lincolnshire are worried that Boris Johnson will sign a trade deal with America that will be a disaster for our farmers. Your food standards are so much lower than ours, chlorinated chicken for example."

There was no reply from George. She waited, the line was still open. Eventually he spoke.

"The American food safety standards are exemplary. All of our products, those coming from our research, have been approved by the American authorities and the European ones. There's no health problems with our plant varieties. GM foods are perfectly safe."

Taken aback by this Sonya quickly changed tack. "I'm sure that locally we're really grateful for all your support on the new sports centre at Ludthorpe. I believe the project is well ahead of schedule?"

"Yes, it's going well and Stellagenix are happy to be able to support the British by providing facilities for its budding athletes."

"Thank you and may I wish you a Happy Christmas." She put the phone down. Her instincts told her that something had happened in that interview that she wasn't expecting. She played back the tape – all her calls were recorded.

The question about American food standards was contentious – it was meant to be. But it couldn't have been unexpected. National news broadcasters had asked the same question of everyone from the American ambassador to our own farming minister. There was always a reassuring answer about food standards being in line with British ones and chlorinated chicken being totally safe. Yet George had taken the question as relating to his genetically modified grain seed. There had been no intention on Sonya's part to suggest that those products were unsafe. So why had he reacted so strongly? The Shakespearean line 'He protesteth too much!" seemed apt. I wonder, she thought, if there is something wrong with their research.

She would have to get more information on their methods but how? She really hadn't understood the Greek scientist. Her knowledge of GM foods was pretty sparse. Maybe she should do a little desk research first.

In the meantime she needed an interview for tonight's edition. Maybe she could get hold of Andrew Eastwood. He was normally good for a few sound bites.

She rang his mobile and it was answered immediately.

"Hi Andrew, it's Sonya Arkle I wondered if we could do a quick telephone interview on the run-up to the election, how the canvassing is going, the main concerns you're encountering from voters etc? Can I record this conversation?"

"Hi Sonya. No problem. Glad to take a breather from banging on doors," he chuckled.

She went through her list of questions and was pleased when she got Andrew's comments about the need to improve people's impression of MPs in Westminster. "We're seen as being out of touch with the man in the street. It's not just the Tories, it's all of us at Westminster. Focus groups talk about the man on the London omnibus. They should be looking at the 19-year-old unemployed man in Laceby, or the nurse working extra shifts in Lincoln to pay her rent. Their concerns aren't about Brexit but how their lives can be made easier."

"Is that how they see you Andrew? Out of touch with local issues?"

"Probably. I've had to spend too much time in London recently."

"That's very honest Andrew."

"I always try to be honest with people."

Gold dust thought Sonya after she put the phone down.

She liked Andrew but that comment would make a great intro to the programme. "MPs stuck in London are out of touch says local candidate". Excellent. Dynamite!

She wondered if Andrew was worried about the election. He couldn't be. There was no doubting the Tories would hold the seat. But she detected that he wasn't happy. Maybe she should get over to Otherby and see him. Off the record. Anyway, he might know something about Stellagenix. She remembered that his wife handled their PR. Yes maybe a trip to Otherby might be valuable.

Martha stood by the side of her husband at the reception. She didn't normally go to these Round Table affairs but this was their pre-Christmas special and the meal was to be followed by a talk by one of her favourite TV presenters.

She didn't know that many people and when her husband excused himself to go and get another drink she looked round nervously. She envied the young woman in a simple black cocktail dress who was busy talking to a group of three businessmen. She wondered what she did. Obviously she was well known.

The woman looked over towards her and smiled. A minute later she came across. "You look like you've been marooned here. Can I introduce myself, I'm Sonya Arkle from Lindum Radio."

"Oh yes, I've heard you on the radio." What a banal reply Martha thought. She introduced herself. "I'm here with my husband, he's with Bradshaws in Lincoln."

"And do you work, Martha?"

"I'm a researcher at a firm called Stellagenix, I don't know if you know them?"

"Yes of course. I've met George Krasnik, he's been on my show."

Martha was impressed. She tried to think of something to say.

"So what does a researcher do at Stellagenix then Martha?" Sonya couldn't believe her luck in meeting Martha. Now she could probe what was going on and why George had seemed so defensive.

"I work in a lab. We're developing new strains of barley and wheat."

"And what's so good about these new strains? Drought resistance, disease resistance?"

"We're improving the yields by getting them to grow faster, stronger. The cells to split sooner and so on."

"I don't know much about things like that," said Sonya innocently. "So how do you go about developing new strains?"

"Well we used to try and get mutations in existing strains. There are always some natural ones you know. So you find one that grows quicker for instance and then you try and grow more seeds from that."

"I see. But what if there aren't any natural mutations what do you then? "

"Well we used to induce mutations through introducing certain DNA into the cells of the plant and seeing what effect they have on the plant. All very technical I'm afraid."

"Yes above my paygrade I'm sure. But you say 'used to'?"

"Yes our director of research now uses special gene editing techniques – even more technical I'm afraid!"

"I think I've heard of gene editing. I thought that was for animals though? "

"Oh no, plants and animals can all be edited. They are really the same process."

"When you develop a new strain are you free to start selling it or do you have to get it licensed or something?"

"Oh...... it just has to pass what we call toxicity tests – to see if it poisons you!"

"But might a new edited strain affect your body in some other way? Not just poison?"

Martha looked down. She thought about George's instructions. "No, no. I'm sure it couldn't, sure."

Her husband arrived with their drinks and Martha turned to him anxiously. "This lady's from the radio station why don't you tell her about Bradshaws?"

Sonya noticed the flush in Martha's cheeks. She saw her take a large gulp of her wine. There's something going on here, she thought. I'm sure of it.

Andrew had had another long, hard day canvassing. The wind had been from the North East, straight from the Urals, and carried rain that lashed down as he walked from house to house. He was therefore glad of the warmth in the bar at the Barley Mow. Despite his misgivings about barley he ordered a pint of Fentastic to accompany the whisky. He nodded to a couple of the regulars and walked across to the corner table. He started scrolling through his emails and answering the urgent ones. He was surprised then when someone sat down across the table from him.

The lady pushed back the hood of her parka, shook her hair free and stretched out her hand.

"Hello Andrew, I hoped I'd find you here. I spoke to

Stan and he said you'd probably be drying out here. Don't you ever answer your phone?"

"Sonya! What a pleasure. Sorry it's still on silent." He scrolled up and saw the three missed calls from an unknown number.

"Can I get you a drink Andrew, you look like you need another?"

"No let me, please."

"It's on expenses. This is a business meeting Andrew. Same again?"

"I'd better be careful what I say to you then," he laughed.

He saw one of the regulars nudge his friend as Sonya walked to the bar. "Don't know how he does it. Different one every night!" His words intentionally carried across the bar. Sonya didn't react.

"I thought you had got what you wanted from our telephone interview last week," said Andrew. "Stan wasn't too pleased with the way you led with my 'out-of-touch' bit."

"Yes, sorry about that. Stan had a go at me about that this afternoon! But it's the job you know. Got to keep the listeners tuning in!"

"Well I'll be careful not to say anything contentious tonight."

"No, Andrew, don't worry. Tonight's totally off-the-record. I don't want to ask you anything about the election."

"That's what you journalists always say."

"If it's any consolation I agree with you. Westminster means nothing to people round here. And as you know I'm one of the few here who voted Remain. But I promised not to talk politics. No I wanted your advice on something else."

She started to tell him about her call with George Krasnik and the reaction of Martha. She noticed that he was immediately interested. He hung on her every word.

"I just think there's something funny going on there. And I know your wife does their PR so you probably don't want to talk about it." She paused and looked at him, her brown eyes searching his face for a reaction.

"Tell me again what this Martha woman said to you about cell division."

Sonya's brow furrowed. She tilted her head to one side. All her journalistic instincts were aroused. The question from Andrew was not expected. He seemed to know something about gene editing by the way he had picked on the cell division aspect.

"So what do you know Andrew? You do know something don't you?"

"I don't *know* anything but I am interested to learn exactly what they've done to get that barley growing so fast."

"So what do you know about gene editing, Andrew?"

"Quite a lot more than I did a few weeks ago but if you want to know more you should ask her." He nodded towards the bar. Sara had arrived and was looking inquisitively at the two of them huddled in the corner.

Sara joined them reluctantly and Andrew introduced them. Kevin came across with a bottle of red wine and three glasses. "The guys over there said you might need this!" He grinned and scuttled back to the bar. "My reputation's shot," laughed Andrew. "I hope it won't stop them voting for me next week." He raised a salute to the three men at the bar. As he did so the door opened as another man came in. The blast of cold air reached even their table in the corner. The man wasn't a regular and seemed to know no one. Andrew had a feeling he'd seen him somewhere before but gave it no further consideration.

As soon as Sara learned that Sonya was interested in the goings on at Stellagenix and had met one of the researchers her mood changed. She sat forward and asked almost the same question as Andrew. "Did she tell you what methods they use to get the cells to split quicker?"

"So what happens now? Sara looked across at Andrew. Sonya had left promising to stay in touch and to report anything she found out about Stellagenix. Sara said the same.

"When will you get the results of the genome map of those three bulls?"

"I'm not sure. With Christmas coming up the labs are going to be closed. It could be a few weeks."

"I agree with Sonya that they are trying to cover something up and it would seem that they've discovered a safety issue but until and unless we get definitive proof we cannot go accusing them. We've still no proof of a connection between the barley and those bulls."

"Or the beer and Colin's twins," added Sara.

They continued to discuss the problem until Andrew said he had better head off as he had an early start in the morning. "I've got an early start too," grinned Sara. "Shall I set an alarm for us?"

They left the pub and headed for Limetree House.

47

It was nearly three o'clock in the morning that West Lincs election results were announced. There were few spectators. No one had expected anything but a Tory win and following the early results being broadcast on TV it was obvious that Boris's Tories were making gains everywhere.

Andrew shook hands with his opponents and made a short speech for the benefit of the two local media representatives. He then walked up the street to the hotel where he had booked in for the night. He was glad the canvassing was over. But he wasn't hopeful that anything could now be done to stop Boris pushing for a quick, hard Brexit.

When he awoke a few hours later he turned on the TV and caught up with the news of the landslide victory. The local news section mentioned him and several other Lincolnshire MPs who had been re-elected with increased majorities. He was about to switch off and go for his shower when the local news flashed up pictures of a car accident. The newsreader explained how emergency services had been called to a fatal crash near Ancaster. Police reported that the dead woman was a research chemist at Stellagenix and appeared to have lost control of her vehicle which crashed into a wall. The woman was not named but Andrew had a sinking feeling he knew exactly who it was.

An hour later Sonya rang his mobile. "Looks as if we've lost our source of information on Stellagenix. She seemed such a nice woman too and had two young children. It was pretty cold last night and the police are saying she could have hit some black ice."

"Are you convinced it was an accident?"

"There's nothing apparently to suggest it wasn't. It'd be easy to jump to conclusions but I think that would be a conspiracy theory too far."

"You're still going to keep on investigating then Sonya?"

"Absolutely."

Sara and Andrew spent another night together before he headed back to Wandsworth. Sara was planning to spend Christmas with her parents in Salamanca, coming back around New Year. Andrew knew that there would be a heavy workload for him back in London and didn't expect to be back in Otherby until the New Year either.

On his drive down to London he thought back to the past year. It hadn't panned out at all as he had wanted or had expected. Politically the Brexiteers had won, got rid of Theresa May and installed their own champion. Andrew had been powerless to influence things. Wasn't that why he had wanted to be an MP? To influence major national and international decisions? And what precisely had he achieved? He'd managed to get a sports complex built for residents of Lincolnshire, sorted out a few problems for constituents and tried to shake up the local hospital administration. Not really what he had planned.

Lincolnshire hadn't provided him with the solace he was looking for either. He'd imagined a rural idyll, weekends with Claire and the boys away from the grime and crime of London. But Claire had rarely been up there and the boys were now more accustomed to walks to McDonalds with the Austrian au pair than country walks with Dad.

On the other hand he had come to have a new respect for farmers and a new interest in genetics. He had a greater appreciation of what drove rural communities and it was very different from that which drove the metropolitan elite.

Then there was Sara. What was he doing there? He was happily married to Claire. They had had a good thing going. She shared his ambitions, he hers. They had built successful careers together and had the twins. Sara was very attractive, that was a given and her Spanishness added some novelty. He had come to love her sense of humour but most of all he loved her dedication to making the world a better place. As a vet she understood the farmers' problems, she cared about the animals. But she was also a people person. She engaged with them. And she had certainly engaged with him. He wouldn't have contemplated an affair before he met her. It had all seemed so natural. The past few days, or more particularly the nights had added a new depth to their relationship. But it was one that couldn't continue. He wasn't going to risk his marriage. He would have to end his relationship. Yes, he thought. I'll end it. After Christmas when I'm back in Otherby we need to have a serious talk. Maybe we can still be friends.

His thoughts turned to Claire. Had she become more distant with him or was it just the pressure of their jobs? There was no doubt that she was absorbed in her work and doing very well at the Agency. But he didn't like the way she seemed to have to go away, leaving him and the boys so often. Barcelona was getting like a second home to her. He'd hoped Otherby would become their second home.

What about her client Stellagenix? He didn't know how that would influence things. She had been so defensive about them when he had dared to suggest that their work might be causing unnatural births. It was right that she should feel protective of one of her clients but she had reacted so vigorously. He was increasingly worried that Stellagenix might have something to hide and he was only too aware of the close relationship George Krasnik seemed to have not only with his wife but with senior Tories too. He remembered how George had suggested he invest in the company before the test results were announced. Andrew knew Amir had invested more. He was always on the lookout for rising stocks. Maybe Claire had given him a little bit of a heads up. George seemed to know a lot about Claire. In fact he seemed to know rather a lot about everything. He was glad George lived a long way from Otherby. That one time he had come over for a drink and met Sara he seemed to upset her. And now there was the accident that had killed Martha the researcher. Conspiracy theories? Maybe, but it was still perturbing.

No doubt Claire and he would be getting together

with the 'gang' around Christmas and he might be able to get some perspective from them on Stellagenix. After all Indra had done pharmacy and Lucy had read biology at Cambridge.

The boys were excited to see him after three weeks. "Did you win Daddy?" asked Marshall. He spent the rest of the afternoon playing with them and hearing all about their school which they obviously enjoyed. "Would you like to go up to Otherby again?" he asked.

Both boys thought for a moment. "We like going to McDonalds here. They haven't got one up there," said Miles.

"But what about the tractors, and the animals?"

"Oh yes. The tractor was good. I like tractors." Miles perked up.

"I like that man who was making beer," added Marshall keen not to be outdone. "And the animal doctor."

Claire got home shortly before seven and was obviously bushed. She gave him a big hug and congratulated him on winning. "Not that it was ever in doubt!" She shook off her coat and ran her fingers through her hair. "Hell of a day. And the tube was so packed. I really need to get changed and take a quick shower. Make me a drink will you darling?"

"Do you want to go out for dinner?"

"Oh not tonight, I'm so tired. And you must be. Let's just eat something here. Analiese can you conjure something up?"

They ate in the kitchen with Analiese. It was a simple pasta dish followed by fruit and cheese and washed down with a couple of bottles of excellent red wine. Andrew regaled them both with stories of his canvassing and some of the reactions he had received

Analiese wanted to know how the election would change things, particularly Brexit negotiations and Andrew told her truthfully that he feared the outcome would be bad.

In bed that night Claire and Andrew made love. It was quick and comforting and both fell asleep instantly afterwards.

48

DECEMBER 13TH 2019, LINCOLNSHIRE

George Krasnik looked across his desk at the Greek. He shifted in his chair. Suitable words of consolation didn't come to him. He was uncomfortable seeing a grown man cry.

George had suffered many tragedies in his life. There had been deaths, business failures and his rejection by the right university. But he had never cried. Albanians don't cry. His father had taught him that.

"We don't show weakness, even if we're wrong. Sometimes you've just gotta do whatever it takes to make sure you win."

George thought about his father's words now. The breakthroughs at Stellagenix with wheat and barley were all that mattered. The result of the producing the new strains would be to alleviate hunger for millions of the world's poor. It would also ensure that he, George, would become very rich.

Losing a researcher was unfortunate, the circumstances sad, but it was for the good of others.

He knew the Greek biologist wouldn't have seen it that way. Dimitri's job was to handle the laboratory work. George's role was to bring the result of that work to market.

"I just don't understand why she would be driving so fast. She was always a very careful driver," sobbed Dimitri.

"Black ice. Nasty stuff. Skidded on it myself this morning." George resisted the temptation to reach for a Snickers bar. Insensitive.

"I don't know how I'll manage without her." The Greek reached for another tissue from the box George had pushed across.

"What about Katriona? Is she good enough to carry on Martha's work?"

Katriona was a problem that George still had to deal with. He had, however, come up with a plan. George always had a plan.

The next morning when Claire announced that she was going to be flying to the States later that week Andrew was far from happy. "You know I'm going to be up to my eyes in work at Westminster between now and Christmas, and Analiese is going home for Christmas too."

Claire explained that it was imperative that she accompanied George Krasnik back to the States where she would be meeting the US PR agency to work on a big announcement.

"What's so big that it can't wait until after Christmas?"

"I can't tell you that. It's embargoed."

"How long will you be away?"

"Only three or four days. I'll be back on the 22nd. You know you really should be more supportive of Stellagenix. George has done a lot for you. But he says that you seem to have something against them."

Andrew thought back to his meeting with Sonya and Sara. He thought about the accident that had killed Martha the researcher.

"What's given him that idea?"

"Well he said something to me about needing to work on the local media as you seemed to be spending a lot of time with a local radio presenter who is criticising them. Is that true?"

"Well you know I am concerned to know about their research methods. We're worried about all these twin births with the cows. You were going to ask him, remember?"

"Look the success they've had with the barley seed, and what they expect from the wheat seed is going to have a massive effect on food productivity. As a politician you should really appreciate that instead of your damn conspiracy theories."

"So you told him I was concerned?"

"No, I didn't mention it at all. Look since I've worked on this account their share price has rocketed and that's good for us. And GE foods are going to be good for your sustainable world. You keep on about saving the planet. You've got to feed the people too."

"Good for us?" Andrew picked up on Claire's words about Stellagenix benefiting them.

"Well good for the Agency and my bonus. And it's good for you and your constituents. After all you're getting more jobs and a new sports centre. And good for the Tories. There are a lot of senior Tories who are glad of the support they're getting from George."

49

DECEMBER 16TH 2019, LONDON.

It was on Monday morning that Andrew got the call from George.

"Hi Andrew, how's it going? Look I'm sorry to be taking your wife off just before Christmas. I know you've got a lot happening but it's really important. I'm sure you've guessed what it's about or has Claire told you?"

"Claire has told me nothing. She says it's a secret."

"Well we certainly wouldn't want the news to get out until we're ready. Claire's going to be really busy for the next two or three weeks telling the world about our barley and wheat successes. We wouldn't want anything to interfere with that would we?"

There was an underlying menace in his voice. Or did Andrew just imagine that?

"I mean, Andrew, we really want your support on this – along with your colleagues of course. I'm sure your local party is grateful even if your little Spanish girlfriend is full of cock and bull stories!" There it was! How the hell did he know about Sara and him? Yes he had met them once but it wasn't unusual to have a meeting with a female constituent. And then there was Claire's remark about Sonya and his connection with her. How did George always seem to know what he was doing?

Andrew thought of a suitable comment. Finally he said "I was really sorry to hear about one of your researchers getting killed in a car accident."

"Yeah, that was tragic. We lost a really good colleague there. I'm due to attend her funeral tomorrow. I don't suppose you'll be coming up for it?"

After the call Andrew sat back and tried to work out what was going on. Why had George phoned? Was it to apologise for taking Claire off? Was that just an excuse to let him warn Andrew not to raise the issue of testing? The references to his Tory colleagues, the donation to the local Conservative Association and his reference to Sara as his 'Spanish girlfriend' were certainly veiled threats. All of which made Andrew more convinced than ever that there was some link between the barley and the twin calves outbreak.

Back at Stellagenix George had put down the phone and now turned to Dimitri. "That should have stopped him," he smiled. "I don't think we need worry about Mr Eastwood shooting his mouth off to the media. Not if he wants to keep his marriage!"

Dimitri didn't smile. "He mentioned Martha? Why did he do that? It was an accident after all."

That's the problem with you scientists, thought George. You're all so gullible. Dimitri didn't realise what a problem had been solved through Martha's unfortunate death. In a few weeks' time the market would be euphoric about the increased yields Stellagenix could offer, the share price would go higher and the value of their all-share offer for Calapharm would make the takeover unstoppable.

In Victoria Street Andrew decided to call Sara. He wanted to tell her about George. His call went unanswered, switching instead to voice mail. She's probably got her hand up a cow's arse, thought Andrew smiling to himself at the thought. But for the rest of the day he waited for the phone to ring.

When eventually she called back Andrew's phone was on silent. He was in a meeting with the Secretary of State for Health and the Prime Minister's Special Advisor. Parliament was being recalled tomorrow when they would elect the Speaker and each MP would then go through a ceremony of swearing allegiance to the Crown. Then on Thursday the State Opening of Parliament would take place and there was much work to be done on the Queen's Speech before then. The Special Advisor, or SPAD, was grilling Andrew on what progress had been made to bring failing hospital trusts into line. Andrew outlined his misgivings about the efficiency of many of the administrations but also pointed out that Brexit was not making it easy to recruit more nurses. That earned him a tongue whipping from the SPAD.

Claire's day had been eventful too. With only two days before she flew to America she had a lot to sort out with her other clients. She would miss the office Christmas party on Wednesday. Clifton hadn't been pleased. "You know you're the only reason I go to the dreadful do," he said. "If you're not going to be there I think I'll give it a miss."

She had lunch with her boss Paul Devorian. He wanted to know all about the reasons behind the trip. Since Claire had been appointed to the account it had grown considerably and was now the Agency's biggest account. Paul liked to keep his finger on everything. Impressed as he was with Claire he would have liked to have a stronger relationship with George himself.

"What's so important that it can't wait until after Christmas?"

"Well we've got the results of the latest trials and they're outstanding. They want them publicised globally so that the share price goes up further. We've already got it up nearly 20% so far this year, mainly on rumours. A proper presentation of the results and some extrapolation of how their market share could grow should get it up another 20%. I'm to work out a joint pitch to the media with Papplewicks their US Agency."

"I see. That's great of course and good news for the shareholders. I've got a small stake-holding myself!"

"So have I, Paul, but don't tell Andrew. Conflict of interest and all that!" She smiled as she thought of her meeting with Amir. His advice on the share options had meant that she already stood to make more from Stellagenix's shares than her annual salary. The last thing she needed was Andrew to start spouting his conspiracy theories about pregnant cows eating barley. She loved Andrew and she had always admired his principles but someone had to make sure they would be able to afford the school fees.

50

The mood at Stellagenix was sombre. People were quietly getting on with their work but the usual buzz of conversation was missing. The death of Martha had affected all those who had known her, and most employees of Stellagenix did. That morning George had called them all into the main meeting room where he spoke of how much he had admired Martha and her work. He said how he would personally miss her and that he had passed on everyone's condolences to her husband.

After the meeting George walked down from his office to the main research lab. Katriona was sitting at her computer in the office she previously shared with Martha. She was gazing blankly at the screen. She looked up guiltily when he entered.

"Katriona, I know you and Martha were close and I appreciate that your workload is going to increase before we can get you an assistant." George perched himself uncomfortably on the end of her desk. He would have to play this well, he knew. The desk creaked as he shifted his weight.

"Assistant?" Katriona looked at the large American. She had seldom spoken to him before on her own. She had been happy to be Martha's assistant. Now she was being offered an assistant of her own. Did this mean promotion?

"The work you, Martha and Dimitri have done here is going to result in enormous benefits for mankind." George watched Katriona's face for a reaction. He had emphasised the benefits to humanity, not the commercial benefits to Stellagenix and him. He continued. "I want Martha to be remembered for the success of our new barley and wheat. Its success will be a kind of ongoing memorial. I guess she would have liked that."

Katriona nodded in agreement.

"I don't want anything to delay the introduction of our new grains." He heaved himself up from the desk. "That's why I'm asking you to take over Martha's role. I know you are capable of it."

Katriona looked down at her lap. She was torn. She was flattered to think George rated her so highly but how could she possibly put in all the extra hours it entailed?

As if reading her mind, George started speaking again.

"I am aware, Katriona, that you have a lot of commitments at home and maybe you feel they might prevent you from taking on an increased role. But I believe this project is too important to delay, and it's only fair that Martha should be remembered for her work."

Katriona was shocked. She had no idea that George had known about her brother. Martha had known, of course.

She had always been understanding when she had to leave early or take a day off to help with her brother's care. Maybe she had told George about it.

"I know Katriona that you and your mother have the responsibility as carers for Hamish. Being confined to a wheelchair since his accident has put great strains on both of you. That's why I've decided that, if you'll take over Martha's work, and see to it that nothing delays us launching as planned, then Stellagenix will pay for a full-time carer." He paused. He had calculated that his offer would not only persuade her to take the job but that she would ensure nothing detrimental got to the media. She would have too much to lose.

Later in his office George allowed a smile to spread across his face. The secrets of the gene editing were safe. Dimitri was only too happy to ignore any health risks. He wanted the personal recognition for his work. He despised the media anyway. Katriona was too shy to talk to the media and would comply with any request from George in order to preserve the care package for her brother. And Martha was dead.

He reached for a Snickers bar.

51

The boys were reaching fever pitch as Christmas approached and were tearful when they heard that Mummy was going away to America. "You must get back quickly so we can write our letters to Santa Claus. You will be coming back quickly won't you?"

But they were in bed before either Claire or Andrew returned from work on Tuesday night. Claire had been frantically trying to finish everything off at the Agency and prepare her proposals for Stellagenix to take out. Andrew had been in the Chamber going through the rigmarole electing the Speaker and swearing allegiance. It all took a long time.

With no desire to talk when he eventually got home, Andrew offered to drive Claire to Heathrow in the morning.

It was as they were heading onto the M4 that Sara returned his call. The control panel on the Nissan flashed up the name 'Sara'. Claire looked at him quizzically. "Well are you going to answer it?"

Andrew pressed the button on the steering column. "Hi Sara, Can I ring you back. I'm driving my wife to the airport right now."

"Well yes, of course. We can speak later."

"New girlfriend?" Claire teased.

"No it was Sara. You remember, the vet? The one who baby-sat for us? She's got trouble with her visa and she's going back to Spain for Christmas. I think she wants reassurance that we'll let her back in!"

He dropped her as close to the terminal as he could. "Have a good trip and don't worry about a thing. I'll keep the boys out of trouble."

"Love you darling. Give my regards to the Queen tomorrow!"

With that she slung her laptop case over her shoulder and set off into the terminal dragging her small suitcase behind her.

Andrew turned the car towards London. A few miles on and he pulled into the services for coffee. He rang Sara.

"Andrew! I'm glad you phoned back. I'm at the airport here in Manchester. Just waiting for my flight to Madrid. But I wanted to tell you the good news. My friend who's doing the DNA tests on those bulls. He's sure he can get the results in the next couple of days, before Christmas anyway. I have arranged to meet him when I fly back after Christmas on the 30th. I'll meet him here at the airport when my Iberia flight lands."

"Great news. Anyway, have a great Christmas. I'm sure you're glad to be seeing your parents again."

"Yes, it's been a long time. But Andrew…"

"Yes?"

"I hope I didn't get you into trouble with Claire when I phoned?"

Andrew laughed. "I told her you were worried about Brexit and visas!"

"I do love you, you know Andrew."

With that the call ended. Andrew sat looking at the phone for some time as if expecting it to suddenly ring. He thought about his decision to cool their relationship. He thought about Claire. Life was beginning to go too fast. He had a feeling that it was rapidly coming to the time when he had to make a decision. A decision not based on careful analysis of data but on emotion. He couldn't have his cake and eat it. He would have to choose between a successful marriage and loving family and a beautiful Spanish girl who seemed so in tune with his aspirations to improve the world.

A little later George Krasnik was similarly staring at his phone. The recording of Andrew's call to Sara had just been played. It was decision time for him too. The DNA results would soon be in Sara's possession. Something must be done.

Claire boarded the American Airlines flight and settled down in her business class seat. She had expected George to join her on the flight but he'd rung to say he would not be coming over for another couple of days. "There's something I gotta do here first. I'm sure you can sort things out with Papplewicks. Just make sure they understand the importance of the British angle and what we've achieved here in Lincolnshire. They'll fill you in on the take-over talks."

So here she was. The international jet-setter. Flying off

to the States to meet with top brass. Claire Eastwood, the PR super-star. It felt good. This is what life was about. Being in the right place at the right time. Meeting with the movers and shakers. Making money!

She thought about her investment in Stellagenix shares. The options that she had taken on Amir's advice were due to mature straight after Christmas. If her campaign to promote Stellagenix resulted in a successful takeover bid they would go even higher. Already she stood to make a small fortune as the price was 20% above her option price. If it went up another 20% then she'd be looking at a seriously large profit. Amir had warned her that if the share price were to have dropped her options would be worthless and she would lose all her investment. But that was never going to happen.

She pushed the lingering thought of Andrew's conspiracy theory to the back of her mind. Nothing was going to stop her from succeeding. Donald Trump might boast about deal making but she had really done it. Behind the Donald's rhetoric there was a litany of failed investments. On the other hand her deal was a sure-fire thing.

She looked out of the cabin window as the plane levelled off having broken through the thick winter cloud cover and the low sun flickered its rays along the fuselage. She accepted the glass of Champagne from the steward.

"To life as it's meant to be lived!" she toasted herself. The man across the aisle smiled at her and raised his glass.

5 2

DECEMBER 31ST 2019, WANDSWORTH

Amir raised his glass to the guests. "Here's to a happy and prosperous 2020!"

It was New Year's Eve and the eight people around the table were in high spirits. Claire and Andrew had been forced to bring the twins with them as Analiese still hadn't returned from Austria. They were sleeping upstairs in the spare room.

Bob and Jane and Caroline and Connor raised their glasses in response.

"It's certainly a prosperous evening for me," laughed Bob. Our pubs are going to be crammed tonight. Best night of the year!"

"There'll still be a few people sitting at home watching a film. Just wish it was one of ours though. I mean, how many times can you watch 'The Italian Job' or 'Where Eagles Dare'?" Connor had two new films in production but they weren't ready for release.

"I just like the fact that my husband's been home for the past 10 days instead of at work." Jane was wearing a particularly revealing dress and Connor's eyes sparkled mischievously.

"We Brits do seem to be better at taking holidays than the Americans. Two days off for Christmas and they're back at their desks." Claire had been forced to go into the Agency twice since Christmas.

"Oh yes, I'd almost forgotten," said Amir, "How is our globe-trotting superstar? Getting ready to launch her stellar client into orbit?"

"Amir says they're making great breakthroughs in gene editing." Indra, the pharmacist, had been following the progress happening with CRISPR and was keen to know more about Stellagenix.

"Well yes. We have developed a new strain of barley that grows faster and bigger than any existing ones. We'll be announcing the latest results in the next few days. It will help produce more food for the world," she said proudly.

"So that's why you had to go off to the States just before Christmas?" Bob knew nothing about gene editing but did fly to the States frequently.

"Yes. I had to finalise our plans with the American PR company. But don't say anything to anyone. We're not making the announcement yet and when we do the share price is going to rocket," she said proudly.

Bob shook his head. "I don't even know what this gene editing business is. What did you have to do to get this new barley strain?"

It was Indra who answered. "Gene editing is one of the most exciting breakthroughs in biology ever. Scientists and biologists now have a way of changing the genome of a plant or an animal by cutting out bits of their DNA and replacing them with different bits. It could lead to curing all sorts of diseases."

"Or improving the yields of grain crops," added Claire. "Our laboratory in Lincolnshire has used this new technique to change the make-up of grain and wheat so that they grow faster and stronger."

Connor looked perplexed. "How the hell do you change someone's DNA? I thought everyone's was different and that's how detectives solved crimes. Now you're telling me that you can just go ahead and change them."

Claire looked at Indra for an answer. "It's complicated but now we can read a plant's or animal's genome – that's the millions-long sequence of their amino acids in their DNA - we can identify which bits cause certain traits, like a particular disease. Then we can work on their DNA or more accurately RNA and change it."

Andrew had been silent to this point. Now he broke in. "You may wonder how anyone could carry out this surgery on such a tiny, tiny thing. Something so small that you can't even see it under a microscope. But scientists have discovered ways of using a special bacteria which they can programme to find the precise bit of the genome and cut it out and replace it with some new sequence. I don't understand it really but it's something like that and Indra is right. It's going to revolutionise microbiology. We'll soon be able to design the perfect baby – one as clever as Amir and as beautiful as Indra!"

The group laughed. All except Indra. She looked worried. "It's a wonderful breakthrough but it's dangerous too. Interfering with a creature's genome could lead to unforeseen problems. After all don't they say every action has a reciprocal action or something like that? We might cure something but cause something else. There's a lot about this CRISPR research that worries me."

"Yes but Stellagenix's new grains are all approved by the relevant health bodies. They aren't going to poison anyone!" Claire spoke like a true PR manager. Andrew looked down at his drink. The response from Claire was like that of George when Sonya had asked him about American food exports. It was too glib. Toxicity tests were fine but those didn't allow for other changes that ingesting the product might cause. Had Stellagenix realised that their barley had unwanted side effects on people and animals that weren't picked up by toxicity tests?

"Wow, you're doing my head in. I never was good at biology at school," said Bob. "Let's talk about something more on my level."

"Do we really have to descend to sex again?" Connor smiled at his friend and once again there was laughter from the group.

Andrew joined in, but the talk had made him think of Sara. She had been due back in the UK yesterday and would have the results of the bulls' DNA tests. Maybe she'd give him a ring tomorrow. Or maybe it would be better if he rang her.

It wasn't until two days later that Andrew rang Sara's number. It went immediately to voicemail saying the number was not obtainable.

Andrew checked the number again. He was using his

new i-phone that Claire had given him for Christmas. Maybe he'd transferred the number wrong. But it checked out. He resolved to try a little later. He didn't want Claire around when he did it.

53

JANUARY 2ND 2020, LINCOLNSHIRE

The days in January are short in the Northern hemisphere. The further north, the shorter the day. Even the 150 miles between Wandsworth and Lincoln make a difference. The temperature can be colder too.

January 2nd was no exception. The sun, when it rose, was hidden by a thick layer of cloud. The temperature was barely a degree above freezing. The thick mist or fog that had lain across the flat ground still persisted. Few people ventured out unless they had to. It was the first day back at work for most although farmers maintained they worked 365 days a year.

For Thomas, a fitter who worked for a local farm equipment dealer, it was a chore to drive over to Grantham that morning. He drove slowly, aware of the danger of black ice and struggling to see more than a few yards ahead at times. But after a bit the wind got up and the fog began to lift although the temperature measurement on the van's dashboard still showed zero degrees.

He passed Otherby and approached the sharp bend that he navigated five days a week. The fields either side had been ploughed just before Christmas and now he looked at them with the eye of someone who made his living working on tractors. There was little traffic around and so he was still looking towards the deep dyke as he started to take the bend. He saw the deep scar in the verge and as his eyes followed the line of it he saw something glinting on the frozen water.

Concerned, he stopped the car and checking that there was nothing coming up behind him reversed towards the bend. He put on his hazards and got out. Almost immediately he changed his mind. It was bloody cold and what had he seen anyway? He got back into the van. But the image of the object in the icy dyke remained with him. What had it reminded him of? It was, it was a wheel. Yes, in that split second of seeing it he had realised that it was a wheel. Suddenly everything made sense. The scar across the verge, the wheel. Oh God. It could be an accident. A car could have gone off the road and into the dyke.

He got out again and pulled his coat around him. He walked back to the bend.

The phone reception wasn't great in this area but he managed to get through to the police. He described what he had found. It was definitely a vehicle, a small one by the size of the wheel protruding through the ice. The skid marks suggested it had left the road at high speed and the frozen water meant that it had happened a day or two before. He gave the policewoman the location details and his contact number. He had to get to work but they would phone him later once they'd investigated.

Thomas got back in the van and headed for Grantham.

It was Monday morning 6th January when Sonya Arkle phoned Andrew with the news. Police had recovered the car and Sara's body. Reports of the accident were on the local news including Lindum Radio but it wasn't until calls had been made to the Spanish police and Sara's parents had been informed that the details were released to the media.

Andrew was in his office in Victoria Street trying to catch up on issues affecting the NHS. He had a series of meetings fixed for the next few days. He also knew he would be spending a lot of time in the House of Commons. The whole House would be debating the Withdrawal Bill and seeking amendments over the next two days. Every vote was crucial. The news was mainly about Iran's response to the US killing of one of their top generals. The Labour Party was licking its wounds after its general election defeat and trying to sort out how to elect a new leader. The Scottish Nationalists were incensed by Boris's railroading of the Withdrawal Bill in December and were determined to lead the debate in Parliament. It might be Andrew's last chance to try and overturn the Brexit deal.

When Sonya gave him the news he was silent for a long time.

"Are you still there Andrew?"

Andrew mumbled something. His mind was racing. He felt his heart rate rise. But no words came. All he could see in his mind was the laughing face of a beautiful Spanish girl. He realised he would never again see her. Never again share a joke or share a bed. A huge part of his life, he realised, had been torn out. There was a gaping hole.

Sonya was filling in the details of the crash but Andrew hardly registered her words. He realised that he was crying.

The door to his office opened and his secretary looked at him. He waved her away with his hand and reached for a handkerchief.

He blew his nose, shook his head and started to listen to Sonya.

"She was on her way back from Manchester airport. It was dark and had started to snow. The police said her car left the road at the bend and turned upside down in the dyke. The roof was all bashed in and she might have been knocked unconscious. She was still strapped in when they found her."

Andrew's tears turned to anger.

"You know who did this, don't you? This was no bloody accident. She had the results of the DNA tests on the bulls. It's Stellagenix. They must have killed her to prevent her telling us the results."

"I think you might be right Andrew. It's just too convenient that first Martha and then Sara die in car accidents. But we can't be sure. I mean how would they know she was on her way back? How would they know she had the results? Did you know? I certainly didn't, so how could they?"

"I don't know but I'm sure it was them."

"Be careful Andrew. You're accusing someone here of murder. The police still think it was just an accident in bad weather."

"Sonya, you and I know it was murder. I'm coming up there. I'll leave first thing tomorrow. In the meantime keep me informed of any more news. Oh, and Sonya, take care. We don't want another 'accident'.

He sat at his desk, hunched over the document he had been reading on the shortage of nurses. He was still angry.

He wanted to hit something or someone but instead he kept clenching and unclenching his fists. He needed to think. Slowly his brain cleared and the analytical Andrew began to go through the events.

Sara was due to return from Madrid on the 30th. She had told him that when he phoned her. She had told him she was going to meet her friend with the DNA results at the airport. She would then have driven back that evening to Otherby. If he was right about the accident not being an accident it meant that someone at Stellagenix knew exactly when she would be driving that route. But how?

How did George Krasnik always seem to know what Andrew was doing? He had made that veiled threat about 'your Spanish girlfriend'. How did he know? He knew that Andrew had been meeting with Sonya too. How did he know these things?

The first thought was that Claire had told him. After all she spoke with George a lot. She had even been to the States with him.

Yet it couldn't be that. Claire certainly didn't know about his relationship with Sara. He went cold for a moment at the thought of her finding out. He might have mentioned that he had discussed the research methods of Stellagenix with Sonya and she certainly might have told George about Sara's suspicions about the twin calves. But that wouldn't explain how George knew exactly when Sara was due back in Manchester and that she was meeting her friend with the DNA results.

He tried to think back to the meeting with Sonya and Sara in the pub that evening. Something was swimming around in his head that he couldn't bring into focus. He had the feeling that something had happened that he had noticed as unusual. What was it?

He remembered the evening clearly. The jealous look on Sara's face when she had seen him huddled in conversation with Sonya. Then that intense concentration he loved as she discussed genome editing with Sonya. Then he thought back to their walk back to Limetree Cottage and their subsequent love-making. He realised the tears were rolling down his cheeks. The memories were too painful.

There was a knock on his door and his secretary poked a nervous head around it.

"Come in," he mumbled.

"Is everything alright Andrew?"

She knew it clearly wasn't. Junior ministers like Andrew weren't prone to tears. He was clearly upset.

"I've just heard that a very dear friend of mine has been killed in a car accident," said Andrew blowing his nose again. "I'm sorry, it's upset me."

"Oh I am sorry. Is there anything I can do? You have a meeting with the General Medical Council at 11.00. Shall I give them your apologies?"

"No. I'll be there." He looked at his watch. It was 10.55. "I may just be a little late."

"I'll tell them."

"Oh, and I won't be in Westminster tomorrow."

"But the debate?"

Across the city Claire was getting ready for a meeting too. Prospect Insurance were due in to discuss their decision to close their London office. The landslide victory for Boris Johnson and the other Brexiteers had made the decision inevitable.

"We're headed for a hard Brexit now. There's going to be a major problem with 'passporting'. If we have a hard Brexit, which I think we will, things could get really tricky for our finance sector in the City. Already many have done what we have and set up divisions in Europe. I just think that's the tip of the iceberg. Unless Boris gets agreement to 'passporting' in the next few months there'll be a mass exodus from the City."

"But closing your London office. That's pretty drastic. What about your UK business?"

"Well that's what we need to talk about. We don't want the news to get out yet, obviously. So we need to work on a strategy to control that. Let's meet."

"Will you be moving to Barcelona permanently?"

"Well I'll certainly be spending a lot more time there. I'm buying a property out there. Maybe you'd like to see it?"

Claire had mixed feelings as she waited for Clifton to arrive. She had just spent several days at home. At home with her husband and her children. She realised how much she had missed recently. Her life had certainly been full. It wasn't boring. She felt important, appreciated, worthy. Yes worthy. She was doing something that her clients appreciated. She was respected for her skills, something she had missed when her boys were younger and she was stuck at home.

But she realised that life was a trade-off. While she was jetting to Barcelona or New York, it was the Austrian au pair who was hearing the stories of what her boys had done at school that day. She wasn't there always to hear about their little adventures. And then there was Andrew. He was wrapped up in his new career but they seldom had time to talk about it. He worked late into the evenings when he was in Westminster or away at weekends in that little village in Lincs. Who did he get to talk to? Who did he now find to unburden himself on as he used to do before?

Then there came the guilt. It wasn't just that she wasn't spending enough time with the boys or Andrew. It was the deception. The affair with Clifton. Wasn't that selfish?

She had fallen in love with Andrew because he was serious about things. He cared about doing the right thing. He wasn't just an adrenaline junkie like so many of the other traders. To them, life was a game. And they played the game to win. For Andrew it was something to be worked at, to succeed at but not at the cost of others.

Did he care more about the twins than she did? It was she who had had to go through all the trials and tribulations of IVF when natural conception hadn't worked. Surely that meant she was committed to them? All he had done was to read a sexy magazine and provide a sample. No that was unfair. He had worried and worked at finding a solution too. But it was she who had to undergo all those intrusive tests. It was she who had submitted her body to the scientists. When the miracle happened and she became pregnant it all seemed so worthwhile. Yet now, here she was, rushing around with little or no time to nurture those very children she had conceived.

Andrew, on the other hand, seemed to be hell bent on changing the world to provide a better place for his children. His passion for saving the planet, for defeating Brexit and other things were all aimed at providing a better future for their children. What was she doing?

Paul Devorian, her boss, came over to her desk full of enthusiasm.

"So Claire. How did it go? Did you get everything sorted with the Yanks?"

Claire's brain switched back to Stellagenix. The trip had gone well. Very well in fact. The first two days she had worked with the American agency putting together the story for the media about how the takeover of Western Calapharm would be a natural fit. They had developed the narrative that agrochem and pharmaceuticals were an obvious combination now both could use the new CRISPR breakthrough to develop both medicines and new crops. The technology was the same for both. Gene editing that could improve plant yields could also be the solution to fighting disease. The manufacturing facilities that Calapharm had would be useful too. They had a subsidiary that made surgical masks and bandages which could be promoted to the NHS.

As she explained all this to Paul she could see his excitement and she felt it too. She also knew that her share options which matured in a few days were going to be worth a fortune once the merger was announced.

She explained how George had arrived on her last day and approved her plans for the UK. In fact he had seemed, for once, slightly distracted. It was probably the fact that he was looking forward to spending Christmas back in the US with his family. "He just said great to everything. Approved it then and there."

"So we're all ready to announce the results of the barley trials?"

"Absolutely. Just as soon as I can get the information pack ready. We should be on course to go next week. I'll try and get up to Lincolnshire early next week just to confirm some details with George and his geek Dimitri."

Once Paul left she turned her thoughts back to Clifton and Prospect Insurance decision to leave London. What would it mean for her? What would it mean for the Agency? Most of their work had been with UK-based investors, the UK financial press and other media. If Prospect switched the emphasis to Barcelona would they be looking to have a Spanish agency? What would this mean to her? The Barcelona visits might come to an end. She had always known that her affair with Clifton wasn't serious but somehow she had come to look forward to every trip. She loved the attention he paid her, and let's be honest she thought, I love the sex too.

Whenever Clifton came to the Agency in London he was careful to act professionally. He didn't even flirt with her. So far, she believed, Paul Devorian had no idea of her relationship with Clifton. Even Prithi seemed to accept that there was nothing in their relationship.

So when Clifton arrived, together with his marketing manager later that morning, she was wearing her business hat. The three of them sat and discussed the ramifications of moving out of London and what it meant. Nicole, his marketing manager knew Claire well as they often spoke about campaigns in England and the wording of press releases. When Clifton took a break and headed for the gents, Nicole turned to Claire and said. "You know he's in love with you, don't you?"

Claire was flabbergasted. She had assumed that no one at Prospect knew of their relationship either. What had Clifton been saying?

"Oh don't be silly." Claire ran her fingers nervously through her blonde hair and gave Nicole her most innocent smile. At least she hoped it was an innocent smile. She could feel her cheeks reddening. Did Nicole know that they slept together in Barcelona? Had Clifton told her, even boasted about it?

"I'm serious Claire. He's always talking about you and he says he wants you to come and work with Prospect in Barcelona."

"I'm flattered that he should think I'm that good but that doesn't mean he's in love with me. You know Clifton, he's always a one for the women. Comes out with the most outrageous things. He's not serious."

"He's deadly serious about you coming to live and work in Barcelona. He just hasn't summoned up the courage to ask you."

She was late home that night. The work for Prospect and Stellagenix meant she would be working flat out for several days. Despite Nicole's words Clifton had said nothing about her moving to Barcelona but he had asked her to put together proposals of how Repute could handle the account once it was headquartered there and not in London. George had rung her twice from the States to check on progress on the announcement of the barley yields and was due to meet her the following week when he got back to Britain.

So she was not happy when Andrew told her he was going to Otherby early the next morning.

"I thought you had a lot of work at the Ministry? What' so important that you have to drop everything and go up North? I thought the whips told every MP to be in the House to vote?"

She looked at Andrew who turned away before replying. "There's something serious come up with one of my constituents. I've got to be at a meeting in Lincoln to try and find out what's happened."

He couldn't face telling Claire what had really happened. Not yet anyway. It was all too raw. If he were right about Stellagenix it would cause a major issue with Claire too. He needed to find out more first.

"Can't you get Stan to sort it out? I thought that was an agent's job? Surely Brexit is more important?"

"No. Not this time. He doesn't know the background. I have to do it. I'll only be away a couple of days."

"Well it's really very inconvenient. I've got so much work on. You know we're going to announce the Stellagenix results next week. I'm going to have to be up there on Monday. Can't your meeting wait until then?"

"No."

"Look, Andrew, I shouldn't be telling you this but you'll know soon enough anyway. Stellagenix are making a bid for a firm called Western Calapharm. They are big in pharmaceuticals and medical equipment. I need to get the results really well promoted. It's the biggest challenge of my career." She didn't add that it would also ensure a massive profit for the Eastwoods when she exercised her share options. Andrew didn't need to know about that.

Still Andrew insisted that he had to go to Lincoln in the morning. "I'll try and be back early on Wednesday."

54

Andrew left early in the morning. It was still dark but the traffic leaving London was light. By the time he reached the A1M dawn was breaking and silhouettes of trees started to appear along the sides of the road. He headed North at a steady pace, a few miles per hour faster than the legal limit but not fast enough to attract a police car. He had arranged to meet Sonya in Lincoln so his journey didn't take him past the scene of Sara's 'accident'. He still was trying to figure out how George knew so much about him and exactly when Sara was returning from Spain. Despite Sonya's warnings not to jump to conclusions he was convinced that George was responsible for the deaths of both Martha and Sara. When Claire had told him about the prospective takeover bid it all made sense.

It was essential that nothing threw any doubt on the safety of the new barley strain. The announcement of the amazing field test results would send the share price even higher and make the subsequent takeover offer more likely to succeed. He knew that George's future depended on that successful outcome. It was motive enough to cover up what he suspected were the dangerous side effects of animals and humans consuming the GE barley.

The mystery of how George knew the details of Sara's movements, and indeed of their relationship remained.

It was Sonya who was first to solve the latter.

"I've been thinking," she said as she sipped her coffee. They had met in her small office at the Radio Station and were drinking machine coffee out of disposable cups. "You remember that night when we all met at the Barley Mow?"

"Yes"

"Well it was a really cold night as I recall. Every time someone came in you felt the draught of cold air. Well I looked up when Sara came in but she looked daggers at me and headed for the bar. But then almost immediately after there was another draught of cold air as someone else came in. I saw you look at him so I turned round. It was obvious he was a stranger. He didn't acknowledge anyone. I think he was following Sara. Did he stay long after I left?"

Andrew thought back. He remembered the stranger. He remembered thinking he had seen him somewhere before at the time. Was he still there when he and Sara left to go to the cottage? He couldn't remember He hadn't given it a thought. But it was strange. Otherby was hardly on any tourist trail or main road. He remembered the first time he had gone in how everyone had looked at him. You didn't get strangers in the Barley Mow very often. Perhaps Sonya was right.

"Have you found out anything more about Stellagenix from Claire?"

Andrew considered his reply. He was an MP after all and she was a news reporter. The takeover was absolutely confidential.

"Well I know they propose to release the results of the field tests next week. That's going to be really good for their share price."

"So that would make it easier for them to win a takeover battle wouldn't it?" said Sonya.

Andrew looked at her. She was the same age as Claire but wore her hair in a short style that accentuated her fine features. Her eyes, browny green he decided, were staring into his. There was a slight smile on her lips which he noticed were a darker shade than he remembered. Perhaps it was a new lipstick. She continued to stare at him, the muscles around her mouth twitching as she waited for him to reply.

"What takeover?" He tried hard to act innocently.

"Well I've been doing some digging on Stellagenix and I talked to a journalist in New York this morning. He says there's a rumour going round that Stellagenix is planning a bid for another company but no one knows which."

Andrew nodded. "Yes I think you could be right. But you didn't get that from me, or Claire. "

"So it's true?"

"I didn't say that."

"You didn't need to. That's our motive right there."

She continued to ask about the type of company Stellagenix might take over but Andrew tried to change the subject.

"Look Sonya, even if you're right about that stranger in the bar, it doesn't explain how they could have known precisely when she was flying back. And anyway they wouldn't have known that she was getting the bulls' DNA tested."

"Claire could have mentioned it."

"No Claire was already on a flight to New York when I spoke to Sara. That's when Sara told me of the tests, and when she was flying back. She told me she was meeting her friend at the airport after she landed."

"And you didn't tell Claire this?"

"No." Andrew looked embarrassed.

"No I suppose you wouldn't want Claire to know about you and Sara."

Andrew nodded sheepishly. "No one knew about Sara and me."

"That's not true. I knew, and that stranger in the pub probably knew too."

"How did you know? Who told you?"

"Andrew, it was obvious. The chemistry between you two was clear to see. I didn't need to be a journalist to see that."

There was silence for a few seconds. Andrew's brow furrowed. It always did when he was calculating. Sonya watched him. She knew not to interrupt.

"Do you think my phone was bugged?"

"Why?"

"Well I have to assume that Sara hadn't told anyone else about her flight arrangements or about meeting her friend with the results. Maybe she might have told the Vet Practice when she was returning but that wouldn't explain how George knew. She told me. It was me who phoned her back. Maybe Stellagenix hacked my phone. "

"In which case they know we're meeting now?" Sonya

looked worried. She had taken Andrew's advice about being careful. She didn't want to end up like Martha or Sara.

Andrew looked down at his phone.

"Look Andrew we've got a really good techie here. One of the sound engineers. What he doesn't know about phones isn't worth tuppence. Give me your phone. Let's get him to check it."

She picked up the desk phone and dialled. A few moments later a tall youth wearing an Iron Maiden T-shirt strolled in. Sonya explained that she thought Andrew's phone might have been hacked. He took Andrew's phone and gave it a cursory look. "The new i-Phone. Tasty. How long have you had it?"

"Only a week or so. My wife got it for me for Christmas."

Andrew looked as the youth swiftly slid off the rear casing revealing the battery and circuit board. He examined it briefly before clipping the case back on and passing it back.

"There's two ways to hack into a phone. Software and hardware. The i-Phone is more secure than an Android one. It's unlikely to be hacked. Maybe they could get your stored messages, like those reporters did years ago," he smiled at Sonya, "but they wouldn't be able to listen to your live phone calls."

"So that theory is blown!"

"No. I said there were two ways. The other is hardware. I've read some stuff and you can insert something in the phone that replicates it. Every time the user makes a call it also calls another number, the hackers. They can just listen in."

"But you said that someone would have to put that into the phone, physically?"

"Yes. There's nothing in this one but maybe your old phone?"

Sonya was listening intently. Now she spoke. "How could anyone get hold of your phone? Unless?"

"Yes?"

"When you go to Stellagenix what's the security like? I would assume it's pretty tight.

"Yes you go through a metal detector and all," said Andrew. "and you have to leave your phone with reception!"

"So what are you going to do, Andrew?"

"I should tell the police immediately, get them to look at both Martha and Sara's deaths as murder, not accidental."

"But you have no proof Andrew. Nobody witnessed either accident. The cars will have been examined for things like cut brake lines or whatever I'm sure. If the cars weren't tampered with what case have you got?"

Andrew thought for a moment. Part of him wanted to call the police and accuse Stellagenix right out. The other part of him, his usual analytical side called for a different approach. Sonya was right. He would need more evidence. He could get his old phone examined to see if it had been tampered with. Even that wouldn't be evidence that anyone, let alone George Krasnik, had caused the women's deaths.

There was also the fact that any accusation he made would be countered by Stellagenix claiming, accurately, that Sara and he were having an affair. He couldn't risk that with Claire. Yet to do nothing would leave him forever feeling guilty for Sara's death.

Sonya had a programme to present at lunch-time so Andrew left her, promising to keep in touch and headed for Otherby.

On the way he had second thoughts. He would go to the police in Lincoln and ask them what examination they had made of Sara's car. It would be the action of a concerned MP for a constituent. He would also need to get the contact details for Sara's parents. He must call them and see what he could do to help.

He turned the car round and headed back to Lincoln.

He spent the afternoon with not only the Chief Constable but also with the Registrar at Lincoln Hospital. The policeman was insistent that the weather conditions were responsible for Sara's crash. "We've taken measurements of the skid marks on the verge and it's clear that the young lady was travelling much too fast in those conditions. Probably hurrying to get home before the snow got worse and forgot about that bend. Easy to do in the dark. We get a lot of speeders on that road." He confirmed that the car controls seemed to be fine. "The car was pretty badly damaged. The roof had caved in when the car turned over and she may well have been knocked unconscious. We'll have to wait for the pathologist's report. They're doing the post-mortem right now."

The police chief looked at Andrew when he then asked about Martha's accident. "It's been a bad time for accidents recently in the county. We've been trying to get the speeding message out to the driving public but it seems we're fighting a losing battle. We don't have the manpower to patrol many roads and I guess people just think they're free to speed. Very unfortunate for that lady. She was a mother too. Very tragic."

"And you checked the controls on that car too?"

"What are you getting at Mr Eastwood? You're suggesting there's a link between these two incidents?"

"No, I'm not saying that. I'm just curious that both accidents seem to have happened with no witnesses and no other vehicles involved."

The Chief Constable regarded Andrew for a minute. Andrew wasn't saying that. He wasn't accusing anyone yet the policeman intuitively felt there was something Andrew wasn't telling him. He decided to have a word with the traffic sergeant who had attended each incident. He had to be careful these days to be seen to be doing his job right. There was an independent police commissioner now. He didn't need anything to upset him especially as his retirement was only months away.

Andrew unlocked the door to the cottage. He pushed open the door and stepped over the small pile of post before switching on the light. The place felt cold and empty despite the fact he'd left the heating on low over the Christmas break.

He went to the kitchen and opened the fridge. There was very little in it. Some eggs and a couple of yoghurts that were no doubt past their sell-by date. He thought back to that last morning when he had said goodbye to Sara. They had finished the bread, toasting the slices to have with scrambled egg that Sara prepared. She'd insisted on washing everything and tidying up before leaving.

He switched on the Nespresso machine and made himself a black coffee taking it into his study. He checked his watch. It was just after 7 here in England, an hour later in Spain. He took his mobile out and dialled the number. He didn't know whether her parents spoke English.

The Mendozas were extremely polite. In good English

they thanked him for his concern and offers of help to arrange for them to come over to England and collect Sara's body. "She was very fond of you, you know. She was always speaking about you. You'd been very kind."

Andrew's mouth went dry. He felt tears welling up. He still couldn't come to terms with her death. He still felt a responsibility. He could have, should have done more to stop Stellagenix.

He wondered if he should tell her mother that he believed her death not to be an accident. Would that make it better? No, it would probably make things worse. A car accident is like an act of God. Something that couldn't be foreseen, something that was unfortunate, unexpected. There was only God to blame. If he couldn't prove foul play from Stellagenix there was no point in distressing her parents more.

After the call Andrew stared for a long time out of the window. It was dark and rain was streaking down the glass. There were no lights. Everything was obscured. Without Sara there was just a big black hole.

He shook his head in a determination to stop wallowing in self-pity. He realised that he was hungry, having eaten little or nothing all day. The Barley Mow would provide him with food and maybe companionship. He felt a desperate need to re-join the world, to shed light on the darkness that lay outside the window.

By the time he had covered the few hundred yards to the pub, his anorak was wet-through and his trousers were damp and muddy. He pushed open the door and stepped into the light and warmth. Some coats were hanging on the hooks by the door and the matting was soaking wet from the dripping clothes. He added his anorak to the collection, ran his fingers through his hair causing a spray of water droplets to run down his jacket and face.

There were few people drinking. The night was not inviting for a walk to the pub. He walked over to the three men perched on stools by the bar. He was surprised to see one of them was Colin, the father of twins who had lost his wife so tragically. He realised that his theory about Stellagenix meant they would be responsible for her death too.

The men greeted him warmly and he pulled up a stool. Kevin, the barman, came over.

"Pint of bitter? We've got a new one now. No more Fentastic. This one's called Fentasy! Tastes the same to me but Jason says it's a bit stronger and he's used a new crop of barley."

Andrew turned to Colin. "It's good to see you Colin. How are the girls?"

"Yes I don't get out so much these days. The girls certainly keep me busy. They're growing so fast. Going to be strapping lasses I'm sure. The doctor says I must be feeding them too much!"

Andrew sipped his pint. The men were silent. They looked embarrassed, nervous. Eventually Ben, the oldest, spoke. "We were so sorry to hear about Sara, the vet. Such a terrible thing. And I know you and her were quite close."

"Yes we were," said Andrew realising that for the first time he wasn't denying their relationship. "I shall really miss her."

"I don't know how it could happen," said Ben. "She knows that road, like we all do, like the back of her hand. I just don't know what went wrong."

"I've been talking to the police today. They believe she was going much too fast and just lost control. There was nothing they could find wrong with the car."

"Terrible, terrible," Colin added looking morosely at his beer.

The conversation turned to other news. It was as if all four men wanted to try and forget the accident. Life had to go on.

Andrew ate his ham and chips without tasting them. He bought his companions a round of drinks and then headed back to Limetree House alone. He watched the end of the debate in Parliament on the television. He slept badly and was on the road back to London early.

55

Claire walked out of Paul Devorian's office along with Leonora. She had presented her plans for announcing the barley test results and also the subsequent announcement of the takeover bid for Calapharm. Leonora had made a couple of suggestions but overall her plans were approved enthusiastically.

"I just love the climate-change angle you've brought in," said Paul. "You've really captured the current mood. Greta Thunberg is making headlines all over the world at the moment and our telling people that the new strains of barley will help them grow stronger and more quickly with less water is going to get broader coverage than just the business pages."

"Yes, and if we follow that a couple of weeks later with Stellagenix's plans to link up with Calapharm and develop ways of improving human health too that should really ensure the deal goes through." Claire looked proudly at her two colleagues.

"And we'll have yet another big client to work on." Leonora smiled at the prospect.

Andrew had gone straight home. The first thing he did was to go to a local mobile phone shop and buy a basic phone and a put £20 of credit on it. He used it to make a quick call to Sonya and give her the number. You couldn't be too careful. Then he headed to Westminster ready to face the wrath of the Tory whips.

For once though his mind was not on the future of Britain and the EU. He knew that he had to decide what to do about Stellagenix. Back home he had pulled out his old phone from the desk drawer. He had no idea if the phone had been tampered with but would take the gadget back to Otherby and get Sonya's geek to look at it. He still believed that was the most likely way for George to be so informed about him and Sara.

By the time he got back home it was nearly midnight. Claire was waiting up for him. She was tired but excited to tell Andrew about her presentation on Stellagenix.

"I'm planning to go up there on Monday. I've sent the proposals to George this evening and just need to talk with Dimitri to check what he's going to say at the press conference."

"Press conference?"

"Yes. This is really big news and climate change is a big hook for the media. I'm emailing invitations to the farming media and the local media tomorrow. I've also prepared a pack for the financial press. The news should give a further kick to the share price and then next week we'll drop the bombshell that we're making a bid for Calapharm."

Claire reached across the table and picked up the bottle of Sauvignon Blanc. She topped up her glass. She raised it and looked for Andrew to do the same. But he hesitated. His brain was working overtime. How could he let her publicise the success of the barley trials when he knew that the new barley strain was responsible for both cattle and humans giving birth to 'super' twins? But he didn't know that did he? He believed it but he couldn't prove it. That was what the bulls' DNA results might have proved but those results were lost in the icy waters of the Lincolnshire Fens. If he accused Stellagenix then George would surely carry out his veiled threat to tell Claire about his affair with Sara. But if he didn't, it could lead to deaths for pregnant women like Colin's wife and he couldn't have that on his conscience. Whichever path he took there was an unhappy ending.

"What's the matter Andrew? Aren't you pleased for me? Paul Devorian is really happy, reckons we'll get the Calapharm account as well. I'll certainly get a great bonus." She could have added that when she traded her share options next week she would make an even bigger return on her investment.

"I'm worried that something's not right at Stellagenix and that they're trying to cover it up." There he'd said it.

"What are you talking about? The yields are fantastic, right off the charts. The new strain is a sure-fire winner. And I can tell you that we're expecting similar results from the new wheat strain we've been trialling." She didn't notice that she was identifying herself with her client, but Andrew did. It was 'we' not 'they' throughout.

"I think that the barley may be causing changes in both

cattle and humans that leads to cows and women developing twins, and fast-growing twins at that!"

"What nonsense! Where did you get that idea? The barley has passed all the regulatory tests. That's rubbish."

"I don't think it's rubbish. And I think your mate George knows there's a problem. The regulatory tests are for toxicity. OK so the new barley won't poison you or your animals but it does seem to have an effect on male sperm that produces twins and rapid growth!"

"Where did you get all this from? Since when were you an expert on biology?" Claire was tired but she wasn't going to allow Andrew to ruin her moment of success with Stellagenix.

"I've been doing a lot of research."

"You always do! What sort of research? What do you know about how we've produced this better strain of barley?" Andrew noted the use of 'we' again. He understood Claire's determination to make a success of her work for Repute, her agency. He knew that if the connection between the barley and the twins syndrome were proved that it would cause a major financial blow to Stellagenix and Repute.

"That's the problem. We don't know how Stellagenix produced this new strain. We believe they may have done gene editing to change the speed at which cells divide and grow, but we don't know. Stellagenix won't tell us. I asked you to ask George but I've not had an answer."

"Well that's a commercial secret. It's like asking for the formula for Coca Cola! Anyway I told you they are using the new CRISPR techniques like a lot of companies. Even Indra knew about that."

"Stellagenix are obviously determined to keep the actual

genome changes secret – they'll stop at nothing. Just look at what happened to Martha when they thought she was going to talk with a journalist."

Claire shook her head. She was confused. "Who's Martha?"

"Who *was* Martha you mean. She's dead. She was Dimitri's right-hand researcher and she was going to talk to Lindum Radio."

Claire was silent for a minute. Then she asked Andrew "I may have met her once but I don't remember. How did she die?"

"She apparently lost control of her car and smashed into a bridge."

"Well that doesn't prove Stellagenix wanted her killed. That's preposterous. Very tragic, I'll admit, but car accidents do happen."

"Rather too frequently it seems. "

"What do you mean?"

"Sara's dead too!" The words came out in a low whisper. His eyes were moist. He reached in his pocket for a handkerchief and blew his nose.

"Sara?"

"You remember, the Spanish vet who babysat for us? She's been concerned from the start about the incidence of twin calves. She believes, believed, that it was caused by two bulls eating cattle food made from the Stellagenix barley. She thinks that it was also behind Colin's wife dying giving birth to the twins after Colin had ingested the barley through the local beer." As he said this Andrew knew it sounded far-fetched yet the results of the bulls' genome testing would have proved it one way or another.

Claire wasn't thinking about the implausibility of the accusation. She was looking at her husband. She knew her husband well. He was meticulous when it came to research. He was always unimpressed by arguments that weren't backed up by facts, yet here he was spouting wild theories raised by some young Spanish girl. What hold had this girl had on him?

She thought back to the time she had met Sara. There was something at the time that had briefly flashed a warning to her subconscious. What was it? She couldn't recall. She'd not given it further thought. But now… She looked at Andrew as he blew his nose again.

"What happened to her?"

Andrew started to explain how she was meeting a friend to get the genome testing results of the bulls. How she had then left to drive to Otherby but had ended up dead in a dyke on the way. "She was lovely. She was too good to die like that!" He realised he was sobbing. He couldn't help it. His anger of the past two days had finally turned to grief.

Call it feminine intuition but Claire instantly knew. "Were you sleeping with her?"

Andrew regarded her with tear-filled eyes. He hesitated. His analytical brain computed as he formulated his answer. To admit it would cause unknown consequences for his marriage. But to deny it would mean lying to his wife. And if he went ahead with his denouncement of Stellagenix George would undoubtedly tell Claire about his affair anyway.

He didn't need to reply. His hesitation was enough to convince Claire.

"You were, weren't you? Don't deny it. I can see it in your face. How could you! And then spouting all this nonsense about bulls' genome!"

Then she burst into tears. "How could you, Andrew?"

"I'm sorry, so sorry Claire."

"Don't touch me. Go away!"

She stormed out of the kitchen and ran upstairs to their bedroom.

Andrew slept on the sofa that night.

5 6

Claire was up early. It was obvious to Andrew that she had
slept badly. She was made up, had a smart business suit on
but her eyes looked bloodshot. He tried to engage her in
conversation, to continue the previous evening's discussion
but she ignored him.

"I don't want to talk to you right now. You've hurt me."
She left for the office without even a cup of coffee.

Andrew went up to the bedroom where he showered and
shaved before joining Analiese and the boys for breakfast. If
Analiese had heard them arguing the previous evening she
didn't let on. He offered to take the boys to school. It wasn't
far and he walked with them through the crowded streets.
They ran into the playground, happy and oblivious to the
fact that their parents weren't even speaking.

As he was walking back to the house his phone rang. It
was Sara's boss. Andrew had spoken to him briefly earlier in

the week to get the phone number for Sara's parents. "Hello Andrew. I just wanted to check if you're down in London right now or are planning to come back up here."

"Both, I'm due to meet someone in Lincoln this afternoon."

"I just wondered. You see Sara's Dad phoned last night to say they were both coming to England this morning to identify Sara's body and make arrangements. They're flying into Heathrow about 10.30 this morning."

"I could pick them up and drive them up with me to Lincoln."

"Exactly. I thought you might want to do that. Poor people, they're so distraught. We all miss her terribly."

The Mendozas were surprised but grateful when he met them at Terminal 2 Heathrow. "We thought we'd have to rent a car and drive to Lincoln. After what happened to Sara we weren't happy to drive on your English roads." Mr Mendoza was a stocky man of about 60, Andrew reckoned. He had a quiet manner and took Andrew's hand in both of his when they shook. He wore a thick dark brown leather coat, but no hat. His grey hair was cut short but showed no signs of receding. Indeed it was thick and wavy and Andrew mused that Sara had inherited her hair from him. He was wheeling a small overnight travel case as was his wife. Mrs Mendoza was as tall as her husband but far slimmer. She wore a dark blue wool coat that came to mid-calf. Long brown leather boots peeped from below. Andrew was struck by her resemblance to Sara. Twice her age and with dark black hair that was cropped short and probably dyed. Nevertheless the features of her face and in particular the eyes painfully reminded him of what he had lost.

As they drove north it was Mrs Mendoza who carried the conversation. Indeed it was as if by talking she could keep her grieving at bay. She told Andrew how proud they were of her, how they had known from her early age that she would end up working with animals. "And she was very fond of you, Andrew. She said you were kind and helped her with her visa."

Andrew looked at Mrs Mendoza's reflection in his driving mirror. He couldn't tell if Sara had told them about her affair with him.

"I was very fond of her too. I feel like I've lost one of my best friends."

"I'll take you to Otherby where Sara lived first. I have a house there and you can stay if you'd like."

Her mother smiled. "That's so kind but I think it would be better if we stayed at a hotel in Otherby."

"Well I'm afraid Otherby doesn't boast a hotel but before I bought the house I used to stay at the village pub. Not exactly the Ritz but quite comfortable and you'd be close to Sara's flat."

They both nodded. "That will do fine if you can arrange it. But then we must go to Lincoln to see the, the, Sara." Mr Mendoza swallowed hard.

Andrew nodded and mumbled '"No problem."

There was a long silence as the three of them stared out of the window at the passing fields.

The Murco sign was illuminated and appeared ahead out of the mist rather as a runway landing light does at Heathrow. Andrew lifted his foot off the accelerator and car slowed as it approached the light. It was only three in the afternoon but the January days were short here with the mist suspended in the cold air.

The garage was still open which was important. Andrew had been running on the reserve tank since turning off the A1. Thirty miles of twisting, flat road and deep dykes lay behind him. He hadn't passed a petrol station. He was used to that by now; the relative isolation of his constituency. The lack of traffic, of shopping malls, of industry.

They drove first to the Barley Mow where Kevin welcomed the Mendozas and showed them their room. Then they headed off to Lincoln.

Andrew dropped them at the hospital having arranged for them to be taken to the morgue. "I have a meeting in the city but afterwards I'll pick you up and we'll go back to Otherby unless you have other plans."

"We have no plans." Mr Mendoza turned sadly to Andrew, "We haven't had time to plan. It's all been such a shock."

His English was impeccable and he spoke clearly and deliberately. "Well ring me as soon as you are ready here. "

Sonya was waiting for him at the radio station and he handed her his old phone. Her sound engineer man joined them. He unclipped the back and looked inside. He nodded. He then shook his head as if in disbelief. Finally he pulled out a very small screwdriver. Seconds later he held up a slim silver box about the size of postage stamp. A wire dangled from it. "Very neat. Not seen one like this before. But it's definitely not an original part of the phone. You've been bugged mate!" He handed it to Andrew.

"Don't lose that Andrew. You'll need it as evidence." Sonya spat the words out and he realised that she was thinking, like him, that this was proof that Sara had been killed on George's orders. Proof to Sonya and him but not to a court.

"I've just dropped her parents off at the morgue. I brought them up from Heathrow. They're such nice people. So polite. But I can tell they're dying inside."

"Yes, no one deserves to have a child die before them. Do they still believe it was an accident?"

"Yes, I think so. They said something about British roads."

"Do they know about you and Sara?" Sonya was used to interviewing guests and was not pulling her punches with Andrew.

"I don't know. She'd obviously told them that she knew me and I'd helped her. I don't know if she'd said anything else."

"So Andrew what are you going to do? You've got a lot of evidence now against Mr Krasnik but there's other things to consider." She looked meaningfully at him. "If you bring this out George is going to tell your wife all about you and Sara. Are you prepared to do that?"

"I've already done it. She knows we were lovers."

"He's told her?"

"No I did, last night."

"What did you say?"

"Well nothing really. She just sort of guessed. She didn't give me time to deny it."

Sonya nodded slowly. She reached across the desk and took Andrew's hand. "We women can read men like a book. How did she react?"

"She was pretty upset. I mean it wasn't just the affair. We'd been arguing about Stellagenix. I told her of our suspicions of foul play and a cover up of the harmful effects of the barley. She just said it was all my imagination. It's her biggest client and she's just about to present the results to the nation's press. It would destroy her career."

Did you tell her about your phone?"

"No, I didn't get round to that. Nor did I mention that strange man in the Barley Mow. I didn't go into details about the local brewery nor the fact that Sara had identified the two bulls. Before I could tell her any of that she just came out and said "So you were sleeping with her then?""

Sonya patted his hand. "I can see where she's coming from. It must have been pretty devastating. First of all you want to destroy her biggest client and thus her career and then she discovers you've been unfaithful. I'm surprised she didn't kick you out."

They talked for a while longer. Finally Sonya stood up. "Look Andrew it's your call. As I see it, and I'm trying to be dispassionate although I'm seething underneath, you can go public with your allegations that the barley causes birth defects but you haven't got definitive proof of that. You don't have the bulls' genome results. You could go further and accuse Stellagenix of killing both Sara and Martha but the only real evidence you have is that little silver box there. Or you could do nothing, try and patch things up with Claire and move on."

"If I did that how would I live with myself if there were further incidences of dangerous pregnancies caused by the barley? What if someone else lost their wife like Colin did?"

"I don't think that's likely. I'm sure the brewery will use different barley in future."

"Yes, they are already. But if this barley goes into full

production then every brewery in the country might be using it."

"There's one hell of a story here. I'd love to be the one to break it." Sonya's journalistic traits were kicking in. "But I need you to support me. Stellagenix is pretty popular round here what with the new sports centre and promises of more jobs. Also I wouldn't want George going for a hat-trick of murders, I am pretty keen to stay alive."

Andrew nodded. She was right. Was there enough evidence to convict George Krasnik? The phone bugging was not evidence that he had arranged for Sara to be killed, let alone Martha. Would an exposé of the health effects of the new barley and the skulduggery of Stellagenix in trying to suppress the information be enough? What would be the effect of that on the Mendozas? What would it do to Claire's career and their marriage?

"Look, I've got my programme starting in 30 minutes so I need to go and prepare. Maybe we can catch up again tomorrow?" Sonya picked up the files from her desk. Andrew's phone rang.

"I'm on my way. I'll see you at the main entrance."

57

Claire was the first to arrive at the Agency. She let herself in and, nursing a coffee, started to go through the final preparations for the Stellagenix Results launch. So when the phone rang she at first decided to leave it. Eventually though she picked it up, half expecting it to be Andrew.

It wasn't. George Krasnik had been brought up on early meetings and didn't consider that the British were rarely at their desks before nine.

"I got your proposals, Claire, and they're great. Simple but great. That's exactly what we need. After all with increased yields north of 20% the press should go wild."

"Not to mention the shareholders," said Claire thinking about the value of her share options she had bought. They were executable on Monday.

"Indeed and our friends at Calapharm are going to be wagging their tails with excitement to be taken over by us." Claire said nothing. "I see you didn't want poor Dimitri speaking at the press do?" There was an implied criticism in George's comment and she hesitated before answering.

It was true that she had proposed he be kept away from the press. She hadn't understood half of what he had gone on about last time and the press didn't seem interested. They were interested in the results not the method. But at the back of her mind were the accusations that Andrew had made last night. She had to admit that she didn't know herself exactly how Dimitri and his team had modified the plant to get such results.

"Well George, I've been thinking about that. He's not a great speaker, is he? On the other hand maybe the press would like to know about our research methods. I mean you've obviously been gene editing to transform the plant. Maybe you should give some details of exactly what that involved."

"Or maybe not, Claire. Some people get very touchy about gene editing although how they expect us to improve plants without it beats me."

"But the new strain has passed all the tests hasn't it? I mean the regulators are happy."

"Hey Claire, what are you driving at? Of course the product's safe. What makes you think it isn't?"

Like Sonya, Claire was amazed at the vehemence of George's defence of the product. She had only mentioned the regulators yet he seemed too eager to kill the conversation.

"That husband of yours hasn't been filling your head with his conspiracy theories has he?"

"No, of course not," she answered.

"Good. Well get everything printed and I'll see you here on Monday."

After she put the phone down she was thoughtful. There was something about that conversation that worried her. She had been mad with Andrew for raising doubts about the product's safety and then shocked to learn of his infidelity. She hadn't slept much. But why did George ask her if Andrew had raised the issue of safety? How did he know that Andrew and Sara had been investigating? That was the problem with George. He always seemed to know what was going on. He knew an awful lot about Claire and Andrew's life it seemed.

She thought about ringing Andrew but decided not to. She hadn't forgiven him. She sat, trying to work out what to do. In all their years of marriage they had never failed to make up after an argument. But this hadn't been an argument. It had been a confession. A confession that her husband had been having an affair with a younger woman! She had been tired and reacted badly when he had gone on about Stellagenix causing birth defects. It was preposterous and he didn't seem to realise how undermining that was. She had left the Agency last night in a euphoric mood, everyone had loved her work on the presentation and then her husband wanted to pull the rug from under her. And in the midst of that scene he had admitted adultery!

Now she tried to be practical, to consider things carefully. That's what Andrew always did. Having just spoken to George she was beginning to think that just maybe Andrew and Sara had something. She hadn't actually let Andrew explain any details of their investigation. She had just dismissed it out of hand. She thought bitterly about the discovery that he'd had an affair with Sara. What had he actually said? She realised that he hadn't said anything. It was her who had accused him, out of the blue. He hadn't admitted it. But then he didn't need to. She knew Andrew too well. His hesitation, his face, said it all. No he had definitely been sleeping with Sara. She looked at the calendar on her desk. It was a pictorial one of Barcelona. Wasn't she just as guilty as Andrew? She had managed to convince herself that her flings with Clifton weren't anything serious and Andrew would never know. Was Andrew's affair with Sara any different?

What should she do? She realised that she had been so caught up with her work that she had neglected Andrew. She hadn't gone up at weekends to Limetree House. She really hadn't made any attempt to get to know his constituency. There had been so much to do here in London. Life was full on. With Prospect Insurance, Stellagenix and the electric car account it was no wonder she didn't have time to play the MP's wife. Andrew couldn't expect her to.

She thought about the money she was earning. Wasn't that necessary now Andrew's salary was so much lower than at Templeton? She continued to try and justify it to herself

The real question was what she should do. Last night she had thought about divorce, she was so mad at him. But now, well, she couldn't keep up her anger. So, he had had an affair. So had she. His wasn't going to continue, Sara was dead. She still continued to see Clifton. In fact she had learned yesterday that he wanted her to move out to Barcelona with him and work for Prospect. Didn't that make her worse than him?

Then there was Stellagenix. Obviously Andrew had fallen for Sara's cock and bull story (she smiled at the pun) of the barley turning into cattle feed and causing multiple births although she couldn't remember how he had then said the barley was causing human births to be affected too. I mean, he had obviously been captivated by the young Spanish girl and that was clouding his judgement. If she sat him down and talked it through sensibly she could persuade him that he was barking up the wrong tree. Then maybe they could make up. She would go ahead with the press launch, she'd tell him about her killing on the shares that she had bought through Amir and would promise to try and spend more time up in Lincs. She would agree to forget about his dalliance with Sara and she would call an end to her romance with Clifton, at least for now. Barcelona was just not on.

She phoned home but the call went unanswered. She looked at her watch. It was nine o'clock and the office was beginning to fill with people. Andrew is probably taking the kids to school she thought. I'll try later.

Her phone rang again. She picked it up ready to talk to Andrew. Again it was George.

"Claire, where's your husband today? Are you bringing him up to the press launch on Monday? I mean it's good for his image to be seen with Stellagenix."

"I don't know if he can come up on Monday. There's still so much happening on the Withdrawal Bill in Parliament. I think he'll have to be in Westminster." She didn't answer his question concerning Andrew's current whereabouts.

"I thought he must be taking a vacation. I haven't heard a word from him since Christmas. Is he still with you in London?"

"Yes, yes of course. He's just very busy I think with Parliamentary things, you know."

She put the phone down. How strange? Why would

George expect to hear from Andrew in the past couple of weeks? Did Andrew normally ring him a lot? She didn't think so. Why did he want to know where he was? If it had anything to do with Stellagenix, the sports centre or such like he would surely have asked her. She was his PR manager after all. The Sports Centre had undoubtedly been good for Andrew's re-election campaign but other than that Andrew had no reason to call him. Except that he had. The safety issue, of course, Andrew might have rung him about that. But no. George was complaining that he hadn't heard from Andrew, not that Andrew was pursuing an investigation against him. Another thought struck her. George had only just got back from the States. So of course he hadn't been in touch. Why would he suddenly be asking what Andrew had been up to since Christmas?

Claire's anger at Andrew had totally subsided. In its place was a nagging doubt that he might just be right about Stellagenix. Something wasn't right.

Andrew was sitting in the Barley Mow having dinner with the Mendozas when Claire called him. The Mendozas looked exhausted. It wasn't surprising with the travel and the ordeal of identifying their daughter's body. He realised that they had hardly eaten all day. Kevin had done everything to make them feel at home and prepared the meal. He had refused to charge for the room. "I wouldn't hear of it. You're Sara's parents and we all loved Sara."

He saw Claire's name on the screen. He was about to answer when a thought struck him. He was using his new mobile but Claire still had her trusty Samsung. He needed to be careful. He pressed the button and spoke rapidly.

"Claire, I'm sorry, I'm with someone right now. Can I call you back? Are you at home?"

He hated to cut her off. He didn't know whether she was still mad at him. He supposed she was and refusing her call wouldn't help.

He excused himself and got up from the table. He walked to a quiet part of the bar and rang the house land line.

Claire answered the phone immediately.

"That was quick!"

"Yes, I didn't want to talk to you on your mobile, I can't explain now."

There was no reply from Claire. He wondered why she had rung him.

"Look Claire. I'm so sorry. I know I've hurt you, I.."

"You have but that's not why I'm phoning." She took a breath before continuing. "Andrew I know you believe in all these conspiracy theories and must be very upset at what happened to Sara but we need to talk about it. "

"I'm actually with her parents now. They've come over to sort out her things."

"No I'm not talking about her. I mean we need to talk about Stellagenix."

There was a silence. Andrew couldn't believe what he'd heard. Here he was with the grieving parents of his, his dead girlfriend, and his wife wanted to talk about her bloody client presentation. At least she wasn't still yelling at him for sleeping with Sara.

"Andrew, there may be something in what you say about their research methods, I don't know and I'm certainly not going to pull out of Monday's launch. But maybe I should come up and we could talk about it, and everything else."

"What about the boys? Will they be alright with Analiese?"

"Yes, she's happy to do that. Your Mum has said she'll come over and help too. I said that you'd come back either Saturday night or Sunday morning. I'm assuming you have a lot of catching up to do in Westminster now the Withdrawal Bill has been passed. I'll stay at Limetree House and go over to Stellagenix on Monday morning."

She had it all worked out, thought Andrew. So typical of her. She gets an idea into her head and runs with it. Nevertheless he wanted to talk. He knew he'd hurt her by sleeping with Sara. And he needed to tell her about the phone.

5 8

Andrew watched from the station entrance as the train from Kings Cross pulled into Grantham. He waved to Claire as she struggled through the barrier with a wheeled suitcase, a laptop bag and a small rucksack.

He took the case from her and led the way to his car. He didn't kiss her. He was nervous, just like a person on their first date. Not knowing whether he would be rebuffed if he tried. After all, her last words to him in London had been "Don't touch me!"

She smiled at him as she fastened her seat belt. "You know we're going to have to get a second car if we keep doing this."

Andrew's heart leaped. His worst fears receded. She wasn't going to break up with him because of what he'd done. She was talking of a future together.

"Train pretty bad was it? Very crowded?"

"No plenty of room but it's just getting through London. Wandsworth to Kings Cross took almost as long as the train to Grantham."

"That's the problem with London. It's so congested." Andrew was still trying to convince her that the countryside, even the bare fields of Lincolnshire, were preferable to stinking London."

"Do you fancy some lunch? I think there's quite a nice place near Ancaster if you like."

"Why don't we go straight to Otherby? That local of yours serves some sort of food doesn't it?" For a young woman used to the choice of world cuisine always available, always close by, her expectations of pub food in Lincolnshire were not high.

When they arrived at the Barley Mow it was practically deserted. Kevin was standing behind the bar talking to a couple of men Andrew didn't recognise. He broke away to greet Andrew and Claire. "Sara's parents have gone off to her flat to try and sort things out. Dave's with them. He came over and offered to drive them down. Terrible for them." He looked at Claire. "Such a lovely lass too."

"Yes, tragic," said Claire. She wasn't sure how she felt about Sara's accident.

They sat at the table in the corner. Andrew felt safer that they were talking on neutral ground, not in the cottage. He hoped it would prevent Claire making a scene. On the ride back from Grantham she had said little of consequence, mainly remarking on the bleak landscape and how few cars were on the road. When they came to the bend outside Otherby she had leaned forward and looked across to the dyke. "Was this where it happened?"

"Yes. The car just ploughed straight through over there."

The grass still bore the scars of the heavy trucks called to winch the car out of the water.

Claire said nothing more but she was thinking hard. She couldn't help thinking that Sara must have been driving very fast to miss the signs and chevrons that marked the bend. She was a local after all. Obviously not a careful driver.

Once Kevin had brought them their food, scampi and chips for Andrew and an omelette and salad for Claire, she spoke about Stellagenix for the first time.

"Tell me Andrew exactly why you think there's something wrong with the new barley?"

Andrew described how Sara had brought up the incidence of several twin births with cows in the area and how it was unusual. He told her that Sara had discovered all the twins were the result of cows mating with just two bulls. She had then checked back to earlier years but these bulls had not fathered twins. So she put it down to their feed. Something, she said, had changed them genetically which was causing them to father twins.

"That can't be right," Claire interjected. "You know as well as me that it's the female that causes twins. I thought you knew that after all we went through with the IVF?"

"Yes I know. Twins like ours occur when more than one egg is fertilised at the same time and can happen naturally if the woman produces two eggs at the same time. So the man doesn't cause that. Identical twins however are when a single egg is fertilised and then splits in two producing two children of the same sex sharing exactly the same DNA. What causes it to split we don't know. So that could be something caused by the male."

"And all these calves were identical twins were they?"

"Apparently yes, although one calf looks the same as any other as far as I'm concerned." Andrew tried to lighten the conversation. It felt strange to be talking genetics with a wife who only yesterday he thought might be going to divorce him. He marvelled at the fact that she seemed more interested in talking about cows than their future together. But then, he mused, that's so typical of her. That's what had attracted her to him straightaway. She latched onto an idea and ran with it but then was capable of completely switching horses and racing off in a different direction.

"So what's the connection to barley from Stellagenix? After all we've not started selling it yet. It's only just passed its trials."

"Well that's the thing you see. Some of the trial barley was sold. Animal feed to the farmer who owned the bulls and a little brewery that makes the beer here. They both bought it cheaply from the farmer who grew it for Stellagenix."

He went on to explain the theory that Colin's identical twins were a result of Colin drinking beer made with Stellagenix barley.

"OK. I admit that there is a coincidence that twins were born after cattle-feed and beer made from the same barley but that's hardly proof that the barley was responsible. I mean how could eating or drinking barley change things like that? It sounds preposterous."

"We don't know what Stellagenix had done to get the new strain to grow so fast. But there's obviously a connection with growth here. The quicker cells split the faster growth you get. That's the problem with cancer cells. With the barley, faster cell growth is a bonus, a big bonus. But if it made animal cells, even the initial fertilised egg, split and grow too quickly that would be dangerous."

Claire looked at him. She knew how he had prepared his arguments for investing in certain companies at Templeton. There was the build-up and then the sucker punch as he revealed news of an imminent takeover, or innovation. There was always a sucker punch. She waited.

"The calves are growing up much faster than normal, and so are Colin's two girls. 'Strapping lasses' he calls them."

"But that's still not evidence that there's something wrong with the barley."

"No, that's why Sara had arranged to get the bulls' DNA tested alongside two normal bulls. The genome sequencing would show if there was any difference in the genes. She had the results with her when she crashed. I've asked the police if they found her laptop. I haven't heard."

Claire picked at her omelette. So this was Andrew's great theory. She had to admit that it was plausible although she didn't understand all the ins and outs of gene-editing and the use of CRISPR or whatever he had called it. But she knew Andrew had studied it and was not prone to conspiracy theories. She also had a strange feeling after her last conversation with George. Was there something she didn't know about. After all he had been reluctant to bring Dimitri out into the open again. Another thought struck her.

"Andrew, why did you answer my call and say you were with someone and then immediately phone me back? That didn't make sense."

Andrew explained about finding his phone had been bugged and his worries that her phone had also been tampered with. "I didn't want George knowing I was up here."

She nodded and turned her attention to her omelette. They ate in silence for a while. Andrew waited for her to speak. He anticipated that she would start to probe about his affair with Sara. He still didn't know how to reply to her accusations. It would be trite and untrue to say that it had meant nothing, it was just a one-night-stand. But to admit that he had had formed a deep relationship with the young girl would hurt Claire even more.

Finally she looked up from her food, wiped her mouth with the paper napkin and spoke to Andrew. "So what you're saying is that George knows there's a health risk with this new barley and that George was prepared to kill two people to keep it quiet in case it affected the Calapharm takeover?"

Surprised, Andrew nodded. "Exactly. That's exactly what we think."

"We?"

"Sonya and me. Maybe we can't prove it yet but we're convinced. The phone bugging is the clincher."

"And Sonya is who? Another one of your girlfriends?"

Andrew explained his connection with Sonya and was relieved to see that Claire accepted his explanation. In fact he couldn't get over the fact that she seemed to be more concerned about his theory on Stellagenix than his adultery with Sara. So far she had asked nothing about that.

"So what are you and this Sonya going to do?"

"I don't know. I just don't know. "

"If it's true and you can prove it then you realise that I'll probably lose my job. You could lose your seat too as I'm sure your relationship with Sara would be exposed. Your constituents wouldn't approve of that. They're so conservative up here."

Again Andrew marvelled at his wife's approach to life. She was, for the moment at least, not the screaming wronged wife, all emotion and accusations. She was taking an approach more like his own. A practical approach. Weighing up the evidence and trying to come to a decision that would be best. Best for who? Best for Stellagenix? For her career? For his career? For their marriage?

He realised that she was waiting for him to reply. "As I said, I really don't know what to do. I can't prove anything yet. I've got to try and get more proof."

"And the press announcement is less than three days away."

"Yes, I know."

"I think I have to go ahead with the press launch of the results. I'm not as convinced as you that there's any connection between the barley and the cell-splitting problem you're suggesting. You may be right but the jury's still out."

Andrew said nothing.

Kevin came across to clear their plates. "Anything else?"

"Yes can I have a glass of white wine? Sauvignon Blanc if you have it please?" Claire looked at Andrew again. "Anything for you?"

"Yes, I'll have the same."

They had both been drinking mineral water up until now. Andrew took it as a good sign.

They drove the few hundred yards to the cottage. Claire walked around the rooms as if she had never seen them. Was she looking for signs of Sara having lived there? Andrew didn't know. He followed her on her tour of inspection. Finally, back in the kitchen she opened the fridge which revealed its meagre contents. "You really need to get yourself sorted in here. It's like a student flat. You need to get it stocked up."

"I've not been up here recently," he apologised.

"We need to go shopping. Where's the nearest supermarket. If I'm staying up here until Tuesday I need some food in the place."

59

The sun was barely above the horizon as Andrew and Claire set off for Grantham. Claire was driving and she adjusted the car mirror to prevent the sun's reflected rays blinging her. There was hardly any traffic at all on the flat roads as they wound their way first to Ancaster and then on to Grantham.

She dropped Andrew outside the station and headed back to Otherby.

The train from Newcastle was late and Andrew walked up and down the platform clutching a polystyrene cup of coffee while he waited. It had made sense for Claire to keep the car. She would need it for her meeting with Stellagenix tomorrow and he would be using public transport in London anyway.

The train was later still by the time they arrived in Kings Cross. Andrew had passed the journey reading two of the Sunday papers and their coverage of the week's shenanigans in Parliament. He hadn't looked at his phone to see if there were any more emails since last night. He still didn't quite know what Claire was thinking. They hadn't spoken about Sara at all on Saturday. After a shopping trip to Sleaford they had had a meeting with Stan.

Stan had not been pleased. Why hadn't Andrew been in Parliament on Tuesday for the first day of the Withdrawal Agreement debate? "What was so important that you had to rush up here? Why couldn't I have done whatever it was?"

Andrew had looked at Claire before responding as if seeking approval for what he was about to say. He explained that one of his constituents in Otherby had died in a car crash and that he felt he had to see if he could help as her parents were in Spain. Stan had obviously not been convinced and had continued to grumble.

Claire and he had slept together in the cottage but there was no intimacy. It seemed Claire was determined to concentrate on her role at Stellagenix and put off talk of Sara until later. Andrew was content for that.

He took the Underground from Kings Cross to Vauxhall and a cab from there to his home.

He was surprised not to find anyone in. There was an appetising cooking smell from the kitchen and he saw that there was a chicken cooking in the oven. On closer inspection he realised the oven had switched off – presumably on a timer. There were vegetables cut and in a saucepan on the table. He looked at his watch. It was nearly 2pm. Why was no one here? Why wasn't the Sunday lunch ready?

He had phoned his mother first thing that morning and told her he would be arriving around 1pm.

He looked at his phone to see if there were any messages

or missed phone calls. No. Then he saw the note on the table. "We've gone to church. We'll be back by 12.00. Just in case you get here earlier than you said. Mum."

They're very late, he thought. He went to the fridge, helped himself to a beer he found there and switched on the small television set.

The newsreader was speaking. "Police and the anti-terrorism squad have been on the scene in Wandsworth for nearly two hours now but there is still no sign of the gunman or his hostages. Our security correspondent says that police will be reluctant to force entry into the church if the terrorist has strapped explosives to himself or any of the congregation. They must hope that they can negotiate a way out."

Andrew collapsed into a chair. His mind raced. He was overcome with a deep sense of foreboding. He was already suffering grief from the death of Sara. Now he was faced with the unthinkable. His twin boys were locked inside a church with an armed terrorist who was threatening to blow them sky high. He had been worrying about Stellagenix and his marriage. All the time his children were in danger.

He watched as the cameras panned onto the front of the church. He recognised it. They had taken the children there for a carol concert before Christmas. His mother liked to go to church and there was no doubt this is where she would have taken them. He wondered if Analiese had gone with them too. Maybe she was elsewhere, thankful to have a day off as his mother was looking after the boys.

The church was less than a mile away and Andrew ran most of the way. It's my fault, he kept thinking. If I hadn't had an affair with Sara I wouldn't have been up in Lincolnshire. I would have been here looking after my children.

The police were keeping people a considerable distance from the church. The whole area around the church had been cordoned off and there were dozens of police cars and black vans parked haphazardly in the street. There were also already three TV news camera teams jockeying for position. He pushed forward until he reached the front of the crowd held back by the police tape. He explained to the officer who he was and that his mother and children were in the church. The policeman was polite, recognising that Andrew was an MP, but refusing to let him go any further.

Andrew was forced to wait as he watched reporters talking to camera and police marksmen crouched behind cars, their weapons trained on the front of the church. He felt an overwhelming sense of dread. He had been so caught up with Stellagenix and Sara's death that he had given little or no thought about his own children here in London. Now they were possibly going to be blown to bits by a terrorist and he was powerless to help. He realised that he was shaking. The sweat was trickling down his back, whether caused by his running or his fear he didn't know. He watched the church and waited.

A few minutes later there was a flurry of activity and everyone's attention switched to a side door of the church. The marksmen adjusted their aim. Then Andrew saw the door open and a female figure emerge, her hands held high. She was in the robes of an Anglican priest. A small woman, probably no more than 5 foot three with short-cropped hair. He couldn't see her clearly enough to judge her age. A helmeted and heavily-padded police officer rushed to her and rather unceremoniously patted her down for weapons or explosives. Andrew could see her gesticulating to the door and speaking urgently to the policeman. Then she turned and walked back to the door. She emerged a few seconds later leading a young man by the hand. His other hand was raised above his head in surrender. A posse of policemen rushed over and forced him to the ground. He was handcuffed and quickly pushed into a black police van that reversed up to the church.

The main doors to the church then opened and a phalanx of police formed on the steps as the congregation started to descend. Some of the people were crying, others were looking around nervously to see if their friends or loved ones were in the crowd.

Andrew caught sight of his mother, her arms around the shoulders of Marshall and Miles. They looked around at the crowd, obviously frightened by the sight of so many police. The crowd surged forward and broke through the police tape as relatives rushed to embrace the bewildered churchgoers and the police tried to get contact details from the worshippers.

Andrew wrapped his arms around his mother and the boys. They swayed together in a group hug. Finally, taking hold of the boys' hands he looked at his mother and asked the inevitable question. "Yes dear, I'm fine," she said. "And the boys were very brave but it's all down to the vicar. I've never seen anyone so brave. She was just magnificent. But now, let's go home. There's a chicken cooking in the oven!"

Later as they spoke to Claire on the phone Andrew's mother explained how the vicar had approached the terrorist and insisted he told why he wanted to blow everyone up. "She just sat with him and listened and then gave him reassurance. I don't know how she did it but in the end she persuaded him that she could get the police to not shoot him if he gave himself up. She promised to help him and his family back in Syria. It was amazing really. She was just so calm and convincing."

Claire hadn't heard the news but was now anxious to know just how upset the boys were. Andrew reassured her that they were fine. "I think they found it all rather exciting actually. They want to tell all their friends about it." He assured her that there was no need for her to come home. "You've got an important day tomorrow. Concentrate on that. I'm here and I'll make sure they're OK."

Andrew was, in fact, the one who wasn't OK. He was still beset by images of what might have happened. His sense of guilt remained. The boys by contrast seemed unfazed, not understanding how close they had come to death and more interested in being able to tell their friends that they had been on TV.

Andrew was a long time getting to sleep that night. He kept thinking what might have happened and he couldn't help thinking that the boys would be safer away from London.

6 0

Claire had been working at Andrew's desk in the study
that afternoon. It was beginning to get dark when Andrew
had rung her about the boys and the terrorist. She had
gone into the sitting room and switched on the little TV
to see the latest news. The story being carried was of the
vicar's role in preventing a disaster and because the event
was over without incident Claire didn't suffer the fears of
not knowing that Andrew had had. She was used to bomb
scares, demonstrations, marches in London. They were a
regular occurrence. It was just something you had to learn
to live with in the bustling capital.

She returned to her work on the press announcement
for Stellagenix. She tried to compartmentalise her thoughts.
She was presenting all the benefits of the new wonder barley
and how it would help feed more people and compensate
for global warming. She was also struggling with the theory

put forward by Andrew that the barley changed the genes of cattle and humans who ingested it which then led to reproduction problems. She instinctively believed Andrew and therefore that Stellagenix might have caused the deaths of two women, Martha and Sara. But she couldn't prove that. Not yet anyway. She had to go ahead as if everything was alright. Tomorrow she could exercise her share options, then sell the shares at a great profit and thus ensure she and Andrew were financially secure. Then maybe she could find out more about the techniques Stellagenix had used to alter the barley's genome. Or maybe she could just forget the whole thing and continue her role as PR spokesperson for Stellagenix. Then there was the case of Andrew's infidelity with Sara and her own with Clifton. She still hadn't heard from Clifton. Would he really ask her to come and live in Barcelona? What would she say?

By six o'clock she was exhausted. Everything was prepared for tomorrow's meeting and she still had no clear idea of what she would do after tomorrow about Andrew, Clifton and Stellagenix's development methods.

She went to the kitchen and looked at the few items she had bought. She didn't feel like cooking yet she was hungry. Like her husband, she settled on going to the pub. She wasn't bothered about eating alone in a pub. No one thought twice about that in London. It didn't occur to her that here in Lincolnshire attitudes were rather different.

61

MONDAY JANUARY 13ᵀᴴ 2020,
LINCOLNSHIRE

It was still dark as Claire drove away from Limetree House. She followed the instructions on the satnav and was soon on the way towards Stellagenix's headquarters. The temperature was still below freezing and the frost on the grass verges sparkled as her headlights illuminated them. She drove carefully, the memory of those awful tyre tracks leading to the dyke where Sara had died still fresh in her memory.

As she drove the blackness gradually gave way to an indeterminate grey as dawn broke and by the time she arrived a watery sun was rising to her right throwing long shadows from the Stellagenix buildings.

She checked her watch. Ten minutes before eight o'clock. George's Mercedes was parked to the side of the main entrance. It would probably be another hour before most of the staff arrived and the press briefing was scheduled for 11.

She parked in the first of the 'visitors' spaces and lifted her laptop off the passenger seat. She had rehearsed her part of the presentation several times the previous afternoon sitting at Andrew's desk in the cottage. She was confident that she knew it word perfectly. What she needed to do now was concentrate on delivery. She needed to sound convincing, enthusiastic, assured. That was the problem. The more she thought about what Andrew had told her on Saturday in the Barley Mow, the more she was convinced that George was covering up something. The phone hacking had been the clincher. When Andrew had produced the little silver box taken from his old phone it was the first real solid evidence that someone had been tapping his phone. And that someone had to be George Krasnik. She was convinced that was why he had always seemed to know what she and Andrew were doing. The fact that Andrew had changed his phone at Christmas helped to explain Friday's call from George querying where Andrew was and why he hadn't been in touch.

She imagined that her phone might similarly have been doctored although they hadn't checked. Andrew had said if they opened it and removed any device it would alert George.

Accepting that George might be monitoring phone calls was one thing. Accepting that he had ordered the murder of two women was quite another and Claire was still not convinced. Partly this was because she was deliberately trying not to think about Sara. In any other circumstance the fact that she had discovered her husband had been unfaithful would have eclipsed every other thought. But her brain was full of too many other thoughts. The success of this presentation and the subsequent announcement of the takeover bid would make her very rich. She could exercise her share options and bank a six figure sum Amir had reckoned. But if the new strain of barley was shown to have serious health risks it could mean a loss of her investment completely.

Then there was the effect on Andrew and his career. If news got out about his affair with Sara and her own involvement with promoting the barley he might face deselection by the local party. They could both find themselves looking for a job. Another thought struck her. If her phone conversations were being monitored it meant that all her conversations with her other clients were compromised. What about her calls with Clifton? She thought they had always been careful to sound business-like in their exchanges but were there a couple of times in Barcelona when she had had to contact him and been less discreet? Did George already know about her affair too?

She looked up at the building as she approached from the parking lot. George's office was on the first floor above the main entrance. She saw him standing at the window. He raised his hand in greeting. She put on her best business face as she entered his office moments later.

"I think we've got everything sorted here," she said, "I've run through it several times and I think it will get the message across about meeting the demands of a climate-challenged world."

"Fine, fine. I expected nothing less from my number-one PR guru." He smiled and sat down. He reached into the bowl on his desk and extracted a Snickers bar. He started to unwrap it without taking his eyes from Claire's face. His flattery rang hollow. Even his smile was cold. She wondered if he had always been like this and she hadn't noticed or whether her suspicions were causing her to doubt the sincerity of his words.

She watched as he bit into the chocolate bar. He took his time chewing before speaking. "There's a change of plan, Claire, but I'm sure you can handle it. In fact I think you'll really love it!"

There were a few more journalists than previously gathered in the conference room at 11 although no more than a couple of dozen. Despite Claire's emphasis on climate change and revolutionary plant yields there were no national papers present. The group consisted mainly of farming press and local media. She noted Sonya had come with a sound recordist and was talking with the cameraman from Anglia TV.

Claire had not been optimistic of national journalists braving the freezing fens to hear about growing barley. That's why she had arranged for Stellagenix to film the whole presentation which she would then circulate on social media to a long list of media she hoped would pick up the story.

Now, with the change of plans that George had announced three hours earlier, that filming would be crucial. No longer was this just a story about genetically-engineered barley and the economic benefits it would bestow upon a climate-challenged world. Now it should cause headlines in every business paper tomorrow morning. And long before that the news wires would be clattering with the news of the Calapharm bid.

"There's no way we could keep the lid on this baby,"

George had informed her. "The Boston Globe was threatening to run the story this morning – US Eastern time – lunchtime here in Britain. They've had a journo snooping around and putting two and two together. They know we're planning takeover of a pharma company – they just don't know which. I'm going to tell'm today!"

On the dot of eleven o'clock Claire walked onto the raised platform installed at the end of the conference room and coughed nervously in attempt to silence the chattering journalists. A few taps on her water glass with her laser stick got their attention.

"Good morning ladies and gentlemen and I thank you for braving the elements this morning to come and hear some very exciting news from Stellagenix. We have two major pieces of news to impart which I am sure will be of considerable interest to your readers, listeners, or viewers. Some of you were at our previous press conference when we explained that we were getting extremely good results from our first field trials of a new strain of barley. Today we shall be hearing from George Krasnik, CEO of Stellagenix UK, how those early test results have been confirmed, indeed improved, and now approved by the American FDA for full-scale manufacturing."

She handed her microphone to George who beamed at the audience before nodding to his technician who pressed play on the video. Pictures of vast fields or barley and wheat lit up the huge screen behind them accompanied by a soundtrack of "This land is my land". Then the pictures changed to show parched, cracked African earth, flooded Asian fields and dried-up reservoirs. Images of Australian and Californian bush fires alternated with city scenes of crowded trains and huge gatherings of people. The soundtrack changed to rap music and words about poverty, hunger and stress.

When it finished, George started to speak.

"Tomorrow's world is going to be very different. There's going to be a water shortage. There's going to be droughts and floods, pestilence and pain."

Claire winced as he said this. He was sounding like a Southern Baptist preacher and Brits weren't as impressed with that type of delivery as George's countrymen were. She listened as he explained how it was Stellagenix's mission to alleviate these effects of global warming by improving the yields of cereal crops and making them more drought-resistant and thus feeding a rapidly growing world population.

"Fortunately we have a little trick up our sleeve which has enabled us to achieve these results ahead of any of our competitors. I won't tell you exactly how we've achieved this," he paused, "I'd have to kill you if I did." He waited for the appreciative laughter. There was little. He continued. "But many of you will have heard about the amazing developments in genome mapping. Why, you guys here in Cambridge have mapped one hundred thousand people's genomes to find out exactly what makes human beings tick, what makes them strong, what makes them sick. It's all to do with the make-up of your DNA – you've heard of that, the police use it to solve crimes!" He paused for laughter again. "Well plants have DNA too. And our scientists here in Lincolnshire have examined the genome of various cereal products to identify what genes help make the plant stronger, grow more quickly and so on. And we've looked at other plants and even animals too to see what makes them grow stronger. Now here's the clever bit! We've used a special, just-discovered, method of finding those exact genes in barley, for instance, and replacing them with a new stronger gene. It's real sci-fi. Revolutionary! Extraordinary and we've done it here in Lincolnshire. Now I'd like to take you through some slides here that demonstrate just how much greater yields we have achieved in our trials."

The journalists watched the screen as George took them through a series of slides showing how well the Stellagenix barley performed against 'normal' barley.

"That's going to increase your farmers' yields and that means they're going to make more profit!" George was in full stride now and sounding like he was offering listeners the kingdom of heaven. He was interrupted by Sonya.

"It'll make Stellagenix more money too won't it?"

"That it will indeed. It'll make our company even more successful." George smiled as Sonya had just fed him the perfect link to the takeover bid. "As I said earlier, our expertise in manipulating plant genomes can be used also to improve the health of people too. Just think how good that would be. And that is why I am very pleased to announce that, just before I started speaking to you, my directors in the US of A announced their intention to take over Western Calapharm, a major pharmaceutical company. The merger of these two companies will create one of the most exciting biotech companies in the world. You are the first to hear about this, so I hope you'll be spreading the news to your readers and viewers."

The journalists fired a series of questions at George. Some were on the performance of the barley and the cost of seeds. These questions came from the agricultural media. Others wanted more information on what exactly had been done to 'normal' barley to create this 'super' barley but George refused to be specific saying it was really too technical to answer here and anyway the precise details were a closely-guarded secret.

It was Sonya who asked the question about local employment and Stellagenix's plans for expansion.

"George, it is obviously good news for those employees here but previously you've talked about expanding production and providing more jobs. But will these be specialist jobs or will they be for the lower-skilled youngsters that we have around here?"

"The takeover of Calapharm should provide a lot more opportunities, particularly if the UK does a trade deal with the US of A. A lot of Calapharm's products could be sold here in the UK, maybe to your NHS and the packaging and distribution of them could provide that type of employment you are seeking. I'm sure Andrew Eastwood your local MP would do all he could to facilitate that trade deal. It's a pity that Brexit has kept him from attending this morning." He looked pointedly at Claire.

"Are you satisfied that your new barley strain, the one you've messed around with, is entirely safe for human consumption?" Sonya had waited for this moment.

George glared at her. "Man has been modifying plants for thousands of years. Our barley has been passed by all the relevant American authorities. It's nonsense to suggest it isn't safe."

Sonya smiled at him. "I wasn't suggesting it was unsafe, I was just asking whether it had got all the necessary approvals."

After the journalists had left and Claire had posted the video on social media and the company's website she joined George for a late lunch in the canteen. He was tucking into a large hamburger and fries with obvious lack of concern for his ever-increasing girth. He waved his phone at Claire who brought her chicken salad over. "We're up more than 3 dollars a share since the news broke!" He passed her his phone so she could see the Bloomberg screen. The New York Stock Exchange had just opened. "That's tremendous George." She grinned at him all the time thinking how much she stood to make if she exercised her share options that afternoon.

"Where was Dimitri?" Sonya had been surprised to see neither Dimitri nor his research assistant at the conference.

"Like you said, Claire, he's not the world's best speaker and I didn't want him letting any of our secrets out of the bag!"

I bet you didn't, thought Claire.

"And do we have secrets?"

George wiped the ketchup from his lips with a paper napkin before replying. "I'm sure you and Andrew wouldn't want anything to spoil our success. After all it's good for his career and no doubt you're hoping Calapharm appoint your agency to handle their PR."

Was there a veiled threat there along with the dangled carrot? Claire's emotions were so mixed up. She had to admit she was feeling excited at the way the press conference had gone, how the share price had reacted and the thought of the hundreds of thousands of pounds she would make selling her shares was fantastic. At the back of her mind however was the Sara situation. Her husband's erstwhile mistress. Now dead. Suspiciously killed. There was the phone hacking, the feeling that George knew too much about what was happening in her life.

"I need to get going. I've got to get back to London."

"Are you sure?"

"Yes I have to. I need to get back to my kids. They were involved in that terrorist attack in the church yesterday."

62

Andrew walked with the boys to their school that morning. He was still worried about their ordeal the day before. He had dreamed that night that he had been unable to get to them in time to rescue them. He was running down endless streets and every time he turned a corner there was another long street with the church at the end. People kept getting in his way and he was forced to push them aside. Then he had seen Sara coming towards him smiling. But just as she drew near she suddenly fell through the pavement and disappeared. He looked down and saw a car upside down in a frozen ditch. He had woken in a cold sweat.

Realising how close he had come to losing the boys, he was anxious to be with them as much as possible. Reluctantly he waved goodbye at the school gate and returned slowly to his house. His mother was still there and seemed none the worse for her experience. Analiese, however, was very subdued. "I have spoken with my mother on the telephone," she said as she made Andrew a coffee. "She is unhappy that I stay here. She thinks London is too dangerous now."

Andrew tried remonstrating with her but realised it was doing no good. "Things are not the same now," she said. "The British don't like foreigners living here. I hear them talking about it. I think I will have to leave. I will stay for a month while you find someone else. I shall miss the boys."

Andrew arrived at his office in Victoria Street around 11.00. His secretary was pleased to see him. "Are you alright Minister? I hope you managed to sort things out up at your constituency."

Nodding, Andrew suggested she fetched him a coffee and brought him up to date.

"The Secretary of State wasn't happy that you weren't in Parliament at the end of last week. The whips wanted all MPs in the chamber for the withdrawal agreement debate. It was pretty important." She still wondered what had been so important that Andrew had rushed off and missed speaking in the most important debate of the year. She knew he had been very much opposed to leaving the EU. What could have been more important?

"I can't be in two places at once," snapped Andrew. "I had to go to Lincoln. My vote wouldn't have made any difference, the PMs not for turning and he's leading us like lemmings over a cliff."

His secretary looked aghast. She said nothing. While she liked Andrew and respected the fact that he treated her better than many other ministers did, she didn't expect to hear him sound off quite so vehemently. If others heard him like this he could find himself demoted at the next reshuffle and she didn't want a new boss.

"My sons could have been killed yesterday, you know. They were in that church. Hostages to that terrorist."

"Oh my goodness, I had no idea. Are they alright?"

"I took them to school myself this morning."

"Of course. And your wife must have been really worried. She was with them?"

"No she's still up at Otherby. She's got an important client presentation in Lincoln."

They sipped their coffees in silence for several minutes. Then she ran through the meetings planned for that week. There was little to occupy Andrew in the Chamber, mainly statements about the Iran situation. He would spend most of the week in committee meetings or catching up with reports. There would be no late-night sittings to keep him away from the kids this week. He wondered how Claire would be. She still hadn't broached the subject of Sara. She wouldn't be pleased to hear that Analiese was leaving. Life seemed unpredictable.

The boys were in bed asleep by the time an exhausted Claire arrived home. The weather had made the roads treacherous and she had endured a half-hour delay on the A1 near Peterborough while police cleared an accident.

As if she knew Claire and Andrew had rowed, Analiese had gone to her room and left Andrew to sort out something for Claire to eat.

The first thing Claire did was to go upstairs and look at the boys. Andrew waited downstairs in the kitchen. He was still on tenterhooks about how Claire might react to the Sara situation. They hadn't talked in Otherby. It seemed as if Claire had pushed it aside and was focusing solely on her

Stellagenix presentation. Now that was over would she take up the issue of his infidelity?

He was at least glad that she seemed to be concerned about the boys and their experience in the church. Her reaction when he had phoned with the news on Sunday had been underwhelming. She had not seemed particularly bothered in fact. Having been assured that the boys were back home safe she seemed to have just turned her attention back to Stellagenix.

He waited anxiously sipping at his second glass of wine. Claire came down a few minutes later. She had changed into her loungers and thanked him as he handed her a glass of wine. "I need this after the day I've had."

"How did the presentation go?" asked Andrew anxious to get her talking about anything rather than Sara.

"Really well actually. There weren't as many there as I'd hoped but I spoke to Leonora on my way back and she said they had been fielding calls from the nationals on the Calapharm takeover already. The share price is up to 14 dollars!"

She had wanted to phone Amir and get him to exercise her share options so she could then sell them. But she was worried that her phone might have been tampered with and she didn't want George to know she had been investing in Stellagenix. She would phone Amir in the morning from a landline.

"How was George?"

"Very sure of himself. Sounded like a Southern Baptist Minister!"

"Did you ask him about the safety issues?"

"No, but your friend Sonya did. And he wasn't happy. I

think you're right. He is worried that there might be health issues but he's insistent that it's met all the standards, got all the approvals."

Andrew nodded but didn't comment. His desk research had convinced him that whatever tests had been applied to the barley wouldn't have picked up the effect the reconstituted barley was having on animal and human germ cells. Finally, he broke the silence.

"What are we going to do? We know George is behind our phones being hacked, we need to check yours by the way. We know that two people at least have been killed in an effort to keep secret the harmful effects of the barley. What are we going to do about it?"

"We don't know those things Andrew. Not for sure. We can't just go accusing him without more proof."

"How much more proof do you need?"

"I don't need any more proof. I believe you are right. I have a very bad feeling about George. He's capable of anything. But proving it to a judge or a jury is something else. And it won't bring Sara back."

Andrew had been dreading talking about Sara. He had tried not to bring it up, but here Claire had said it. He felt the tears welling up again.

Claire continued. "I met her parents last night in the Barley Mow. Such nice people. It's so terrible for them to lose a child. I don't know how they'll ever get over it."

"I thought we might have lost our boys yesterday. It was terrible Claire. I couldn't do anything. I just had to stand there in the crowd looking on expecting the building to erupt at any moment. I've had terrible dreams since."

Claire placed her hand on his. "I can't imagine. When

you phoned me it was all over. No one had been hurt, the boys were safe. I didn't have to worry. You were with them. I'm sorry, I just didn't think what you must have been going through. And after the Sara thing too."

There she had brought up Sara again.

"I'm so sorry darling about Sara. I know I've hurt you and I wouldn't ever want to do that. It just sort of happened." He realised that this sounded pathetic and braced himself for Claire's response.

"I don't want to hear about it. I haven't forgiven you but I'm prepared to forget it right now. I think we need to concentrate on what we're going to do. Our life has changed over the past year. We never seem to have time together. You're always working late or up in Lincolnshire and I admit I've been pretty caught up with work at the Agency. We need to change things."

For more than an hour they sat and talked. Andrew realised how little time they had had to talk recently. Even over Christmas there always seemed to be things that needed doing, children to mind, meals to prepare.

Andrew talked of his frustration with the government. He'd become an MP because he thought he could play a role in tempering or even reversing Brexit, but that had proved impossible. Since last month's election that gave Boris's Tories an 80-seat majority it seemed a lost cause. Boris was determined to leave come what may. Never a man to worry himself with detail he was likely to sign up to a very poor deal.

Andrew was also appalled by the cronyism and corruption that seemed to be rife. When he had tried to raise his fears about Stellagenix he was promptly warned off because of

Stellagenix's donations to the party. He had begun to realise that individual MPs had little power to influence decisions.

Claire's experiences over the past few months had been very different. She had relished the pressure upon her to perform. She had embraced the Agency life. She had enjoyed the trips to the US and, in particular, to Barcelona.

She realised that she'd been ignoring the boys and Andrew and knew that had to change. She knew that she would have to speak with Clifton soon and he would push her to relocate to Barcelona. That wasn't going to happen. Andrew's affair with Sara had been cut short. She would have to break off with Clifton if she wanted her marriage to succeed.

She had been thinking about this and about what to do with George Krasnik as she had driven down. She had an idea and she explained it to Andrew.

He agreed.

63

TUESDAY JANUARY 14TH 2020, LONDON

Tuesday morning dawned and Claire set off to carry out the first part of her plan.

The train from Clapham Junction was crowded as usual. It was only two stops and Claire steeled herself for the journey. It was too congested to be able to read a paper. She found herself pressed against the back of a large man in a dark raincoat. Her view consisted of his shoulders and the nape of his neck. She looked disgustedly at the sprinkling of dandruff on the collar of raincoat. She tried to shift her position to the side but it was impossible. Her laptop shoulder bag was now wedged between the large man and another traveller. It prevented her from turning. She braced herself as the train jerked forward. The crowd was so packed that it moved as a single force, rocking forward and then back in rhythm with the train. She closed her eyes and waited. Two stops and then she could escape to the underground.

Prithi greeted her as she walked into her office. "The conquering hero returns! How was the presentation?"

Claire struggled out of her coat. Despite the January temperature outside she was perspiring after two uncomfortable train rides and she felt dirty. "I'll tell you in a minute. I need to go freshen up first and I could murder a cup of coffee."

Leonora joined her shortly afterwards and Claire started to go through yesterday's press do in detail. Leonora had news of the press reaction and Prithi brought in several newspapers to show the coverage for Stellagenix.

"The share price is up over $14 and George has been on to Paul Devorian already this morning telling him he wants to talk about the PR for Calapharm. We've really scored there!" Leonora was obviously pleased with her protégé and wanting to be part of the success.

Claire began her plan.

"It's all very positive but we do need to be careful about one thing."

"What? Calapharm?"

"No, I think the takeover is assured now. We need to make sure that we handle the opponents to GM foods. I'm concerned that we don't know exactly what Stellagenix did to the barley to get their results. I think we need to make sure we know and that we can defend any attacks from the tree-huggers."

"I would have thought that's something you would have already discussed with George? I mean, I know they want to preserve their commercial secrets but we are their PR company for goodness sake."

"George won't really talk to me about it. Either he doesn't

402

understand the science himself, quite possible I would say, or he doesn't want anyone to know and that worries me."

"So what are you suggesting we do?" said Leonora.

Claire explained her plan. Well parts of her plan. The parts that involved the Agency. The rest of the plan she kept to herself.

Prithi had said little until then. Now she spoke. "What about Prospect Insurance? Clifton was on the phone yesterday wanting to speak to you quite urgently. I told him you were travelling and would ring him this morning."

Claire nodded. She had made up her mind but wasn't looking forward to telling Clifton.

Clifton had insisted on lunch. He was due to fly to Barcelona that evening and needed to talk urgently.

She watched him as he tasted the wine before nodding to the sommelier and waving his hand in her direction as an instruction for him to pour her a glass. He was so attractive, thought Claire. No wonder he had such a reputation.

He smiled at her as if reading her mind. "I'm glad you've found time from your other clients to grace me with your presence!"

"Well I can always find time for you." She smiled back at him and sipped her wine.

"You know I'm planning to move to Barcelona? I'll be setting up our EU office there and it's going to be very busy. I wondered if you might consider coming out there and working with me?"

Claire had been expecting this but was surprised he had broached the subject so early in their lunch.

"You know I'm married with a family, Clifton. There's

absolutely no way I could move to Barcelona. Sorry, but non-negotiable!"

He paused while the waiter brought their food. Then he put on a 'little boy lost' face. "Oh what will I do without you?" But he broke into a broad grin. "We've had such good times in Barcelona haven't we?"

They shared the joke.

"What about the account though Clifton? We've done a great job for you and I'd like to think we could still handle things from here."

"I think we'll have to appoint a Spanish agency for our European work but there is still a role for Repute here in the UK."

It was the chance for Claire to introduce her plan. She had to be careful. She didn't want to lose the account but her plan meant things would change radically. Most of all she would not be flying out for sex-filled weekends with Clifton.

"What are your plans for your Docklands office? I mean you are going to be moving a lot of staff to Barcelona."

"I fear that most of our clerical staff will not want to move. Hopefully some of the senior management will. The clerical work for Europe at least is likely to be done from Barcelona, by Europeans."

"So your lovely offices are going to be pretty empty. Will you get rid of them?"

"We're coming up to a break period in our lease in around six months so it's certainly a possibility. It all depends on what sort of deal Boris manages to negotiate, whether we'll get guarantees on passporting etc. Even if we do, we will have moved a lot of our business to Spain so we won't need nearly as much space."

"And it doesn't have to be here in London, does it?" Claire cut off a good piece of her steak. It was funny how she wanted steak today. She was really hungry. Normally she'd have settled for a prawn salad. Must be all the travelling I've done, she thought.

"Well I suppose not. But we've always been in the City. I'm not sure we could run things so well elsewhere. And anyway wouldn't that make us look provincial if we moved out of London? How would that sit with the 'major-player' reputation you've helped us to build?"

"Aren't American Express and Western Union major players?"

"Of course."

"Well last time I looked Amex were based in Brighton and Western Union had their big office in Peterborough. So you wouldn't have to be in London."

Clifton thought for a minute. He poured more wine from the bottle of Rioja. Claire had a point. If their operation in Britain was largely clerical and their international business moved to Barcelona, did they really need to pay expensive London rents?

It was then that Claire dropped her proposal. She had come up with the idea while sitting motionless in her car on the A1 the evening before.

"I've been giving some thought to how we could make a move out of London, to smaller premises, look like a really progressive move rather than a cost-saving exercise. Climate change!"

"Climate change?"

"Yes. Next year Glasgow is hosting COP26 – a major international gathering to tackle climate change. If you were to move out of London it would cut down on everyone's commuting. Lower their carbon footprint. Smaller offices would need less heating and lighting. Lower carbon footprint!"

"You're suggesting we move to Glasgow?" He looked disgusted at the thought.

"No, I'm suggesting you move to somewhere like Peterborough, or Grantham or Newark for instance. But more than that I'm suggesting you make your offices really energy-efficient, really environmentally friendly. Then we could trumpet about your social responsibility and everything and that could really help set you apart."

"But why Peterborough or Newark for goodness sake. What is there up there?"

"Me."

"What?"

"I'm thinking of relocating so I can spend more time with Andrew and the family. You know we actually bought a house in Lincolnshire?"

"But Andrew's an MP. He works down here in London. So do you."

"Yes, but I'm looking ahead. I'm not sure London's a good place to bring up our boys. Apart from all the pollution and lack of green space it's dangerous." She explained how the boys had been held hostage in the Church on Sunday.

"I didn't know you were there! I watched it on TV. I had no idea."

"That's just it. I wasn't there. Neither was Andrew. We'd both been in Lincs. Andrew came down on that day. I had a meeting with Stellagenix up there so stayed till yesterday. That's why I'm thinking maybe I should move up there. It

406

would be better for the boys, I'd be close to Stellagenix and Andrew could spend more time with his constituents."

"But Claire, that's not you. You love London, the art galleries, the restaurants, the theatre. You'd hate it up there."

Claire had thought the same. Giving up her life and work in London would be a wrench. She was already thinking how they could sell the Wandsworth house and buy a small flat in the West End. They could come down for weekends. Or maybe it would be useful for Andrew when he had to be in Parliament. She could come down with him if she could find someone to look after the boys. The main thing would be that the kids would be in a safer environment.

"Look Clifton. Everything is changing. You're having to relocate to Spain, we don't know what's happening with Brexit. We can't ignore climate change. All I'm suggesting is that you look at relocating your UK office. I'd be very happy to look at possible sites for you – all part of the Repute service."

There, she'd said it. Not that anyone at Repute yet knew of her intentions. One step at a time. Firstly take a few weeks holiday up in Lincolnshire. Repute owed her some holiday anyway. It would help if she could say Clifton had asked her to look out for new offices up there. Being up there would also give her more time to see what was happening at Stellagenix. Andrew was not going to give up investigating, she knew.

64

FEBRUARY 1ST 2020, LINCOLNSHIRE

'Rise and Shine, it's a glorious new Britain.' *Daily Express.*

'Killer virus. 2 cases in Britain.' *Evening Standard*

Britain was out of Europe and Claire and Andrew were out of London. Neither felt the need to celebrate cutting the ties with our closest neighbours and biggest trading partners.

It was a new beginning for Britain and Claire hoped it would be a new beginning for the family too. Officially she was taking a month's leave (although with the promise that she would be visiting Stellagenix and looking round for suitable offices for Prospect.)

Leonora had been sympathetic when she explained the trauma of the Church terrorist incident and the fact that she needed to spend some time with Andrew and the boys after her hectic schedule around Christmas.

Andrew was delighted to be leaving London and

Westminster. Since Boris's triumphant election there had been a change of atmosphere among the Tories. The Remainers, like him, had largely been side-lined. Jeremy Hunt, recently Boris's successor as Foreign Secretary had now to be satisfied with chairing the Health and Social Care Committee. There was a new, young administration at Number 10 and, as if to emphasise it, Boris announced that he was to be a father again, as Carrie was pregnant. That may well have accounted for the fact that now the Brexit deal was done Boris decided to take time off too!

The Brexiteer MPs were in full cry and Andrew had been busy preparing data on the NHS that he suspected were going to be used to woo the Americans to a trade deal. It was all too depressing for Andrew who realised that his bid to try and save the country from a hard Brexit had finally been defeated.

His mind had still been preoccupied with thoughts about Sara and the links between the Stellagenix barley and the twins outbreak. He thought of Colin trying to bring up two daughters alone. He wondered how he would feel if he lost Claire. His affair with Sara had risked losing his wife, the mother of his boys. The risk was still there although there seemed to at least be a truce. Claire had not talked to him again about his affair and seemed, after the church terrorist attack, to be keener than ever to spend time with him and the boys.

In his usual methodical way, he prepared the case against Stellagenix. The coincidences were too great to ignore. The animal feed, the local brewery, the sudden death of the one person who might have been able to tell him what had gone on in the Stellagenix labs. And then Sara's 'accident' that had destroyed his chance of knowing the DNA results. Then there was his bugged phone. The motive for George to conceal the effects of the barley at all costs was obvious too. The takeover of Calapharm had proved that. Yet there was no proof that would stand up in court. If he was to bring George to justice he would need hard evidence that both Martha and Sara had been murdered and the police were still maintaining that the deaths were accidental.

He arranged to meet the Minister and also the under-secretary from Defra. He walked into the Minister's office and was surprised to find two other men there. The Chief Whip scowled at him as he entered while the other man was introduced to him as working for the Chairman of the Party.

The Minister settled himself at the head of the small table and the others took their seats. He smiled at Andrew. "Now Andrew I believe you have some concerns about the safety of GM foods? I know you have strong connections with one of the Party's major donors, Stellagenix, and I'm sure they are very keen to expand their investment in our country. And indeed invest in your constituency. A brand-new sports centre I believe? Just what we need to help with levelling up."

There it was. The warning shot not to rock any boat that a major donor might be sitting in. A blatant admission that Stellagenix, a foreign-owned corporation was making political donations to the Party. Stan had nudged him and winked, saying there were ways of donating without the authorities knowing. He had been right.

The Chief Whip spoke. "So what exactly are you proposing we do? What are the problems, if any, with GM foods?"

Andrew looked nervously at his notes. His carefully-prepared case linking Stellagenix to the twin calves, and the human twins was concisely outlined in a document he took out of his case. The three copies he had made for distribution remained in the case.

He paraphrased the report, stressing the connections between the barley and the animal foodstuff and beer. He went on to try and explain how CRISPR was now enabling laboratories to replace strands of DNA, genes, with other genes.

The four other men sat through his speech in silence. When he had finished it was the man from Defra that spoke first.

"Andrew, I know that a lot of people are frightened with the prospect of GM foods but they are nothing new and indeed are essential if we are going to be able to feed an increasing world population. Whilst I understand your concern for your constituents," he paused and looked at the Chief Whip, "there is only a very tenuous link between this trial barley and the incidences you outlined. Nothing more than coincidence perhaps. The barley has, after all, been approved by the US authorities and shows no harmful effects on animals."

Andrew realised that the Defra minister had been well briefed on the issue. He wondered who had alerted him to Andrew's concerns. Why was he even at this meeting? "Yes I know it has passed US tests but I believe those are merely concerned with possible toxicity. What we are looking at here is the effect the gene-edited barley is having on the germ cells of animals and humans leading to an early splitting of cells and an increased risk of multiple births."

The chief whip interrupted. "All very technical, I'm sure. Something for the scientists to worry about. Maybe even get some of our guys at Cambridge to set up a study if we can find the money." He smiled at the Minister. "Not a lot of money available for the NHS as it is, I believe?"

Andrew tried another tack. "Stellagenix seem very reluctant to say how they have edited the barley. And indeed one of their researchers who might have been willing to tell us unfortunately was killed in a road accident."

"Very tragic I know. Most unfortunate. But Stellagenix is a commercial operation and its formulas are a valuable asset that it naturally needs to protect. I really feel that you'll have to let this one go. There are far more important health issues for us to worry about." The Minister stood up to signify the meeting was over. The others joined him. The man from the Party who had remained silent throughout now came over to Andrew. "Look Andrew, you've done very well as a new MP and the people in your constituency are grateful to you for getting Stellagenix to build them a new sports centre, and promise them more jobs. We wouldn't want anything to upset that. Not that we're likely to lose such a safe seat. That constituency is rock solid Tory. Any candidate could win there." The threat was unstated but obvious. Drop the investigation or you'll be dropped as a candidate in the next election.

His one meeting that had been worthwhile was with the scientists up at Cambridge. Having visited them earlier last year when they successfully completed the human genome mapping project he had stayed in touch with Emil, one of the leading researchers. He wanted to run by him his suspicions about the new barley and its effects on animals and humans. He hadn't got the results of the bulls' DNA tests that Sara had arranged with some friend in Manchester and he had no way of contacting that friend. But he felt he should run his theories by Emil and see whether he thought them plausible.

Andrew had returned from his visit armed with a lot more facts and he attempted to explain them to Claire that evening.

Claire, while secretly believing that George had been hiding certain things was still prepared to play devil's advocate.

"The problem is Andrew that a lot of ignorant people are just against GM foods and make a lot of unsubstantiated claims. I mean we've been changing plants and animal's genes for years to improve flavour, resist disease etc. This new CRISPR method just makes it quicker and easier to change a plant's genes. It's better than the old methods like exposing it to radiation for instance."

Andrew refilled their glasses. Amazing! Other couples would be shouting at each other about his infidelity. Yet he and Claire were discussing the intricacies of gene editing! "There's a difference between what CRISPR does though. In fact it should be better as it normally works to just change the performance of a plant's existing genes rather than inserting a foreign gene into it as has been done in the past. It's much more precise."

"But getting back to regulations I thought it took years to get a new strain or a genetically modified product approved for human consumption? So how can Stellagenix have got the approvals so quickly?" Claire was still clinging to the hope that there wasn't a health issue with the barley.

She was well aware however that this did not excuse George's involvement in Sara and Martha's deaths – if in fact he had been.

"You're right Claire, it is unusual but not so unusual as it used to be. You used to have to go through a long-winded process in the US. Jurisdiction was split between the Food and Drug Administration, the Environmental Protection Agency and the US Department of Agriculture. The result was long and expensive and kept many smaller firms out of the GM market. The big boys were left to run the market. But it's changed recently since Trump got in and a lot of the checks seem to have been quietly dropped and products are getting by the USDA without tests. It gives smaller companies like Stellagenix a chance to benefit from gene modifying and the CRISPR breakthrough means it's much cheaper and easier to edit the genome than ever before."

"Right, I see." Claire picked a handful of nuts from the dish and started chewing them. "So you're saying there is a definite link between the trial barley and the animal feed that these bulls were fed? You're also saying the same barley was used to make that local beer you drank? And you're saying this resulted in cows having twins and your friend's wife having twins, from which she died?"

"Yes, I am. And there is also some evidence that these twin calves and girls are growing faster than normal."

"But there's no absolute proof?"

"No."

"And if a link were proven, the value of Stellagenix's shares would suffer a setback?"

"A massive setback I should say. That's why George is so

keen to keep everything hushed up. Keen enough to arrange the deaths of two women!"

"But again, we have no proof Andrew." Claire toyed with the idea of telling Andrew about her gamble on the Stellagenix shares. The money had gone into her account. She would have to tell him sometime. But perhaps not right now.

"We have the phone bug. That's real. Someone bugged me. Let me look at your phone."

She handed it over. Andrew fetched a small screwdriver from the kitchen drawer and prised off the back panel as the IT guy in Lincoln had. Sure enough, there was the same little silver box and the two wires. He showed it to Claire.

"What should we do Andrew?"

"I think we need to be very careful. If George knows we're on to him he might try to silence us too! The fact that I changed my phone means he doesn't know I found the device. But if you take your device out he'll know we're on to him."

Claire got up and went over to Andrew. She leant forward and kissed him on the head. "I'm so sorry about Sara."

Andrew reached up and clasped her arm. It was the first time they had been affectionate since he had confessed. They stayed like that for several seconds. Thoughts of his time with Sara filled his head. He pictured her long dark hair, her eyes that sparkled mischievously when she laughed. Then he thought about Claire. She was being forgiving. She was even being sympathetic. He loved her for this. He let go of her arm and stood up. "Right we need to plan carefully."

"I've got some ideas," said Claire. Andrew knew that when Claire had a new idea there was no stopping her.

The next morning after they had given the boys their breakfast they set out for Lincoln. The boys were excited and wanted to know if Andrew was taking them to the farm which had the big tractors. But this was not the plan. First they visited a mobile phone shop and purchased a new phone for Claire. Then they headed across to the radio station where they had arranged to meet Sonya.

The boys were fascinated by all the studios and equipment and were left in the care of Sonya's production assistant while they talked.

Claire explained her plan to Sonya. "Be careful, Claire. If we're right about George he's dangerous. If he suspects that you're checking him out ......" Her voice trailed off.

"I need to find out more detail about what tests the barley has passed. I need to talk to Dimitri and find out just what editing he did to the barley genome. Then Andrew could run it by his friend in Cambridge."

"Couldn't we just get some more DNA samples from those two bulls and get Andrew's friend to run the same tests?"

Andrew interjected. "I know which farms they were from. I'm sure I could get the necessary samples from the farmers. They are my constituents after all."

"In the meantime," said Sonya, "I'm going to keep digging with the police. I'm sure those 'accidents' weren't accidents at all."

It was Andrew's turn to urge caution. "If George knows you're investigating those deaths it could be really dangerous for you too."

Sonya looked at Claire and Andrew. She wondered what Claire had said about Sara. Claire was looking tired and

Sonya smiled at her. "You look tired Claire. You've had a lot on and I am sure a few weeks up here away from London will be a tonic."

Claire did feel tired. Tired and hungry. She suggested they left, took the boys home and had an early supper.

65

If they had thought their stay in Otherby was going to be a holiday, they were soon disillusioned. Claire had left the next morning to call on George at Stellagenix. It was all part of her plan to get to the bottom of the health risks in the new barley.

She had prepared herself well with promises to get substantially more media coverage now she could spend more time with George and his team.

"I want to really push this 'saviour of the world' theme. You know, rising world population, need for more food, scientific breakthroughs thanks to brilliant Stellagenix researchers. That sort of thing. Should play really well. We might even be able to get some TV production company interested in doing a 'fly-on-the-wall' piece."

George looked at her. He nodded but didn't comment. He reached in the bowl for another Snickers bar. Finally he answered. "I'm not sure I would want a TV crew poking around the labs here. What we do is real cutting edge. Our competitors would love to know how old Dimitri did it, but I don't want them finding out from some Panorama documentary."

"OK, OK. I get that but this whole gene editing thing is going to be increasingly talked about and it's important that Stellagenix are seen to be leaders in the field." Claire fidgeted on her chair trying to get comfortable. The sight of George munching the chocolate bar made her feel queasy. The leather of her chair squeaked as she rearranged her posture. She noticed that George was looking at her legs. Her skirt had risen up as she shuffled. "Can I at least go and have a chat with Dimitri and get him to give me some more information – nothing too precise – but just so I know what I'm talking about when I see the journalists?"

"OK Claire. I'll fix that for your next visit. In the meantime I want to talk about Calapharm. There's great potential there and I can see Repute really driving that forward for us."

Claire leaned forward, tugging at her skirt hem as she did so. "What exactly are the plans for Calapharm and how do they affect things here in Britain?"

"Well you know the interesting thing?" He looked at her again. His intensity was unnerving her. She shook her head.

"Tell me," she said.

"It turns out they've been having a good go at this CRISPR thing too. Looking at how they can develop drugs with it. Maybe vaccines. They tell me that that's where the future is. Developing drugs that can work with particular individuals – a sort of bespoke medical treatment rather than the one-size-fits-all approach used at the moment."

"Great but how does that affect us here in Lincs?"

"Well of course that remains to be seen. But if the US becomes more involved with your NHS here, say we do a good trade deal with Boris, then some of Calapharm's products could be manufactured here."

"How likely is that?" Claire was beginning to feel a little faint and wondered whether she should help herself to one of the remaining chocolate bars.

"A trade deal? I don't know. That'd be up to the politicians like your husband. But it's the research I'm interested in for now. Apparently there's some cutting edge stuff being undertaken by the Chinese in a place called Wuhan. My team have been out there and I'm going to get a briefing about a possible collaboration. I'm leaving for the States on Thursday."

Claire was glad to be back in Otherby. The journey back from Stellagenix had been awful. The rain had come down so strongly that the Nissan's windscreen wipers had trouble clearing the screen. The low clouds had stolen any light from the sun and she had had full headlights on in order to navigate the narrow roads.

Andrew was inside with the boys. He had a big fire going in the sitting room and the carpet was littered with Lego.

"Are you alright Claire? You look exhausted. How did you get on with George? Is he going to let you speak to Dimitri?"

"I am tired and the drive back was dreadful. The wind really whips across these fields doesn't it and the rain was literally bouncing of the roof. I could hear it. It was like being inside a drum."

She related everything that had happened at Stellagenix. She clutched the mug of tea tightly. She had turned down the offer of a whisky. She had a feeling that something wasn't quite normal. She tried to think back over the past couple of months. How long had it been?

Seeing her frowning and concentrating, Andrew asked what was wrong.

"I'm not sure anything's wrong darling. But I think I might need to take a trip to Boots tomorrow."

"For medicine?" Andrew walked over taking the mug from her.

"No, for a pregnancy testing kit. Andrew I think I might be pregnant!"

Claire had had difficulty in conceiving. For several years nothing had happened. Eventually after tests had shown that both she and Andrew were perfectly fertile they took a course of IVF and Marshall and Miles were the result. Five years later she had given up expecting to fall pregnant, she was convinced she couldn't. But she now realised that she hadn't had her period since well before Christmas.

George Krasnik sat at the boardroom table. No one else was in the room. Distracted, he munched another Snickers bar. It helped him think. He was thinking about Claire. According to the phone records which he had in front of him she had said nothing about the accidents to Martha and Sara, nor about any DNA testing of bulls. On the face of it, and with the telephone transcripts since Christmas before him it would appear that she had none of her husband's concerns about the new barley. He no longer had any transcripts from Andrew's phone. It was bad luck that Andrew had got a new phone at Christmas. Obviously he hadn't found the device that had been installed in the old one and Claire clearly hadn't realised her phone was bugged. There had been hardly any calls from Claire to Andrew and none that suggested any concern about the product safety.

Yet he had a nagging feeling that Claire suspected something. For all her apparent support of Stellagenix he had noticed a change in her attitude to him. Nothing he could put his finger on but still. She had been pushing to talk to Dimitri and learn more about their research methods. Was that to be expected from a good PR consultant? Maybe. Or was she digging like that Sonya woman from Lindum Radio? She and Claire seemed a little too friendly.

He thought back to the recent press conference. Claire had been perfect. She had presented well and seemed genuinely delighted that the share price had reacted so favourably to the takeover news. At least she was pleased. That husband of hers hadn't wanted to know when he'd been given the nod to invest before the yield results were published. What was wrong with him? His Tory colleagues had been only too grateful to receive George's calls.

George knew he could get Andrew to do what he needed if he had to. Andrew wouldn't want his wife to know about his affair with that Spanish vet. Oh no, even an honest MP like Andrew would succumb rather than have his marriage ruined. George smiled to himself. That's how you got on in business. You just had to know things about your competitors or critics that they wished to hide.

He picked up the telephone transcripts and walked out of the room. Back in his office he checked with his PA about tomorrow's flights. Then his mobile rang. He looked at the screen and waved at his PA to leave.

"Yes. What's up?" He held the phone close to his mouth, speaking quietly.

"The MP and his wife are back in the village. They've got their kids there too." The man's Albanian accent was barely discernible.

"I already knew. Just find out how long they're staying. Let me know when they leave."

"Nothing else? You happy to let them alone?"

George thought for a moment. If he was right about Claire becoming suspicious, and her husband still pursuing his questions with the police maybe it would be safer if they were out of the way. As long as it didn't look suspicious. After all two 'accidents' could be coincidence, three would look like something else.

"Not yet. Maybe later I might need you to do something. In the meantime I'm paying you to keep tabs on them. Weekly report eh? And, oh, let me know if they see the woman from Lindum Radio, "

"OK boss we do that." He rang off.

"I think Harry will be back here soon. He's just down in the lower field." Madge was a small woman with a thin, weathered face. She looked at Andrew closely. She didn't often have a visitor as important as him sitting in her kitchen. She wasn't interested in politics. When Andrew had driven into the farmyard that morning she had thought it was the John Deere salesman. He had a similar Off Roader.

Now she was trying to make conversation with Andrew while they waited for her husband.

They heard the door open and the sound of boots being wiped on the mat. "Whose car is that in the yard Madge?"

Harry was twice the size of his wife. He wore navy blue dungarees and he took off his hat to reveal an almost bald head. He looked suspiciously at Andrew who stood up and extended his hand.

"Good morning. I'm Andrew Eastwood, your MP."

"I didn't know there was another election due." Harry scowled at him. "That's the only time we get politicians coming out here."

"No, no there's no election. We just had one. I'm not here about your vote."

"Good because I voted for your lot to get this Brexit thing done and dusted. So what do you want?"

"I wanted to ask you about your two bulls." Andrew was not fazed by Harry's bluntness. He was getting used to some of the locals' way of speaking with strangers.

"Which bulls? I've only got one at present."

"I thought you had two bulls that were pretty prolific – good stud animals?"

"Oh them. Yes I had two really fine bulls but I sold them."

"You sold them?"

"That's what I said. Got a damn good price for them too."

"Who did you sell them to? When?"

"You ask a lot of questions. Why are you so interested in my bulls?"

"Well it was something that Sara Mendoza said to me before she died."

"Oh yes, nice girl that. Very tragic. I was sorry to hear about her accident."

"Yes, very tragic. She told me she had asked you for DNA samples from your bulls."

"That's right. She had some theory about twin calves but I don't think anything came of it. She came over and took the samples before Christmas. Never heard another word."

Andrew reached for his notebook and asked, "Who did you sell them to?"

"Well I hadn't thought of selling them. After all they were nice little earners those two. But the man came and made me such an offer it would have been mad not to accept. Nothing wrong with that is there?"

"No, not at all. Just a little strange. Who was this man?"

"He said he was a beef farmer from the Cotswolds. Came with his trailer the next day too. Brought the cash too."

"Cash? Surely you got thousands of pounds for prize bulls like that?"

Harry looked at his wife. "He said he was in a rush to get them and I've never trusted strangers with chequebooks. And in case you're wondering I'll be reporting it on my tax return." He looked nervously at his wife again.

"Of course," said Andrew "very understandable. But do you have his name and the farm's address."

"Must have a note of it somewhere but not sure I can find it now. Somewhere over Cheltenham way I think."

Andrew realised he was getting nowhere. Someone had removed the bulls, there was no chance of getting more DNA. He had a pretty good idea who had been behind it.

When Claire phoned Stellagenix later that week to speak to Dimitri she was told by his PA that he was in the States with

George. Frustrated, she called Andrew who had gone down to London. She was careful to use her new mobile.

"It seems that we're not going to find out about their research methods anytime soon and we've got no chance of finding those bulls either. I think there's a big cover-up going on." Her days of playing devil's advocate had passed. She was now firmly convinced that George had something to hide. She also realised that he could be responsible for two women's deaths too.

Her hand went to her stomach and rubbed it. The test kit had shown a positive result.

66

FEBRUARY 2020, LINCOLNSHIRE

"I got a right bollocking from the Minister!" Andrew had returned from London on Saturday morning in a bad mood. Over coffee he filled Claire in. There had been more complaints about the Lincolnshire Hospital Trust and Matt Hancock was going to be facing questions in committee about their failure to implement many of the recommendations of the CQC report.

"He's blaming me as I'm the local MP."

"And Junior Minister for Health, Andrew. I think you need to sort things out there. After all I might need them come August!"

"Oh we'll be back down in London before then. There's only so long that Repute will let you stay up here." Andrew was pleased that Claire had suggested spending time up at Otherby but he doubted she could put up with being cut off from her restaurants, galleries and theatres for long. "How have the boys been?"

"They're getting a little fed up with this weather. It just keeps on raining which means they can't go out. And I actually think they're missing school. I think I'll have to go back to the office in a couple of weeks and I think it will be good for them to get back to school."

"I thought you were wanting to move up here? We could get them into the local school, or there's a good one in Sleaford."

"I don't know Andrew. I am still worried about bringing them up in London but so far I just haven't really got to know anyone up here."

Andrew nodded. Their social life hadn't exactly been a mad merry-go-round. In fact they had hardly been out at all.

"OK, let's give it a chance. I'll spend time trying to sort out the hospital, we'll look at local schools and maybe have a dinner party or two."

"A dinner party with who?"

Andrew thought hard. "Well there's David who runs the vets, and maybe Sonya would come over?"

"Maybe we should meet up with Sonya again. I'm as convinced now as you that there's something fishy with this new barley."

"In the meantime I'm hungry. What do you say we take the boys to the Barley Mow?"

"Oh yes, the Barley Mow. The centre of the universe for residents of Otherby! Well it's too far to drive to a McDonalds but maybe they can get chicken nuggets at the Barley Mow."

The boys seemed only too happy to go anywhere having been stuck indoors for days and the family set off in their wet-weather gear to walk to the pub.

"Who are those men?" asked Marshall pointing to a white van parked outside the pub. Andrew looked and through the rain-streaked glass could just make out two figures sitting in the van.

"I don't know. Perhaps they've just arrived and are getting ready to have a drink like us."

"No I've seen them in that van yesterday. They just sit in it, they don't get out."

"Yes I've seen them too Daddy."

Andrew shook his head and smiled. "Come on it's wet and I want to get those chicken nuggets." They pushed open the door to the Barley Mow.

The next two weeks proved busy for the Eastwoods. In between trips to Peterborough and Grantham to look for new Prospect Insurance offices, Claire also took it upon herself to find a suitable local school. Unlike Wandsworth there didn't appear to be any private prep schools around so she ended up visiting the two local state primaries.

She still hadn't reconciled herself to moving 'into the sticks' but her pregnancy was causing her to reconsider her life. With another baby her ability to jet-set off to Barcelona was over. Spending more time supporting Andrew had been one of her goals. Her relationship with Clifton would have to be over. She thought back to the nights in Barcelona. She had only seen him once since their last night in December.

She still wanted to get to the bottom of the Stellagenix affair even though it might jeopardise the Agency. She was more convinced than ever that George had been hiding something and she was still no closer to discovering what methods Dimitri had used. She knew Andrew was grateful for her support.

She had told him about her share options investment and how much money she had made from those Stellagenix shares. She had expected an outburst from him. Instead he had seemed almost pleased. His only question was whether George knew. "I wouldn't want Stellagenix to have anything they could use against us."

She could see that he was getting more and more disillusioned with the goings on in Westminster.

Meanwhile Andrew had been kept busy with constituency work. He had made three visits to Lincoln for meetings with the hospital trust and also met Stan in Sleaford to discuss the lack of progress on a new bypass. He had taken over parenting duties while Claire was away since they no longer had Analiese to look after the boys. He found that he enjoyed teaching them things but it meant that he often had to catch up with work in the evenings.

One evening he had a call from his contact in Cambridge. The biologist said he had been thinking about the link between the barley and the apparent birth changes.

"Look Andrew, there's no real evidence that eating (or drinking) genetically-edited barley could in anyway change the germ cells of an animal or a human. I mean bacteria can cause changes to certain cells we know and indeed this whole CRISPR breakthrough uses harmless bacteria in proteins to edit sections of DNA. But we don't have any evidence that this particular barley was carrying any particular bacteria."

"So you're saying that it couldn't have been linked?"

"No I'm not saying that. There is certainly some circumstantial evidence that links those bulls and the brewery to the animals and people who had twins. We just don't know how."

"But you've mapped the whole genome so surely you'd be able to tell?"

"Well we haven't actually mapped it all. You see there's a whole lot of our DNA that just seems to be repeats, exactly the same code for long stretches of the chain. So it's impossible for us to put them together in the correct order."

"I don't understand."

"Well to map the genome we have to break the long chain of millions of lines of code if you will, and then look at each section separately. We then piece them all back together. The problem is, it's like a jigsaw. It's easy to put detailed pieces back together in the right place but if you've got lots of pieces with just blue sky on them it's a lot more difficult. Maybe someday soon we'll have powerful enough programs to do it, but not yet."

"And these 'repeating sequences' are all the same?"

"Well at least nearly the same so we just supposed that they aren't important. But we could be wrong. Maybe there's a little bit more to the DNA helix than we thought. There's a new technique called nanopore – I won't bore you with the details - but it looks as if in time we might be able to sequence things much, much faster and more accurately. We won't need to cut up the chain into little pieces. It will simply start at the beginning and work right through to the end. But it's only a theory at the moment."

"It all sounds terribly complicated."

"It is. Did you know that the genome of bread wheat for instance is five times the length of the human one? So there's a hell of a lot we don't know. "

"So that's it? Nothing we can do?"

"Well we will learn something if we can compare the DNA of those two bulls you mentioned against a couple of other bulls. I think that's what your vet friend was trying to do wasn't she?"

"Yes."

"Well if you give me the samples of the two bulls I'll get the guys here to run a test. I'd be really interested in doing that. Might take us a few weeks but we'd learn something I'm sure."

"There's a problem. We don't know where the bulls are anymore."

67

MARCH 2020, LONDON

Claire's pregnancy had been confirmed not only by the test kit but by a visit to her GP back in London She had decided to combine a visit to the Agency with a doctor appointment. She didn't tell anyone at Repute.

She was some three months into the pregnancy and, knowing her history, the doctor recommended that she take things very easy as this was a critical time for miscarriages.

Andrew had seemed very pleased with her news although she sensed some concern. His affair with Sara had not been discussed further and Claire had decided not to pursue it. The affair was over now that Sara was dead and she still had concerns of her own over her affair with Clifton.

She had rung Clifton from her office to report on her office search in Peterborough. She hadn't mentioned that she was pregnant.

She had also told Leonora about her success in finding some suitable candidate offices for Prospect. She said that she hoped to get Clifton to come up and take a look.

Leonora was more interested to know what was happening with Calapharm and Stellagenix. "How are you getting on with George? Has he said anything about getting us involved with Calapharm?"

Claire explained that he still hadn't returned from the States but had definitely said there was a good possibility of Repute being given any PR work for Calapharm if they began operations in the UK.

On the train back to Grantham that evening she started to think about what George had said. She still felt there was a veiled threat to not dig into the barley research in too much detail if she wanted the Calapharm business. He had seemed really excited about Calapharm's prospects, or perhaps he saw his own success linked to Calapharm. He hadn't said how long he would be away but it was now nearly two weeks. She determined to phone his PA tomorrow and see when he was due back.

"I don't know when they'll be back. Apparently they've both been struck down with some kind of bug. George felt poorly last week and thought it was flu but it's got a lot worse. He's even having to take oxygen to help him breathe. It's the same with Dimitri." The PA sounded very concerned as Claire questioned her.

"Maybe they caught something on the plane?"

"I don't think so. They think the Chinese guy might have given it to them. He's in intensive care now in New York. You've heard that there's some virus linked to China and it is believed to have started in Wuhan. That's where the research unit is."

68

MARCH 26TH 2020, LINCOLNSHIRE

"So that's it then," said Andrew. "We're stuck here."

Claire nodded. The Covid lockdown had started. No one could go out for more than a hour a day and then only for essential exercise. Social distancing was imposed. All-but-essential shops were closed and the Barley Mow was locked up tight.

It was difficult to believe so much had happened so fast. Little more than a month ago when Claire had learned about George Krasnik falling ill, the new bug, Covid, seemed just another flu-type virus that would have no more effect in Britain than SARS or Avian Flu had had. In those few weeks the virus had spread worldwide and thousands were dying or had died. George and Dimitri had both succumbed. Neither had returned from the States. Dimitri had hung on the longest. George's demise had been rapid. Rushed into hospital and seriously overweight he had been put onto a mechanical ventilator immediately. Two days later he was pronounced dead.

There was no way that Claire and Andrew were going to return to London now. As the implications of Covid became apparent and the infections rose Claire didn't want to risk anything that might affect her pregnancy. They both agreed that they were much safer here in rural Lincolnshire than in overcrowded London. They had originally fled London to avoid terrorism. Now it appeared there was a deadlier reason to keep out of the metropolis. At least for a few weeks until the pandemic was over.

She looked out of the study window at the boys playing in the garden and smiled. "The boys seem so much happier too. It's a pity if they can't start school next month. We'll just have to do online lessons with them."

"If we can get the bloody broadband to work better," said Andrew. He had been fighting with BT for weeks to try and get a better connection. Streaming video was a nightmare. He had taken up the cause with constituents and had been trying to get some action from OffCom without any noticeable success. One of the disadvantages of living outside a big city.

He was at his laptop now trying to download more information on breakthroughs in genome sequencing, still worried about the infamous barley. He was worried too about Claire. Her pregnancy had been so unexpected. What had changed that she had suddenly conceived? He couldn't help thinking about Colin and his wife. He had been drinking Fentastic just as Andrew had.

Claire was due to have a scan which would show if she was having twins. But that had been arranged with their GP down in Wandsworth. They hadn't got round to signing on to a local practice. And with this lockdown it would be a few weeks before they could venture down to London.

One thing was settled though. The urgency to find evidence against George for the deaths of Martha and Sara was now unnecessary. There was no retribution to be sought. Covid had seen to that. George was dead and there was nothing to be gained by pursuing it. There was, however, reason to worry about the barley. Andrew had turned his attention to trying to get changes to the UK testing of genetically modified and edited animal foodstuffs. He'd managed to get a colleague at the Ministry of Agriculture interested and hoped they might get a private member's bill through. Stan, his agent, wasn't hopeful and warned him not to criticise Stellagenix. There was, after all, a new sports complex nearing completion and Stellagenix had been very generous to the Tory party as well. "Don't rock our boat, Andrew. We've got too much to lose."

The lockdown and other Covid restrictions had prevented Claire and Andrew having their planned dinner parties. As her pregnancy progressed Claire was also anxious to avoid any chance of infection. The news every night on the TV was about hospitals struggling to save Covid patients.

Life had been completely turned upside down. The family now spent all day together, something they had never managed before. They amused themselves with simple pleasures, walking, working in the garden playing board games with the boys. Andrew managed to get some paint delivered and they spent time sprucing up the cottage and preparing the nursery.

The computer was now used for teaching the boys or Zoom meetings with constituents and fellow MPs. Brexit had been forced from the newsreels by this new worldwide pandemic.

As for Stellagenix the running of the UK company had fallen to a young British accountant that George had appointed to head up the financial side. He tried to carry out the instructions he received regularly from the States. The research team was now seriously depleted since Dimitri's death. They had already lost their chief research assistant, Martha. The team was now led by a Japanese biologist who had been sent over by the US board shortly after George's death. Claire had spoken a couple of times with him and had been promised a meeting 'when the pandemic is over'.

She had several calls with Clifton although the lockdown had prevented him from visiting Peterborough and Newark. He was beset with problems setting up the new office in Barcelona and the even-stricter lockdown rules in Spain had prevented him going down there.

"I'm stuck here in London. All the clubs and restaurants are closed and my top consultant is hiding herself away in the bloody fens!" he joked during one Zoom meeting. "You look like you're getting plenty of good food up there."

She had decided not to comment and still hadn't mentioned her pregnancy. The beauty of Zoom calls was that you could choose how much of your body you showed.

69

JULY 2020, LINCOLNSHIRE

The family had quite enjoyed the last four months of Covid restrictions. Their all-too-busy lives had suddenly eased. They had never spent so much time together. The boys had enjoyed having both parents at home rather than just an au pair. Both parents had enjoyed the excellent weather that had enabled them to go for long country walks, garden and generally enjoy a quieter life.

In many ways the enforced isolation that the Government's Covid rules necessitated provided them with the opportunity to spend more time with the boys and more with each other. It was certainly safer in the country although Covid was spreading fast here too.

Although Claire had managed to operate relatively well without meeting clients or colleagues, it had not been so easy for Andrew.

It had become obvious that the NHS was totally unprepared for a major pandemic. The lessons from the

2016 'war games' undertaken by the Cameron Government had not been acted upon. There were major shortages of PPE (personal protection equipment) for the struggling medical staff. Although the Ministers and Cabinet members in London continued to meet, most MPs were bunkered down in their constituencies. Most civil servants were also stuck at home.

Andrew had been forced to return to London for a few days to meet with the Secretary of State for Health. He soon realised that those civil servants who were working weren't up to the task of procuring the much-needed equipment quickly enough. They showed an appalling lack of commercial experience. In panic, the Minister and the Prime Minister had called up their friends in the hope that they might be able to procure equipment from their contacts abroad.

That evening he spoke with his friend Amir about his worries. Amir was scathing. "They've no idea about ordering things from China or Turkey or wherever. They're handing out contracts to friends who have no experience in medical equipment!"

When Andrew met with the Minister the next morning he expressed his concerns. "I'm worried that we won't get the right quality equipment, or not get it in time."

The Minister reacted to the criticism explaining that he was doing his best in unprecedented circumstances. "What about your friends up at Stellagenix? They've got a pharmaceutical company now. Maybe you can pull strings there and get us some masks or whatever."

Andrew shook his head. "I'm more concerned with finding out what they did to alter the barley and what effects it's having on animals and babies."

"I've got better things to worry about right now." The minister looked at his watch and picked up a phone. The interview was over.

The next day Andrew returned to Otherby still angry at his treatment in London. He was relieved to find that his efforts to get BT to improve the broadband had finally borne fruit. Claire delightedly demonstrated the new router and pointed to the line of disturbed earth in the front garden that marked where the new fibre cable been installed. Obviously being a Minister, even a junior one, had benefits.

So Zoom meetings would now enable both of them to continue keeping in touch with work colleagues, clients or departments.

It was by Zoom that Andrew learned that he was no longer a Junior Minister. There had been no further meeting in Westminster, just a Zoom call from Downing Street. He was left in no doubt that his sacking was because he continued to press for an investigation into the Stellagenix barley. This had made him even more determined to find out more about the effects of the gene editing and try and tighten the testing requirements.

70

JULY 2020, LINCOLNSHIRE

The days passed slowly, but pleasantly. Claire continued to grow but no longer felt nauseous. The slow pace of rural life under Covid seemed to be doing her good.

She had been furloughed by Repute since there was little to do to promote their clients whose offices were empty of staff. Covid was dominating the news stories. She had spoken twice to the new Japanese head of research at Stellagenix but learned nothing about the research methods implemented by his Greek predecessor.

All she had learned was that the winter wheat project had been put on hold for a few months. She wondered why. The takeover of Calapharm had occurred but progress in integrating the two companies was slow due to the pandemic.

The only real problem the lockdown had caused Andrew and Claire had been getting any medical treatment. Everything had to be done by phone or Zoom meetings. Her London GP had arranged for midwife care in Otherby.

Claire had been visited by Julie the local midwife a couple of times although it had all been rather strange with Julie masked up and insisting on scrupulous hand-washing and open windows before examining Claire. On her first visit they had talked briefly about her friend Sara and her tragic death. "She was a very good friend," said Julie.

Claire hadn't been able to get a scan but Julie assured her that everything seemed to be progressing just fine and judging by the size of her she felt certain that it wasn't going to be twins. Claire and Andrew were less certain. Claire had not been very large when she had had the boys. She seemed now to be just as bloated as before to Andrew's eye. Maybe it was just all the good food and country air, or maybe not.

It was becoming clear that she might be going to Lincoln for the birth and Andrew was also worried about that. He hadn't been able to visit the hospital since the first lockdown and he was hearing stories of chaos with all the Covid cases being treated there. Hopefully it would have improved by the time Claire was due. It was still several weeks away.

They were sitting in the study overlooking the back garden. The view was obscured by the heavy rain that streaked down the windows. The old windows rattled as the gusts buffeted them. The beautiful weather of the first lockdown had suddenly this week changed into rain of biblical proportions. There were reports of houses being flooded and rivers breaching their banks from several parts of the county. Andrew had received calls from several constituents complaining that promised flood precautions had not been executed.

When he had ventured out to the Barley Mow yesterday, now that pubs were allowed to open once again, he met one of the village's older residents. "All this weather reminds me of 1960. Time of the great flood. Killed people over in Horncastle. If it keeps on like this we could see the same again. They got floods last year too."

"We're going to need to get some more food in," Claire had said. "And it would be a good idea to get some stuff for the baby. There could be shortages of things. I know it's still weeks away but we shouldn't leave everything to the last minute, especially if there are floods."

Andrew didn't argue. Actually he was rather pleased to have an excuse to get out of the house. Much as he loved Otherby he was, like lots of the population, beginning to get a little stir crazy.

"Do me a list and I'll motor over to the big supermarket in Grantham and get a load of things in. I'll go now before the weather gets even worse."

He set off and followed the flat road until he came to Sara's Bend as he now called it. The field from the road to the dyke was already flooded and the spray from the Nissan's big tyres fountained up as he took the bend. He was glad he had four-wheel drive but even so on some stretches of the road the water was nearly a foot deep and the car struggled to get through. Either side the flat fields stretched to the horizon, an horizon obscured by dark menacing clouds.

The further he drove the more worried he became. This weather was horrendous. He would get a really good stock of things at the supermarket so he didn't have to do this trip again soon. The wipers flopped left and right with a rhythmic thud and Andrew found himself thinking about everything that happened in the past six months since Sara's death. Claire seemed to have forgiven him for his affair and had instead worked with him to try and uncover the role of George in Sara's accident. When George himself was killed by Covid there seemed to be some divine retribution and it made proving his involvement less urgent. The effect that the new barley would have on animal and human germ cells was, however, much more of a concern to Andrew. He couldn't help worrying about Claire's new baby. Had he drunk enough of the Fentastic to cause a problem? Was she in fact due to have twins despite what Julie thought? After all they hadn't had the luxury of having any scans. So much was unknown.

He pressed on through the driving rain.

He got to Grantham and rushed around the store piling up groceries and toiletries until his cart was nearly overflowing. He splashed his way across the car park to his car. His trouser legs were soaked and the rain seemed even heavier. He drove out of the car park heading back towards Ancaster. His headlamps cut through the curtain of falling rain while those of the oncoming traffic diffused into shooting stars of light. He concentrated hard to avoid the deepest of the puddles. At one point he was met with a 'Road Closed' sign and had to detour for several miles before re-joining his route. It was completely dark by now. He wished he had waited until the morning before setting out. It was much harder in the dark.

He switched the car radio to Lindum Radio and heard Sonya's voice describing the reports of severe flooding. This was followed by a report from the Lincoln Hospital where the already-overburdened staff were having to deal with colleagues unable to get through to the hospital because of the floods.

The reporter described how there had been breakdowns on the main approach road to the city which had caused the police to describe it as unpassable. Andrew drove on, grateful that he wasn't having to go to Lincoln tonight.

His mobile phone started to ring and he pushed the button on the console to go hands free. Claire's voice cut through the noise of the engine and the throbbing windscreen wipers.

"Andrew. Where are you? I need you back here now. My waters have broken! I think the contractions have started. There's no one here, just the boys and they are frightened. Where are you? How soon will you be back? "

"I'm still an hour away I reckon. I had to detour because of the floods. The roads are really bad. Look, phone Julie, the midwife. She'll be able to get over, she doesn't live far away. I'll get back as fast as I can."

He started to drive faster along the flooded roads. Eventually he found himself speeding down the stretch of road before Sara's Bend. He started to brake and felt the car aquaplane. He pumped the brake pedal up and down in an attempt to gain traction. The car began to judder as it lost speed. But the car had already reached the sharp bend. He pulled the steering wheel hard left and pressed even harder on the brake pedal. The car rocked as it slewed around the bend, its four-wheel drive struggling to deal with the excess water. For a sickening moment he felt the nearside wheels lift off the road and the car tipped towards the field and the dyke. He spun the wheel the other way and the nearside wheels thumped back onto the tarmac. He fought to straighten the car, as he felt the right front wheel tear into the grass verge on the far side. The car came to an abrupt halt on the wrong side of the road. The engine cut out leaving just the sound of water hissing off the hot exhaust and the crescendo of raindrops beating on the metal roof.

Andrew turned the ignition key and the engine coughed into life. He glanced at the road ahead leading to Otherby, relieved not to see an oncoming vehicle. He put the car in gear and headed for Otherby. That had been too close. That was no way to help Claire.

Julie's little car was parked outside the house. The front door was unlocked and he pushed it open and squelched into the hall. The two boys rushed towards him. They had been sitting on the bottom stair – the 'naughty step' as Claire called it.

"Daddy, Daddy. Mummy's having the baby. The nurse is here but we're not allowed to go in." They clung to his legs oblivious to the wet cloth.

He took the stairs two at a time and found Claire lying on the bed, her knees raised and Julie staring intently between them.

"Andrew get some clean towels right now, fast as you can. And wash your hands." Julie didn't look at him. She continued to focus on Claire. Claire moaned and then swore.

"Right, that's it. Now push!" He heard Julie's urgent instruction to Claire. He fumbled in the bathroom and gathered every towel he could find and rushed back to the bedroom. Julie turned her head. "Put them down there Andrew and now go look after your boys."

The three of them sat at the bottom of the stairs. "Is Mummy alright, she keeps screaming," said Miles looking at his father.

"Yes, yes she'll be fine." Andrew tried to sound confident but his brain was hardly functioning. What was wrong? She wasn't due for a month or more. Colin's wife had been a month early too. And she had been able to go to hospital. And she was dead.

He clutched both boys and held them close. "We have to be very brave, just like Mummy and then everything will be alright."

The boys started to sob and he realised he was crying himself. He reached for his handkerchief and blew his nose, trying to stop the tears.

Upstairs the screaming had stopped. There was no sound at all. Ignoring Julie's instructions he climbed back up the stairs, taking them two at a time, and pushed open the door.

He was met with the sight of Julie holding a small blood-stained baby upside down and slapping it. It started to cry. Julie looked up at Andrew and smiled. "Congratulations Andrew, you have a beautiful daughter."

A little later he brought the two boys up the stairs to meet their new sister. Julie had tidied up and eventually allowed him to return. Claire was sitting up, her hair combed and cuddling her daughter. The two boys looked at their sister in awe. Finally Marshall said, "She's got lots of black hair Mummy"

"Yes she has," said Claire smiling.

"What's her name Mummy?"

Claire looked at Andrew. "I think we should call her Sara."

If you've enjoyed reading this book you might find *Outdriven* by Laurie Rogers equally satisfying. It tells the story of Maggie.

When Maggie is tragically widowed, she cannot imagine how she will manage without her husband. Then her ninety-nine-year-old golf club suddenly faces collapse in an unprecedented financial crisis and she finds herself cast in the role as saviour.

Together with her young Polish lodger, she launches a bold plan to save the club's centenary and make her own life more rewarding. But when he mysteriously disappears along with her money, Maggie must face the biggest challenge of her life.

Set in 2008 at the start of the great financial crisis, this inspiring book charts Maggie's year as she struggles against increasing odds to overcome male prejudice, a family catastrophe and grasping bankers. A gripping read.

Available from good bookshops or direct from Troubador:
troubador.co.uk/bookshop/contemporary/outdriven

This book is printed on paper from sustainable sources managed under the Forest Stewardship Council (FSC) scheme.

It has been printed in the UK to reduce transportation miles and their impact upon the environment.

For every new title that Troubador publishes, we plant a tree to offset CO_2, partnering with the More Trees scheme.

For more about how Troubador offsets its environmental impact, see www.troubador.co.uk/sustainability-and-community